25% OFF

C000228800

3751 4808

Bryn looked up at Gabriel sharply. 'I don't see how, when my name and appearance are so different from five years ago.'

He gave a humourless smile. 'It's unlikely I'd ever forget the young woman who glared her hatred across a courtroom at me for days on end; those eyes alone would have given you away.'

Bryn had never forgotten him either, but for quite a different reason.

Gabriel D'Angelo was quite simply the most charismatic and darkly intriguing man she had ever set eyes on. But it was more than that—*he* was more than that. Gabriel had awakened something deep inside the eighteen-year-old Sabryna that had filled her night-time fantasies for weeks before her father's arrest, and months after the trial had ended.

The same fantasies had filled all of her nights since meeting Gabriel again a week ago. The same desire had caused her breath to catch in her throat when she turned to look at him. This man—Gabriel—awakened that hunger inside her just by being in the same room with her.

A BARGAIN
WITH THE ENEMY

BY
CAROLE MORTIMER

MILLS
BOON

Published in Great Britain 2014
by Mills & Boon, an imprint of Harlequin (UK) Limited,
Eton House, 18-24 Paradise Road, Richmond, Surrey, TW9 1SR

© 2014 Carole Mortimer

ISBN: 978-0-263-25413-6

Printed and bound in Spain
by Blackprint CPI, Barcelona

THE DEVILISH D'ANGELOS

Sinners named for saints…

Known around the world for the prestigious
Archangel auction houses and galleries, in London,
New York and Paris, the D'Angelo brothers are
notorious for their prowess in the art world…and even
more so for their exploits in their personal lives.

These Italian heartthrobs might have been named
for angels, but their ruthless natures and powerful
personas make them *anything* but angelic…

Soar to LONDON for *Gabriel D'Angelo's* story in:
A BARGAIN WITH THE ENEMY

Sail to NEW YORK for *Raphael D'Angelo's* story in:
A PRIZE BEYOND JEWELS

Fly to PARIS for *Michael D'Angelo's* story in:
A D'ANGELO LIKE NO OTHER

Enter the exclusive world of the D'Angelos
in this dazzling new trilogy from
Carole Mortimer!

To my six wonderful sons. I am so proud of you all.

Carole Mortimer was born in England, the youngest of three children. She began writing in 1978, and has now written over one hundred and fifty books for Harlequin Mills & Boon®. Carole has six sons: Matthew, Joshua, Timothy, Michael, David and Peter. She says, 'I'm happily married to Peter senior; we're best friends as well as lovers, which is probably the best recipe for a successful relationship. We live in a lovely part of England.'

Recent titles by the same author:

RUMOURS ON THE RED CARPET
  (Scandal in the Spotlight)
A TOUCH OF NOTORIETY
A TASTE OF THE FORBIDDEN
  (Buenos Aires Nights)
HIS REPUTATION PRECEDES HIM
  (The Lyonedes Legacy)

Did you know these are also available as eBooks?
Visit www.millsandboon.co.uk

PROLOGUE

'Don't worry, Mik, he'll be here.'

'Take your damned feet off the desk,' Michael snapped in reply to his brother's reassurance, not even glancing up from the papers he was currently reading in the study at Archangel's Rest, the secluded Berkshire home of the D'Angelo family. 'And I'm not worried.'

'Like hell you're not!' Rafe drawled lazily, making no effort to swing his black-booted feet down from where they rested on the front of his older brother's desk.

'I'm really not, Rafe,' Michael assured mildly.

'Do you know if—?'

'I'm sure it can't have escaped your notice that I'm trying to read!' Michael sighed his impatience as he glared across the desk. He was dressed formally, as usual, in a pale blue shirt and neatly knotted navy blue silk tie, dark waistcoat and tailored trousers, the jacket to his suit draped over the back of his leather chair.

It had always been something of a family joke that their mother had chosen to name her three sons Michael, Raphael and Gabriel to go with the surname D'Angelo, and the three brothers had certainly taken their fair share of teasing about it when they were at boarding school. Not so much now they were all in their thirties, and the three of them had been able to utilise their names by making the three Archangel auction houses and galleries in London, New York and Paris the most prestigious privately owned galleries in the world.

Their grandfather, Carlo D'Angelo, had managed to bring his wealth with him when he fled Italy and settled in England almost seventy years ago before marrying an English girl, and producing a son, Giorgio: Michael, Raphael and Gabriel's father.

Like his father before him, Giorgio had been an astute businessman, opening the first Archangel auction house and gallery in London thirty years ago, and adding to the D'Angelo wealth. When Giorgio retired ten years ago and he and his wife Ellen settled permanently in their Florida home, their three sons had turned that comfortable wealth into a veritable fortune by opening up similar Archangel galleries in New York and Paris, resulting in them now all being millionaires many times over.

'And don't call me Mik,' Michael instructed harshly as he continued to read from the file in front of him. 'You know how much I hate it.'

Of course Rafe knew that, and he considered it part of his job description as a younger brother to annoy the hell out of his older sibling!

Not that he had as many opportunities to do that nowadays with the three brothers usually at a different gallery at any one time. But they always made a point of meeting up for Christmas and each of their birthdays, and today was Michael's thirty-fifth birthday. Rafe was a year younger and Gabriel, the 'baby' of the family, another year younger at thirty-three.

'I last spoke to Gabriel a week or so ago.' Rafe made a face.

'Why the grimace?' Michael quirked a dark brow.

'No reason in particular—we all know that Gabe's

been in a bad mood for the past five years. I never understood the attraction myself.' He shrugged. 'She looked a mousy little thing to me, with just those big—'

'Rafe!' Michael cautioned in a growl.

'—grey eyes to recommend her,' Rafe completed dryly.

Michael's mouth thinned. 'I spoke to Gabriel two days ago.'

'And?' Rafe prompted impatiently when it became obvious his older brother was doing his usual clam impersonation.

Michael shrugged. 'And he said he would arrive here in time for dinner this evening.'

'Why the hell couldn't you have just told me that earlier?'

Rafe swung his booted feet impatiently down onto the carpeted floor before rising restlessly to his feet. He ran an irritated hand through the short thickness of his sable-dark hair as he paced the room, tall and leanly muscled in a fitted black T-shirt and faded denims. 'That would have been too easy, I suppose.' He paused his pacing to glower at his older brother.

'No doubt.' Michael gave the ghost of a smile, eyes dark and unreadable, also as usual.

The three brothers had similar colouring, height and build; all a couple inches over six feet tall, with the same sable-black hair. Michael kept his hair short, his eyes so dark a brown they gleamed black and unfathomable.

Rafe's hair was long enough to curl down onto his shoulders, his eyes so pale a brown they glowed a deep gold.

'Well?' he rasped impatiently as Michael added nothing to his earlier statement.

'Well, what?' His brother arched an arrogant brow as he relaxed back in his leather chair.

'How was he?'

Michael shrugged. 'As you said, as bad tempered as ever.'

Rafe grimaced. 'You two are the pot and the kettle!'

'I'm not bad tempered, Rafe, I just don't choose to suffer fools gladly.'

He raised dark brows. 'I trust I wasn't included in that sweeping statement…?'

'Hardly.' Michael relaxed slightly. 'And I prefer to think of all three of us as perhaps being just a little… intense.'

Some of Rafe's own tension eased as he gave a rueful grin in acknowledgement of the probable reason none of them had ever married. The women they met were more often than not attracted to that dangerous edge so prevalent in the D'Angelo men, as much as they were to their obvious wealth. Obviously not a basis for a relationship other than the purely—or not so purely!—physical.

'Maybe,' he conceded dryly. 'So what's in the file you've been looking at so intently since I arrived?'

'Ah.' Michael grimaced.

Rafe eyed him warily. 'Why do I have the feeling I'm not going to like this…?'

'Probably because you aren't.' His brother turned the file around and pushed it across the desk.

Rafe read the name at the top of the file. 'And who might Bryn Jones be?'

'One of the entrants for the New Artists Exhibition being held at the London gallery next month,' Michael supplied tersely.

'Damn it, *that's* the reason you knew Gabriel would be back today!' He glared at his brother. 'I'd totally forgotten that Gabriel's taking over from you in London during the organisation of the exhibition.'

'And I get to go to Paris for a while, yes,' Michael drawled with satisfaction.

'Intending to see the beautiful Lisette while you're there?' He eyed his brother knowingly.

Michael's mouth tightened. 'Who?'

The dismissive tone of his brother's voice was enough to tell Rafe that Michael's relationship with the 'beautiful Lisette' was not only over, but already forgotten. 'So what's so special about this Bryn Jones that you have a security file on him?'

Rafe knew there had to be a reason for Michael's interest in this particular artist. There had been dozens of eager applicants for the New Artists Exhibition; since Gabriel had organised the first one in Paris three months ago and it had been such a success, they had decided to go ahead and hold a similar one in London next month.

'Bryn Jones is a she,' Michael corrected dryly.

Rafe's brows rose. 'I see....'

'Somehow I doubt that,' his brother drawled dismissively. 'Maybe this picture will help....' Michael lifted the top sheet of paper to pull out a black and white photograph. 'I had Security download the image from one of the security discs at Archangel yesterday—' which explained the slightly grainy quality of the picture '—when she came into the gallery to personally deliver her portfolio to Eric Sanders.' Eric was their in-house art expert at the London gallery.

Rafe picked up the photograph so that he could take a closer look at the young woman pictured coming through the glass doors into the marbled entrance hall of the London gallery.

She was probably in her early to mid-twenties. The

black-and-white photograph made it difficult to tell her exact colouring. Her just-below-ear-length hair, in a perky flicked-up style, looked to be light in shade, her appearance businesslike in a dark jacket and knee-length skirt, with a pale blouse beneath the jacket—none of which detracted in the least from the curvaceous body beneath!

She had a hauntingly beautiful face, Rafe acknowledged as he continued to study the photograph: heart-shaped, eyes light in colour, pert little nose between high cheekbones, her lips full and poutingly sensual with a delicately pointed chin above the slenderness of her throat.

A very arresting, and slightly familiar, face.

'Why do I have the feeling that I know her?' Rafe asked, lifting his head.

'Probably because you do. We all do,' Michael added tersely. 'Try imagining her slightly more…rounded, with heavy, black-framed glasses, and long mousy-brown hair.'

'Doesn't sound like the sort of woman any of us would ever be attracted to—' Rafe broke off abruptly, his gaze narrowing sharply, suspiciously, on the black-and-white photograph in front of him.

'Oh, yes…. I forgot to mention that perhaps you should look closely at…the eyes,' Michael drawled dryly.

Rafe glanced up quickly. 'It can't be! Can it?' He studied the photograph more closely. 'Are you saying this beautiful woman is Sabryna Harper?'

'Yes,' Michael bit out crisply.

'William Harper's daughter?'

'The same.' Michael nodded grimly.

Rafe's jaw tightened as he easily recalled the uproar five years ago when William Harper had offered a supposedly previously unknown Turner for sale at their London gallery. Ordinarily the painting would have remained a secret until after authentication had been made and confirmed by the experts, but somehow its existence had been leaked to the press, sending the art world and the media into an excited frenzy as speculation about the painting's authenticity became rife.

Gabriel had been in charge of the London gallery at the time, had gone to the Harper family home several times to discuss the painting while it was being authenticated, meeting both the wife and daughter of William Harper on those occasions. This made it doubly difficult for him when he'd had to declare the painting, having undergone extensive examination by the experts they had brought in from all over the world, to be a near-perfect forgery. Worse than that, the police investigation had proved that William Harper was solely responsible for the forgery, resulting in the other man being arrested and sent to prison for his crime.

His wife and teenage daughter had been hounded by the media throughout the trial and the whole sorry story had blown up again when Harper had died in prison just four months later, after which his wife and daughter had simply disappeared.

Until now, it would seem....

Rafe eyed Michael warily. 'Are you absolutely sure it's her?'

'The file you're looking at is from the private investigator I hired after I saw her at the gallery yesterday—'

'You *spoke* to her?'

Michael shook his head. 'I was passing through the entrance hall when Eric walked by with her. As I said, I thought I recognised her, and the private investigator was able to establish that Mary Harper resumed using her maiden name just weeks after her husband's death, and her daughter's surname was changed to the same by deed poll.'

'And this Bryn Jones is really her?'

'Yes.'

'And what do you intend doing about it?'

'Doing about what?'

Rafe breathed his impatience with his brother's continued calm. 'Well, she obviously can't be one of the six new artists exhibited at Archangel next month.'

Michael raised dark brows. 'Why can't she?'

'Well, for one thing her father was put in prison for attempting to involve one of our galleries in selling a forged painting!' He eyed his brother. 'Not only that, but Gabriel went to court and helped to put him there!'

'And the sins of the father are to be passed down onto the daughter, is that it?'

'No, of course that isn't it! But—with a father like that, how do you even know the paintings in her portfolio are her own?'

'They are.' Michael nodded. 'It's all in the file. She attained a first-class arts degree. Has been trying to sell her paintings to other galleries for the past two years with very little success. I've looked at her portfolio, Rafe, and, despite what those other galleries may have thought, she's good. More than good, she's original, which is probably why the other galleries refused to take a chance on her work. Their loss is our gain. So much so that I have every intention of buying a Bryn Jones painting for my own collection.'

'She's going to be one of the final six artists?'

'Without a doubt.'

'And what about Gabriel?'

'What about him?'

'We warned him repeatedly but he refused to listen. She's the reason he's been in a bad mood for five years— how do you think he's going to feel when he realises exactly who Bryn Jones really is?' Rafe bit out exasperately.

'Well, I think you'll agree, she's definitely improved with age!' Michael said dryly.

There was no doubt about that. 'This is just— Damn it, Michael!'

Michael's mouth firmed. 'Bryn Jones is a very talented artist, and she deserves her chance of being exhibited at Archangel.'

'Have you even stopped to think *why* she might be doing this?' Rafe frowned. 'That she might have some ulterior motive, maybe some sort of revenge plot against us or Gabriel for what happened to her father?'

'It did occur to me, yes.' Michael nodded calmly.

'And?'

He shrugged. 'I'm willing to give her the benefit of the doubt at this stage.'

'And Gabriel?'

'Has assured me on numerous occasions that he's an adult, and certainly doesn't need his big brother interfering in his life, thank you very much!' Michael drawled dryly.

Rafe gave an exasperated shake of his head as he began pacing the study. 'You seriously don't intend to tell Gabriel who she is?'

'As I said, not at this stage,' Michael confirmed. 'Do you?'

Rafe had no idea yet what he was going to do with this information....

CHAPTER ONE

One week later...

SHE WAS ENTERING the enemy camp—again!—Bryn realised with a frown as she paused outside on the pavement to look up at the marble frontispiece of the biggest
and the best of the privately owned galleries and auction houses in London, the name Archangel in large gold
italics glittering in the sunlight above the wide glass entrance doors. Doors that swung open automatically as
she stepped forward before walking purposefully into
the high-ceilinged entrance hall.

Purposefully, because this really was the enemy camp
as far as Bryn was concerned. The D'Angelos, Gabriel
in particular, had been responsible for both breaking her
heart and sending her father to prison five years ago....

She couldn't think of that now, couldn't allow herself
to think of that now. She had to focus on the fact that
the past two years of rejection from gallery after gallery
were what had brought her to this desperate moment.
The same two years, after leaving university with her
degree, when she had believed the world was now her
oyster, only to learn that the recognition she craved for
her paintings was ever elusive.

Many of her friends from university had caved to the

pressure of family and stretched finances and entered advertising or teaching instead of following their real dream of painting for a living. But not Bryn. Oh, no, she had stuck doggedly to her desire to have her paintings exhibited in a London gallery, believing that one day she would be able to make her mother proud of her and erase the shame of her family's past.

Two years later she had been forced to admit defeat, not by abandoning her paintings, but by being left with no choice but to enter the New Artists competition at Archangel.

'Miss Jones?'

She turned to look enquiringly at one of the two receptionists sitting behind the elegant cream-and-rose marble desk, which was an exact match for the rest of the marbled entrance hall; several huge columns in the same marble stretched from floor to ceiling, with beautiful glass cabinets protecting the priceless artefacts and magnificent jewellery on display.

And this was only the entrance hall; Bryn knew from her previous visit to the Archangel Gallery that the six salons leading off this vast hallway all housed yet more unique and beautiful treasures, and there were many more being prepared for auction in the vast basement beneath the building.

She straightened, determined not to be intimidated— or at least not to *reveal* that she was intimidated—by her elegant surroundings, or by the cool blonde and elegant receptionist who couldn't be much older than her own twenty-three years. 'Yes, I'm Miss Jones.'

'Linda,' the other woman supplied as she stood up from behind the desk and walked across the entrance hall, the three-inch heels of her black shoes clicking on the marble floor as she joined a hesitant Bryn still standing near the doorway.

Bryn felt distinctly underdressed in the fitted black trousers and loose flowered silk shirt she had chosen to wear for her second meeting with Eric Sanders, the gallery's in-house art expert. 'I have an appointment with Mr Sanders,' she supplied softly.

Linda nodded. 'If you would care to follow me to the lift? Mr D'Angelo left instructions for me to take you upstairs to his office as soon as you arrived.'

Bryn instantly stiffened, her feet suddenly feeling so leaden they appeared to have become weighted to the marble floor. 'My appointment is with Mr Sanders.'

Linda turned with a swish of that perfectly groomed blonde hair as she realised Bryn wasn't following her. 'Mr D'Angelo is conducting the interviews this morning.'

Bryn's tongue felt as if it were stuck to the roof of her suddenly dry mouth. 'Mr D'Angelo?' she managed to squeak.

The older woman nodded. 'One of the three brothers who own this gallery.' Bryn knew exactly who the three D'Angelo brothers were. She just had no idea which one Linda was referring to when she said 'Mr D'Angelo'. The haughty and cold Michael? The arrogant playboy Raphael? Or the cruel Gabriel, who had taken her naive heart and trampled all over it?

It didn't really matter which of the D'Angelo brothers it was; they were all arrogant and ruthless as far as Bryn was concerned, and she wouldn't have come within twenty feet of a single one of them if not for the fact that she was as determined to become one of the six artists chosen to take part in the Archangel New Artists Exhibition next month, as she was desperate.

She gave a slow shake of her head. 'I think there's

been some sort of mistake.' She frowned. 'Mr Sanders'
secretary phoned me and made the appointment.'

'Because Mr D'Angelo was out of the country at the
time,' Linda said, nodding.

Bryn could only stand and stare at the other woman,
wondering if it was too late for her to just cut and run
while she still had the chance....

Gabriel rested his elbows on his desktop as he watched
the link to the security camera in the entrance hall of the
gallery on his laptop.

He had recognised Bryn Jones the moment she entered the gallery, of course. Seen the way she hesitated,
before her expression turned to one of confusion as Linda
spoke to her, followed by total stillness as her face went
completely blank, making it easy for Gabriel to guess
the moment Linda had told her that her appointment this
morning was now with him rather than Eric.

Bryn Jones...

Or, more accurately, Sabryna Harper.

The last time Gabriel had seen Sabryna had been five
years ago, day after day across a crowded courtroom. She
had glared her dislike of him with glittering but velvet-
soft dove-grey eyes from behind dark-framed glasses
every time she so much as glanced at him. And she had
glanced at him a lot!

Sabryna Harper had only been eighteen at the time,
her figure voluptuously rounded, her manner a little
clumsy and self-conscious, light brown hair growing
silky and straight to just below her shoulders, dark-
framed glasses making her eyes appear large and vulnerable. A vulnerability and appeal that Gabriel had been
inexplicably drawn to.

Her figure had slimmed down to a svelte elegance that

was shown to full advantage in a loose floral blouse and fitted trousers. The light brown hair looked as if it had been given blonde highlights, as well as being expertly cut and styled as it winged out perkily about her ears, nape and creamy, smooth brow. And she had dispensed with the dark-framed glasses, probably in favour of contact lenses. She also possessed a new self-confidence that had allowed her to walk into Archangel with purpose and determination.

The loss of weight was even more noticeable in her face; there were now slight hollows in her cheeks, revealing sculptured cheekbones either side of a pert little nose. Her mouth— Thank God Rafe had warned him about that sexy mouth. As it was, he had an arousal that would need several minutes to subside—the same minutes it would take Linda to bring Bryn Jones to his office, he hoped.

Would Gabriel have recognised this beautiful and confident young woman as the Sabryna Harper of five years ago if Rafe hadn't prewarned him of her real identity, after Michael had decided to act with his usual arrogance by remaining silent on the subject?

Oh, yes, Gabriel had no doubts he would have recognised Sabryna. Voluptuous or slender, glasses or no glasses, slightly gauche or elegantly poised, he would have known Sabryna under any guise she cared to take on.

The question was, would she betray by word or deed that she remembered him too?

Delicious, decadent, sinful, melted-chocolate brown. It was the only way to describe the colour of Gabriel D'Angelo's eyes, Bryn acknowledged with self-disgust as, Linda having delivered her to his office, she now stood in front of the marble desk looking at the man she had long considered her nemesis. The man who, with the whiplash of his arrogant and ruthless tongue, had not only helped to send her father to prison, but also succeeded in killing Sabryna Harper and necessitating that Bryn Jones rise from her ashes.

The same man that the youthful Sabryna had been beguiled by, kissed by and lost her heart to five years ago.

The same man who only weeks later had stood in a courtroom and condemned her father to prison.

The same man that Sabryna had looked at across that courtroom and known that she still wanted, despite what he was doing to her father. Just looking at him had aroused her when she should have felt nothing but hatred for him, robbing her of both breath and speech.

A reaction, a dangerous attraction, that in the years that followed Bryn had convinced herself she hadn't felt. That the emotions that had bombarded her whenever she looked at him must have been dislike, perhaps even hate, because she couldn't have still been attracted to him after what he had done to her family.

One look at him now and Bryn knew that she had been lying to herself for all these years; that Gabriel D'Angelo, despite being the one man she should never have been attracted to, never have allowed herself to be flattered by or allowed to kiss her, had then, and still now, held a dangerous fascination for her.

So much so that she could feel how his overpowering presence managed to dominate the dramatic and opulent elegance of the huge office with floor-to-ceiling windows looking out over the London skyline and original artwork adorning all of the delicate pink-silk-covered walls.

Gabriel D'Angelo...

A man who should by now—Bryn had many times

wished it so!—be balding, running to fat, with lines of
dissipation etched into his overbloated and self-indulgent
face.

Instead, he was still well over six feet of taut, lean
muscle, all shown to advantage in a dark and tailored
designer-label suit that probably cost as much as a year
of Bryn's university fees! And his hair was just as thick
and dark as she remembered it too, brushed casually back
from his face to fall in silky ebony waves to just below
the collar of his cream silk shirt.

As for his face…!

It was the face of a male model. The sort of face that
women of all ages would have drooled over before buying whatever it was he was selling; a high intelligent
brow above those sinful brown eyes, his nose aquiline,
cheekbones high and sharply defined against light olive
skin—with not a line in sight, of dissipation or otherwise!
He had perfect chiselled lips—the top one fuller than the
bottom—and the strong line of his jaw was exactly as
Bryn remembered it: square and ruthlessly determined.

'Miss Jones.' His cultured voice, as Bryn had discovered five years ago, wasn't in the least accented, as might
have been expected from his name, but was as English
as her own. The same deep and husky rumble of a voice
that had once caused Bryn's knees to quake, and had still
done so even as she had listened to that voice condemn
her father and seal his fate.

Bryn almost took a step back as Gabriel D'Angelo
stood up and moved out from behind the marble desk.
She managed to stand her ground as she realised he had
only risen to his feet in order to hold out his hand to her
in greeting. A lean and elegant hand totally in keeping
with the strength Bryn could discern in every leanly
muscled inch of him.

The sort of strength that she had no doubts was capable of crushing every bone in her own much smaller hand, if he chose to exert it.

Bryn gave an inward jolt as she realised he was studying her just as closely through narrowed lids, those melted chocolate-brown eyes appearing to see everything and miss nothing.

Would he recognise her as Sabryna Harper? Somehow she doubted it, given the fact that the gauche Sabryna, despite Gabriel having kissed her once, would have made very little impact on the life of a man like Gabriel D'Angelo, and there would have been so many other women in his life—and his bed!—during the past five years.

Besides which, her name was different, and she looked dramatically different: she was twenty pounds lighter, her hair was now cut short with blonde highlights, her face thinner, more angled, and she wore contact lenses rather than dark-framed glasses.

But was it possible—could Gabriel D'Angelo have recognised her, despite those changes?

Bryn moved one sweat-dampened hand surreptitiously against the thigh of her trousers before raising it with the intention of brushing it as briefly as possible against his much larger hand. A move Gabriel D'Angelo instantly circumvented as those long, lean fingers closed firmly about, and retained hold, of Bryn's—instantly renewing and deepening that jolt of electricity, the sexual awareness, as it throbbed from his hand into hers, moving the length of her arm before settling in the fullness of her breasts, causing her nipples to tingle and harden beneath her blouse.

A jolt that Gabriel D'Angelo also felt, if the tightening

of his fingers about hers and the increased narrowing of those captivating eyes, was any indication.

'We meet at last, Miss Jones,' Gabriel murmured as he deliberately continued to hold the slenderness of her hand firmly within his own.

Bryn blinked, her expression suddenly wary, those dove-grey eyes even more beautiful now that they weren't hidden behind glasses. 'I—I'm not sure what you mean.'

Gabriel wasn't completely sure what he meant either!

Rafe's advice, when the two brothers had met for dinner before he flew back to New York five days ago, had been that the easiest and best way for Gabriel to avoid any further unpleasantness with the Harper family was to simply tell Eric Sanders to take Bryn Jones off the list of possible candidates for the upcoming New Artists Exhibition.

And on a professional level Gabriel understood exactly why his brother had given him that advice; given the circumstances of his past history with her late father William Harper, it was sound, even necessary, advice.

Except…

Gabriel had a history with Bryn too. Brief, admittedly, just a stolen kiss when he had driven her home from visiting Archangel one evening, but he had hoped for more at the time, had thought of Bryn often the past five years, had wondered, speculated, what would have become of the two of them if not for the scandal that had ripped them apart.

Gabriel wasn't in the least proud of the part he had played in the events of five years ago. Not William Harper's conviction and incarceration for fraud, his death in prison just months later or the way in which his wife and teenage daughter had been hounded and harassed during the whole ordeal.

Against his brother's advice Gabriel had tried to see
Sabryna, both during the trial and after her father was
sent to prison, but she had turned him away every time,
refusing to answer the door to him and changing her
number so he couldn't call her either. Gabriel had decided to step back, to give her time, before approaching
her again. And then William Harper had died in prison,
putting an end to any hopes Gabriel might have had for
himself and Sabryna ever having a relationship.

He had also taken an objective look, a purely professional look, over the past few days at the paintings Bryn
Jones had submitted to the competition. They were really good—her still-life paintings so delicately executed
it was almost possible for him to smell the rose petals
falling gently down from the vase. To want to reach out
and touch the ethereal beauty in a woman's eyes as she
looked down at the baby she held in her arms.

Gabriel could see genuine talent in every brush stroke,
the sort of rare artistic talent that would one day make
Bryn Jones' paintings highly collectable, as both objects
of beauty as well as a sound investment. Because of this
Gabriel didn't feel he could eliminate her as a candidate
for the New Artists Exhibition just to save himself from
the discomfort of facing her and having her hate every
breath of air he took.

He did, however, have every intention of keeping the
question of Bryn Jones' own motivation for entering the
competition in the forefront of any of his future deal-
ings with her.

Gabriel released her hand abruptly before moving to
retake his seat behind the desk, very aware that his earlier arousal had returned with a vengeance the moment
he had touched the silky softness of Bryn's hand. 'I was
referring to the fact that you're the seventh, and last, can-

didate to have been interviewed in the past two days.' The only candidate that Gabriel was interviewing personally, but she didn't need to know that.

Her cheeks slowly paled. 'The *seventh* candidate?'

He gave a dismissive shrug. 'It's always best to have a reserve, don't you think?'

She was a *reserve*?

Bryn had been so desperate she had swallowed her pride, her dislike of all things D'Angelo, to enter their damned competition, only to be told she was a reserve?

Bryn had thought—*believed*—that being asked to come in to Archangel for another interview meant that she had been chosen as one of the final six artists for the Archangel New Artists Exhibition. And now Gabriel D'Angelo was telling her she was a reserve! Like an actor who was expected to learn all the lines and then stand in the wings of the theatre every night, in the full knowledge they might never have the chance to appear on the stage!

Had she been recognised after all? And if she had, was this Gabriel D'Angelo's idea of amusing himself, of extracting further retribution for the scandal her father had brought upon the Archangel Gallery, and the three brothers who owned it, five years ago?

'Are you quite well, Miss Jones?' A frown now creased Gabriel's brow as he stood up once again and moved round the desk. 'You've gone very pale....'

No, Bryn wasn't 'well'. In fact she was feeling far from well! So much so that she didn't even attempt to back away as Gabriel moved far too close to her. She had swallowed her pride, risked everything, the whole persona and life she had made for herself these past five years, by even bringing herself to the attention of the

D'Angelo brothers, only to now be told she wasn't good enough!

'I— Is it possible I could have a glass of water?' She raised a slightly shaking hand up to the dampness of her brow.

'Of course.' Gabriel was still frowning darkly as he strode across to the bar.

She was a reserve.

How disappointing was that?

How humiliating was that?

Damn it, she had been living in a state of nervous tension since entering the competition and this was the thanks she got at the end of all that anxiety, all that swallowed pride: to be made the reserve artist for the Exhibition!

'I've changed my mind about the water,' she snapped tautly as she straightened. 'Do you have any whisky in there?'

Gabriel turned slowly, eyes narrowing as he saw that colour had returned to Bryn Jones' cheeks, her eyes taking on a similar angry glow. A glow he easily recognised as being the same one he had felt directed at him across the courtroom. Why was Bryn suddenly so angry? They had been in the middle of a conversation about—

Ah. Gabriel had stated she was the seventh candidate being interviewed in a six-candidate competition.

Gabriel strolled back with the glass of whisky she had asked for. 'I believe there's been a misunderstanding—'

'There certainly has.' She nodded, taking the crystal glass of whisky he held out to her and drinking it down in one swallow, only to breathe in with a gasp before coughing as the fiery alcohol hit the back of her throat.

'I think you'll find that thirty-year-old single-malt whisky is meant to be sipped and savoured rather than guzzled down like lemonade at a child's birthday party,' Gabriel drawled dryly as he took the empty glass from her slightly lax fingers and placed it safely on his desk as she bent over at the waist, obviously still fighting for breath. 'Should I—?'

'Do not even think about slapping me on the back!' she warned through gritted teeth as she straightened and saw his raised hand, her cheeks now a fiery red, eyes ringed with unshed tears caused by her choking fit.

At least, Gabriel hoped they were caused by her choking fit and not from disappointment. She had obviously misunderstood his earlier comment; he had caused this woman enough heartache already in her young life. 'Would you care for that glass of water now…?'

She glared even more fiercely. 'I'll be fine,' she snapped. 'As for your offer, Mr D'Angelo—'

'Gabriel.'

She blinked long silky lashes. 'I beg your pardon?'

'I asked that you call me Gabriel,' he invited warmly.

A frown settled on her face. 'What possible reason could I have for wanting to do that?'

Gabriel eyed her mockingly; with her hair styled in that short spiky fashion, at the moment she looked very much like a bristly, indignant hedgehog! 'I thought, perhaps, in the interest of…a friendlier working relationship?'

She gave an inelegant snort. 'We have no relationship, Mr D'Angelo, friendly, working or otherwise.' She picked up her shoulder bag from where it had fallen to the floor during her choking fit. 'And, while I'm sure many artists would feel flattered to be chosen seventh out of a six-candidate competition, I'm afraid I'm not one of them.' She turned sharply on her heel and marched towards the door.

'Bryn.'

She came to an abrupt halt at hearing her name spoken in that throaty rumble through those perfectly sculptured lips. The same chiselled lips that had once kissed her, that had filled her fantasies every night for months before, during, and after her father's trial and incarceration.

Her name sounded…sensual, when spoken in that husky voice. Soft, seductive and definitely sensual. A sensuality Bryn's body instantly responded to, her breasts once again feeling fuller, the nipples firming, aching.

Bryn turned slowly, her expression wary as she acknowledged, inwardly at least, that her traitorous body still thought Gabriel D'Angelo was the most decadent, wickedly attractive man she had ever set eyes on.

And it shouldn't.

She shouldn't.

How could she possibly still feel this way when this man had been instrumental in destroying her family?

They had been five tough years for both Bryn and her mother. The two of them had remained living in London while her father was in prison, only changing their surname and moving out of London after he had died.

On top of their grief had come the ordeal of finding somewhere to live, finally moving into the cottage they had found to rent in a little Welsh village.

Then had come the difficulty of Bryn finding and getting into a university that allowed her to live at home; she hadn't wanted to leave her still-devastated mother on her own. Her mother was a trained nurse, and had found a job at a local hospital, but Bryn had had to settle for working in a local café and fitting her hours of study around her work shifts.

In amongst all that change and struggle there hadn't been a lot of time for men in Bryn's life—the odd date

here and there, but never anything prolonged or intimate. Besides which, any serious involvement would
have eventually necessitated that she confide her real
name wasn't Bryn Jones at all, and that her father had
been William Harper, something she had been loath to
do.

At least Bryn had thought, until now, that was the reason she had avoided any serious involvement....

To look at Gabriel D'Angelo now, however, to hear
his voice again, and realise that *he* was the reason behind her lack of interest in other men, was humiliating
in the extreme.

To realise, to know, that it was this man's sensual good
looks, that deep voice, that filled her senses and created
a sexual tension within her without even trying.

To acknowledge that the hateful Gabriel D'Angelo, a
man who had kissed her just the once, a kiss he had no
doubt regretted as soon as it had happened, had been the
yardstick against which Bryn had judged all other men
for the past five years, was not only masochistic madness on her part, but disloyal to both her mother, and her
father's memory....

CHAPTER TWO

'YOU'VE GONE PALE again,' Gabriel said, striding determinedly towards where Bryn now stood transfixed and unmoving by the closed door of his office. A dark scowl creased his brow as he saw how the colour had once again leeched from those creamily smooth cheeks. 'Perhaps you should sit down for a minute—'

'Please don't!' She stepped back and away from the hand Gabriel had raised with the intention of lightly grasping her arm, her fingers tightly clutching her bag, her eyes deep pools of dark and angry velvet-grey as she gave a determined shake of her head. 'I have to go.'

Gabriel's mouth tightened at her aversion to his even touching her. 'We haven't finished our discussion yet, Bryn—'

'Oh, it's definitely finished, Mr D'Angelo,' she assured him spiritedly. 'As I said, thank you for the—the honour, of being chosen as the seventh candidate, but I really have no interest, or time, to waste on being a runner-up.' Her eyes flashed darkly. 'And I have no idea why you would ever have thought that I—'

'You were far and away the best of the six candidates to be chosen for the exhibition, Bryn,' Gabriel bit out briskly—before she had chance to dig a bigger hole for herself by insulting him even further. 'I saved the best till last,' he added dryly.

'That I might be, so thank you for your interest, but—' She broke off her tirade to stare up at him blankly as his words finally trickled through the haze of her anger. She moistened her lips—those sexily pouting lips!— with the tip of her tongue before speaking again. 'Did you just say…?'

'I did,' Gabriel confirmed grimly.

'But earlier you said— You told me that I was the seventh person being interviewed—'

'And one of the previous six is the reserve. And happy to be so,' he added harshly.

Bryn stared up at Gabriel as the full horror of what she had just done, what she had said, was replayed back to her in stark detail. At the same time realising he was right; at no time had Gabriel said she was the seventh-place candidate, only that she was the seventh artist being interviewed.

She swallowed as the nausea washed over her, and then swallowed again, to absolutely no avail, the single-malt whisky she had 'guzzled down like lemonade at a child's birthday party' obviously at war with her empty stomach; she had been far too tense about coming back to the gallery to be able to eat any breakfast this morning. 'I think I'm going to be sick!' she gasped as she raised a hand over her mouth.

'The bathroom is this way,' Gabriel said quickly, lightly grasping her arm and pulling her towards a closed door on the opposite side of the office.

Bryn didn't fight his hold on her this time, too busy trying to control the nausea to bother resisting as he threw open the bathroom door and pushed her inside. Bathroom? It was more like something you would find in a private home, with a full glass-enclosed walk-in shower along one wall, along with the cream porcelain facilities, and had to be as big as the whole of the bedsit in which Bryn had lived and painted this past year!

Bryn dropped her bag to the floor and ran across the room to hang her head over the toilet only just in time, as she immediately lost her battle with the nausea and was violently and disgustingly sick.

'Well, that really was a complete waste of a thirty-year-old single-malt whisky!' Gabriel commented dryly some minutes later, when it became obvious from Bryn's dry retching that she had nothing else left in her stomach to bring up.

Adding further to her humiliation Bryn realised he must have remained in the bathroom the whole time she was being physically ill. 'I'll buy you a replacement bottle,' she muttered as she flushed the toilet, and avoided so much as glancing at the dark figure looming in the doorway as she moved to the sink to turn on one of the gold taps and splash cold water onto her clammy cheeks.

'At a thousand pounds a bottle?'

Bryn's eyes were round with shock as she lowered the towel she had been patting against her cheeks, before turning to look at him as he leaned against the doorframe, arms folded across the broad width of his muscled chest.

She instantly wished she hadn't looked at him as mockery gleamed evidently in his eyes. 'Who pays that sort of money for—? You do, obviously,' she acknowledged heavily as he raised his dark brows. 'Okay, so maybe I can't afford to buy you a replacement bottle right now.'

He gave an appreciative and throaty chuckle. And instantly threw Bryn into a state of rapid, heart-thumping awareness.

It had been years since she had seen Gabriel laugh—there had been no room for humour or soft words between them once her father had been arrested!—and the transformation that laughter made to his harshly handsome face reminded her of exactly why she had fallen so hard for him all those years ago.

She had believed—hoped—that if they should ever meet by chance, she wouldn't still respond to him like this, but the warmth that now shone in his eyes, the laughter lines beside those eyes and the grooves that had appeared in his chiselled cheeks, along with the flash of straight white teeth between those sculptured and deeply sensual lips, instantly proved how wrong she had been to hope. Gabriel might be sinfully handsome when he wasn't smiling, but he became lethally so when he was!

Bryn abruptly averted her gaze to finish drying her face and hands before checking her appearance in the mirror behind the sink—dark shadows beneath tired eyes, pale cheeks, throat slender and vulnerable. A vulnerability she simply couldn't afford in this man's presence.

She took a deep, controlling breath before turning back to face Gabriel. 'I apologise for my comments earlier, Mr D'Angelo. They were both rude and premature—'

'Stop there, Bryn,' he interrupted as he straightened. 'Abject apology doesn't sit well on your defensive shoulders,' he explained as she looked at him warily.

Angry colour rushed back into her cheeks. 'You could have at least let me finish my apology before mocking me.'

He was obviously having difficulty holding back another smile as he answered her. 'As I just said, abject apology doesn't appear to come naturally to you!'

She sighed at the deserved rebuke. 'I apologise once again.' Bryn didn't even attempt to meet his mocking gaze now as she instead kept her gaze fixed on the beautiful marble floor. She might know exactly why she harboured such resentment against this man, but as she had guessed—hoped—Gabriel didn't remember her at all, and she didn't want to do or say anything that would make him do so either.

'Shall we go and finish our conversation now?' he prompted briskly. 'Or do you need to hang over my toilet for a while longer?'

Bryn gave a pained frown. 'It was the whisky on top of an empty stomach.' And the fact that she knew, as did he, that she had prejudged his words without so much as a single hesitation!

'Of course it was,' Gabriel humoured dryly as he stood aside for Bryn to precede him back into the office, only too well aware that it was her resentment towards him for past deeds that was responsible for her having jumped to the wrong conclusions. 'And it's sacrilege to drink single-malt whisky any other way but neat.'

'At that price I can see that it would be, yes,' he heard Bryn mutter derisively. A mutter he chose to ignore as he instead returned to the reason for her being there in the first place. 'As I said, you are definitely one of the six candidates to have been chosen for the New Artists Exhibition being held in the gallery next month. Shall we sit down and discuss the details?' He indicated the comfortable brown leather sofa and chairs arranged about the coffee table in front of those floor-to-ceiling picture windows.

'Of course.' She noticeably chose to sit in one of the

armchairs, rather than on the sofa, before crossing one of her knees neatly over the other and looking up at him questioningly.

Gabriel didn't join her immediately, but went to the bar instead to take a bottle of water from the refrigerator, collecting a clean glass as well, then walking back to place them both down on the coffee table in front of her before lowering his length down into the chair opposite hers.

'Thank you,' she murmured softly, taking the top off the bottle and pouring the water into the glass. She took a long, grateful swallow before speaking again. 'Mr Sanders told me some of the details last week but obviously I'm interested in knowing more…' Her tone was businesslike.

Gabriel studied her through narrowed lids as they went on to discuss the details of the exhibition more fully, Bryn writing down the details in a notebook she had taken from her bulky shoulder bag.

Five years ago this woman had still been sweetly innocent, a young woman poised on the cusp of womanhood, a combination that had both intrigued and fascinated him. The passing of those years had stripped away all that innocence, in regard to people and events, at least; Gabriel had no way of knowing whether Bryn was still physically innocent, although somehow he doubted it. Five years was a long time.

But not only had Bryn grown more beautiful during those years, she had also grown in confidence, especially where her art was concerned, and she talked on the subject with great knowledge and appreciation.

'Have you ever thought of working in a gallery like Archangel?' Gabriel prompted as their conversation drew to an end half an hour later.

Bryn looked up from placing her notebook back into her handbag. 'Sorry?'

He shrugged. 'You're obviously knowledgeable on the subject, enthusiastic and bright, and those things would make you an asset to any gallery, not just Archangel.'

Bryn frowned as she looked warily at Gabriel across the glass coffee table, not sure if she had understood him correctly. 'Are you offering me a job?' she finally prompted incredulously.

He returned her gaze unblinkingly. 'And if I was?'

'Then my answer would have to be no! Thank you,' she added belatedly as she realised she was once again being rude, a rudeness that was totally out of keeping with her expected role as one of the grateful finalists in the New Artists Exhibition.

'Why would it?'

'Why?' She gave an impatient shake of her head at his even having to ask that question. 'Because I want my paintings to hang in a gallery, to hopefully be sold in a gallery, not to work as an assistant in one!'

He shrugged. 'Do you have something against taking a job to help pay the bills until that happens?'

Bryn eyed him guardedly, only too aware that her rent was due to be paid next week and that she had other bills that had reached the red-reminder stage too. And yes, a job did help to pay the bills, but she already had a job, at yet another café, even if it didn't pay nearly well enough to cover both her monthly rent and the bills, no matter how much she tried to economise.

It was almost as if Gabriel had guessed that and was offering her charity....

She instantly chided herself; of course Gabriel D'Angelo wasn't trying to help her. He just knew, as she did, that she was more than capable of doing the job he was offering, and he had no doubt assumed she would jump at the chance to work at Archangel, based on the fact that, historically, artists were known for starving in garrets.

Bryn wasn't starving, exactly, she just didn't eat some days. And while her third-floor bedsit wasn't exactly a garret, it was barely big enough to swing the proverbial cat in, with one half of the room put aside for sleeping and cooking and the other half utilised as her studio.

'No, of course not,' she answered him lightly. 'But I already have a job—'

'At another gallery?'

Bryn frowned as she heard the sharpness in his tone. 'What does it matter where I work?'

He raised dark brows. 'It matters in this case because it would hardly be appropriate for your paintings to be displayed at Archangel when you're working for another gallery.'

Good point, Bryn acknowledged ruefully. 'Right.' She nodded. 'Well, I don't work for another gallery. But I do have a job,' she continued briskly as she bent down to retrieve her bag from the floor. 'And my next shift starts in half an hour, so—'

'Your next…shift?'

'Yes, my next shift,' Bryn confirmed abruptly, stung by the incredulity in his cultured voice. 'I work behind the counter in a well-known coffee-shop franchise.'

His brows rose. 'Latte, cappuccino, espresso and a low-calorie muffin? That sort of coffee-shop franchise?'

The previous half an hour of conversation had gone smoothly; it had even been enjoyable at times, as they'd discussed which paintings from her portfolio Bryn was going to show at the exhibition next month, the timelines and other necessary details. But that had so obviously only been a brief lull in the tension between them if Gabriel had now decided to pull his arrogant-millionaire rank on her. Bryn eyed him challengingly. 'You have something against coffee shops?'

Those sculptured lips thinned. 'I don't recall ever having been inside one.'

Of course he hadn't; people as rich as Gabriel D'Angelo frequented exclusive restaurants and fashionable bars, not high-street coffee shops.

'But I do have something against one of my artists working in one of them, yes,' he continued evenly.

She stiffened. 'One of your artists?'

'This will be your first public exhibition, I believe?' he prompted evenly.

'I've sold one or two paintings in smaller galleries in the past couple years,' she came back with defensively.

'But am I right in thinking this will be the first time that so many Bryn Jones paintings have been shown together in an official exhibition?'

'Yes…' Bryn confirmed slowly.

He nodded. 'Then in future, whether you like it or not, your name will be linked with the Archangel Gallery.'

Bryn certainly didn't like it. It had felt as if she were being forced to walk over burning-hot coals by even entering her paintings in a competition being run by the hateful D'Angelo brothers; she certainly didn't like the idea of her name being for ever linked with either them or their galleries.

She hadn't even told her mother of the desperation that had forced her to enter the competition, dreaded thinking how her mother would react if she were to ever find out Bryn was having her work shown at *this* gallery!

And maybe Bryn should have thought about that a

little more deeply before deciding to walk over those burning hot coals and enter the competition.

Gabriel could almost actually see the war being waged inside Bryn's head. The natural desire to have her artistic talent not only shown for the first time but also recognised for the talent that it was, obviously totally at war with her desire not to be in the least beholden, or associated with in the future, either the D'Angelo name or the Archangel Gallery. Yet another indication of how much she still disliked him and all he stood for. If he had needed any. Which he didn't.

'Your point being?' Bryn now prompted guardedly.

He grimaced. 'I think it would look better in the catalogue being printed and sent out to our clients before the exhibition if you weren't listed as currently working in a coffee shop.'

'Better for whom?'

Gabriel bit back his irritation with her challenging tone, having no intention of admitting that he had already known about her working in a coffee shop—and that it was him, personally, who didn't like the idea of her working there. He might never have been into such an establishment, but he had driven past them numerous times, and the thought of Bryn being run ragged in such an establishment, day after day—evening after evening— just so that she could pay her bills every month, wasn't particularly appealing.

Besides which, Gabriel also knew, from the discreet enquiries he had made about her once Rafe had told him exactly who she was, that Bryn Jones suffered a constant struggle to pay those bills. A job as an assistant at Archangel would go a long way to relieving her of that burden, at least.

A dark frown creased his brow. 'What possible rea-

son could you have for refusing a job here if it was offered to you?'

'Let me see...' She lifted a finger to her chin in exag-
gerated thought. 'First, I don't want to work in a gallery.
Second, I don't want to work in a gallery. And third, I
don't want to work in a gallery!' Her eyes glittered determinedly.

'This gallery in particular, or just any gallery?' Gabriel questioned evenly.

'Any gallery,' Bryn answered firmly. 'Besides,
couldn't it be considered as a little...incestuous, if I were
to start working at Archangel now?' she forestalled Gabriel D'Angelo's next comment lightly.

'Because of your inclusion in the exhibition?'

'Exactly,' she confirmed with satisfaction.

His mouth tightened. 'And that's your final answer?'

'It is.'

He scowled darkly. 'You're very...intractable in your
attitude, Miss Jones.'

'I prefer to think of it as maintaining my independence, Mr D'Angelo,' Bryn came back sharply.

'Perhaps,' he drawled as he stood up in one fluid
movement, the dryness of his tone implying he thought
the opposite. 'I think we've said all that needs to be said
for today. I have another appointment in—' he glanced
at the expensive-looking gold watch on his wrist '—ten
minutes or so.' He looked at her expectantly as she remained seated.

'Oh. Right.' Bryn stood up so hastily she accidentally
kicked her bag across the floor, instantly scattering the
contents far and wide. 'Hells bells and blast it!' She immediately dropped to her knees on the carpeted floor,
her cheeks flushing with embarrassment as she began
collecting up her scattered belongings, some of which

were personal in the extreme, and cramming them back into her handbag.

'I've always wondered what women kept in their handbags,' Gabriel D'Angelo drawled in amusement.

'Well, now you know!' Bryn had paused to glare up at him, and instantly became aware of how his well over six feet of lean muscle towered over her so ominously. 'And I would get this done a whole lot quicker if you were to help rather than just stand there grinning!' Like an idiot, she could have added, but didn't, because it wouldn't have been the truth.

The last thing Gabriel was, or looked like when he grinned in that way, was an idiot; devilishly rakish, devastatingly attractive—lazily, sensuously so—and maybe even boyishly mischievous, as that grin knocked years off his age, but he certainly didn't look like an idiot.

Besides which he had stopped grinning now, those chocolate-brown eyes narrowed on her in totally male assessment.

A frown creased Gabriel's brow as he looked down at Bryn on her hands and knees in front of him. It was a… provocative pose, to say the least. As the ever-increasing bulge in his trousers testified.

Bryn's cheeks were flushed, her lips slightly moist and parted and it should be illegal what those black trousers did for her heart-shaped bottom—and Gabriel's arousal—bent over like that…!

'Right,' he rasped harshly as he crouched down beside her, his gaze averted as he gathered up the notebook and pen she had been using to make notes in earlier, as well as a small bottle of hand cream and a lip salve. 'Hell's bells and blast it…?' he prompted gruffly, aware of her perfume now; nothing so anaemic as something floral for Bryn Jones, she was a mixture of spices, with an underlying hint of sensual woman.

He saw her shrug out of the corner of his eye. 'My mother has never approved of a woman swearing, so I learnt to improvise at an early age.'

Gabriel only half listened to her answer as he moved down onto his knees. The smell of those spices—cinnamon, something fruity, maybe a hint of honey and that more elusive smell of sensual woman—all served to increase his awareness of the woman beside him. 'A pot of white pepper, Bryn?' he questioned as he held it up for inspection.

'It's cheaper than pepper spray!' She snatched the pot from his hand before thrusting it back into her bag.

Gabriel sat back on his heels to look at her. 'Pepper spray?'

'I have to walk home late at night several times a week.' She dismissed his concern without looking up, missing the frown of disapproval that clouded Gabriel's face.

'From the coffee shop,' he said stiffly.

She gave him a brief glance before looking away again. 'Why does that bother you so much?'

Good question. But not one Gabriel could answer. Not without revealing that he knew exactly who she was, and the part he felt he had played in her current circumstances—something her defensive attitude told him she definitely didn't want from him.

And the past half hour in Bryn Jones' company was enough to tell him that what she claimed as independence was actually defensive pride, and that she had more than her fair share of it.

Because of the scandal involving her father five years

ago? No doubt that was a contributing factor, but Gabriel had a feeling she would have always been more than a little prickly; her feistiness was all too apparent in those flashing eyes and the stubborn tilt of her pointed chin.

'I thought you had another appointment in a few minutes?' She gave Gabriel a pointed look as he knelt unmoving beside her.

Make that a whole lot prickly! 'I was just wondering what a third party, if they should walk into my office right now, would make of the two of us being down here on the floor together like this,' Gabriel came back with deliberate and husky provocation.

'We may just find out if your next appointment arrives early!' Colour warmed her cheeks as she bent over to retrieve a lipstick from beneath the coffee table.

As that next appointment was the elderly Lord David Simmons, an avid art collector, Gabriel worried the other man might have a heart attack on the spot if he should catch so much as a glimpse of Bryn's shapely backside!

'Did I say something amusing?' Bryn sat back on her heels to look at Gabriel, who was grinning again, his dark hair having fallen rakishly over his forehead, causing Bryn's hands to curl into fists as she resisted the impulse to touch those silky dark locks.

'Private joke.' His grin faded, his eyes deepening almost to black as he continued to look at her intently.

Except Gabriel wasn't looking at all of her, Bryn realised self-consciously, just her lips. Moist and slightly parted lips that she immediately clamped shut as she rose abruptly to her feet and slung her bag over her shoulder.

Only to as quickly freeze in place as she realised, with their difference in height, that Gabriel's face was now level with her breasts.

A fact he took full advantage of as he made no effort
to hide his interest in the fact that he could see Bryn's
bared breasts beneath the gauzy material of her floral
blouse....

CHAPTER THREE

'MR D'ANGELO...?'

'Hmm?' Gabriel couldn't look up from the mesmerising view he currently had of Bryn's breasts, full and perfect breasts, tipped by rosy areolas and plump nipples. Rapidly firming nipples that deepened in colour even as he continued to gaze at them.

'Mr D'Angelo? Gabriel!' Bryn's voice became more urgent as he failed to respond.

Gabriel ran the tip of his tongue moistly over his lips as he imagined taking those nipples into his mouth and suckling hungrily, his roused shaft instantly throbbing its approval of the idea. 'You aren't wearing a bra....'

'No. I—'

'Do you intend to wear this blouse to work today?' He scowled at the thought of Bryn's seminaked breasts being ogled by other men across the counter of a high-street coffee shop.

'We're all required to wear a black T-shirt with the franchise logo on it,' Bryn answered him dismissively. 'And will you please get up!' She grasped hold of his arm and tried to pull him to his feet.

A move that jiggled those plumped and roused breasts temptingly in front of Gabriel's heated gaze. If he just moved forward, ever so slightly, he would be able to put his mouth on them and actually taste—

'Damn it, Gabriel, someone is knocking on the door!' Bryn hissed. The urgency of her tone, as much as the words, finally broke through Gabriel's sexual haze, causing him to frown darkly as he realised exactly what he was doing. What he had been thinking of doing.

And with whom....

Bryn breathed out shakily as Gabriel finally rose abruptly to his feet, running his fingers impatiently through his hair as he shot her a scowling glance before striding across the room to wrench open the outer door.

'I'm sorry, Mr D'Angelo, I didn't realise Miss Jones was still here.' The receptionist took a wary step back as she obviously saw and recognised the aggression in Gabriel's scowling expression.

'Good to see you again, Gabriel!' The elderly man at the receptionist's side appeared less concerned as he greeted the younger man warmly before stepping into the room and giving Bryn a friendly if curious glance. 'Are you going to introduce me to your young lady?' he prompted Gabriel.

'I'm just Mr D'Angelo's previous appointment,' Bryn supplied quickly, dismissing even the suggestion of her and the arrogant Gabriel D'Angelo ever being a couple. 'And I've already taken up far too much of his time,' she added lightly as she joined them near the open doorway before turning a cool gaze on the still-frowning Gabriel.

Damn it, she was doing her best to allay the speculation she had seen in the receptionist's eyes and the curiosity in Gabriel's visitor's. The least Gabriel could do was try to reciprocate rather than continuing to scowl his irritation at the interruption!

An interruption of what? Bryn wondered....

There had been no doubting the hunger she had seen in those seductive eyes as Gabriel had looked at her breasts so appreciatively, or the flush of arousal high in those sculptured cheeks as he had begun to lean towards her. Evidence that, if they hadn't been interrupted by the knock on the door, he would have acted on that unmistakable hunger, and actually kissed her breasts? Perhaps more than kissed them?

Bryn felt her knees go weak just thinking of having those sculptured lips latching on to her aroused nipple, suckling deeply, his tongue a hot and arousing rasp—

'Bryn, this is Lord David Simmons.' Gabriel's voice was harsh as he made the introduction. 'David, this is Bryn Jones.' His tone softened to politeness. 'One of the six artists whose paintings will be appearing in the New Artists Exhibition next month.'

'Indeed?' David Simmons' warm blue eyes lit up with pleasure as he and Bryn shook hands. 'I'm very much looking forward to attending the exhibition,' he informed Bryn warmly as he retained a hold on her hand. 'I flew over to Paris two months ago to attend the New Artists Exhibition at the Archangel Gallery there, and I can assure you you're in good hands with Gabriel here. He has a definite eye for recognising new talent.'

Bryn's smile froze on her lips, not just at being told she was in good hands with Gabriel but also because she knew, only too well, that Gabriel had a definite eye for spotting a forgery too. She released her hand from David Simmons'.

'Then no doubt I'll see you again next month, Lord Simmons—'

'Please, call me David,' he invited warmly.

'Bryn,' she returned tautly, very much aware of Gabriel's brooding presence beside her. 'Now, if you will all excuse me…? I have another appointment as well.'

Gabriel knew Bryn's other 'appointment' was her shift at the coffee shop, a fact that still displeased him greatly. His bad mood was added to by the way David Simmons, a man old enough to be Bryn's grandfather, had maintained far too long a hold of her hand when introduced.

'Linda, please make an appointment for Miss Jones, before she leaves, for her to see Eric on Monday,' Gabriel instructed abruptly.

'Certainly, Mr D'Angelo,' the receptionist responded brightly.

Bryn blinked her long lashes. 'May I ask what for?'

Gabriel's mouth tightened. 'We need more personal information and photographs for the catalogue we're sending out to existing clients—as I believe we discussed earlier?'

Her cheeks coloured slightly at the rebuke, and a flash of anger illuminated her eyes. 'Obviously I must have been so overwhelmed at being told I was one of the six artists chosen for the exhibition that I didn't hear all the details that followed.'

Some of Gabriel's tension eased as he saw the continued anger in Bryn's eyes accompany her too-sweetly-made statement. It also reminded him that Bryn had actually been physically ill, rather than 'overwhelmed', once he had fully explained her inclusion in the exhibition, a nausea she had no doubt still been suffering from when the two of them had sat down together and discussed the details of what still had to be done before the exhibition.

Not to mention the distracting attention he had given her breasts a few minutes ago!

Not that Gabriel was particularly proud of that lapse;

he had recognised five years ago that she represented a danger to his self-control, and his meeting today with the older and more self-assured—even more beautiful!— Bryn Jones had shown him that danger still existed. Very much so...

Perhaps he should have taken Rafe's advice after all and stayed well away from Bryn Jones.

'Just make the appointment, Bryn,' he bit out tersely. 'I'll instruct Eric that he needs to explain those details to you again on Monday.'

She turned to give the older man a warm smile. 'It was a pleasure to meet you, Lord Simmons. Mr D'Angelo.' Her voice had noticeably cooled, and there was no smile, or mention of her feeling any of that same pleasure in meeting Gabriel.

'Pretty girl,' David Simmons remarked as the two men watched Bryn join Linda out in the hallway before closing the door firmly behind her.

'Linda?' Gabriel deliberately misunderstood the older man.

David gave him a knowing glance. 'Does Miss Jones paint as beautifully as she looks?'

'More so, if anything,' Gabriel answered truthfully; Bryn's work really was exceptional, and he had no doubt that David Simmons would recognise that talent as easily as he had, and would most likely be happy to buy one of her paintings in the exhibition next month.

'Interesting...' The older man nodded as he followed Gabriel to the seating area in front of the window.

It wasn't until much later, after his business with David had been concluded and Linda had escorted the older man down the stairs that Gabriel was able to pause and replay his meeting with Bryn from earlier.

The prickly outspokenness she had been unable to

hide had shown that she hadn't even begun to forgive him for the part he had played in her father's downfall. A defensive manner that was also an indication of the resentment she felt at having to be even slightly beholden to the D'Angelo family—clearly telling Gabriel that Bryn wouldn't have entered the New Artists competition, or the Archangel Gallery, if she hadn't considered it the very last resort. It was—

A glance across the office showed something glinting from beneath one of the armchairs. A something that, upon closer inspection, proved to be an item that he knew must have fallen out of Bryn's handbag earlier.

'And what can I get you to drink this evening— Gabriel?' The last word came out much louder than Bryn would have wished after glancing up and seeing that her next customer was Gabriel D'Angelo.

A Gabriel D'Angelo who was much more casually dressed—but no less lethally attractive—than he had been in his office earlier today; he wore a thin black cashmere sweater, the sleeves pulled up to just below his elbows—which emphasised every toned muscle and dip of those broad shoulders, chest, and the flatness of his stomach—with faded denims resting comfortably on the leanness of his hips. His overlong dark hair had also been slightly tousled by the warm evening breeze outside and fell softly, rakishly, onto his brow.

He'd claimed earlier never to have been inside a coffee shop, which posed the question of what was he doing in one now? And not just any coffee shop, but the one in which Bryn worked, because there was no way she believed his being here was just a coincidence.

She frowned slightly as she realised the people in the queue behind Gabriel were getting restless; six o'clock in the evening was one of their busiest times, when the people leaving work called in to collect a drink and something to eat on their way home, or to linger in the coffee shop while they relaxed for an hour or so with friends. It was even busier as it was a Friday evening, and the end of the working week for most people.

'What can I get for you this evening, Mr D'Angelo?' she repeated tightly.

He looked up at the board behind her. 'Black coffee?'

'Black coffee,' she repeated slowly; the coffee shop served six different brands of coffee and just as many types, as well as several flavoured teas, all of which could have milk, runny or whipped cream or several different flavoured shots, and Gabriel was asking for black coffee!

He nodded. 'If it's not too much trouble,' he drawled derisively.

'It's no trouble at all.' Bryn was aware of the keen eyes of the manager fixed beadily on the two of them as she watched Bryn ring up the sale and take Gabriel's money—unless, of course, Sally was just enjoying the chance to ogle the six feet three inches of hot, heart-poundingly attractive man standing on the other side of the counter.

Which appeared to be what all the other women in the coffee shop were doing—surreptitiously by the ones with a man of their own, the others openly eating Gabriel up with their eyes!

'If you would like to follow me,' Bryn instructed sharply as she moved farther down the crowded counter to fill his order, at the same time allowing one of the other assistants to take her place and serve the next customer. 'What are you doing here, Mr D'Angelo?' she muttered under her breath as she prepared his tray.

'Sorry?'

'I said—'

'You'll have to speak up a little, Bryn,' he drawled. 'I can't hear you with all the other noise and chatter in the room.'

She shot him an irritated frown as she raised her voice slightly. 'I asked what you're doing here.'

'Oh.' He nodded. 'You left something of yours on my office floor when you left earlier today, and I thought you might want them back.'

Bryn stilled, her breath catching in her throat, as she realised that the half a dozen or so people standing closest to them had fallen silent as they overheard his remark, their eyes wide as they obviously drew their own conclusions as to what Bryn might possibly have left on Gabriel D'Angelo's office floor....

'Did you do that on purpose?'

Gabriel looked up at Bryn a short time later as she came over to wipe and clear the table next to the one where he sat in a comfortable armchair, enjoying his mug of surprisingly good Colombian coffee. 'Did I do what on purpose?'

She frowned, her skin appearing creamier than ever against the black T-shirt she now wore in place of the gauzy blouse of earlier. 'You implied— You deliberately gave the impression a few minutes ago that I had left an item of clothing on the floor of your office earlier today!'

He raised dark brows. 'I did?'

Bryn's mouth thinned as she pretended to wipe his table. 'You know you did.'

He had, yes. Because, until she had seen him, Bryn had looked relaxed and smiling as she served customers, that smile instantly replaced by an annoyed frown the moment she'd recognised him, arousing his own feelings of irritation.

It had been a mistake for him to come here at all; he accepted that now. He should have just passed her property on to Eric Sanders to give back to her on Monday, or bagged it up and had it delivered by courier to her tomorrow rather than come here personally.

He knew he should stay well away from Bryn, that it was better for both of them if he did so; she so obviously wanted nothing to do with him outside Archangel, and he knew from their meeting how dangerous she was to his self-control.

It seemed he just hadn't been able to stop himself from coming here when the opportunity presented itself.

His jaw tightened. 'I do have something of yours that I thought you might need returning to you sooner rather than later.'

'Really?' She eyed him sceptically.

Gabriel leaned back in the leather armchair to look up at her through narrowed lids. 'You know, Bryn, I've found your attitude towards me to be…less than polite since meeting you. Surprisingly so, considering that I'm one of the owners of the gallery where your paintings are going to be exhibited. If you have a problem with me, or my gallery, then perhaps now might be a good time for you to tell me what that problem is?'

A delicate blush coloured her cheeks as she chewed on her bottom lip, her artistic ambitions obviously once again at war with the past—and present—resentment Bryn felt towards him.

It was a resentment Gabriel understood, and sympathised with, but it rankled that Bryn still so obviously held him to blame for what had happened in the past; Gabriel wasn't responsible for William Harper's attempt to sell a forged Turner to the D'Angelos. Only for showing the other man up as the charlatan he so obviously was.

Bryn had initially talked herself into entering her paintings in the New Artists competition by reassuring herself that in all likelihood she would never have to meet any of the three D'Angelo brothers personally. She now found it totally disconcerting that she had met and spoken with one of them—twice in one day!—and that that one should happen be Gabriel!

Even so, she knew she deserved Gabriel's criticism. She *was* guilty of allowing the past to influence her manner towards him, something he must consider highly disrespectful, as well as puzzling, given that he only knew her as Bryn Jones, aspiring artist, and had given no indication of recognising her as Sabryna Harper. If Gabriel ever learned the truth, it would no doubt result in that seventh, reserve artist being asked to take her place in the exhibition!

'I apologise if I've seemed less than...grateful, Mr D'Angelo,' she muttered stiffly. 'Obviously it's a privilege and an honour to be chosen as one of the new artists to display their paintings in a gallery as prestigious as Archangel—'

'As I told you earlier, Bryn, abject apology doesn't sit well on your slender shoulders,' he drawled, dark eyes gleaming with mocking humour.

Her gaze fell from his. 'In that case, I believe you said you came here this evening to return something of mine?'

'I did, yes.'

'And?' she prompted.

He glanced down at the gold watch on his wrist. 'What time do you finish this evening?'

Bryn frowned. 'In a couple hours.'

'Eight o'clock?'

'Eight-fifteen,' she corrected warily.

He nodded. 'Then I'll meet you outside at eight-fifteen.'

Bryn's brows rose. 'I don't understand.'

He shrugged those broad shoulders. 'I think it would be a good idea for the two of us to have dinner together, so that we can discuss, and hopefully dispose of, whatever your problem is with me or my gallery.'

Bryn's mouth gaped open. Had she imagined it or had Gabriel just— Had he just invited her to have dinner with him tonight?

No, of course he hadn't, Bryn answered her own question; Gabriel had made a statement, not asked a question. Because he was a man used to issuing orders and then expecting them to be obeyed? Or simply because it didn't even occur to him that Bryn—or any other woman, for that matter—would ever think of turning down a dinner invitation with the darkly attractive and eminently eligible Gabriel D'Angelo?

Bryn had a feeling that both of those things were true, but going out to dinner with him, discussing whatever her problem was with him or his gallery, was *not* an option.

Gabriel could almost see the struggle going on inside Bryn's beautiful head as she tried to find a polite way of refusing his invitation.

An invitation Gabriel knew he never should have made when he couldn't even look at Bryn without wanting her and she so obviously detested the very sight of him.

This prickly Bryn was so different from the Sabryna of five years ago, but even then Gabriel had known how much her beauty and innocence had appealed to him. He had only kissed her the once, a sweet and yet arousing kiss, a kiss that had affected him so deeply he had continued to think about her for months after her father's trial was over and she had refused to so much as see Gabriel again, and off and on in the years that followed too, as he'd found himself wondering what she was doing with her life, if she was happy.

That single meeting with her earlier today had shown him that the woman she had become, the woman she was now, had just as deep an effect on him.

So much so that being alone in his office with her, knowing he would have been able to touch her soft and creamy skin if he had just lifted his hand, and that unique spicy, womanly smell of her had invaded his senses, had resulting in his thinking of nothing else but her for the past six hours.

As for his arousal…! That had been a pounding ache for those same six hours, and even now the hardness of his shaft was pressing painfully against the restricting material of his jeans.

Which was as good a reason as any for him to get the hell as far away from Bryn Jones as was possible.

'Obviously not,' he dismissed harshly, pushing his cooling mug of coffee away from him before standing up abruptly. 'These are yours, I believe,' he rasped abruptly as he withdrew a silver metal tube from the front pocket of his jeans.

Bryn was still so shocked by Gabriel's suggestion that the two of them have dinner together this evening that it took several seconds for her to register the significance of the metal tube he held out to her. 'My reading glasses…' she finally recognised softly as she took the tube from him, glancing up at him quickly—guiltily— as she realised he really had come here this evening to return something that had obviously fallen out of her handbag earlier.

She moistened her lips with the tip of her tongue before speaking. 'It was very kind of you to return them to me so promptly and in person.'

He gave a hard, derisive smile. 'That sounded as if it actually hurt.'

'Of course it didn't.' Her cheeks had warmed at the taunt. 'And I apologise if you think my manner towards you has been…less than polite. I really am grateful for the opportunity to show my paintings at Archangel.'

'As far as you're concerned, Bryn, I *am* the Archangel Gallery,' he admonished harshly.

And quite what she was going to do about that Bryn had no idea; she only knew, having come this far, having worked so hard and for so many years towards this, it was now totally unthinkable she should be forced to withdraw her paintings from the exhibition because of the man who owned and ran the gallery! Or for Gabriel to decide her manner was so unacceptable he decided to withdraw them for her.

'I'm not sure what you mean by that, Mr D'Angelo,' she prompted uncertainly; she hadn't forgotten those few brief moments of intimacy between them in his office earlier, when she had been certain that he was going to touch or kiss her breasts. But, grateful as she was that he hadn't recognised her, if Gabriel believed for one moment that his position as owner of the Archangel Gallery gave him some sort of power over her, then—

'I'm not sure I like your implication either, Bryn!' he responded, dismissing that illusion.

Her throat moved as she swallowed before speaking. 'Maybe we could go somewhere and grab a bite this evening after all? Talk this through—'

'I can see no point in us even attempting to do that unless you're going to be completely honest with me.' Those brown eyes glittered as he looked down the length of his nose at her. 'Are you going to be honest with me, Bryn?'

Bryn's breath caught in her throat as she looked up at him sharply, searchingly. Had Gabriel realised who she was after all?

Of course he hadn't! For one thing Bryn doubted this man had ever given so much as a single thought towards William Harper's wife and daughter once her father had been sent to prison. For another, she had changed so much in the past five years, not just her name, but the way she looked and behaved too that he couldn't possibly have recognised her as the gauche teenager he had once kissed. And last, if he had known who she really was, he would never have allowed her anywhere near him or his gallery—

'Bryn, I need you to go back on the counter now.' There was an underlying edge of steel to her manager's tone as her rebuke cut across the tension between Gabriel and Bryn.

Bryn gave a guilty start as she turned to face Sally, knowing that the pointed remark was deserved; she had been talking with Gabriel D'Angelo for far too long. 'I'll be right there,' she promised lightly before turning back to Gabriel. 'Shall I meet you outside at eight-fifteen?'

For a moment Gabriel thought about refusing, about walking away from this woman and not looking back.

The plans for the exhibition were well in hand, and as such there was absolutely no reason why the two of them should even meet again before the night of that exhibition. Eric was more than capable of handling any and all future meetings with Bryn Jones.

And there were far too many reasons why Gabriel should keep his distance from her....

CHAPTER FOUR

GABRIEL WAS STILL having second, third—and fourth!—thoughts as to the wisdom of meeting up with Bryn Jones again this evening as he sat in his parked car waiting for her to emerge from the coffee shop.

It didn't take too much intelligence to know what Bryn had been thinking earlier. Or to know why she had thought it. Gabriel's behaviour earlier hadn't exactly been businesslike, most especially that remark about her not wearing a bra. Especially considering the fact that he had been down on his knees in front of her, staring at her breasts, when he'd made it!

Which was, Gabriel had reasoned with himself, all the more reason for him to meet with her again this evening, if only to reassure her that the two of them were to have a business relationship in future and nothing more.

Gabriel's senses all went on full alert—making a complete nonsense of that last sentiment—as he looked through the smoked glass of the window beside him and saw Bryn step out of the coffee shop at last, a short denim jacket over top of the gauzy blouse she had worn earlier today, a frown darkening her creamy brow as she looked for him amongst the crush of people still milling about on the busy pavement.

No doubt she was adding tardiness, or standing her up completely, to Gabriel's already long list of sins.

'Bryn.'

She turned in the direction of Gabriel's voice, giving a rueful grimace as she saw he had emerged from the sleek black sports car parked illegally outside the coffee shop. The smoky black windows had prevented her from seeing him seated inside. 'Mr D'Angelo,' she greeted as she hurried over to where he stood. 'I hope I haven't kept you waiting long?' she murmured politely.

'Not in the least.' He just as politely opened the passenger door of the car before standing back to allow her to get inside. 'And it's Gabriel,' he reminded her gently.

Bryn didn't move, or respond to his comment. 'Er— there's a pizza place just round the corner.'

He grimaced. 'I saw it. And trust me, Bryn, what they serve isn't real Italian pizza.'

'But—'

'The name is D'Angelo, Bryn.' He quirked dark, pointed brows.

It hadn't been part of Bryn's plans for this evening to go off somewhere in Gabriel's car with him. She had envisaged them getting a quick slice at the place round the corner, an hour or so of—hopefully—pleasant conversation, before they each went their separate ways. But, considering this was supposed to be a conciliatory meeting, it would look petty for her to refuse him now— besides which, with his Italian ancestry he probably did know more about pizza than she did!

'Fine.' She gave a bright, unconcerned smile as she moved forward to slide into the black-leather passenger seat, determined that this evening was going to go better than their previous two meetings had. Determined that she was going to act more like the fledgling-artist-grateful-to-the-art-gallery-owner-for-this-opportunity that she was supposed to be.

She had to push firmly to the back of her mind that the sleek sports car, the interior smelling richly of leather, along with a spicy, totally male smell that was pure Gabriel, was so reminiscent of that evening he had kissed her.

Gabriel closed the passenger door once Bryn had settled into the seat, before moving back to the other side of the car and resuming his seat behind the wheel. 'You didn't have any trouble after I left earlier?' he prompted as he fastened his seat belt and turned on the ignition.

'No, it was fine,' she dismissed; there was no need to tell him of the lecture she had received from Sally earlier about not spending her time talking to one of the customers, no matter how hot he was, and how there were plenty of other people who would like her job if she didn't want it. 'Where are we going exactly?' Bryn prompted interestedly as Gabriel manoeuvred the vehicle out into the evening flow of traffic.

'It's a little family-run place I know in a back street in the East End— Trust me on this, Bryn,' he drawled as he noticed her surprise.

'I'm sure it's fine. I was just— It doesn't sound like your sort of place,' she amended awkwardly.

'My sort of place being…?'

Bryn realised she was once again on shaky ground as she heard the hard challenge in Gabriel's tone; it hadn't taken long for the tension to return between them, despite her earlier promise with herself to keep the conversation light and pleasant. 'I have absolutely no idea,' she answered honestly.

'Good answer, Bryn.' Gabriel chuckled wryly, his seat

all the way back to accommodate his long legs, and appearing very relaxed as his hands moved lightly on the steering wheel of the powerful sports car.

He had nice hands, Bryn noted abstractedly. Long and artistic, and yet gracefully powerful at the same time. 'How did you become such an art expert?' she prompted interestedly. 'Do you paint yourself? Or did you inherit the galleries?'

It was clear to Gabriel that Bryn had decided to make a concerted effort to be more polite to him and to keep their conversation impersonal rather than personal, if possible. Unfortunately she had chosen the wrong subject if that was her intention.

'I wanted to paint,' he answered abruptly. 'I even took a degree in art with that intention, only to very quickly realise that I'm someone who can appreciate art rather than be good enough to participate.'

'That's…unfortunate.'

'Very.' One of the biggest disappointments of Gabriel's life was realising that his real artistic talent was for the visual rather than painting itself.

Bryn was frowning slightly as she turned sideways in her seat to look at him. 'I can't imagine not being able to express myself through my painting.'

'The art world would be all the poorer for it too,' he assured gruffly. Knowing it was true, that Bryn showed an insight in her paintings, a sense, a knowing, for what was inside her subject, even a dying rose, rather than what was only visible with the naked eye; it was the quality that made her paintings so unique.

'The art world hasn't exactly been beating a path to my door before now,' she said with a shrug.

Gabriel gave her a sideways glance. 'That's probably because the galleries you've approached with your work

before now have all been looking for chocolate-box paintings, stuff they can sell to the tourists to hang in their
sitting rooms when they get back home to remind them
of their visit to London. Your paintings are too good for
that. Archangel would have no interest in showing them
if they weren't.'

Bryn had stilled beside him. 'I don't remember men-
tioning what galleries I've approached in the past.'

'You didn't need to,' Gabriel dismissed lightly, having
no intention of reigniting the tension between them by
confiding that he now had a file on her at Archangel—
another file on her. Michael apparently had one too, a
security file, although Gabriel hadn't seen that one. To be
fair, they now had a professional file on all seven of the
finalists of the competition, which listed previous sales,
of which Bryn had three. But Gabriel had good reason
to know that Bryn was more sensitive than most—quite
rightly so—about sharing the personal details of her life.

'But—'

'We're here,' Gabriel announced as he saw they had
reached Antonio's; just in the nick of time too, as Bryn
seemed intent on pursuing a subject he would rather not
continue. 'Don't be misled by the exterior. Or the interior either, for that matter,' he added dryly as he parked
the car in front of the small bistro before getting out and
moving around to open Bryn's door for her. 'Antonio
makes the best Italian food in London, and none of his
customers gives a damn about the decor.'

Bryn was glad of the warning as they walked into
the brightly lit interior. There was a strong smell of gar-
lic in the air, crowded tables covered with plastic red-
and-white-checked tablecloths, artificial plants dangling
from every conceivable nook and cranny and an overly
enthusiastic Italian tenor playing over the audio system.

'Toni sings and records all his own songs,' Gabriel explained as he saw Bryn wince at a particularly off-key moment.

'Something else I'm going to have to trust you on, hmm?' she came back teasingly. Only to stiffen as she realised what she had just said. And Gabriel D'Angelo was the very last man she should ever trust. For any reason.

'Gabrielo!' A round-faced and portly man rushed across the room to greet them, standing at least a foot shorter than Gabriel as he shook the younger man's hand enthusiastically. 'We 'ave not seen you 'ere for some time.'

'That's because I've been in Paris—'

'Aha, I see what has kept you away from us, Gabrielo.' Warm brown eyes had settled knowingly on Bryn. 'You 'ave brought your young lady to meet Mamma and me, yes?'

'No—' Bryn started to interrupt.

'I promised Bryn one of your famous pizzas with everything on, and a bottle of your best Chianti, Toni,' Gabriel interjected, cutting lightly across Bryn's denial as he took a firm hold of her elbow and squeezed warningly.

'No problem.' The older man beamed. 'You will find somewhere for you and your young lady to sit, and I will 'ave Mamma bring the wine to you.' He waddled off in the direction of the door at the back of the room marked Kitchen, stopping often to chat with one or other of his many customers.

Finding somewhere to sit wasn't as easy as it sounded; Gabriel was right, the place was heaving, despite the decor and the music. Luckily a young couple with a baby were just preparing to leave, and Bryn and Gabriel were able to grab their table before someone else did.

'This is wonderfully mad,' Bryn murmured a few

minutes later, feeling slightly bemused by all the people around them talking in loud voices, most of them in Italian, and gesticulating with their hands to emphasise a point.

Gabriel grinned. 'My mother always refers to Antonio's as "picturesque".'

Bryn looked across the table at him. 'Your mother comes here too?'

He nodded. 'My father insists on coming to eat here at least once a week whenever my parents are back in London.'

Bryn slipped off her jacket as she settled more comfortably on her chair. Talking about Gabriel's parents might not be ideal but it was certainly a safer subject than her own family. 'Where do your parents live?'

'They moved to Florida ten years ago when my father retired, and left the running of the original Archangel Gallery, which was all we had at the time, to myself and my two brothers.' Gabriel shrugged, surprising Bryn by appearing totally relaxed in his surroundings.

She smiled slightly. 'That would be Raphael and Michael.'

He grimaced. 'My mother's romantic choice of names rather than my father's.'

'And you've opened two more galleries since then, one in New York and one in Paris. With the Italian connection, why not Rome?'

'The D'Angelos have always visited Italy for pleasure, not work.' He gave one of those totally disarming smiles that made him appear several years younger and which made it all too easy for Bryn to guess exactly what sort of 'pleasure' the three D'Angelo brothers enjoyed when in Italy.

'Have you—?'

'Gabrielo!' A tall, voluptuous, dark-haired woman—no doubt Toni's wife—descended on them, placing a raffia-bottomed bottle of Chianti and two glasses down on the table before pulling a now-standing Gabriel in tightly against her overabundant bosom as she burst into a flourish of Italian.

'English, please, Maria.' Gabriel chuckled.

'You are as 'andsome as ever, I see!' She leant back to beam up at him. 'Ah, if I were only twenty years younger!' she added wistfully.

'Even if you were you would never leave Antonio.' Gabriel smiled at her warmly.

Bryn felt a bit disconcerted, both by the friendly way that Toni and Maria had greeted Gabriel, and his warm response to them in return. It was much easier for her to keep her own distance from Gabriel when she could continue to think of him as that cold and ruthless man who had sealed her father's fate. The warmth shown to him by Toni and Maria, and his own obvious and long-standing affection for both of them, revealed a completely different side to the arrogantly ruthless Gabriel D'Angelo than the one Bryn had come to expect. Especially following so quickly on the heels of those moments of intimacy between them in his office.

'Toni tells me you 'ave brought your young lady with you?' Maria eyed Bryn speculatively as she stepped away from Gabriel.

'No embarrassing Bryn, please, Maria!' Gabriel warned quickly as he slipped off his jacket and hung it on the back of his chair, wondering if it had been a wise move on his part to bring Bryn to Antonio's. The Italian couple were always asking when he intended settling down and having *bambinos*, and Bryn was the first woman he had ever brought here.

In his defence, bringing Bryn to Antonio's had been a knee-jerk reaction to her obvious belief that he was a man who thought himself far above frequenting high-street coffee shops, or little Italian bistros, instead favouring exclusive restaurants and bars. Gabriel had just forgotten to factor in the consequences of bringing a woman to Antonio's for the first time; in the past he had only ever come to the bistro with members of his family, knowing the women he usually dated wouldn't give a damn how good the food was—this little bistro simply wasn't fashionable enough or exclusive enough for their 'sophisticated' tastes.

Not that he thought Bryn unsophisticated. His sole reason for bringing her here had been to show her that he wasn't the arrogant sophisticate she so obviously believed him to be.

Nor should he think of this as being a date—

Oh, to hell with this; whatever his reason for bringing Bryn here, she was here now, and it was his own fault if he had to suffer Toni and Maria's teasing speculation. 'Maria, Bryn. Bryn, Toni's wife, Maria,' he introduced stiffly.

'None of this is what you expected, is it...?'

Bryn took a sip of the Chianti that Gabriel had poured into the two glasses, Maria having hurried off to the kitchen shortly after the introductions to see if their pizza was ready. Introductions where, Bryn had noted, Gabriel had made no effort to correct Maria's assumption as to who Bryn was—or wasn't!

And no, this disorganised and noisy bistro wasn't the sort of place Bryn would ever have imagined seeing the Gabriel D'Angelo she had met earlier at Archangel, when he had looked every inch a wealthy and arrogant D'Angelo brother in his designer-label suit and silk shirt and tie.

'I have every reason to hope the pizza will be as delicious as this Chianti,' she murmured noncommittally.

'Oh, it will be.' Gabriel nodded, dark eyes hooded as he looked across the table at her. 'But I probably should have taken you somewhere a little more...upmarket, to celebrate your inclusion in the New Artists Exhibition.'

Her brows rose. 'Then shouldn't the other five finalists, and the reserve, have been invited too?'

He gave a hard smile. 'No.'

'Oh.' Bryn could feel her cheeks warm, but wisely said nothing; she had already made one wrong assumption about Gabriel this evening, an assumption he had taken exception to, and she wasn't inclined to make another. 'Well, this is absolutely fine for me,' she continued quickly. 'I would probably have felt out of my depth somewhere overly sophisticated anyway. Dining out hasn't exactly been something I've done a lot of since— This is fine,' she repeated flatly, lowering her eyes to avoid meeting his suddenly piercing and probing gaze. She had almost—almost—said 'since my father went to prison'. A slip that could have been extremely costly to her inclusion in the exhibition.

Bryn had no doubts that it was the very informality of their surroundings that was responsible for her feeling so relaxed she had almost spoken without thinking, rather than the man seated opposite her. There was nothing about Gabriel that caused her to feel in the least relaxed—not his dangerous good looks, or her own unwelcome response to them.

'To you, Bryn.' Gabriel held up his glass in a toast, seeming unaware of her inner turmoil. 'Let's hope that the Archangel exhibition is not only a successful one but also the first of many for you.'

'I'll drink to that!' Bryn took a grateful sip of her own wine. 'Do you—? Oh, wow!' Her eyes widened as she saw Maria winding her way deftly through the other diners towards their table, holding aloft the biggest pizza Bryn had ever seen in her life. Maria placed the hot plate down in the centre of their table with the beaming instruction to 'Enjoy!' before she hurried off again.

Bryn's mouth watered as she stared down at the laden pizza, seeing pepperoni, mushrooms, onions, spinach, ham and aubergines.

'I hope you don't mind that there are no anchovies?' Gabriel shrugged ruefully. 'Toni knows that I don't like them.'

'Are you kidding? Who would ever miss them with all these other toppings?' Bryn laughed delightedly as she continued to look at the pizza.

Gabriel felt his mouth go dry as he drank in the sight of Bryn relaxed and smiling; those dove-grey eyes warm and glowing, her creamy cheeks slightly flushed, her full and sensual lips—that had no need of the lip gloss so many women wore and which Gabriel, for one, found such a turn-off—delectably plump and rosy.

And watching those tempting lips as Bryn ate the pizza was going to be nothing short of physical torture for him!

'Tuck in before it gets cold,' he encouraged gruffly. 'There are no knives and forks,' he added dryly as Bryn frowned slightly at the obvious omission of utensils from the table. 'The only way to eat pizza is with your fingers,' he explained as she looked up at him questioningly.

'Is that another Gabrielism?' she teased as she helped herself to a slice of the pizza.

'Trust me,' Gabriel murmured softly.

She stilled before raising suddenly guarded eyes. 'You keep saying that....'

Yes, he did. Because, after meeting Bryn again, after spending time with her this evening knowing that she believed he had no idea who she was, and knowing how much he still wanted her, Gabriel did want Bryn to trust him.

'I had a really good time this evening, thank you,' Bryn murmured as she and Gabriel sat together in the darkened interior of his sports car. He had parked outside the old Victorian building where she lived, only the moonlight from above illuminating the quiet residential street.

Apart from the fact that it wasn't raining, it was an end to the evening so reminiscent of the one five years ago. A memory that had remained etched in Bryn's mind.

She had been mooning about Gabriel for weeks by that time, totally infatuated with his dark good looks and confident air. After he had come to her parents' house to talk with her father a couple times, she had taken to calling in to the Archangel Gallery several times a week on the off chance she might see him again.

That evening she had hung around outside at closing time, telling herself it was because she was waiting for the rain to ease off before making a dash for the bus stop, but in reality she had been hoping to catch a glimpse of Gabriel as he left the gallery.

Her breath had caught in her throat when she'd seen him coming out of the main doors, a fiery blush on her cheeks as he'd looked up and seen her, his face going blank for several seconds before recognition had widened those chocolate-brown eyes and he'd stopped to chat with her. It had been a blushingly stilted conversation on Bryn's part, and she had been rendered completely speechless when Gabriel had asked if he could drive her home.

She had been so aware of Gabriel's proximity once they were seated in the confines of his sleek sports car, the silence between them on the drive to her home seeming heavy with possibility and causing Bryn to tremble with nervous anticipation.

She had given him a shy glance from beneath dark lashes once he'd stopped the car outside her parents' house. 'Thank you for driving me home.' She had groaned inwardly at her lack of sophistication.

'You're welcome.' His voice had been husky as he'd turned in his seat to look at her. 'Sabryna, I— Tomorrow there's going to be—' He had broken off, frowning darkly. 'Oh, to hell with it, if I'm going to burn I may as well go down in a ball of flames!' he had muttered fiercely before his head had swooped down and his lips had captured hers.

It had been the most exquisite kiss of Bryn's young life, slow and searching, but at the same time so erotically charged she had felt as if she might drown in the feelings, emotions, coursing through her body.

She had been totally dazed by those emotions as Gabriel had suddenly wrenched his mouth from hers to look down at her briefly with hot, passionate eyes before moving back and turning away.

'You should go in,' he muttered darkly. 'And try not to— Never mind,' he had bitten out abruptly as he'd turned to look at her with tortured eyes. 'I'm sorry, Sabryna.'

She had blinked. 'For kissing me?'

'No,' he had rasped harshly. 'I'll never be sorry I did that. Just— Try not to hate me too much, okay?'

At the time Bryn had believed she could never hate Gabriel, that she loved him too much to ever hate him.

The following day, that 'tomorrow' Gabriel had referred to so obliquely, her world had blown up in her face, as her father had been arrested for forgery, with Gabriel lined up as the prosecution's lead witness against him.

'I'm glad,' Gabriel murmured now in answer to her earlier comment.

Bryn came back to the present with a bump. 'I'd ask you in for coffee, but…' She trailed off with hard dismissal.

It had been a surprisingly enjoyable evening, Bryn acknowledged self-disgustedly, knowing that the past shouldn't have allowed her to enjoy an evening with the hateful Gabriel D'Angelo.

But she had….

The food had been so excellent and the decor, the crowded room and loud conversation had all become part of that enjoyment. Two glasses of wine and she had even become fond of Toni's off-key renditions of classical Italian arias!

As for the company… Gabriel had proved to be an amusing and entertaining dining companion, as they discussed their favourite artists as they ate, along with some of the funnier stories from Gabriel's years of running the Archangel Galleries with his brothers.

Bryn had felt totally relaxed in his company by the time they left the bistro, from the good food, the wine and the good company, so much so that it had seemed like the most natural thing in the world to agree to Gabriel driving her home.

Enjoyable as the evening had been though, she admittedly inwardly that she found Gabriel even more disturbing now than she had five years ago.

As Gabriel D'Angelo he was unmistakably intelligent, sinfully handsome, as well as being equally sinfully rich and powerful.

As Gabriel he was obviously intelligent and handsome, but he was also relaxed and charming, plus he had a slightly wicked sense of humour, and a warmth that had allowed him to accept, without so much as a blink, the enthusiastic kiss Maria had planted on his lips, with the plea to 'come back and see me soon', before they left the bistro earlier.

All of those things, together with those dark and mesmerising good looks, that Bryn had become so increasingly aware of as the evening progressed made her very aware that she was in danger of falling under this man's spell for the second time in her life.

'But?' Gabriel turned in his seat to prompt Bryn out of her continued silence.

She raised startled eyes. 'Sorry?'

'"I'd ask you in for coffee, but…"' he reminded her.

She smiled ruefully. 'That's a woman's polite way of saying thank you for the evening but now it's over.'

'You don't have any coffee?'

'I always have coffee.'

'Then why not invite me in?'

She blinked long lashes. 'I—well—it's late.'

'It's only eleven o'clock.' Although it was obvious to Gabriel that Bryn didn't want to invite him into her home, and he knew she was right to feel that caution, he wanted so badly for her to change her mind.

He hadn't thought it was possible, but his attraction to her had deepened in the past few hours and he was now desperate to taste and feel those plump lips that had been tormenting him all evening.

So desperate he moved to close the distance that separated them. 'Bryn—'

'Please don't!' She immediately held her hands up defensively, her eyes wide with alarm as she leaned back against the door behind her.

'Why not?' Gabriel prompted.

She ran the moistness of her tongue over her lips before answering him. 'Why ruin a perfectly good evening?'

He frowned darkly. 'My kissing you would ruin the evening?'

'Please, Gabriel—'

'But that's what I want to do, Bryn— To please you!' He closed the last of the distance between them as he pulled her gently forward into his arms before looking down at her hungrily.

'I can't!' Her eyes glittered with unshed tears, her hands still held up defensively between them, not pushing Gabriel away, but desperately trying not to touch him either. 'I can't, Gabriel,' she repeated achingly.

It was the despair in her voice, along with those unshed tears glistening in her beautiful eyes, that caused an icy chill down the length of Gabriel's spine as he stilled. 'Talk to me, Bryn,' he encouraged gruffly. 'For God's sake, talk to me!'

'I can't.' She gave another desperate shake of her head.

'I have to kiss you, damn it,' he said, wanting Bryn, but more than that wanting her to trust him.

With her body. With her emotions. With her past....

She looked up at him searchingly in the moonlight for several tense, timeless seconds, before she gave another slow and determined shake of her head. 'I really can't,' she repeated flatly.

'Not good enough, Bryn!' he rasped. 'Tell me you

don't want me to kiss you, that you don't want that as much as I do, that you haven't ached for it all evening, and I won't ask you again,' he encouraged gruffly.

Her throat moved as she swallowed convulsively. 'I can't do that either,' she acknowledged achingly, her voice carrying a desperate sob.

'You want me to make that decision for both of us, is that it?' he bit out harshly.

Bryn was no longer sure what she wanted!

Well... She was, but what she wanted—to kiss and to be kissed by Gabriel—was what she shouldn't want.

He was a D'Angelo, for goodness' sake. And no matter how charming and entertaining he had been this evening, underneath all that charm he was still the cold and ruthless Gabriel D'Angelo from all those years ago. To allow— To *want* to kiss and be kissed by that man went against every instinct of loyalty she had, as well as every shred of self-preservation she possessed.

Except... She couldn't escape the fact that the man she had met earlier today, the man she had just spent the evening with—the same man who made her pulse race and caused her body to be so achingly aware of everything about him—wasn't in the least cold or ruthless, but was instead hot and seductive. *That* man she desperately wanted and longed to kiss.

Which was utter madness, when she knew exactly how Gabriel would react if he knew who she really was.

'Please let me, Bryn.'

She couldn't breathe as she looked up at Gabriel, unable to make a move to stop him as his hands moved up to cup her cheeks and lift her face to his, feeling herself drowning, becoming totally lost in the dark and enticingly warm depths of his piercing brown eyes as his mouth slowly descended towards hers.

CHAPTER FIVE

BRYN MELTED AS Gabriel first sipped, tasted and then devoured her as he crushed her lips beneath his, hearing the low groan in his throat as her fingers became entwined in the dark hair at his nape. Her breasts were heavy and aroused as they pressed against the hardness of his chest, Gabriel having pulled her in as tightly against him as was possible in the confines of the car as he continued to kiss her with an ever-deepening hunger.

A hunger that Bryn couldn't help but feel in return, groaning low in her throat as she felt the brush of Gabriel's tongue against her bottom lip, light, questing, possessing as her lips parted and his tongue surged inside, licking and tasting, learning every nuance, every dip and curve, his hands a restless caress along the length of her spine.

Bryn broke their kiss, her slender neck arching as she felt Gabriel's hand push her blouse up, his fingers lightly caressing the bareness of her spine, her abdomen, before his hand cupped beneath the bared fullness of her breast.

The soft pad of his thumb was a light, sweeping torture across her aroused nipple, his lips a hot caress against Bryn's throat as pleasure coursed hotly through her body, heating, dampening between her thighs, as he captured her aching nipple between thumb and finger, squeezing lightly.

His ragged breath burned against her throat as his other hand moved to unfasten the buttons of her blouse, allowing his questing lips to move lower, his tongue a sweeping, hungry caress against the tops of her breasts before dipping lower as he sucked her aching, straining nipple into the moist heat of his mouth.

Bryn's head fell back against the headrest behind her, her fingers becoming entwined in the dark thickness of Gabriel's hair as she held him against her, the intense pleasure of the dual assault of Gabriel's lips and fingers against her breasts almost too much to bear.

Almost.

The pleasure was just too good, too exquisite, as it built higher, and then higher still, as Gabriel continued to draw deeply on her nipple, his tongue a moist and rasping caress against that burgeoning heat, rising higher, deeper, until she felt as if she would explode into a million pieces that could surely never be completely put back together again.

Never.

'Gabriel, you have to stop!'

Gabriel was so aroused by the taste of Bryn and the desire that had raged so deeply, so out of control between them, that it took him several moments to realise that her hands were now pushing against his chest, her face turned away from him as she struggled to free herself from his arms.

He backed off the instant he realised what she was doing; he had never forced himself on a woman in his life before and he certainly wasn't about to start now. He desired Bryn too much to ever want to do anything that she didn't want, ache for, as much as he did.

Gabriel's breathing sounded harsh in the confines of the car. 'Hell, I totally forgot where we were.' He gave a wince as he realised they were still sitting in his car parked outside the building where Bryn lived, and that although the side windows of the car were darkened glass, the windscreen certainly wasn't. 'I'm sorry, Bryn.' He ran an agitated hand restlessly through the dark thickness of his hair.

She avoided so much as looking at him as she straightened and refastened her blouse with hands that shook slightly, her face pale in the moonlight.

'Bryn?'

'Not now, Gabriel. In fact, not ever!' she insisted shakily. 'I have to go.' She turned to look out of the side window. 'I— Thank you for dinner. I enjoyed Antonio's.'

'Just not what followed?' Gabriel murmured knowingly.

Bryn gave a pained grimace. 'I'm sure you'll agree it wasn't the most sensible thing either of us has ever done—'

'Bryn, will you, for the love of God, look at me?' he rasped his frustration with the situation. 'Talk to me, damn it!'

She turned slowly, eyes huge and shadowed, her cheeks as pale as ivory in the moonlight. 'I don't know what you want me to say.'

'Don't you?'

She looked away from the intensity of his gaze. 'How about, this should never have happened?' She gave a shake of her head. 'We both know that already.'

'Do we?'

'Yes.' Bryn looked at him searchingly. 'Unless— Is this standard procedure? Did you think, expect, that I would be so grateful to be included in the exhibition at

Archangel I would—?' She broke off abruptly as she obviously saw, and recognised, the tightening of Gabriel's jaw and the anger now glittering in the darkness of his eyes.

'I'm getting a little tired of that accusation, Bryn.' He spoke softly, dangerously so. 'And no, kissing me isn't the price you're expected to pay for inclusion in the exhibition!'

She winced. 'I didn't exactly say that—'

'You didn't *exactly* have to!' Gabriel bit out harshly, wondering if he had ever been this angry in his life before. 'What the hell sort of man do you think I am? Don't answer that,' he immediately amended. He already knew what sort of man Bryn thought he was.

Gabriel had thought, believed, that after a rocky start they had managed to spend a relaxed evening together, that Bryn was starting to see beyond what happened in the past—starting to see him beyond that—and instead she now thought him capable of using his position as one of the owners of the gallery to— What an idiot, what a fool he was, to think that Bryn could ever see him as anything more than the man who had helped to put her father in prison....

'You're right, Bryn. You should go inside now,' he growled coldly. 'Before you think of something else to say to insult me.'

Bryn hesitated, continuing to look at Gabriel searchingly, unable to read anything from his suddenly closed expression. 'It wasn't my intention to insult you—'

'Then heaven help me if you ever do mean it,' he muttered disgustedly.

She moistened her lips with the tip of her tongue. 'I was— I just— Our going out to dinner earlier, what happened just now, it was a mistake.'

'Mine or yours?'

'For both of us,' she insisted firmly. 'And I think it would be better, for the sake of the exhibition, if it didn't happen again. If we keep things on a purely business footing between the two of us from now on,' she added.

'As opposed to?'

'Anything less than a business footing,' she maintained determinedly.

Gabriel gave a grim smile. 'Do you really think that's possible after what just happened?'

Bryn wasn't sure a business footing had ever been a possibility between herself and Gabriel—and she was utterly convinced of it after her response to him just now. Gabriel had only needed to kiss her, to touch her, to caress her and she had forgotten everything but him and the moment. Nothing else had mattered at that moment. Nothing.

And it had to. It must. Because she wasn't about to allow herself to suffer the heartache of falling in love with Gabriel D'Angelo.

Not again.

Gabriel took in the stubborn lifting of Bryn's chin, the determined glitter in her eyes, and knew that she meant it when she said she wanted the two of them to go back to having a business relationship only.

If not for the reason she stated.

He was thirty-three years old, had been sexually active for almost seventeen of those years, and he was experienced enough to know when a woman desired him. And, whether she liked it or not, Bryn had been looking at him all evening as if she desired him as much as he desired her, and what had happened just now had been a direct result of that mutual desire. Bryn might wish it weren't so, might believe it was insanity on her part to be attracted to Gabriel while still carrying the pain of the past, but none of that changed the fact that she *did* want him.

Whether or not she actually *liked* him was something else entirely.

And that mattered to Gabriel.

Because he not only desired Bryn, he liked her. He had liked her five years ago too, even before he had seen her unshakeable loyalty to her father, and the quiet strength she had offered her mother as the two of them had sat together in the courtroom day after day.

Just as he admired Bryn's determination since meeting her again, her tenacity to succeed so intense that she had even been willing to become involved with the Archangel Gallery, to meet with at least one of the detested D'Angelo brothers, in order to achieve the success she so desired.

Kissing and embracing Bryn while knowing she didn't return that liking was not an option for Gabriel. Not with this particular woman. 'Okay, Bryn—' he nodded tersely '—if that's how you want it, then that's how it will be from now on,' he bit out abruptly.

She blinked. 'You're saying you agree to—to just a business relationship between the two of us?'

His jaw tightened. 'I believe I just said so, yes. Do you not believe me?' he rasped as she continued to look at him warily.

Of course Bryn believed Gabriel; why shouldn't she, when he had never done anything, five years ago or now, to give her cause not to believe he always did and meant what he said?

It was just— She didn't— Damn it! Part of her was actually irritated and hurt that Gabriel had agreed so easily to the two of them resuming a business relationship. Even if it had been her suggestion.

Which was utterly ridiculous. The exhibition wasn't until next month, and she knew from the things Gabriel had told her earlier—she had heard at least some of what he had to say—that she would be expected to go to Archangel often during the next few weeks, sit for photographs and provide the contents for the blurb for the catalogue, and to oversee and approve the framing of her paintings. And it would be far better, for everyone involved, if she and Gabriel could manage to maintain at least a semblance of politeness between the two of them during that time.

Bryn knew all that.

Logically, she accepted all of that.

Illogically, she knew that the attraction she had felt towards Gabriel five years ago might have been buried, might have remained dormant for those same five years, but that it was still very much alive inside her, and had only needed for her to see him again, to be with him again, for it to be rekindled.

To rage out of control.

As she had been out of control a few minutes ago, so much so that she had been balanced on the edge of orgasm just from the touch of Gabriel's lips and hands on her body.

What made it all so much worse, so much harder to fight that desire the second time around, was knowing that Gabriel obviously returned the attraction.

An attraction he felt for Bryn Jones. A desire he felt for Bryn Jones.

Because he wouldn't have allowed Sabryna Harper within ten feet of him!

Which was why the two of them couldn't do this

again, why they had to set down the rules right now for any future meetings between them. 'That's good.' She nodded as she bent to collect her shoulder bag from the floor of the car before turning to open the door.

'Wait there,' Gabriel instructed tersely as he turned, climbed out of the car and came round to open her door for her. 'My mother taught me it's polite, and safer, to always walk a lady to her door,' he explained as Bryn looked up at him questioningly.

A courtesy that Bryn wasn't sure, with her own lack of politeness to Gabriel just now, that she deserved. 'Once again, thank you for dinner and introducing me to Antonio's. It's definitely the place for pizza,' she murmured as she searched for her keys in her bag once they were standing outside her door.

He nodded tersely. 'I'm going away on business for a few days, so I probably won't see you on Monday.' He shrugged. 'But you've already met and like Eric?'

'Yes.' Was that sudden, heavy feeling in her chest disappointment because she now knew there wasn't even a possibility of her seeing Gabriel again on Monday? If so, then she was in more emotional trouble than she had thought she was. 'Are you going anywhere interesting?' she prompted conversationally.

'Rome,' he replied.

Bryn's eyes widened as she remembered Gabriel telling her earlier that he only went to Rome for 'pleasure'.

And, having stated that she was only interested in a business relationship with him, she had absolutely no right to show the least curiosity—let alone feel that curl of jealousy in the pit of her stomach—about the reason for his going there now.

And yet she knew she did.

'Bryn?'

She forced herself to look up and smile unconcernedly as she unlocked the front door of the house before stepping inside and turning back to face him. 'Enjoy Rome.'

'I usually do,' Gabriel accepted distractedly as he looked down at her searchingly for several long seconds, before accepting there was nothing else for them to say. He turned and returned to his car, part of him wondering if he had imagined the way Bryn had gone suddenly quiet after he had mentioned going away on business, and the slight edge to her tone when she did speak. And if he hadn't imagined it, what did it mean?

Not what he hoped it did, he answered himself derisively. No, all it indicated was that Bryn was relieved, because even the possibility of the two of them meeting again on Monday had now been removed. If he thought it had been for any other reason then he was only fooling himself; Bryn had made it more than clear what she thought of him a few minutes ago. What she believed had been his reason for kissing her.

When his real reason had been because he just hadn't been able to resist any longer. Hadn't been able to fight the fact that she was the last woman on earth he should get involved with because the need, the hunger he felt to taste her was too great. And she had tasted so damned good. She might try to deny it to herself, but she had responded to those kisses and made no protest when Gabriel had touched her breasts.

He now needed this time away from her, to put some distance—literally—between himself and Bryn. And hopefully, by the time he saw her again, he would have his desire for her back under his control.

It was several hours later—several hours and half a bottle of single-malt whisky later—as he relived the evening over and over in his mind, that Gabriel remembered he had told Bryn that he only ever went to Rome for 'pleasure'.

He wondered—hoped—that might be the reason for that edge to her tone.

'That looks amazing, Eric.' Bryn's face glowed as she looked admiringly at the silver gilt frame that had been put on the painting she always referred to in her mind as *Death of a Rose*. It represented so much more than the death of a single bloom, of course; it was symbolic of any death: love, hope, dreams. And, as they had hoped, the silver gilt frame was perfect against the misty background, the blood-red bloom weeping dew and petals onto the base of the canvas.

Bryn had spent most of her free time at Archangel the past four days, safe in the knowledge that Gabriel was still away in Rome. The highlight of each day had been the hours she spent in the cavernous basement of the gallery with Eric choosing the frames they thought suited to bring out the best in the ten paintings she was to exhibit at the gallery next month. This evening was no exception.

As far as Bryn was aware, Gabriel had spent those same four days—and nights—in Rome, no doubt indulging his every 'pleasure'.

Bryn had kept busy while at the same time determinedly not thinking of Gabriel, the evening they had spent together, or the ways in which he might now be indulging his pleasure in Rome!

And she wasn't going to think about him now either. 'It's perfect!' Bryn enthused as she continued to gaze at the painting in the silver gilt frame.

Eric nodded. 'Gabriel will have the final yay or nay,

of course, but I think he'll like what we've done so far. No doubt he'll change it if not,' he added ruefully.

Bryn's smile faded at mention of Gabriel. 'He will?'

'He has a really good eye for this stuff.' Eric shrugged.

'Better than you?'

'Much better,' Eric confirmed without rancour. 'All of the D'Angelo brothers do. They're the reason I wanted to work for the Archangel Galleries.'

Eric took the painting down off the wall where they had hung it so as best to appreciate the effect of the framing. 'Feel like going for a drink somewhere when we've finished here?' he suggested lightly as he stored the painting away safely.

'I—'

'I believe you'll find that Bryn doesn't believe in mixing business with pleasure.'

Bryn's heart stopped beating at the harsh sound of Gabriel's voice behind her. She whipped round quickly to find him standing in the doorway just feet away. And looking—

Looking more lethally attractive than when she had last seen him—if that was possible—his dark brown bespoke suit obviously designer label, his cream shirt and tie of the finest silk, his ebony hair slightly tousled in that just-got-out-of-bed style, his face tanned a deeper gold, intensifying the colour of his warm, chocolate-brown eyes.

No, his eyes weren't warm this evening. They were icy. Like a deep arctic chill.

An arctic chill that swept contemptuously over Bryn as the coldness of that gaze moved over her slowly from head to toe and then back again. Gabriel's top lip curled back derisively as he took in her casual appearance in a black short-sleeved T-shirt and black low-rider denims and a face that was completely bare of make-up. At the very least Bryn felt she looked like the penniless student she had once been—still was?—compared to Gabriel's expensive and sartorial elegance.

Bryn looked more stunningly beautiful than ever, Gabriel acknowledged irritably, her eyes glowing a warm dove-grey, her cheeks flushed with becoming colour.

At least, her eyes *had* been glowing a warm dove-grey, and there *had* been colour in her cheeks too, as she obviously enjoyed Eric's company.

Until she turned to look at Gabriel, at which point her gaze had quickly become guarded and her cheeks had paled.

His mouth tightened as he glanced across at Eric. 'If you've finished with Bryn for this evening, I need to speak with her for a few minutes.' It was a statement rather than a question, Gabriel having no intention of taking no for an answer. From either Eric or Bryn.

'Actually,' Bryn began tentatively, 'I—'

'I think it's best if we go upstairs to my office for this conversation, Bryn.' Gabriel held the door open pointedly.

Her eyes widened, her creamy throat moving as she swallowed then wet the dryness of her lips with the tip of her tongue. 'I— Yes, of course.' Her hands were gripped tightly together in front of her, knuckles showing white. 'A rain check on that drink, Eric?'

Eric gave a relaxed smile, obviously completely oblivious to the underlying tension between Gabriel and Bryn. 'No problem,' he agreed easily.

Which was perhaps as well; Gabriel had always had a healthy respect and liking for their London in-house art expert, and he would hate to ruin their working relationship by having to exert his executive power. 'Bryn?' he prompted tersely.

She grabbed her denim jacket and shoulder bag from a chair before hurrying across the room to join him, pressing her spine back against the door frame so as not to come into contact with him as she slipped out into the hallway, her expression apprehensive as she waited for Gabriel to join her.

An entirely appropriate apprehension, as it happened. 'Whisky?'

Bryn stood awkwardly in the middle of Gabriel's elegant office watching as he removed his jacket and draped it over a chair before moving to the bar in long, easy strides. They had travelled up in the lift together in complete silence. Bryn's apprehensive. Gabriel's grimly foreboding.

It didn't help that Bryn was still uncomfortably aware of how young and gauche she must appear to him, in her casual clothes and wearing no make-up, only to then chastise herself for even caring what, if anything, he might think of her appearance. Gabriel D'Angelo was one of the owners of the gallery where her paintings were to be exhibited next month, nothing more. She couldn't allow him to be any more than that.

'It's a little early in the evening for me, thanks,' she refused lightly. 'Unless you think I might need it?' she added uncertainly as she saw the hard implacability of his expression.

A hard implacability that showed her just how relaxed Gabriel had been on the previous occasions the two of them had met and spent time together....

Gabriel made no comment as he poured an inch of whisky into two crystal glasses before crossing the room and holding one out to Bryn.

The past four days had been successful ones for him as far as business went, but far less so on a personal level, as Gabriel hadn't been able to shake off thoughts and memories of Bryn. Of that last evening with her, when the desire the two of them felt for each other had raged so out of control.

As Gabriel had no doubt it would rage out of control again, despite the business-only arrangement Bryn had suggested and Gabriel had reluctantly agreed to. Gabriel had wanted this woman five years ago, and he wanted her still. A fact that had been brought painfully home to him after he had spent an evening with the beautiful Lucia while in Rome, and then politely walked her to the door of her apartment before leaving again, rather than spending the night with her as he would normally have done. He hadn't felt a shred of desire to bed the raven-haired beauty because Bryn was the woman he wanted. In his arms. In his bed. In his possession! And that was never going to happen while the events of the past were allowed to continue to lurk in the shadows between them.

'You're going to need it,' he confirmed gruffly. 'We both are,' he added with hard self-derision, taking a much-needed sip from his own whisky glass as Bryn's perfume, that heady spice and desirable woman, invaded his senses.

Her hand moved up and her fingers curled around the proffered glass, a hand that shook as she made no effort to drink any of it. 'How was Rome?'

'Beautiful, as always.' Gabriel stepped away from her to stand with his back to one of the floor-to-ceiling picture windows, needing to put space between himself and Bryn—between himself and that insidious perfume invading his senses. 'It took some persuading but I fi-

nally managed to acquire the two magnificent frescoes
for the gallery that I went to look at.'

'Oh?'

His mouth twisted mockingly as he saw, and recognised, the surprise in her expression. 'I did tell you I was
going away on business.'

Yes, he had, but Bryn hadn't believed him, after his
previous comment. Not that it really mattered whether
or not she believed him, then or now; it was none of her
business what Gabriel had been doing in Rome for the
past few days.

At the same time as she knew part of her wanted
to know, had anguished over it during those days and
nights, as to what woman, or women, Gabriel was spending his time with in Rome.

Nor did she feel in the least reassured about his mood
now as she saw the grimness of his expression. 'So what
was it you wanted to talk to me about?' she prompted
with forced lightness.

'Sabryna Harper.'

CHAPTER SIX

'BRYN, SIT DOWN here, put your head between your knees and just breathe, damn it! Yes, that's right,' Gabriel rasped harshly, slamming his glass down on the coffee table before guiding Bryn over to an armchair to push her head down between her knees as she drew huge gasping breaths of air into her starved lungs. 'Damn it, woman, do you have something against my thirty-year-old single-malt whisky?'

Gabriel bent down to retrieve the glass from where Bryn had dropped it a minute or so ago as she'd looked in danger of passing out completely. He put the glass back on the bar and grabbed a cloth to soak up the golden puddle of whisky that had seeped into the pale carpet.

'What did you say?' He frowned as he heard her mutter something in the vicinity of her knees.

'I said,' she bit out succinctly as she raised her head to glare at him, her face deathly pale, eyes deep grey wells of anguish, 'I don't give a damn about your thirty-year-old single-malt whisky!'

'I doubt you'll feel that way when I take the price of the bottle out of the sale of your paintings,' Gabriel assured her dryly as he sat back on his heels.

'What sale?' she came back bitterly, sitting up in the chair now that the first danger of her fainting had obviously passed, her expression one of proud fragility. 'How could you do that?' she continued accusingly before he could answer. 'How could you just come out with a statement like that without—without giving me some sort of prior warning?'

Well, it hadn't taken long for her to recover from the initial shock, Gabriel appreciated ruefully. 'What sort of warning should I have given you, Bryn?' he challenged as he stood up to throw the sticky whisky-soaked cloth disgustedly down onto the bar. '"Oh, by the way, I think the two of us may have met before across a crowded courtroom"? Or, "You look a lot like Sabryna Harper, the daughter of—"? Do not collapse on me again, Bryn!' he warned harshly as her face took on a grey tinge, her chest barely moving beneath the black T-shirt as she breathed shallowly.

'I'm not about to collapse.' Instead, she stood up abruptly, taking a few seconds to steady herself before straightening determinedly, her chin held high. 'How long have you known?'

He quirked one dark brow. 'That Bryn Jones is Sabryna Harper?'

'Yes!' she hissed, jaw clenching.

Gabriel gave a dismissive shrug. 'Since the beginning.'

'Since…?' Bryn gasped, reaching down to grasp the arm of the chair as she felt herself sway again, despite her earlier claim that she wouldn't collapse again. She gave a shake of her head. 'You can't have done!'

Brown eyes looked across at her calmly. 'Why can't I?'

'Because— Well, because— Because you can't!' Her mouth firmed as she shied away from listing those reasons why. 'I would never have got this far in the competition if you had known who I was from the beginning!'

He shrugged, his shoulders wide and muscled in the cream silk shirt. 'Admittedly my brother Rafe advised against your inclusion, but I decided—'

'Your brother Raphael knows who I am too?' She stared at him in disbelief.

'You know, Bryn, we're going to get a lot further with this conversation if we work on the understanding that I invariably tell the truth. No matter what the consequences,' he added harshly.

And one of those consequences had been Bryn's father going to prison. An indisputable fact that hung between the two of them, unsaid but there nonetheless.

'It was Michael who recognised you initially,' Gabriel continued calmly. 'He saw you when you came in for an interview with Eric at the gallery that first day, and then he spoke to Rafe about it, who then told me.'

'Quite the secret little coterie of spies, aren't you?' Bryn snapped defensively, still completely thrown and befuddled by Gabriel's admission of having known who she was from that first day.

Something she was still having trouble absorbing. Because if that really was the truth, as Gabriel claimed it was, then he had chosen her as a finalist for the New Artists Exhibition knowing exactly who and what she was.

Had ogled her breasts, that first day here in his office knowing exactly who she was. Had taken her out to dinner at Antonio's knowing exactly who she was. Had kissed her later that same evening in his car knowing exactly who she was.

Which made absolutely no sense to Bryn whatsoever.

'I don't think insulting me, or my brothers, is helpful to this conversation either,' Gabriel drawled.

Gabriel had decided while he was away in Rome and thinking of her constantly that the truth couldn't remain unspoken between them once he returned to London. And if Bryn wouldn't tell him the truth, then it was up to him to do it.

Bryn so obviously disliked, perhaps even hated, Gabriel for the part he had played in her father's trial. Her desire now, her physical response to him, much as she might hate it, and him, was just as undeniable. And Gabriel couldn't see any way forward for the two of them if the truth of who Bryn really was continued to remain unspoken between them.

Of course, there was always the possibility that there was still no way forward for the two of them once they had spoken of it, but Gabriel knew they couldn't go on any longer with this lie standing between them, that the longer he allowed that omission to continue, the less chance there was that he and Bryn could ever come to any sort of understanding of each other.

'I asked you to trust me several times, Bryn, to talk to me,' he reminded huskily.

Her eyes widened. 'And this was what you meant? That I should trust you enough to tell you I'm really Sabryna Harper, William Harper's daughter?'

'Yes,' Gabriel bit out tautly.

Bryn continued to stare at him disbelievingly. 'That's the most ridiculous thing you've ever said to me!'

He gave a derisive smile. 'Nevertheless, it's the truth.'

She gave a dazed shake of her head. 'In what universe did you think that was ever going to happen?' Gabriel seriously expected her to— He had really thought that she would one day trust him enough to tell him, to confide in him. 'It was never going to happen,' she stated flatly.

He drew in a sharp breath. 'That's…unfortunate.'

'I don't see why,' she challenged scathingly. 'Luckily for you, you already have your reserve candidate for the

New Artists Exhibition, so no problem there once you've had the pleasure of kicking me off—'

'I'm not kicking you off anything, Bryn, and I resent the fact that you think it would ever be a pleasure for me to do so,' he cut in harshly, running an agitated hand through the darkness of his hair as he scowled. 'And why the hell would I do that, when you're far and away the best artist in the exhibition?'

'Why would you?' she repeated challengingly. 'I'm William Harper's daughter!' she reminded him—as if saying it repeatedly would help her to accept that Gabriel really did know, had always known, exactly who she was.

'And, as I've already stated, I knew that when you were chosen as one of the six finalists.'

Yes, he had, which again made absolutely no sense to Bryn. Her father's name was so shrouded in scandal that her mother had decided to distance them from it all by changing their last name after he had died. A scandal that had been connected to this very gallery and the D'Angelo name; she couldn't believe that Gabriel would ever want to risk the resurrection of that scandal by exhibiting the paintings of William's daughter. And certainly not intentionally.

She looked across at him guardedly, once again aware of how he owned the elegantly furnished office rather than the opulence dominating the man; Gabriel was such a force in his own right that he seemed to own the very air around him, no matter what his surroundings. Something that had been all too apparent during her father's trial—even the judge hearing the case had treated him with a deference and respect he hadn't shown to anyone else in the courtroom. Something that had no doubt added weight to the evidence Gabriel gave against her father.

Not that any weight had needed to be added; there had been no doubting her father's guilt, not only for attempting to sell a fake Turner, but for having commissioned the forgery in the first place, having paid an artist in Poland a pittance to paint the forgery and then attempting to sell it for millions of pounds to Gabriel and the Archangel Gallery.

'Bryn, even without Michael's help, I would have known who you were the first time I looked at you again....'

She looked up at Gabriel sharply. 'I don't see how when my name and appearance are so different from five years ago.'

He gave a humourless smile. 'It's unlikely I'd ever forget the young woman who glared her hatred across a courtroom at me for days on end. Those eyes alone would have given you away.'

Bryn had never forgotten him either, but for quite a different reason.

Gabriel D'Angelo had, quite simply, been the most charismatic and darkly intriguing man she had ever set eyes on. But it was more than that; *he* was more than that. Gabriel had awakened something deep inside the eighteen-year-old overweight and slightly shy Sabryna that had filled her night fantasies for weeks before her father's arrest, and months after the trial had ended.

The same fantasies that had filled all of her nights since meeting Gabriel again a week ago. The same desire that had awakened in her again, a few minutes ago in the basement, the second she had heard his voice behind her. The same desire that had caused her breath to catch in her throat when she'd turned to look at him. The same desire that raged through her even now, just from seeing how his cream silk shirt fitted so well over the broadness of his shoulders and tapered waist, the tailored brown trousers of his suit draping elegantly from his hips. This man—Gabriel—awakened that hunger inside her just by being in the same room with her.

'How is your mother, Bryn?'

She looked at him warily. 'Why are you asking?' she came back defensively.

He shrugged. 'Because I'd like to know?'

'My mother is fine. She remarried two years ago. Happily.'

'That's good.' He nodded.

'Gabriel, if this is some sort of guilt trip on your part—'

'It's not,' Gabriel cut in harshly. 'Damn it, Bryn, I have nothing—absolutely nothing—to feel guilty about. Am I sorry for the way it happened, the way your mother's and your own life were affected? Yes, I am. But your father was the guilty one, Bryn, not me. Am I sorry that he died in prison only months later? Yes, of course I am,' he rasped. 'But I didn't put him there. He put himself there by his own actions!'

Yes, he had. And part of Bryn had never forgiven her father for that.

Which was something *she* had to live with. 'You kissed me the night before my father was arrested!' she reminded accusingly.

He closed his eyes briefly before opening them again. 'I know that. And I wanted to tell you— Despite being warned by the police, and my lawyers, not to discuss the case with anyone, I almost told you that night! It almost killed me not to do so.' He gave a shake of his head.

'I don't believe you,' she breathed heavily.

'No,' he accepted heavily. 'I tried to see you, Bryn. Against the advice of my lawyers I tried to see you again, after your father was arrested, during the trial, after the trial. I tried, Bryn! I wanted to explain, to— I never wanted to hurt you, Bryn,' he assured earnestly.

'But you did it anyway.'

'I told you, I had no choice, damn it.'

Perhaps he hadn't, but that didn't stop Bryn from resenting his silence. From resenting the fact that he had kissed her that night. From resenting the fact that he had broken her heart the following day....

'I didn't want to see or speak with you again.' She gave an abrupt shake of her head. 'You had nothing to say that I wanted to hear.'

'I guessed that,' he said bleakly.

She breathed in deeply. 'So where do we go from here?'

Gabriel looked at her from beneath hooded lids. 'Where do you want us to go?'

To his bed. On top of his marble desk. On the sofa. Up against a wall! Bryn didn't care about the 'where' as long as Gabriel finished what he had started in his car last Friday evening. The desire she had felt then was nothing compared to what it was now, after days of not seeing him, not being with him.

And she hated herself for it. Hated that in spite of everything, she still felt that way, still wanted him!

She moistened her lips with the tip of her tongue. 'I need to know— Have these past few days all been some sort of sick game? An act of revenge for what my father—'

'I could ask the same of you!' he grated harshly, anger flaring in those deep brown eyes, lips thinned, a nerve pulsing in his aggressively set jaw. His body was rigid with that same tension, his hands clenched at his sides before he reached out to pick up the whisky glass he had put down earlier, drinking down the contents in one swallow. 'In fact, my brothers insist on it!'

'Then ask, damn it,' Bryn bit out shakily. He looked at her guardedly.

'Why did you do it, Bryn? Why did you enter your paintings in a competition being run by the gallery, the man, who helped put your father in prison?'

Bryn drew her breath in sharply, all the colour draining from her cheeks as the starkness of Gabriel's words hammered into her like a blow she wasn't sure she was ever going to recover from.

The truth was completely out in the open now, spoken aloud between them with no going back, and no fooling herself, allowing herself to indulge her desire for this man, by assuring herself that it was okay to do so because Gabriel had no idea who she really was. Because he did know. He had always known.

She avoided meeting that accusing gaze. 'The truth?'

That nerve pulsed in his clenched jaw. 'In the circumstances, I'll accept nothing less.'

Bryn nodded. 'I was desperate. I'm an unknown artist who wants more than anything to succeed, and the best way to do that is to be exhibited in the most prestigious private gallery in London.'

'Thank you,' he accepted derisively.

Her anger flared again at his obvious sarcasm. 'I was stating a fact, not giving a compliment!'

Gabriel knew that. Knew Bryn. Not as well as he wanted to, but he did know her as being determined, gutsy and proud. All traits he could admire. It was the beautiful and desirable that destroyed him!

'Heaven forbid you should ever do that,' he drawled, eyeing the whisky bottle longingly as he placed his empty glass down on the bar before walking away. The enigma that was Bryn might be enough to turn any man to drink, at the same time as that same man—namely Gabriel!—would be well advised to keep his wits about him whenever he was in her company.

'Yes. Well.' She turned to walk over to the long picture windows, hands thrust into the back pockets of her jeans as she stood with her back towards him, her spiky hair in silhouette. 'Believe me, nothing less would have induced me to come anywhere near your gallery or you ever again!'

Gabriel gave a wince. 'Perhaps a little less honesty on your part might be preferable after all.'

'What do you want me to do now, Gabriel?' she continued tersely. 'Quietly withdraw from the exhibition?'

'I've already said that isn't an option,' Gabriel bit out.

She turned back slowly, stance defensive, breasts thrust forward, hands in her pockets. 'Then what are my options?'

That was a good question.

Having made the decision to put an end to this pretence, Gabriel had gone over the possible scenarios of this conversation over and over again in his mind on his flight back from Rome.

There seemed to be only two possible outcomes.

Outcome one—the one that was undoubtedly the best one for Bryn—was that they would continue with the business-only relationship they had agreed upon, and she would exhibit her paintings in the gallery next month. Outcome two—the one that Gabriel disliked the most—was that Bryn would walk away now: from the gallery, the exhibition and from him.

There was a third outcome—the one that Gabriel wanted but knew was never going to happen. In that Bryn continued with the exhibition, and the two of them agreed to put the past behind them and continue from where they had left off on Friday evening!

An outcome that Gabriel knew to be pure fantasy on his part, following on from Bryn's blunt comment.

His mouth tightened. 'What's going on between you and Eric?'

She blinked, lashes long and dark around those dove-grey eyes. 'Sorry?'

Gabriel's days in Rome, persuading an elderly count to sell two small frescoes to the Archangel Gallery, had been something of an ordeal as his thoughts had constantly wandered to the problem of what to do about Bryn rather than concentrating on the task in front of him. And his flight back to England had been consumed with thoughts of the conversation he needed to have with her.

He had only called in at the gallery for a few minutes to drop off some papers in his office before going to Bryn's apartment. He had been surprised to learn from the night security that Miss Jones and Mr Sanders were still in the building. Going down to the basement and seeing Bryn there with Eric, obviously totally at ease with him, laughing with him—being invited to go out for a drink with him—had not improved Gabriel's already taciturn mood.

'If you decide to go ahead with the exhibition at Archangel, and the business-relationship rule, then that rule will apply to all employees of the gallery, not just me,' he bit out harshly.

Bryn gave a slow shake of her head. 'I don't— Are you suggesting— Do you think that Eric and I are involved? Romantically?' she added incredulously.

It had occurred to him, yes.

Eric Sanders was only a year or two older than Gabriel, and pleasant enough to look at. He was also an extremely well qualified and respected art expert, and Archangel was lucky to have him.

Even so, Gabriel knew that he wouldn't hesitate to find some way to dismiss the other man if it should turn out that he and Bryn were now 'romantically involved'.

Bryn stared at Gabriel D'Angelo in disbelief. This was the same man she had almost allowed to make love to her in his car just days ago, a lapse on her part that still made her feel hot all over every time she thought of it—and she had thought of it a lot since Friday evening!

Did Gabriel really think— Did he believe that she would have become involved with another man in the time he had been away in Rome?

'If you bothered to find out a little more personal information about your employees,' she snapped angrily, 'then you would know that Eric is engaged to a very lovely girl called Wendy, and that the two of them are getting married in three months' time!'

Gabriel nodded tersely, lids hooded over those dark brown eyes. 'As it happens, I do know that.'

Her eyes widened. 'But you still think that I— That the two of us have been— You don't think much of me, do you?'

Gabriel thought *about* this woman far too much than was comfortable. Or wise. Or conducive to a calm or logical frame of mind. Which was why he had jumped to the conclusion he had in regard to the friendly ease that obviously existed between Eric and Bryn!

None of which he was about to admit out loud to Bryn when she was this prickly and defensive. 'I'm tired and irritable and I haven't eaten yet this evening.'

Her eyes widened indignantly. 'And that's the excuse you're giving for accusing me of being involved with a man who's happily engaged to another woman?'

Gabriel gritted his teeth. It was definitely the only explanation he was willing to admit to at this moment; admitting his jealousy of the other man wasn't an option. 'It is, yes.'

She gave an impatient shake of her head. 'We seem to be veering off the relevant subject.'

He quirked mocking brows. 'My being hungry isn't relevant to you?'

'You've just dropped the equivalent of a bombshell on top of my head, by revealing that you've been aware from the beginning who I am, so no,' she snapped, 'your being hungry isn't of the least importance to me. Or the fact that you're also tired and insultingly irritable!'

He should have followed his first instinct when they had entered the privacy of his office a short time ago, Gabriel realised ruefully—which had been to strip Bryn naked, pick her up in his arms and carry her over to his desk to lay her down on the top of it, before making fierce and satisfying love to her!

That was what he *should* have done.

What he still wanted to do....

He now wanted that so badly, his erection so hard and aching against the soft material of his trousers, that the past few days might just as well not have happened.

Bryn eyed Gabriel uncertainly, her mouth suddenly dry as he began slowly stalking towards her, a determined glitter in the intensity of his dark gaze. 'Gabriel, what are you doing?' She took a step back, only to feel the cold of the window down the length of her spine as she stood flush against it.

'What I should have done the moment I saw you again,' Gabriel growled as he stood in front of her, the heat of his body not quite touching hers as his hands moved up to rest on the glass of the window on either side of her head, effectively holding her captive within the circle of his arms. His breath was a warm caress across her cheeks, those deep brown eyes holding—possessing—hers as she found it impossible to break away from the intensity of his gaze.

Bryn's heart was pounding rapidly in her chest, and she couldn't breathe, certainly couldn't have moved, even if someone had shouted 'fire'. Because the only fire that mattered to her was right here between the two of them as it blazed fiercely, heatedly, out of control.

'That might have been a bit awkward, considering that Eric was in the room at the time,' she said, attempting to lighten the tension currently sizzling between them.

'Do I look as if I care who else was in the room?' The reckless glitter in his eyes answered with a resounding no to the question. 'You do realise that this—whatever this is—is only going to complicate an already impossible situation?'

He nodded briefly. 'And I'm currently in the mood to complicate the hell out of it!'

Bryn swallowed before running her tongue over her lips.

'Did you know you have a habit of doing that?' Gabriel murmured achingly.

'I do?' Bryn's voice was just as hushed; the whole building was so empty and quiet at this time of night, with none of the sounds from outside penetrating the thick glass behind her either, giving the impression that they were the only two people in the world. The only two that mattered at this moment.

'Mmm.' He nodded, gaze transfixed on her slightly parted lips. 'And every time you do it I want to replace your tongue with mine.'

'You do?' Bryn still couldn't move, her heart beating

even louder, faster in her chest, as a wave of heat washed over her, plumping the lips between her thighs, causing a fire in her belly, swelling her breasts, her nipples becoming engorged against her T-shirt, before that heat licked up the slenderness of her throat and coloured her cheeks.

'Mmm.' Gabriel gave another nod as he raised the fierceness of his gaze to meet hers. 'And the way I see it, you have two choices right now.'

She swallowed. 'Which are?'

He smiled slightly. 'One, you can take me away from here and feed me. Two—and this is my personal favourite—we stay here instead and indulge a very different appetite.'

Against her better judgement, the second choice was Bryn's personal favourite too!

Right here and right now.

Later—much later—she knew she would feel totally differently about that choice, but the two of them were caught in a moment seemingly out of time, where there was no past and no future, only now, her body expectantly aroused, aching with hunger. For Gabriel. For the touch of his hands. The feel of his lips against her skin. Everywhere.

She forced herself to make some effort at resisting that hunger. 'There is the third choice of my just walking away.'

Gabriel shook his head. 'Not this time.'

'But—'

'No buts, Bryn.' He rested the heat of his forehead against hers, those brown eyes now mesmerisingly close to hers. 'It's your choice, Bryn,' he assured huskily. 'But I advise that you choose quickly!' he added urgently.

Bryn felt surrounded by him, held captive by him— his physical presence, his heat, the sensual pull of that muscled body so dangerously close to her own—so much so that she knew that the choice had already been made for her.

CHAPTER SEVEN

GABRIEL FELT AS if time had stopped as he waited for Bryn to answer—an answer that, knowing Bryn, could very well be her deciding to knee him in the groin, rather than choosing either of the two options he had so arrogantly given her!

His only excuse for that arrogance was the need he felt, the burning ache he had, to make love to her—which he doubted the fiery Bryn would see as a reasonable excuse at all.

His jaw was clenched, his forehead slightly damp against Bryn's, his arms rigid as he kept his hands flat on the window on either side of her head. He continued to hold himself back from coming into contact with her body, his arousal a throbbing ache, his shoulders tense as he waited for her to speak. For her to decide, to choose, to determine what happened next.

Bryn's tongue flicked nervously across her lips, only for her to quickly bring a halt to the nervous movement as she saw the way the darkness of Gabriel's gaze was now fixed so intently on those parted and moist lips.

She breathed raggedly, unevenly, her gaze continuing to hold Gabriel's as she spoke in a hushed voice. 'I'm getting a neck ache just looking up at— What are you doing?' She gasped as Gabriel skimmed his hands lightly down her arms, placing them on her waist before moving down onto his knees in front of her. Bryn was forced to reach out and grasp onto the support of his shoulders as she tottered at the suddenness of the movement, Gabriel's eyes now level with her breasts. 'Better?' he murmured throatily.

Better wasn't quite the word Bryn would have used—she would have described their current position as *very* dangerous.

Gabriel was so close now, his face just a breath away, allowing her to see the fire in the depths of those chocolate-brown eyes up close and very personal, the darkness of his hair falling rakishly, enticingly, over his forehead, those sculptured lips parted oh-so-temptingly.

The warmth of his hands on her waist seemed to burn through the cotton of her T-shirt. Big hands. So much so that they almost spanned the slenderness of her waist completely.

Bryn had felt surrounded by Gabriel before, but now she felt totally overwhelmed by his close proximity, the burning heat of his hands on her waist, that same heart burning in his eyes as he looked up at her. 'You do realise this isn't going to change anything, right?'

'I don't want to change anything. I'm more than happy with exactly where we are right now,' he assured huskily, his hands shifting, gaze dropping lower to watch as his fingers slowly pushed up her T-shirt to bare the smooth and silky skin of her abdomen. 'Very happy, in fact….' he murmured throatily, his breath warm against her skin as his lips trailed lightly, caressingly, across her bared flesh.

This wasn't what Bryn had meant, and Gabriel knew it. But she ceased to care at that moment as her every thought, every sensation, came down to the feel of Gabriel's lips and the rasp of his tongue moving caressingly against her skin.

She gasped low in her throat, her back arching, her fingers tightly gripping on to Gabriel's shoulders as his hands now moved up beneath her T-shirt and cupped breasts covered by nothing more than a black lace bra.

'You are so beautiful, Bryn,' he growled softly. 'I've thought of doing this for longer than I care to think about—' he pushed the T-shirt higher so that he could kiss the tops of her breasts '—and this.' He pulled the T-shirt up and over her head before discarding it onto the floor, his eyes dark and hungry. He looked at her appreciatively for several seconds before reaching up to tug the lace cup of her bra down and bare one of her breasts, the rosy nipple already hard and pouting. 'And, oh, God, this!' he groaned, his hands resting on her hips as his mouth closed over the tip of that bared breast and he sucked her roused nipple fully into the heat of his mouth.

Fire surged and swelled inside Bryn, making it difficult for her to breathe at all as she felt that pull on her nipple accompanied by the rasp of Gabriel's tongue, the place between her thighs dampening as her fingers became entwined in the darkness of his hair and she held him closer to her, needing more, wanting more.

Receiving more as Gabriel deftly unclipped and removed her bra completely before suckling and feeding on her other nipple as his hand caressed its twin.

'Could we at least move away from the window? We can be seen from outside the building.' Bryn gasped in half protest, too aroused, too greedy for more, to be able to call a halt to this. Gabriel's breath was hot against the dampness of her breast as he reluctantly released her nipple. 'The windows are reflective. No one can see in. Only we can see out.'

'Oh. Ah!' Bryn gasped breathlessly as Gabriel's hands moved to unfasten the button of her jeans before sliding the zip slowly downwards.

He sat back on his heels, eyes so dark they appeared as black as the lace panties now revealed, the air cool against Bryn's heated flesh as Gabriel slipped off her trainers before slowly pushing her jeans all the way down her legs and removing them completely.

Bryn had never felt so exposed, so desired, as Gabriel glanced up at her briefly, searing her with a single, heated glance, his gaze moving lazily downwards.

Gabriel's hands moved beneath the black lace as he breathed in the scent of her, a perfume that increased his own arousal, demanding that it be set free, to claim what it already knew to be his.

A single glance at Bryn's face had revealed the flush of arousal on her cheeks, the feverish glitter in her eyes. Her fingers tightened almost painfully in his hair as one of his hands cupped her mound, shifting the black lace aside and allowing his fingers to seek out the bare flesh beneath.

Her curls were damp with arousal as his fingers moved lower before moving up and around the roused nubbin. Bryn gasped low in her throat, parting her legs as he slowly stroked her.

Gabriel wanted to taste her, to feel Bryn fall apart as she climaxed. He wanted, needed— 'You do know I just want to rip these panties off you?'

'You're the one who has too many clothes on, Gabriel,' Bryn complained, desperate to touch his naked flesh in the same way he was touching hers. She wanted to run her hands over his bared shoulders, explore the hardness of his chest and stomach, to taste the heat of his skin beneath her lips. 'Please, Gabriel,' she groaned achingly.

'Undress me,' he invited throatily as he sat back on his heels and looked up at her expectantly.

He looked so damned good, wild and seductive as a pagan god, with the darkness of his hair in disarray from her caressing fingers, eyes dark and glittering, his cheeks flushed, lips slightly swollen.

The admiration in Gabriel's eyes as he looked at her dispelled any embarrassment she might have felt at standing almost naked in front of a man for the first time.

Nevertheless, her hands shook slightly as they moved to undo and remove Gabriel's tie, unfastening the buttons of his shirt before pushing it off his shoulders and down his arms to fall onto the carpeted floor with her own clothes.

Bryn's breath caught in her throat as she looked down at his muscled shoulders, a deep V of dark hair covering his chest and leading down over the flatness of his abdomen before disappearing into the waistband of his trousers. 'You're beautiful,' she murmured appreciatively as her hands trailed lightly over all that muscled flesh.

'I believe that should be my line,' Gabriel came back huskily.

She smiled shakily. 'Not from where I'm standing.'

'Then let's not stand any longer.' His grin was entirely roguish as he stood up to sweep Bryn easily into his arms, carrying her over and laying her down on the sofa before straightening to strip off the rest of his clothes.

Bryn watched unashamedly as he slipped off his shoes and socks before unfastening his trousers and allowing them to fall to his feet, carelessly discarding them as if they hadn't cost what Bryn earned in a month.

She had thought him beautiful before, but, wearing only black body-hugging boxers that clearly revealed the lengthy bulge beneath, he had to be the most sinfully gorgeous man Bryn had ever set eyes on: wide and muscled shoulders and chest, his waist tapered, thighs lean and powerful, legs long and lightly sprinkled with dark hair.

Gabriel felt the painful swell of his shaft in response to Bryn's appreciative gaze on him as he hooked his fingers into his boxers before slipping them down his thighs and legs, and then straightening.

She drew her breath in sharply as Gabriel stood naked in front of her, her wide eyes darkening to gunmetal grey as she gazed up at him with open hunger.

A hunger Gabriel was powerless to resist as he stepped closer, his breath catching in his throat as Bryn reached out to trail her fingers lightly down the silken length of his shaft, her face flushed with passion as she traced the engorged blood vessels along the length to the bulbous tip.

Gabriel's jaw clenched, hands fisting at his sides, as Bryn sat up and swung her legs to the floor, her breasts thrusting temptingly as she leaned forward to curl her fingers about his erection, her tongue moving distractedly over her lips as the soft pad of her thumb touched the moistness of that sensitive purple head. She looked up at him briefly before slowly lowering her head and lapping up those escaping juices with the soft rasp of her tongue.

'Sweet—' Gabriel muttered as he drew in a hissing breath, his whole body rigid with tension. 'Are you trying to kill me, Bryn?' he choked as she continued.

'You taste delicious,' she murmured appreciatively. 'Sweet and yet salty too.' The fingers of one hand remained curled about him as she parted her lips before taking him completely into her mouth.

'You *are* trying to kill me!' Gabriel's back arched, his hands becoming entangled in Bryn's hair as he began to thrust slowly, instinctively, into that hot, moist cavern as

Bryn's throaty chuckle of satisfaction vibrated along the length of his pulsing and sensitive shaft.

Bryn hadn't known—had never imagined—anything could taste and feel this good. She felt bold, totally empowered by Gabriel's uninhibited response as her head bobbed in rhythm with his increasingly powerful thrusts, his hips bucking as those thrusts became more urgent still.

'You have to stop, Bryn,' he gasped, his fingers biting into the bareness of her shoulders as he halted her movements. 'Or I'm going to lose this before we've even begun.'

Her lashes rose as she looked up at Gabriel to find him looking down at her, his expression pained; eyes jet-black, cheeks flushed, his mouth twisted into a grimace.

Even so, Bryn was reluctant to release him immediately, moving slowly down his length, lips squeezing just beneath the purple head before she released that pressure. He gave a strangulated groan.

'Now it's my turn to torture you,' he added as Bryn finally sat back to look up at him with wide innocent eyes. 'And I warn you,' he murmured determinedly as he moved down onto his knees between her parted thighs before easing her back against the sofa, 'I'm not going to stop.' His head swooped down as he claimed one pouting nipple into his mouth, suckling deep and hard, as his other hand cupped its twin, finger and thumb plucking, gently squeezing.

Pleasure raged through Bryn like wildfire at this full-on assault to her senses, and she realised that Gabriel had only been teasing her earlier, tantalising her. Her head fell back against the sofa, back arching, as his mouth drew hungrily on her nipple, his thumb and fingers matching that wild rhythm on its twin as heat poured between her thighs like molten lava. The tiny nubbin there pulsing as her hips began to move against him restlessly, pleading, begging for Gabriel's touch.

He growled low in his throat before his lips released her nipple and moved down over her abdomen, his hands moving to grip her hips, holding her unmoving as his lips and tongue sought and easily found the nubbin pouting and swollen amongst her curls.

Her breath caught in her throat, heat engulfing her at the first caress of Gabriel's tongue across that sensitive bundle of nerve endings. He flicked his tongue mercilessly, again and again, across that pulsing nubbin.

Bryn sobbed low in her throat as her hips arched up in rhythm with that torturously flicking tongue, gasping, keening, as Gabriel's hand moved down and he slipped a finger inside her hot and grasping channel, gently thrusting. A second finger joined the first, her pleasure rising to fever pitch as his tongue flattened against her nubbin, pressing to the same rhythm as those thrusting fingers, until Bryn felt the pleasure rising, soaring, completely engulfing her, again and again, until she felt as if she had shattered into a million pieces.

'Are you okay?' Gabriel prompted with concern as he lay down on the sofa beside her and gathered her shaking body close against his.

Bryn in the throes of orgasm had been the most beautiful thing he had ever seen and heard; little throaty sobs had caught at the back of her throat, her face flushed, throat arched, breasts jutting proudly forward, her hips rising to meet each thrust of his fingers as the muscles in her channel gripped tightly with each prolonged spasm of pleasure. A pleasure that Gabriel had drawn out to the fullest until Bryn was sobbing and the tears flowed down her cheeks.

'I'm fine,' she answered him shakily, limp in his arms as she lay draped across his chest. 'Better than fine,' she added. 'That was the most amazing thing— I had no idea— It was truly amazing,' she repeated breathlessly.

'I aim to please, ma'am.' Gabriel chuckled softly.

'Oh, you did! You do,' she amended huskily, hand lightly caressing his shoulder. 'That was truly unbeliev-able. I— Are we going to stop now?'

'Not a chance,' Gabriel assured indulgently. 'I'm just giving you time to recover. You seem a little over-whelmed.'

'A little?' Her laugh was shaky. 'I could become ad-dicted to so much pleasure!'

'You're doing wonderful things for my ego, Bryn,' he murmured wryly.

'I invariably tell the truth too,' she assured quietly.

Gabriel frowned slightly, not wanting either of them to dwell on the reason he had said that to her earlier, not when they were together so intimately. They could deal with the past, and the future, later; right now he just wanted to be with Bryn, with no tension or animosity between them. 'Didn't any of your other lovers pleasure you so well?' he teased.

Her fingers twirled in the curls on his chest. 'What other lovers?'

Gabriel stilled as he looked down at her searchingly, a smile of satisfaction curving her lips as she tweaked one of his nipples and watched as it hardened in response.

She looked up at him. 'Do you like that too?'

'I love it.' He nodded distractedly. 'Bryn—'

'Do we have to talk right now, Gabriel?' She moved to lay between his parted thighs as she flicked her tongue across his hardened nipple, causing Gabriel to draw his breath in sharply as his shaft once again jerked and swelled in response to the caress. 'You do like that,' she murmured with satisfaction, the heat of her breath brushing across his dampened flesh.

'Yes,' he grated between gritted teeth. 'Bryn—'

'Not now, Gabriel.' She glanced up at him pleadingly, her hands looking very pale and slender against his olive skin. 'I don't want to talk—to think—I just want to taste you some more.' She moved sinuously down his body until she knelt between his parted thighs and her hands both curled about the length of his shaft.

Gabriel sat up slightly as he reached down to grasp her wrists and stop those mind-numbing caresses before it was too late. 'Not yet, Bryn. I— Have you had any other lovers at all?' he prompted cautiously.

She frowned as she looked up at him. 'This isn't the part where we confess to past relationships, is it? Because I really would rather skip hearing about all your previous conquests!'

So would Gabriel; there hadn't been so many women for him that he didn't remember their names and their faces, but there had certainly been enough. Not so much during the past five years, but Bryn wasn't ready to hear the reason for that. 'We aren't talking about me, Bryn—'

'Well, we're not going to talk about me either, if this is going to be a one-sided thing!' she assured impatiently. 'Let go of my hands, Gabriel—'

He ignored her request. 'Bryn, are you even on any contraception?' he prompted exasperatedly.

She shrugged. 'I've never had a use for it. Don't tell me a man like you doesn't have a condom or two in his pocket somewhere? Weren't you ever a Boy Scout?'

'Bryn, will you please answer me?' Gabriel sat up, taking her with him, looking down at her intently as he continued to hold both her hands captive in his. 'How many lovers have you had?'

She blinked. 'Why do you need to know?'

'Because this is important, damn it!' he groaned. 'I really need you to answer the question, Bryn.'

She frowned. 'Am I doing something wrong? You seemed happy enough a few minutes ago—'

'I was very happy, Bryn. I *am* happy.'

'You don't look it.'

'That's probably because you keep avoiding answering my question,' he said, sighing his exasperation.

Bryn sat back, completely unconcerned by her own nakedness; Gabriel had seen and touched and licked parts of her that no other person ever had, so it was a little late for her to feel in the least self-conscious now. 'Are you going to make a thing out of this, Gabriel?' she prompted impatiently.

'That would depend on what "this" is,' he answered cautiously.

'Okay, let's just get this out of the way so that we can move on.' She sighed. 'No, I haven't had any previous lovers. Which actually answers your second question, doesn't it, because if I haven't had any lovers then I've obviously never felt the need for contraception either.' She looked up at him uncertainly as he released her to stand up abruptly. A nerve pulsed in his clenched jaw as he stared down at her.

'No lovers?'

'Not until tonight, no.' She slowly shook her head.

'Sweet mother of...' He ran an agitated hand through his already tousled hair as he began to pace restlessly. 'You should have told me, Bryn.'

'Why should I?' she reasoned. 'I should tell you that fierce pacing doesn't have the same impact when you're stark naked.' She fell silent as he quickly pulled on his briefs, trousers and shirt, not bothering to refasten the latter. 'Gabriel?'

He breathed raggedly. 'Just give me a minute, please, Bryn.'

'I believe there were two of us here tonight, not just me,' she continued despite his warning. 'And I don't remember you bothering to ask me any of these questions *before* we both took our clothes off.'

No, he hadn't, had he? Which was more than careless on Gabriel's part. His only excuse—if it could be called one—was that Bryn affected him so deeply he couldn't think of anything else but her when he held her in his arms.

He looked at Bryn now, still unsettled at learning that he was her first lover— Well, her *almost* lover. 'Bryn, I would have— I wouldn't have pushed so hard if I had known of your…inexperience,' he said gently.

She frowned. 'What does that mean?'

He shook his head. 'Well, I wouldn't have made love to you in my office, for one thing.'

'Why not?'

He closed his eyes briefly. 'Your first time should be in a bed, Bryn, preferably a four-poster—'

'I never imagined you as a romantic, Gabriel.'

His jaw tightened. 'Don't mock me, Bryn. Not now.'

'I'm not the one who just spoiled the moment!' She rose lithely to her feet, her face pale as she turned her back on him and began pulling her own clothes back on, her panties and jeans no problem, the bra proving less cooperative, forcing Bryn to thrust it impatiently into her pocket before she pulled her T-shirt on and fluffed out her hair.

'I could have hurt you, Bryn.' He gave a pained frown as he realised what he had just said.

'It's five years too late for you to think of that,' Bryn came back bitterly as she looked up from pulling on her shoes. 'Besides, I don't think either of us was thinking too clearly a few minutes ago. I certainly didn't think I needed to give you a list, or otherwise, of my credentials as a lover before we proceeded.'

He sighed as she stood up to collect her bag in preparation of leaving. 'You can't just leave—'

'Watch me.'

'Why are you so angry, Bryn? Can't the two of us at least talk before you go? Please, Bryn,' he encouraged gruffly.

Her mouth thinned. 'I don't think we have anything to talk about. We had an…encounter, and now it's obviously over.'

It hadn't just been an encounter to Gabriel. No matter what Bryn might think, how many previous lovers he might have had, he had never experienced anything even remotely like the pleasure he had felt with Bryn tonight. She was so beautiful she took his breath away. Responsive beyond belief. And the caress of her hands, the touch of her lips on his body, his shaft, had been so unbelievably arousing he had almost lost control.

He gave a shake of his head. 'I have the feeling that this was your first encounter too?'

Her cheeks warmed with colour. 'I've been a little busy the past five years, okay? Building a new life in Wales for myself and my mother. Getting my degree. Working to pay off the student loans, and the rent, and painting madly in my spare time. Besides which—' she drew in a ragged breath '—I would have felt compelled to explain about the past to anyone I became seriously involved with, and I've never cared enough to want to do that. I'm sorry if that makes me a lousy lover, but I—'

'You're not a lousy lover, Bryn,' Gabriel cut in forcefully. 'Far from it,' he added huskily. 'I just— I'm surprised that you chose me, of all people, to be your first.'

'You of all people,' she echoed bitterly. 'I suppose it is a bit ironic,' she murmured self-derisively. 'But it has a certain rightness about it too, if you think about it. You already know about my past, who I am, who my father was, which means I don't have to confess anything to you.'

In just a few short minutes everything between them had changed once again, and she was back to being her usual defensive and antagonistic self.

Or maybe that responsive woman was the real Bryn?

Gabriel didn't know anymore, and for once in his life he wasn't sure what to do next. Wasn't sure if there was any way they could move forward with Bryn in the mood she was in right now. 'Could we have dinner together tomorrow evening?' he asked tentatively.

Bryn's chin rose stubbornly. 'Not if it's going to result in us having some sort of post-mortem regarding what happened tonight, no.'

'Damn it, Bryn—' He broke off exasperatedly. 'I'm desperately trying to put things right between us, but I could really do with a little cooperation from you.'

'It's a little late in the day for that, isn't it?' she scorned.

'I'm really trying here, Bryn,' he bit out between gritted teeth.

She eyed him suspiciously. 'Put things right between us how?'

He sighed. 'We've skipped over a couple sequences

of a relationship, and I'd like to maybe take those two steps back and start again.'

Bryn looked at him searchingly, not sure where he was going with this. 'We had a sexual encounter, Gabriel, not a relationship.' An encounter that had been life changing for her, although she had a feeling that it was Gabriel himself who had made tonight so special; he was not only an exceptional and experienced lover, but a caring and considerate one too. Even with her own lack of experience Bryn knew that not all men were like that, so maybe she should be thanking Gabriel for the consideration he had shown her, instead of arguing with him.

And maybe she would be—if she didn't feel so confused about how she had allowed tonight to happen in the first place.

Nor did she understand why Gabriel had been thrown so off balance by her lack of experience; didn't men prefer no-ties-no-expectations sex?

And, damn it, she couldn't allow herself to become any more deeply involved with Gabriel than she already was. As it was, she had no idea how she would even begin to explain to her mother about her dinner date with Gabriel, let alone what had happened tonight; accepting another dinner invitation from him would only add to the complication of this situation.

'I appreciate the invitation, Gabriel,' she told him dismissively. 'And I understand what you're trying to say, but I'm really not interested in taking this any further.' She gave him a bright and dismissive smile.

'You're not interested in taking this any further?' he repeated slowly.

'No. You've said you're willing to forget the past, so I suggest we do the same with what happened just now. Let's both just forget it ever happened,' she repeated evenly.

Gabriel had never met another woman even remotely like Bryn Jones. Nor did he ever remember wanting to strangle a woman as much as he did Bryn at this moment.

First, she had aroused him so much that the two of them had almost had unprotected sex on the sofa in his office, of all places, and now she was giving him the brush-off. Unbelievable!

And was that injured pride speaking, or something else?

This woman had him so tied up in knots that Gabriel had no chance of sorting out his emotions. Except to know he wanted to see Bryn again, to be with her.

'Dinner tomorrow evening,' he repeated firmly.

'No,' she refused flatly.

Gabriel's eyes narrowed. 'You already have a date tomorrow night?'

Bryn raised her brows in silent rebuke. 'My shifts at work have worked out that I have three days off together, so I'm travelling home tomorrow morning to see my mother and stepfather. It's also the reason I was working late with Eric this evening,' she added challengingly.

'I see,' Gabriel murmured slowly, not willing to get into that conversation again, or the jealousy he had felt seeing her with Eric.

'How are you getting there?'

'By train.'

'Let me drive you—'

'Don't be ridiculous, Gabriel,' Bryn cut him off sharply, impatiently. 'It's bad enough that the two of us have met again. I don't need to shock my mother by having you turn up on her doorstep with me tomorrow.'

His mouth thinned. 'Are you saying she doesn't even

know about your participation in the exhibition at Arch-angel next month?'

Bryn snorted. 'I wouldn't even know where to start telling her of my reinvolvement with the D'Angelo family!'

'Damn it, Bryn.' Gabriel glared. 'Your mother never hated me in the way that you do—'

'You can't possibly know that,' she cut in dismissively.

As it happened, Gabriel did know that. But it appeared, from what Bryn was saying now, that Mary Harper had never told her daughter of their meetings after William went to prison.

'Bryn, your father—'

'I don't want to talk about him!' Her eyes flashed in warning.

Neither did Gabriel, but at the same time he knew it was a subject they couldn't continue to avoid. 'Bryn, he was a man, not a saint. Just a man,' he repeated heavily. 'His past misdemeanours weren't allowed to come out in court because they would have prejudiced the verdict, but surely you know that your father was a professional conman.'

'How dare you?' she gasped furiously.

Gabriel frowned. 'Not only that, but he brought about his own downfall.'

'You already said that!'

'But I mean this literally.' He sighed. 'Bryn, the reason I came to your home, talked to your father a couple times, was to try to talk him out of going through with trying to sell the painting. Because I knew, deep inside me, here—' he held his hand to his heart '—that the painting was a forgery. I had no proof but that feeling, but that was enough for me to try to stop him from going through with it. The morning after I visited him the second time the headlines of the painting's existence were blazing across half a dozen newspapers.'

'You're saying my father was the one who went to the press?' Bryn gasped.

'Well, I certainly didn't. And if it wasn't me, then it had to be him. If you don't believe me—'

'Of course I don't believe you!' she said scornfully.

He sighed heavily. 'Then ask your mother about him, Bryn,' he encouraged. 'Ask her to tell you about all the years she suffered in silence through William's schemes and machinations. Ask her if he went to the press. You have to ask her, Bryn,' he repeated forcefully.

'I don't have to do anything.' She gave a determined shake of her head. 'I think—' she breathed deeply '—that I may actually hate you for the things you've said tonight.'

Gabriel had no choice but to watch as Bryn left, accepting that if hate was all Bryn had to give him, then he would take even that hate.

CHAPTER EIGHT

'OKAY, YOUNG LADY, time to spill the beans!' Bryn's mother smiled as she placed a jug of fresh lemonade and two glasses down on the picnic table, joining Bryn. They sat outside in the garden at the back of the cottage where she now lived with Rhys Evans, her second husband.

'Spill what beans…?' Bryn straightened in her garden chair as she slowly pushed her sketch pad aside, her expression cautious as she watched her mother pour lemonade into the glasses.

Mary, a slightly older version of Bryn, with shoulder-length brown hair and deep grey eyes, gave her a reproving glance as she dropped down into a seat on the other side of the wooden table. 'This is your mother you're talking to, Bryn. And you've been here for two days already and barely spoken a word since you arrived.'

'I've been busy sketching.' Bryn had found it soothing to lose herself in drawing the beautiful array of coloured flowers that scented her mother's cottage garden, rather than think of the things Gabriel had said about her father before she left London.

'I noticed,' Mary dismissed. 'Now tell me who he is!' she prompted interestedly as she sipped her lemonade.

'He?' Bryn squeaked a reply. She should have known by now how impossible it was to divert her mother's at-

tention once she had made her mind up to something—
which she now seemed to have done on the subject of
Bryn's distraction these past two days.

'The man who's making my normally chatty daughter so introspective.'

Bryn recognised her mother's tone as being the 'and
don't try telling me any nonsense'—in this case, that
there was no man—'because I won't believe you' tone.

And Bryn knew she had been unusually quiet since
coming home to visit her mother and Rhys, that the last
evening with Gabriel had left her in a state of confusion. About the things Gabriel had said about her father
as much as about Gabriel himself.

She gave her mother a searching glance now. 'Are you
happy with Rhys?'

'Absolutely,' her mother answered instantly, a warm
smile curving her lips.

Bryn nodded slowly. 'And were you happy with
Daddy?'

Her mother's smile faded and a frown appeared between her eyes. 'Where's this coming from, Bryn?'

'I don't know.' She stood up restlessly. 'I just— I've
watched you and Rhys together, the teasing, the easy
affection, the total respect you have for each other,
and—and I don't remember ever seeing you and Daddy
together like that.'

'We were happy in the beginning. When you were
little.'

Bryn gave a pained frown. 'But not later on?'

Her mother grimaced. 'It became…complicated. Everything was fine to start with, but then William became
restless working in an office day after day, and started
coming up with these get-rich-quick ideas—all of which
failed miserably. You're old enough to know these things

now, Bryn. William used up all our savings on those ideas, and I never knew what he was going to do next. Or whether we would all still have a roof over our heads the following week.' She shrugged. 'That sort of uncertainty in a partner can test even the best of relationships to its limits, and our marriage was already pretty shaky. It very quickly deteriorated into chaos.'

Which was probably why her mother now appreciated Rhys's steadiness, Bryn's stepfather having been the local and much-respected carpenter for all of his working life.

'But you stayed together....'

Her mother smiled. 'We had you.'

'But did you never think of leaving Daddy?' Bryn looked at her mother searchingly.

'Many times,' Mary admitted truthfully. 'And I'm sure, as much as it would have hurt you, it would have come to that in the end.'

Bryn gave a pained frown. 'And yet, even during the trial, you stood by him.'

'He was my husband. And your father,' her mother added pointedly. 'And you adored him.'

Yes, Bryn had adored her father. But she hadn't been able to get Gabriel's outburst that last evening in London out of her mind. To question, to want to know if the things he had said were true.

Her mother's comments confirmed what Bryn had feared—that William had been the petty crook Gabriel had called him, for almost all of her life, involved in one scam or another. A petty crook who had tried to break into the big time by selling the fake Turner—and failed miserably.

And these past few days Bryn had questioned whether she hadn't always known that, and that it was the knowing that had added to her resentment of Gabriel, not because he had kissed her, not because she had fallen in love with him, not even because of his involvement in her father's downfall, but because that involvement had made him part of the disenchantment she hadn't wanted to acknowledge all these years.

'Why the interest in all of that now, Bryn?' her mother prompted softly, her gaze sharp. 'Has something happened? Something that's made you start thinking, questioning the past?'

Gabriel D'Angelo was what had happened! A man who was making it impossible for Bryn not to question the past. But it wasn't Gabriel's fault; Bryn was the one who had chosen to come into contact with him again when she'd entered the exhibition.

No, it wasn't Gabriel's fault, but Bryn's reaction to meeting him again, her response to him, had set in motion those same feelings of guilt inside her that she had felt five years ago when she had looked across that crowded courtroom and known that, despite everything he was saying and all the damage he was causing to her father and her family, she still wanted him.

It had been bad enough then for Bryn to realise she was infatuated with the arrogant and handsome Gabriel D'Angelo, but she found it harder still to realise, all these years later, that she was still attracted to the man who had helped shatter her world.

Admittedly her mother was happily remarried, but still the past had to overshadow, to make impossible, there ever being any sort of relationship between Bryn and Gabriel. A relationship she would have to tell her mother about.

Even if her traitorous body seemed to have other ideas on the subject!

Just thinking about that last evening with Gabriel, of the depth of intimacy the two of them had shared, the way she had totally fallen apart in his arms, climaxing so spectacularly, was enough to make her blush.

'Okay, now I really want to know who this man is if he can make my sensible daughter blush so prettily,' her mother stated firmly.

'I can't tell you,' Bryn groaned.

'Why on earth not?' Mary looked stunned. 'We've always been able to talk about anything in the past— Bryn, if it's a woman making you feel this way, then I hope you know that I'm broad-minded enough not to—'

'It's not a woman!' She gave a rueful smile. 'But I appreciate knowing how broad minded you are!' she added dryly.

'Is this man involved with someone else, then? Maybe married?' her mother added worriedly.

'It's worse than that!' Bryn groaned as she began to pace the lawn Rhys had recently cut. Her mother's brows rose. 'What could possibly be worse than—? Is he older than you?'

'Marginally.' Bryn shrugged. 'Maybe ten years or so.'

'That's nothing.' Her mother sighed her relief. 'But I still don't understand why you won't tell me who he is.'

'Because I can't.' She sighed heavily. 'He's just not— suitable for me to be involved with, okay?'

'No, of course it's not okay, Bryn.' Mary frowned worriedly. 'I've never known you to— He isn't a drug dealer or something like that, is he?'

'Of course not,' Bryn denied ruefully.

Her mother didn't look reassured. 'But he's unsuitable in some other way?'

'Oh, yes,' Bryn sighed.

Mary continued to look at her searchingly for several long minutes, that worried frown between her eyes. 'Does your interest just now, in the past, have anything to do with your reluctance to talk about this man?' she finally prompted.

'I— Maybe.' Bryn's teeth worried her bottom lip. 'Do you know—? Is it possible that Daddy was the one to tell the press about the painting, as a way of ensuring the D'Angelo gallery, or some other gallery, couldn't just dismiss the painting as a forgery?'

'More than possible, I'm afraid,' her mother sighed. 'You know, Bryn,' she said slowly, evenly, 'it took me years to accept this, but your father was responsible for everything that happened to him.' Exactly the words Gabriel had used to Bryn just days ago.

'Not me. Not you,' her mother continued firmly. 'Not anyone else involved in that mess. Just your father. He gambled not just with his own future but with ours too, and he lost. We all lost. But having met Rhys, finding such happiness with him, has shown me that we don't have to continue to let ourselves be the losers, darling.'

'I'm not a loser—'

'Bryn, I've watched the way you've avoided all involvement with men these past five years,' her mother admonished gently. 'And I'm telling you now that the only way of allowing yourself to go forward is to let go of the past.'

Tears blurred Bryn's vision. 'Sometimes that's easier said than done.'

'But it can be done.' Her mother reached out and grasped Bryn's hand tightly in hers. 'I'm living proof of that.'

Yes, her mother's happiness with Rhys now *was* living proof of that. Except... Gabriel had been directly involved in that past her mother spoke of. Not as a spectator, or someone removed from the situation, but as a full participant.

'We'll see.' She squeezed her mother's hand reassuringly. 'But could we just forget about this for now? Talk about something else?'

Her mother looked less than happy with the idea. 'If that's what you really want.'

'It is.'

Mary nodded. 'You know where I am when and if you want to talk.'

Yes, Bryn knew; she just couldn't see a time she would ever be able to tell her mother of the emotional tangle she had got herself into with Gabriel.

'Did you have a good time in Wales last week?' Gabriel's expression was guarded as he looked down at Bryn and saw the way the colour drained from her cheeks. She slowly looked up from the magazine she was reading at the back of the coffee shop, the girl who had prepared his coffee having told him where Bryn was sitting taking her evening break.

Gabriel knew that Bryn had to have been back in London for four days now, but she hadn't come anywhere near the gallery, or him. Mainly him, Gabriel suspected.

The fact that his unexpected appearance at the coffee shop this evening had caused Bryn's face to pale so dramatically, as well as striking her uncharacteristically dumb, would seem to confirm that suspicion.

He pulled out the chair opposite hers and sat down before placing his mug of coffee down on the table between them. 'Everything all right at home?'

Her throat moved as she swallowed before answering him. 'Fine, thank you.'

'That's good.' Gabriel leaned back in the chair to

stretch his long legs out in front of him as he continued to study Bryn.

She appeared somehow fragile to his critical gaze. Her face was pale, and there were hollows in her cheeks that hadn't been there a week ago, implying that she had lost weight since he saw her last. Her eyes were also shadowed and bruised-looking, as if she hadn't been sleeping well.

Because she had been as disturbed by what had happened between the two of them the previous week as Gabriel still was, rather than the things he had said to her?

Had she talked to her mother, as he had advised? Did she now know the truth where her father was concerned? Or did she still hold Gabriel responsible for everything that had happened in the past?

His determination to find answers to these questions had brought him to the coffee shop.

The past week had been a torturous hell for Gabriel, the first three days spent wondering if Bryn would talk to her mother, what she was thinking if she had, what decision she was going to come to in regard to the two of them while she was away. He had then spent the four days since she'd returned from Wales assuming she had decided to cut him out of her life.

A totally unacceptable decision as far as Gabriel was concerned.

Bryn was totally disconcerted at Gabriel's arrival in the coffee shop, not least because his appearance, in a casual cream polo shirt, faded jeans resting low on lean hips and the darkness of his overlong hair falling casually over his forehead, had literally taken her breath away. How she wanted this man.

More so even than a week ago, she acknowledged achingly as she looked at him from beneath lowered lashes, their time together in Gabriel's office, the intimacies they had shared, having for ever changed the way she now thought and felt about him.

A realisation that made a complete nonsense of her avoidance of him this past week.

'You haven't been to the gallery since you got back.' Gabriel's accusing tone echoed some of her thoughts.

She shrugged. 'I've spoken to Eric several times on the phone, explained that I couldn't make it to the gallery because I've been really busy at work.'

'So he told me.'

Bryn found it impossible to meet the dark shrewdness of Gabriel's gaze. 'Then I don't understand why you're here.'

He lost his relaxed pose as he sat forward and grasped both of her hands in his, his nostrils flaring angrily as Bryn instinctively sat back and tried to pull free. A freedom he wouldn't allow her. 'I'm here so that we can have the conversation we didn't finish a week ago.'

Her tone was pleading. 'Gabriel—'

'Bryn, don't try to freeze me out, or put me, and what happened between us, into some convenient little compartment in your brain never to be opened again,' he warned fiercely, 'because, I assure you, that isn't going to happen. I'm not going to allow it to happen.'

She gave another tug on her hands, once again failing to free herself, her throat moving as she swallowed before speaking. 'I don't know what you mean—'

'Like hell you don't,' Gabriel scorned harshly.

A blush warmed her cheeks as she hissed, 'You're causing a scene, Gabriel.' Several people at neighbouring tables had turned to give them curious glances as they had obviously heard the harshness of Gabriel's tone.

He gave a humourless smile. 'We wouldn't be having

this conversation here at all if you hadn't been too much of a coward to come to Archangel when you got back.'

She gasped. 'I told you, I've been really busy at the coffee shop since I returned—'

'Too busy to so much as bother to telephone the man who is your lover?'

'Gabriel!' she warned fiercely, wrenching her hands painfully from his grasp even as she glanced around them before turning back to glare across the table at him. 'You are *not* my lover.'

'More than any other man has ever been,' he stated uncompromisingly.

And how Bryn regretted ever allowing Gabriel to re-alise that.

Gabriel wasn't enjoying this conversation, not his own part in it, or the fact that it was obviously causing Bryn discomfort. But this past week of not personally hearing so much as a word from her had made him so frustrated that he couldn't seem to help himself.

Just looking at Bryn again as she sat alone in a corner at the back of the coffee shop reading a magazine, taking in the delicate softness of her cheek, the long sweep of her lashes, the silkiness of that defensively spiky hair, had been enough to cause his breath to catch in his throat and his shaft to become hard and aching beneath his jeans—the same painful state of arousal he had been in for most of the past week!

Consequently, he wasn't in the mood to accept the brush-off from Bryn again. 'What time do you finish here tonight?' he prompted.

She blinked. 'Gabriel—'

'We either have this conversation at my apartment later tonight, Bryn, or right here and right now, but we are going to talk sometime this evening,' he assured her.

She gave a shake of her head. 'I'm tired, Gabriel.'

'And you think I'm not?'

Her frown was pained. 'I don't understand.'

'I haven't exactly been sleeping like a baby for the past week as I waited to see what you decided to do about us.'

'There is no "us",' she sighed wearily.

'Oh, yes, Bryn, there most definitely is an "us".'

She gave a shake of her head. 'Doesn't the fact that I haven't bothered to contact you since I returned speak for itself as to how I feel about what happened between us?'

Gabriel gave a humourless smile. 'It tells me you're a coward, nothing more.'

Her chin rose. 'That's the second time you've called me a coward in as many minutes, and I don't like it.'

'Then prove that you aren't one by meeting me once you've finished work tonight.'

She gave him a pitying glance. 'We aren't children playing a game of dare, Gabriel.'

'We aren't children at all, which is why you should stop behaving like one.' His eyes glittered angrily. 'I'm not going anywhere, Bryn, so if you thought I was going to help you get through this situation by going along with pretending last week didn't happen, you were obviously mistaken. It happened, Bryn. I suggest you live with it.'

Bryn had been living with it for the past week. With the knowledge of her complete lack of resistance to this man. With the fact that she'd had no control over what had happened between them in his office a week ago. With the fact that Gabriel had been the one to call a halt to their lovemaking because she hadn't been able to do so.

With the fact that she had only needed to look at Gabriel again tonight to know that she wanted him still.

Her mouth tightened. 'It would have been the gentlemanly thing to do, in the circumstances.'

'Insulting me isn't going to make me get up and walk out of here either, Bryn,' he assured her softly. 'This is way too important for that. To both of us. This past week, waiting, wondering, has been sheer bloody hell.' He ran an agitated hand through his hair.

She looked across at Gabriel searchingly, noting the dark shadows beneath his eyes, the sharp blade of his cheekbones above slightly hollow cheeks, lines etched beside his nose and mouth that she was sure hadn't been there before, and realised that this past week really hadn't been any easier for Gabriel than it had been for her.

'Why won't you just accept that I can't do this, Gabriel?' she groaned achingly.

'Because neither of us knows what this is yet,' he maintained stubbornly. 'And I'm not willing to just give up on it until we do know.'

She gave a shake of her head. 'Isn't it enough that we both know that the events of the past makes this impossible?'

'I refuse to accept that.' His gaze was tormented as he reached across the table to once again take one of her hands in his.

'You have to! We both do.'

Gabriel gave a shake of his head. 'Did you speak to your mother?'

'About you?'

'Obviously not about me,' he drawled knowingly at her shocked expression. 'But did you at least ask her to confirm the things I told you about your father?'

'And what if I did?' Colour warmed her cheeks as she avoided meeting his gaze. 'Knowing who and what my father was, the things he did, changes nothing, Gabriel.'

'It means we can put the past where it belongs—in the past! It can't be undone, or remade, because it is what it is, but if we— If we want each other enough, we should be able to talk about it, to get by it. And I do want you, Bryn, and the trembling of your hand when I touch you is enough to tell me that you still want me too.' His fingers tightened about her shaking ones as she would have pulled away. 'Nothing else matters at this moment but that.'

'And what about later? What happens once the—the wanting has all gone, Gabriel?' Tears glittered in her eyes. 'What happens then?'

'Who says it's ever going to be gone?'

'I do.'

'Then we deal with later when later comes along,' he stated firmly. 'For now I just want us to be together and see where this takes us. Can we do that, do you think?' The soft pad of his thumb caressed the back of her hand as he looked across at her intently.

Could they? This past week had been absolute hell for Bryn too, her desire for this man taking over her every thought as she remembered how it had been between them that night in Gabriel's office. The way they had still responded to each other despite both knowing who the other was, before her feelings of guilt had once again made her deny that desire she still felt for him. A desire that Gabriel so obviously reciprocated and refused to dismiss. Refused to allow her to dismiss.

Could the two of them really have a relationship for however long these feelings lasted and simply ignore the pain of the past?

Could she do that?

CHAPTER NINE

'COME IN AND make yourself at home, Bryn, and I'll pour us both a glass of wine,' Gabriel encouraged huskily as she stood hesitantly in the doorway to the sitting room of his apartment.

He had felt an inner sense of relief earlier, when Bryn had finally capitulated to the idea of the two of them meeting up again when she finished work at ten; he might have deliberately given her the impression he was both confident and unyielding in his demand for them to talk this evening, but inwardly he hadn't been at all sure, until that moment, that Bryn would agree.

Gabriel had been waiting outside in his car for her when she and several of her co-workers left the coffee shop a little after ten o'clock, the two of them not speaking after he climbed out of the car and opened the passenger door for her to get in, or during the short drive to his apartment.

She *had* lost weight, he realised as Bryn finally entered the sitting room, the black denims she wore not quite as figure-hugging as they had been a week ago, her collarbone visible at the open neck of her black shirt, those grey eyes appearing huge in the paleness of her face. Evidence that she was finding fighting the attraction between them as difficult as he was? Gabriel certainly hoped so, because this past week of not seeing her since the two of them had made love together had been sheer torture.

His expression softened as Bryn sank down wearily into the comfort of one of the brown leather armchairs. 'Busy evening?' he prompted as he poured two glasses of pinot grigio.

'Very.' Bryn accepted one of the glasses before taking a welcome sip. 'You have a nice apartment,' she added with an appreciative glance at the obviously masculine decor and original artwork on the walls.

'It isn't mine particularly.' He shrugged. 'We all use it whenever we're in London— Don't worry, Bryn, Michael and Raphael aren't in London at the moment,' he added ruefully as she instantly looked alarmed. 'Michael is in Paris, Raphael in New York.'

Her frown eased slightly. 'They really are wonderful names.'

He nodded. 'The family estate in Berkshire is called Archangel's Rest—and, I assure you, I've heard all the jokes.'

She smiled slightly but it quickly faded. 'Gabriel, I only came back with you tonight because I agree that we need to dispense with this situation once and for all, and then just move on— What are you doing?' she gasped as Gabriel put his glass down on the coffee table before kneeling down at her feet and beginning to unfasten the laces on her shoes.

He looked up to quirk a teasing brow. 'Removing your shoes, obviously.'

'Why?' She tried, and failed, to pull her foot from his grasp as he slipped one shoe off before turning his attention to the other.

Gabriel sat back on his heels after removing the second shoe. 'I'm guessing your feet ache from all that standing?'

'Yes.'

He nodded. 'Then a foot massage should be very welcome about now.'

'A foot— Gabriel, stop that.' She tried to pull away as he took one of her bare feet into both his hands and began to gently knead the aching flesh. 'Gabriel!' Her protest was less convincing this time, and she gave a low sigh of pleasure as his fingers continued to massage the tension from her tired muscles.

'Good?' he prompted.

'Oh, yes.' Her head fell back against the chair, lashes fanning over her cheeks as her lids closed and Gabriel continued to knead and massage her foot.

She had tiny elegant feet, the nails painted a bright— and defiant—red, Gabriel noted indulgently as he turned his attention to her other foot and continued to massage her aching muscles.

Bryn knew she should stop Gabriel doing what he was doing, that his kneeling at her feet was intimate enough, without the sensuous touch of his long fingers massaging her to add to that dangerous intimacy.

She *should* stop him.

But she couldn't.

Because she didn't want to; she was enjoying this far too much to want Gabriel to ever stop.

She had never thought of her feet as being an erogenous zone before now, but they obviously were, the warmth emanating from Gabriel's caressing hands now moving to other parts of her body, her nipples becoming hard and full, a familiar warmth between her thighs. 'You should think about taking this up professionally,' she murmured appreciatively, eyes still closed. 'You could make a fortune!'

Gabriel chuckled throatily. 'I already have a fortune. Besides which,' he added, fingers moving lightly over her ankles and calves now, 'I have no interest in massaging anyone else's feet but yours.'

Bryn raised one lid, her heart beating a loud tattoo in her chest as Gabriel looked back at her, those brown eyes once again as compelling and addictive as chocolate. An addiction Bryn was once again finding hard to resist.

'I think that's enough of that, thank you.' She pulled her feet out of Gabriel's grasp before bending her knees and drawing her legs up into the chair—well away from Gabriel's caressing hands. Her pulse raced as he made no effort to get up from kneeling in front of her. 'It's getting late, Gabriel,' she prompted determinedly. 'I need to leave soon.'

Gabriel sat back on his heels, looking up at her. 'Did you tell your mother that the two of us had met up again?'

'Did I—?' Her eyes had widened. 'Of course not!' Bryn protested impatiently.

His eyes narrowed. 'Why not?'

'Don't be obtuse, Gabriel,' she snapped, glad now that he wasn't still touching her. Because if he had been he would have been able to feel the way just being this close to him caused her to tremble in awareness. 'My mother never knew— She didn't know that we knew each other five years ago. I—I never told anyone about—about that evening you drove me home from the gallery.'

'The evening I kissed you.'

She grimaced. 'I'm surprised you even remember that.'

'It was too memorable to ever forget,' he assured gruffly.

Bryn looked at him sharply. 'I somehow doubt that very much.'

Gabriel looked straight back at her with hot, glittering eyes. 'The timing was all wrong, the circumstances impossible, but even then I wanted to do so much more than kiss you.'

'I— You did?' She was totally flustered by his admission.

He shrugged. 'I was attracted to you then. I'm attracted to you now.'

Bryn gave a scathing snort. 'Five years ago I was a chubby and gauche teenager wearing heavy-framed glasses.' And this man had been lean and sophisticated, with the same dark and wicked good looks that still took her breath away.

He nodded. 'And now you're sleek and elegant, and I'm guessing you wear contact lenses?'

She nodded distractedly. 'Except for when I paint, when I prefer to wear the glasses you returned to me last week.'

'You weren't chubby five years ago, Bryn, you were voluptuous,' he assured her earnestly. 'And your eyes were just as stunningly beautiful behind those glasses as they are tonight.'

She gave a dismissive shake of her head. 'We're veering off the subject, Gabriel.'

'Which is?'

'That just thinking about the distress it would cause my mother if I were to tell her I've met you again now, let alone this—this attraction, between us, is the very reason why it can't continue.'

Gabriel looked up. 'You can't possibly know how your mother would react.'

Bryn frowned her impatience. 'Get real, Gabriel, and

try to imagine how that conversation would go. "Oh, by the way, Mum, guess who I almost had sex with a couple nights ago. Gabriel D'Angelo. How weird is that?"'

Gabriel drew in a sharp breath before pushing up onto his feet to pick up his glass of wine, taking a sip before answering her, knowing Bryn was now spoiling for a fight—probably as her way of putting an end to this situation. But he wasn't about to give it to her, wasn't about to make any of this easy for her after the week of uncertainty he had just suffered through. 'We didn't have sex, Bryn, although we came very close, and, as I said, the location could have been a little more…conventional, but I'm pretty sure there was nothing in the least "weird" about anything we did together.'

Those two wings of colour deepened in her cheeks as she looked up at him with overbright eyes. 'You won't even try to see this from my point of view, will you?'

His jaw tightened. 'I'm not inclined to let you walk away from me just because you *think* your mother might react badly to knowing about the two of us, no.'

'How about if I walk away because *I'm* reacting badly to just the idea of the two of us together?'

His eyes narrowed. 'And are you?'

'Yes!'

'Why?'

She gave an exasperated shake of her head. 'Gabriel, I know you to be an intelligent man—'

'Thank you,' he drawled dryly.

'And as an intelligent man,' she continued firmly, 'you must know how impossible this whole situation is. For goodness' sake, my father went to prison for attempting to defraud you and your family,' she added impatiently when he made no response.

'I'm well aware of what happened five years ago.' He nodded grimly.

'Then you must also be aware— You must have issues of your own about that situation.'

'I deeply regret that I was in the wrong place at the wrong time,' he conceded impatiently. 'But it was sheer coincidence your father chose to bring his painting to Archangel, even more so that I, rather than Michael or Raphael, happened to be in charge of the London gallery when he did.' Something Gabriel had also long had reason to regret.

Except he would never have met Bryn five years ago if not for her father's greed.

She blinked long lashes. 'And you're saying you don't have a problem with that? With the fact that I'm William Harper's daughter?'

'Of course I have a problem with that.' Gabriel swallowed the rest of his wine before placing the empty glass down on the coffee table. 'At the very least it's inconvenient—'

'Inconvenient!' Bryn echoed incredulously.

He nodded. 'Because the past is affecting how you feel about the two of us now.'

Bryn no longer knew how she felt about the past, let alone the here and now.

Five years ago she had been devastated by her father's trial and imprisonment. A month ago she had still been resentful of Gabriel D'Angelo's part in her father's downfall. Even a week ago she had been disgusted with herself for allowing herself to respond to Gabriel in the way that she had.

But Gabriel was asking how she felt about that *now*.

She was still devastated by the events of the past, but the talk she'd had with her mother last week, the things

Mary had told her about the deterioration of her marriage, her daily uncertainty of her own and her daughter's future, how she believed William's get-rich-quick schemes would have eventually caused a complete meltdown in their marriage...

Having spoken with her mother, Bryn now believed that her father, determined to ignore Gabriel's advice to take his painting and just walk away, had instead informed the press of the painting's existence, ballooning the situation beyond anyone's control.

And all of those things put a different slant on that past situation. Bryn had worshipped her father when she was a child, had loved him dearly for the man she had believed him to be. But as an adult she now realised, and was forced to accept, that he had been far from the perfect husband or father.

And, yes, Gabriel had been involved in her father's being sent to prison, but he hadn't done it out of spite, had merely, as he had just pointed out, been caught up in the sequence of events created and executed by Bryn's father, and over which Gabriel himself had no control.

It wasn't the past, or Gabriel's involvement in that past, that made a relationship between the two of them so impossible now; it was how Bryn felt about Gabriel.

Five years ago she had been infatuated, utterly mesmerised, by the dark and devastatingly attractive Gabriel D'Angelo. Since meeting him again, sharing intimacies with him that she had never experienced with any other man, she had realised that it hadn't just been infatuation she had felt for Gabriel five years ago. She had fallen in love with him then, she loved him still, and he—how she felt about him—was why none of the men she had met since had ever held her interest. How could any man compete with Gabriel D'Angelo? Or the fact that Bryn had fallen in love with him all those years ago?

And it was a futile love. Not just because of the past, but because Gabriel, still single at the age of thirty-three, so obviously didn't do falling in love, let alone for ever.

Oh, he was attracted to her, admitted to desiring her, but that was all he felt, and the only way, the only defence Bryn had left against falling even more in love with Gabriel than she already was, was to continue to use the shield of the events of the past to keep him at arm's length.

Gabriel watched through narrowed lids as Bryn swung her feet to the carpeted floor before sitting up.

Her expression was one of cool dismissal. 'I don't feel anything about the two of us now,' she told him coldly.

His jaw tightened. 'That's not—'

'Nor do I think it a good idea for us to be alone together like this again,' she continued firmly. 'You asked that we talk, Gabriel, and we've done that. And I've told you exactly how I feel.' Her chin rose. 'And if anything I've said means you now change your mind about including my paintings in the New Artists Exhibition, then so be it!' she added challengingly as she stood up.

Gabriel eyed her frustratedly, knowing that Bryn was deliberately shutting him out, but he had no idea how to break through the defences she was deliberately putting up against him. The fact that she felt the need to put up those defences at all was surely telling in itself. In what way, Gabriel couldn't be sure. And this stubbornly assertive Bryn obviously wasn't about to enlighten him either.

'I won't change my mind, Bryn,' he assured grimly. 'About anything.' He used the same challenging tone she had to him.

She eyed him guardedly. 'What does that mean?'

Gabriel gave a mocking smile. 'It means that you don't know me very well if you think that anything you've said tonight means I'm going to just walk away from you. It means,' he continued firmly as she would have spoken, 'that, for the two weeks left before the exhibition, I'm going to require that you come to the gallery at least once a day, and that those meetings will be with me, rather than Eric. It means, Bryn, that you can try running away from me, from the attraction between us, but for the next two weeks, at least, I have no intention of allowing you to just ignore me.'

'Why are you doing this?' Tears glistened in those dove-grey eyes.

'Why do you think I'm doing it?' Gabriel rasped, hating being the cause of those tears, but hating even more the idea of giving up on what he knew was between the two of them. Bryn could fight it all she liked, but her responses to him told him that she wanted him as much as he wanted her.

She made a dismissive gesture with her hands. 'Probably because you're the arrogant Gabriel D'Angelo?' she accused huskily. 'Because a D'Angelo doesn't take no for an answer?' She gave a disgusted shake of her head. 'Or possibly because you just enjoy torturing me!'

Gabriel's hands clenched at his sides even as he bared his teeth in a facsimile of a smile. 'Nice try, Bryn, but I've already warned you I'm not backing off because you deliberately insult me.'

'I'm not—'

'Yes, you are, Bryn,' he rasped. 'And yes, I'm arrogant. Enough so that I don't intend taking the answer "no" from the woman I know wants me as much as I want her.'

She drew in a sharp breath.

'You—'

'Your lips might be saying no, Bryn,' he continued remorselessly, 'but the rest of your body, your aroused nipples especially—' he deliberately lowered his gaze to where those hardened nubs were pressed so noticeably against her black cotton shirt '—are definitely saying yes, please!'

Bryn instinctively crossed her arms over her breasts even as she inwardly acknowledged the truth of Gabriel's claim; she *was* aroused from the sensual pleasure of having Gabriel's hands caressing her feet and calves just a few minutes ago, but also because she seemed to be in a constant state of arousal whenever she was in Gabriel's company.

She only had to look at him, into those sultry dark eyes, at those sculptured kissable lips, the long, lean lines of his utterly masculine body, for her own body to become achingly aroused.

And now Gabriel was suggesting—no, ordering—that she spend at least part of every day for the two weeks before the exhibition in his company.

Her eyes glittered with anger now rather than tears. 'I don't even like you very much at this moment, Gabriel.'

He gave another humourless smile as he crossed the distance between them in soft predatory strides. 'If this is not liking me then long may it continue,' he scorned harshly as Bryn took those same steps back, until she could go no farther, her spine pressed flush against the wall as she stared up at him. 'I believe I could become addicted to the way you hate me, Bryn.' Gabriel's expression was grim as he once again held her imprisoned by placing his hands on the wall on either side of her head, his dark gaze deliberately holding hers as his head lowered and his mouth claimed hers.

Bryn groaned low in her throat as, after the briefest hesitation, her arms moved up about Gabriel's shoulders and she met the fierceness of that kiss with a hunger of her own, no room for gentleness as their tongues duelled, Bryn's fingers becoming entangled in the dark thickness of the hair at Gabriel's nape as she moved up on tiptoe to curve her body into his. The softness of her breasts pressed against the hard muscles of Gabriel's chest, her thighs arching as she pressed her mound against the hardness of his arousal, that arousal pulsing in response, growing longer, firmer, as she ground her thighs against his slowly, instinctively seeking that pressure against her hardened nub.

Gabriel wrenched his mouth from hers to hungrily kiss the length of her throat, the tops of her breasts, groaning his frustration as her fastened shirt stopped him from going any lower. A barrier he easily dispensed with by taking hold of both sides of her shirt and simply pulling, several buttons flying off as he pushed the shirt down her arms and let it fall to the floor.

'Oh, yes,' he rasped hotly as he gazed down hungrily at the creamy swell of her breasts visible above a red lace bra. 'I'm going to lick and suck your oh-so-sensitive breasts—' his gaze held hers as one of his hands moved to unfasten the clasp at the back of her bra before dropping it down onto the floor with her shirt '—and I'm going to continue licking, sucking and biting these pretty breasts—' his hands moved up to cup those thrusting globes tipped by swollen strawberry-ripe nipples '—until you come for me again.'

Bryn felt her cheeks pale. 'No, Gabriel—'

'Yes, Bryn,' he ground out harshly, eyes feverish, his skin flushed against the hard blades of his cheekbones. 'You want it as much as I do.'

She did. Oh, yes, she most certainly did. She ached to feel Gabriel's lips and hands on her again, and that amazing, overwhelming feeling when he brought her to climax.

'These are mine, Bryn.' Gabriel's hands squeezed her breasts. 'Do you understand? These are all mine. To lick and suck, to give you pleasure! And I'm not letting you walk out of here tonight until I've proven that to you!' The past few minutes—Bryn's rejection of there ever being a relationship between the two of them, of Gabriel himself—seemed to have stripped him of showing even a veneer of civilised behaviour.

A loss of control that had touched an equally primitive need deep inside Bryn.

Heat gushed between her thighs, the nubbin swelling, pulsing, in the dampness of her curls as Gabriel lowered his head and sucked one nipple deep into the heat of his mouth even as the thumb and finger of his other hand captured and plucked its twin into the same throbbing needing.

Again and again he suckled her nipple, remorselessly caressing and squeezing its twin, both just short of pain, until Bryn was wild, mindless with hunger, with a need that pulsed and ached between her thighs and caused her to groan, to arch her spine, forcing her breast even deeper into the tormenting heat of Gabriel's mouth as he pressed his thigh rhythmically against that swollen nubbin.

'Gabriel?' Bryn gasped in protest as he released her breast to look up at her.

'Come for me, Bryn,' he encouraged throatily. 'Watch me as I take you over the edge. No way, Bryn!' he refused fiercely as she used the last slender thread of her control to defy him by turning her head away. 'Do you want me to stop?' he rasped harshly. 'Look at me now, Bryn, and tell me you want me to stop!'

A sob caught in her throat as she slowly turned back to him, instantly losing herself in the glittering black pools of his feverish gaze.

'Tell me to stop, Bryn, and I will,' he encouraged huskily.

'I—I can't,' she sobbed. 'Don't stop, Gabriel!' she urged achingly as her fingers tightened in his hair, drawing him back towards her breasts. 'Please don't stop!'

'Look at me this time, Bryn,' he encouraged softly, his breath a warm caress across the aching moistness of her swollen nipple. 'I want to look into your eyes as you come for me.' His tongue flicked out, a tormenting lash against her swollen and aching nipple, continuing to rasp that tongue against her, his gaze continuing to hold hers as he released the button of her jeans before sliding the zip slowly down.

Bryn couldn't have looked away if she had tried, her pleasure swelling, rising out of control, at the eroticism of watching Gabriel as he now parted his lips about her nipple before suckling, gently at first, and then more deeply, her breathing hitching, fracturing as she felt his hand against the heat of her abdomen as it slid beneath the red lace of her panties, his fingers lightly circling her swollen nubbin.

Again and again those tormenting fingers stroked, above and then below that swollen nubbin, dipping his fingers into the dampness of her channel before slowly caressing but never quite touching her right where she most craved his touch, never giving her the pressure there that she ached for.

'Please, Gabriel,' Bryn gasped when she couldn't bear the torment a moment longer. 'Please! Oh, yes,' she gasped, her hands clinging to his shoulders, her thighs thrusting up instinctively as his fingers finally brushed lightly over that aching nubbin. 'Harder, Gabriel! Harder!' She cried out as the pleasure built, higher and then higher still as he increased the pressure and speed of his stroking fingers.

'Let go, Bryn,' Gabriel encouraged harshly against the creaminess of her breast. 'Come for me.' He captured the swollen nubbin between his fingers, squeezing as his mouth returned to her breast, drawing greedily on her nipple as he felt that nubbin throb and then pulse between his fingers as Bryn shattered into a shuddering, gasping climax, as he took it all, unwilling, unable to stop, until he had wrung out every last shuddering, trembling ounce of her orgasm.

'Oh, God, oh, God, oh, God!' Her head dropped down weakly onto Gabriel's shoulder as she continued to quiver and shake and cling to him in the aftermath of her pleasure.

Gabriel took her into his arms and held her tightly against his chest, his breathing as ragged and uneven as hers. 'And that, my beautiful Bryn, is why I refuse to walk away from you. From this. From us,' he told her gruffly. 'Not even if you beg me to.'

Bryn wanted to beg, not for Gabriel to walk away, but for him to continue making love to her.

Again and again.

Which was why *she* had to walk away.

CHAPTER TEN

THE NEXT TWO weeks were absolute hell for Bryn, compelled, as Gabriel had promised she would be, to go to Archangel and see him on a daily basis as they dealt with putting the final details of the exhibition into place.

Not that he ever attempted, or even indicated he wished, to repeat the intimacy of that night at his apartment. Oh, no, Gabriel had a much more subtle torment than that, as he took every opportunity to touch her, always seemingly accidentally: brushing lightly against her to emphasise a point, placing his hand on hers, or at the sensitive base of her spine, or the glide of her hips, whenever the opportunity arose.

And he did it all without saying a word or showing outward acknowledgement of the attraction that sparked and burned between the two of them every time they were together.

Bryn quickly realised that Gabriel really was intent on torturing her.

And how well he was succeeding.

As day followed torturous day Bryn's awareness of Gabriel grew to such a degree that she began to tremble and shake even as she approached the Archangel Gallery. Her nerves would be strung tightly, her body tingling with awareness, as she wondered if that would be the day Gabriel would relent and kiss her, caress her, before she went quietly insane with this growing need for him.

By the day of the exhibition Bryn knew she had never been so aware of a man in her life: his smell—that seductive male smell, a spicy musk, that was uniquely Gabriel—the rippling play of muscles across his shoulders and back when he removed his jacket and tie. He'd unfasten the top two buttons of his shirt to reveal a light dusting of dark hair on his chest whenever they weren't in the public galleries, allowing her to fully appreciate that masculinity. Her fingers literally itched to become entangled in the glossy dark hair she could see on his chest, to caress the firm line of his back, the silky hair at his nape.

She only had to get through one more day, just a few more hours of this torture, Bryn told herself on that final morning as she made her way to Archangel and the closed west gallery, where the paintings of the six artists were finally ready to be exhibited at a private invitation-only showing this evening.

Unfortunately, Bryn realised as she came to an abrupt halt in the doorway to the west gallery, today was going to be the most difficult twenty-four hours of the past two weeks of torture. Her breath caught in her throat and her face paled as she saw, and easily recognised, the three men talking quietly together across the room.

Gabriel was instantly recognisable, of course, but the unmistakable likeness between all three men—tall and lean, dark haired, with hewn and handsome olive-skinned faces—told her that the other two men had to be Gabriel's two brothers, Michael and Raphael D'Angelo.

Two men who had absolutely no reason to feel in the least kindly towards Sabryna Harper.

* * *

Gabriel sensed Bryn's presence in the gallery even before he turned and saw her standing pale and still across the room; his senses had become so heightened to her presence during these past two weeks that he now felt a thrum of awareness beneath the surface of his skin whenever she was anywhere near. His shaft would harden, becoming a painful throb just at the smell of her perfume— that exotic spice, and the womanly smell that he knew was all uniquely aroused Bryn—the husky sound of her voice enough to raise the hairs on the back of his neck and send shivers of pleasure down the length of his spine.

Gabriel had lost count of the amount of times he had been tempted to put an end to the torment that made his days a living hell and his nights a sleepless nightmare, to just take Bryn in his arms and make love to her, to keep her there until she admitted she wanted him with the same fierce hunger that he wanted her.

The only thing that held him back from doing that was Bryn herself.

For both their sakes she had to be the one to come to him this time. Through her own choice, and not because of any physical coercion on his part. And if that required that he go quietly out of his mind while he waited— hoped—for that to happen, then so be it!

The fact that Bryn looked small and vulnerable today in a dark grey blouse and black jeans, her eyes apprehensive as she stared across the gallery at the three of them, was enough to tell him that she had found the past two weeks as much of a strain as he had.

'Bryn?' he prompted gently as she made no effort to come farther into the gallery.

Her chin rose. 'I— Excuse me, I just wanted— I didn't realise there was anyone— I'll come back later,' she muttered awkwardly as she turned away with the obvious intention of hurrying from the gallery. And maybe Archangel itself?

'Bryn!' Gabriel called out harshly.

She came to an abrupt halt, her tension visible in the stiffness of her shoulders and spine, her hands clenching and unclenching at her sides as she obviously debated whether or not she was going to turn back and face him or simply continue running.

Gabriel mentally willed her to do the former rather than the latter, to be that strong and confident Bryn that he so admired as well as desired.

Bryn felt slightly light-headed as she forgot to breathe, her heart beating so loud and wildly in her chest that she felt sure the three men standing across the room must be able to hear it.

She hadn't known—hadn't even guessed. No one had thought to warn her—certainly not Gabriel—that his brothers were going to be in London today. For the purpose of attending the exhibition this evening?

Wasn't it bad enough that she had been forced to deal with Gabriel on a daily basis for the past two weeks, that her nerves were shot to hell because of it, without having to now face his two disapproving brothers?

Except there was no escaping the fact that Michael and Raphael D'Angelo were both here, that they were the co-owners of the Archangel Galleries, and as such Bryn knew she had no choice but to face them at some point today. So perhaps it was better if she did so sooner rather than in public later, when the meeting could be even more embarrassing?

Bryn drew in a ragged, steadying breath before turning slowly, her chin tilting defensively as she kept her gaze fixed firmly on Gabriel rather than looking at either of his two brothers. 'I was just—' She moistened the dryness of her lips with the tip of her tongue. 'I thought I would come and take a last look in here before the exhibition this evening.'

'I'm glad you did.' Gabriel nodded, dark eyes hooded, his expression unreadable as he crossed the room in long graceful strides to stand in front of her. 'My brothers would like to meet you,' he encouraged gruffly.

Bryn barely managed to hold back her snort of derision as she looked up at him sceptically; they both knew she was the last person Michael and Raphael D'Angelo would ever wish to be introduced to. 'I thought your brothers didn't approve of my inclusion in the exhibition?' she said loud enough for all three men to hear.

Gabriel's jaw tightened at the directness of her challenge, his gaze dark and disapproving as he frowned down at her.

'We initially questioned your motives for entering the New Artists competition, yes,' one of the two men across the room—Michael or Raphael?—came back just as directly.

'Shut up, Rafe,' Gabriel rasped dismissively.

'Some of us still do.' Raphael ignored him as he strolled across the gallery, dark sable hair long and curling silkily onto his shoulders, more casually dressed than his two brothers in a tight black T-shirt that emphasised the muscled width of his shoulders and chest, faded denims resting low down on the leanness of his hips, heavy black boots on his feet. 'I don't believe Gabriel has bothered to ask you this, but why us and why here, Miss Jones?' He quirked a dark and mocking brow.

'Shut up, Rafe,' the third man instructed harshly—he had to be Michael D'Angelo—as he crossed the room with more forceful strides, his sable hair cropped close to his head, his eyes so dark a brown they appeared black and unfathomable, a three-piece charcoal-grey suit perfectly tailored to his muscular frame, his shirt the palest grey, a darker grey silk tie neatly knotted at his throat. 'I'm Michael D'Angelo, Miss Jones.' His tone was compelling as he held his hand out to her.

Bryn eyed that hand uncertainly even as she felt the compulsion in that voice, enough so that she ran the dampness of her own hand down her denim-clad thighs before raising it to be clasped firmly, briefly, in Michael D'Angelo's much stronger one before he released her again. 'I believe we all know that my name isn't really Jones,' she murmured.

'Confrontational. I like that,' Raphael D'Angelo drawled encouragingly.

'Shut up, Rafe.' Gabriel and Michael spoke together this time, both their tones weary, as if they had suffered years of repeating that same phrase.

Bryn bit her lip uncertainly as she quickly looked at each of the three D'Angelo brothers in turn: Gabriel glowered at Rafe impatiently, Michael also frowned at his sibling while Rafe grinned unrepentantly at both of them before turning to give Bryn a conspiratorial wink.

Her eyes widened as she realised Rafe D'Angelo, rather than seriously challengingly her, was, in fact, deliberately annoying his two brothers.

'I don't understand any of this.' She gave a dazed shake of her head.

'Not even Gabriel?' Raphael came back speculatively.

'Rafe—'

'I know, shut up.' Raphael lightly acknowledged Gabriel's rebuke as he pushed his hands into the front pockets of his denims. 'I don't know why it is, but you and Michael just love to ruin all my fun.' He shrugged.

Bryn really was baffled by Michael and Raphael D'Angelo; she had expected hostility, at least, from the two of them because of who she was and the damage her father could have caused the Archangel Galleries five years ago. A hostility that she realised simply wasn't there.

Admittedly Michael was a little austere, self-contained, restrained, in both appearance and manner, but that seemed to be his normal demeanour, rather than any personal animosity directed towards her.

As for Raphael… Bryn had a feeling, looking into those predatory and shrewd golden eyes, that Rafe D'Angelo was a man who maintained a wickedly irreverent appearance on the outside as a way of keeping his real feelings very close to that beautifully muscled chest.

Gabriel easily saw the bewilderment in Bryn's expression as she looked at his two brothers.

Just as he recognised Rafe's open appreciation for Bryn as he mockingly returned that curious gaze. An appreciation that Gabriel didn't like in the least, following his own two weeks of private hell as he had forced himself not to touch or kiss Bryn.

He put a proprietary hand beneath Bryn's elbow now as he stepped closer to her. 'If the two of you will excuse us, I want to talk to Bryn upstairs in my office for a few minutes.'

'"Talk" to her, Gabriel?' Rafe came back derisively.

He gave his brother a narrow-eyed look of warning. 'I'll see the two of you later this evening.'

'You can count on it,' Rafe came back challengingly. 'I'm very much looking forward to seeing you again this evening, Bryn,' he added huskily.

'For God's sake, Rafe, will you just—?'

'I know, I know. Shut up,' Rafe sighed heavily at Michael's terse admonishment.

Gabriel gave a shake of his head as he and Bryn finally left the gallery together, maintaining his hold on her elbow as the two of them walked towards the private lift at the end of the marble hallway. 'I apologise for Rafe,' he bit out abruptly. 'As you may have gathered, he has a warped sense of humour.' A warped sense of humour that on this occasion had been at Gabriel's expense; Rafe knew and had played upon the fact that Gabriel hadn't liked the interest he had shown in Bryn.

'He seemed...very nice,' Bryn answered him uncertainly as they stepped into the lift together.

'Nice is not a word I would ever use to describe my brother,' Gabriel rasped. 'Annoying, irritating, sometimes infuriating, but never anything as insipid as "nice".' Even as he said it Gabriel knew he was being unfair to Rafe; after all, his brother had been the one to warn him that Bryn Jones was Sabryna Harper after Michael had decided against doing so.

'Both your brothers were far more polite to me than I could ever have expected, in the circumstances,' she murmured softly as they stepped out of the lift and walked down the hallway to Gabriel's office.

Gabriel shot her a sideways glance. 'Than I led you to believe, perhaps?'

'Well... Yes.'

He drew in a sharp breath at the speculation in Bryn's tone. 'I advise you not to complicate an already impossible situation by falling for the charms of one of my brothers!' he bit out harshly.

'I wasn't— I didn't— Why would you even think I might do that?' Bryn reacted with predictable accusation.

'You already know the answer to that question, Bryn,'

Gabriel murmured as they entered his office, closing the door firmly behind them before turning Bryn in his arms, his hands resting lightly on the slenderness of her hips.

'Do I?'

'Yes.' He nodded. 'But just so that there's no misunderstanding—if any of the D'Angelo bothers is going to be allowed to kiss these delectable lips today, then it's going to be me,' Gabriel assured her gruffly as he raised one of his hands to run a fingertip gently over her fuller, sensuous bottom lip.

Her eyes darkened, cheeks suffusing with colour. 'I'm not interested in being kissed by either Raphael or Michael,' she breathed softly.

'I'm glad to hear it.' Gabriel's hand moved beneath her chin and tilted her face up towards his, his other arm moving lightly about her waist as he moulded the softness of her curves against his much harder ones. 'How about me, Bryn? Are you interested in kissing me?'

'Gabriel...' she groaned breathily.

It took every particle of willpower Gabriel possessed not to just take that kiss as he felt the way Bryn's body trembled against his, but he knew that he couldn't, wanting, needing Bryn to make the first move. 'A single kiss, Bryn,' he encouraged throatily. 'For luck. To the success of the exhibition this evening.' His breath caught in his throat as he waited for her answer.

Bryn gazed up at him searchingly, longing, aching to once again feel Gabriel's lips on hers, to lose herself in that pleasure. At the same time as she knew that a single kiss wouldn't be enough, that she wanted so much more from Gabriel than just passion and pleasure. So very much more. And that Gabriel didn't have any more than that to give her.

'I can't,' she breathed softly as she pushed against his chest to be released.

Something dark and primal moved in the depths of his eyes as his arms tightened about her. 'Can't or won't, Bryn?' he rasped harshly.

She closed her eyes briefly before answering him. 'Let me go, Gabriel.'

His mouth thinned, a nerve pulsing in the tightness of his jaw. 'Why are you doing this, Bryn?' he groaned. 'Why are you making us both suffer because of your stubbornness?'

This wasn't about Bryn being stubborn; it was so much more than that—*she* felt so much more than that. 'You know why.'

'Because you're worried about your mother,' Gabriel rasped. 'Because of how you believe she would feel about the two of us being together.'

Tears burned in her eyes. 'And you don't think that's important?' she choked. 'You believe that I should just take what I want and to hell with how it affects anyone else?'

'If I'm what you want, then, yes, damn it, that's exactly what I think you should do!' His eyes glittered darkly.

Bryn gave a shake of her head. 'You said it yourself, Gabriel. This is an impossible situation that doesn't need to be made any more complicated than it already is.'

'And when I said it I was warning you not to take Rafe's flirtation seriously,' he grated harshly.

Bryn blinked back the heat of tears. 'Gabriel, we only have one last day together to get through. Do you think we could try to do that without arguing?'

His expression sharpened. 'You think I'm just going to gracefully bow out of your life after tonight?'

She tensed. 'I was under the impression— Eric told me weeks ago that you would be returning to the Paris gallery after the opening night of the New Artists Exhibition.'

'Did he?' Gabriel gave a humourless smile.

Bryn looked up at him searchingly, a sick feeling forming in the pit of her stomach as he met her gaze unblinkingly. 'You don't intend going back to Paris tomorrow?' she guessed weakly.

'No, I don't,' he answered with satisfaction. 'In fact, Rafe, Michael and I were discussing that very thing when you arrived. Michael is flying to New York tomorrow to take over the gallery there for a month, Rafe is going to Archangel in Paris and I'm staying right here to oversee the rest of the New Artists Exhibition and auction.'

And Bryn knew that the exhibition was being opened to the public tomorrow, the paintings to be on display until they were included in the next Archangel auction in two weeks' time.

Which meant that Gabriel was going to be in London for at least those same two weeks, possibly longer— and his very presence in London would continue to be such a torment and torture that she wouldn't know a moment's peace.

'Let me go, Gabriel,' she instructed. 'Please,' she added as his arms remained firmly about her waist. 'I have to be at the coffee shop by ten o'clock.'

He frowned darkly as he slowly released her. 'You're working today?'

'Of course I'm working today,' she dismissed impatiently as she stepped away from him, finally able to breathe again now that she wasn't pressed up against the disturbing length of his body. 'I haven't sold any of my paintings yet, and I still have my rent to pay at the end of the month,' she added ruefully.

Gabriel moved to lean back against the front of his desk. 'As of this morning, one of your paintings has a reserved sticker on it.'

Her gaze sharpened. 'It does?'

Gabriel nodded. 'Michael wants it.'

Her eyes widened. 'He does?'

Gabriel smiled ruefully. 'Hmm.'

'Which one?'

'The rose.'

The dying red rose, Bryn's representation of the death of hopes and dreams rather than just the flower itself.

Did the austere Michael D'Angelo, a man who gave the appearance of being so totally self-contained, a man who surely had no hopes and dreams to die, appreciate the full meaning of her painting?

'That's— I'm flattered,' Bryn murmured softly.

Gabriel nodded grimly. 'You should be. Michael's private art collection is very exclusive. I have every reason to believe that Lord Simmons is very interested in purchasing one too.'

'That's…amazing.' Bryn's eyes glowed excitedly as she reached out and grasped his hands impulsively. 'This is really going to happen, isn't it, Gabriel? I'm really going to sell some of my paintings, maybe even be able to paint full-time!'

'It's as real as it gets, yes,' Gabriel confirmed huskily as he pulled her in between his parted thighs before placing her hands against his chest. 'Tonight is your night, Bryn.' His hands cupped either side of her face as he gave in to the hunger and kissed her gently on the lips that had haunted and tormented him for the past five years. 'And I want you to enjoy it. Every single moment of it,' he encouraged.

'Oh, I will,' she assured him happily, her hands warm against his chest. 'I— Thank you, Gabriel, for giving me this chance. I really— I know I've been difficult on occasion—' she grimaced '—but I—I really do appreciate everything you've done for me.'

Gabriel could only hope that Bryn still felt that way after tonight.

The past two weeks of being close to Bryn, but never quite close enough, had been enough of a hell for Gabriel to know that the two of them couldn't go on like this indefinitely, that something had to change, and that it wasn't going to be the way he felt about Bryn.

So he had made his arrangements accordingly. Carefully and quietly. Arrangements that would come to full fruition later this evening.

And he wasn't sure Bryn would ever forgive him.

CHAPTER ELEVEN

'IS IT EVERYTHING you hoped it would be?'

Bryn turned to smile warmly at Eric as he came to stand beside her. 'It's so much more!' Her smile widened as he handed her one of the glasses of champagne he carried.

There were over two hundred people crowded into the west gallery for this invitation-only showing, the men all wearing evening suits, the women chic and glittering in their evening gowns and expensive jewellery. Two dozen waiters circulated amongst them carrying trays of finger food and glasses of champagne and half a dozen huge arrangements of flowers perfumed the brightly lit room, all adding to Bryn's light-headed euphoria.

Bryn had chosen to wear a simple black sheath of an above-the-knee length, her only jewellery a simple silver bracelet about one of her wrists and a silver locket at her throat, both of them presents from her mother.

Her smile faded a little at thoughts of her mother, knowing how much Mary would have loved all of this, how proud she would have been of Bryn's success. Instead, Bryn still hadn't so much as dared to tell her mother about the exhibition; how could she when that exhibition was being held at the Archangel Gallery?

As might be expected, the D'Angelo brothers all

looked amazingly handsome in their evening suits as they stood head, and sometimes shoulders, above the other guests, the darkness of their different lengths of hair becoming a sable sheen below the glittering lights of the chandeliers above them. Michael was as remotely austere as ever when he gave her a brief nod of acknowledgement earlier, Rafe as rakishly devil-may-care as he shot her another wink.

But to Bryn's biased gaze Gabriel was far and away the most distinguished man in the room, and she once again found her gaze shifting to the other side of the gallery where he stood in conversation with David Simmons. His mesmerising and dark good looks drew Bryn's gaze to him again and again as if pulled by a magnet, her heart now skipping a beat as Gabriel laughed easily at something the older man had just said to him.

A heart that ached. To be with Gabriel. To make love with him, just once.

Gabriel stilled as he felt a prickle of awareness, of being watched, at his nape and down his spine. Allowing his gaze to move unhurriedly about the room, he sought the source of that awareness even as he continued his conversation with the enthusiastic David Simmons.

Bryn.

Standing beside Eric on the other side of the crowded gallery, her eyes a deep and misty grey as they looked directly into his, the fullness of her lips curving into an enigmatic smile.

Gabriel raised his champagne glass to her in a silent toast; the exhibition was only an hour old but already Bryn's paintings were noticeably attracting the most attention.

Her smile widened as she accepted his silent toast, her eyes glowing. With happiness? Or something else?

'—keep you any longer when I can see I'm keeping you from where you really want to be,' David drawled dryly.

Gabriel drew his gaze reluctantly from Bryn's as he turned back to the other man. 'Sorry?'

The older man chuckled good-naturedly. 'I advise you go to her, man!'

Gabriel gave a rueful smile. 'Is it that obvious?'

David continued to smile indulgently. 'Lovely-looking girl. Beautiful as well as talented. Deadly combination, hmm?'

'Deadly,' Gabriel accepted heavily.

'Then go to it, man.' David gave him an encouraging slap on the shoulder. 'Before that rascal of a brother of yours beats you to it,' he added with a pointed look at Rafe making his way determinedly in Bryn's direction.

'Damn you, Rafe,' Gabriel muttered impatiently even as he placed his empty champagne glass on the tray of one of the passing waiters before striding forcefully across the room to intercept his brother. 'This isn't what we agreed your role would be this evening, Rafe!' He glowered in warning.

Rafe raised mocking brows. 'I just thought I would keep Bryn company while I'm waiting. She looks absolutely stunning this evening, by the way.'

'Hands off, Rafe,' he growled.

His brother grinned unrepentantly. 'Does Bryn know how damned possessive you are over her?'

'Yes.' He frowned grimly, not sure that Bryn wasn't actually going to hate him by the end of this evening.

Rafe chuckled. 'And have you told her how you feel about her yet?'

'Go to hell, Rafe.'

Rafe looked comfortably unconcerned. 'Of course. Why do things the easy way when you can so easily complicate the hell out of them?' He gave a rueful shake of his head. 'At this rate you're going to end up as cold and remote as Michael!'

Gabriel glanced across to where their older brother managed to remain withdrawn even while mingling with their guests. 'He likes his life that way.' He shrugged.

'But you don't, not anymore. Which is why—' Rafe turned back to Gabriel, brows raised '—complicated or not, you should just grab your woman and to hell with everything else!'

'We both know it isn't that simple where Bryn is concerned.' Gabriel grimaced.

'Then I suggest you make it that simple and put the rest of us out of our misery.'

'Your turn will come, Rafe,' Gabriel warned impatiently. 'And when it does we'll see just how well you deal with it. And her.'

Rafe gave a scornful snort. 'There isn't a snowball's chance in hell that I'm going to let some woman—any woman!—come between me and my bachelor lifestyle.'

'Oh, it will come, Rafe, take my word for it, and when it does I'm going to enjoy seeing you have to eat your words.' Gabriel chuckled with satisfaction. 'In the meantime, keep your lethal charms away from Bryn,' he added firmly.

'Just can't stand the competition, hmm?'

'You're too irritating for me to consider you serious competition,' Gabriel drawled dismissively, his gaze once again returning to, and remaining on, Bryn as she chatted with Eric. 'If you'll excuse me, I think I'll go and talk to "my woman".' But before he could even begin to

cross the room to Bryn's side he saw her face pale, her
eyes widening in distress as she stared across at the entrance to the gallery.

And Gabriel knew, without needing to turn and look,
that the moment of truth had arrived.

'Go now, Rafe!' he rasped harshly as he strode towards Bryn.

Bryn was sure she had to be hallucinating, brought about,
no doubt, by the strain of the past two weeks and too
much champagne on an empty stomach; she had been
too excited about this evening to even think about eating today!

Because she couldn't really be looking at her mother
and Rhys standing in the entrance to the gallery; it had
to be her guilty thoughts of a few minutes ago that made
her imagine she could.

Except… Bryn was sure she would never have imagined Rhys looking so handsome in an evening suit; as far
as she was aware her stepfather didn't even own an evening suit. In fact, she didn't think she had ever seen Rhys
in anything other than jeans and casual tops, T-shirts or
sweaters, depending on the time of year. He had worn
a suit at his wedding with Mary, of course, but as far as
Bryn knew that had been put at the back of his wardrobe
the day after the wedding and forgotten about.

Her mother looked slender and beautiful, of course, in
her favourite gown, the same deep grey as her eyes, her
ivory skin flawless, pale peach lip gloss on her parted
lips.

A smile now curved those peach-coloured lips, grey
eyes lighting up with excitement, as Mary looked straight
across at Bryn before her attention was distracted by
Raphael D'Angelo as he joined them in the doorway,

speaking briefly before kissing Mary's hand and shaking Rhys's.

Bryn knew there was no way she could have imagined that.

Which meant her mother and Rhys really were here. How on earth had—?

Gabriel!

Gabriel had to have done this.

But why?

Why would Gabriel do something so potentially destructive to what should have been a glitteringly successful evening for the Archangel Gallery? Was he, despite having consistently denied it, still so absorbed in the past that he was willing to take his revenge against Mary and Bryn at the cost of that success and all the weeks of hard work that had gone into this exhibition?

No.

Bryn couldn't believe that of him. She *wouldn't* believe that of the man she loved and had come to know so well these past few weeks. There had to be another reason, an innocent reason, for Gabriel having deliberately invited her mother and Rhys to the exhibition.

'Bryn? Bryn!'

She turned sharply at the sound of Gabriel's voice, trying to focus through the black spots wavering in front of her eyes. 'Why?' she had time to gasp before those black spots all merged into one huge black hole into which Bryn thankfully fell.

She wasn't aware of being swept up into Gabriel's arms, of the sympathetic gasps of the other guests as he carried her across the room, or her mother's concern as she followed the two of them out of the gallery and up to Gabriel's office, leaving her stepfather and Rafe to deal with providing an explanation for her having fainted.

No, Bryn was aware of none of that as she slowly returned to consciousness and heard her mother and Gabriel talking softly together.

'—should have warned her,' Gabriel muttered disgustedly, holding Bryn's hand tightly in his as he sat beside her limp form on the sofa in his office.

'You wanted it to be a surprise,' Mary soothed.

'And this is the result!' he cursed grimly as he looked down at Bryn, her lashes very dark against the pale delicacy of her face.

'It's just a faint, Gabriel,' Bryn's mother assured ruefully. 'If I know my little girl, she's been too excited about tonight to bother eating today.'

Gabriel stood up abruptly, running an agitated hand through the dark thickness of his hair. 'I just wanted her to have the two of you here tonight to share in her success.'

'I know that, Gabriel,' Mary assured gently. 'And so will Bryn once she's thought things through.'

'You think?' Gabriel knew Bryn well enough by now—knew what she thought of him only too well—to know that she was more than capable of believing he had some Machiavellian reason for inviting her mother and stepfather to the exhibition.

Because he hadn't thought his actions through properly, should have realised the shock it would be for Bryn when Mary and Rhys arrived at the gallery this evening.

'I think,' Mary echoed, having now taken Gabriel's place on the sofa beside Bryn. 'I accept my daughter can be fiery on occasion, Gabriel—part of her Welsh heritage, I'm afraid,' she added ruefully. 'But she isn't so headstrong that she will judge you unfairly. And what you've done for her, in regard to her inclusion in this exhibition at Archangel, and inviting Rhys and I here this evening to share in her success, was incredibly kind of you.'

'Bryn doesn't see me as being in the least kind,' Gabriel drawled ruefully.

'Oh, I think you might be pleasantly surprised at what my daughter sees in you,' Mary murmured dryly.

Bryn knew that last remark was directed towards her rather than Gabriel, that her mother, at least, was aware Bryn had recovered from her faint but was now choosing to appear as if she hadn't.

Mary squeezed her hand to confirm it. 'When she wakes up you need to tell Bryn everything, Gabriel,' she told him—and Bryn—softly. 'She especially needs to know what you did for us five years ago, what you did to help the two of us make a new life together in Wales after William died.'

Bryn frowned at this revelation, at the same time knowing her mother's comment 'when she wakes up' was pointedly directed at her.

And she did need to do that; lying here listening to this conversation was totally unfair to Gabriel. Besides, she very much wanted to hear all about what Gabriel had done for them five years ago.

Mary released Bryn's hand before standing up. 'You're a good man, Gabriel,' she told him. 'And if you give my daughter a chance, I believe you will find she already knows that. Now, I think it's time I returned back downstairs, and left the two of you alone to talk.'

'But—'

'My mother is right, Gabriel,' Bryn spoke at the same time as she opened her eyes and looked up at them both. 'You and I do need to talk.' She swung her legs to the floor and sat up slowly.

'I'm not sure you should do that just yet.' Gabriel stepped swiftly forward and sat down on the sofa beside her before once again taking one of her hands in both of his. 'You're probably a bit shaky still from—'

'Mamma?' Bryn looked up at her mother pointedly.

Mary nodded. 'I'm going downstairs now to bask in some of my daughter's glory,' she murmured indulgently. 'No doubt I will see the two of you sometime later this evening?'

'No doubt,' Bryn nodded distractedly, having eyes only for Gabriel.

'And, Bryn?' Her mother paused in the doorway. 'You're wrong. Gabriel isn't in the least "unsuitable". In any way,' she assured before she left the office and closed the door softly behind her.

CHAPTER TWELVE

'WHAT WAS THAT about?' Gabriel prompted.

Bryn's vision was slightly misty with tears as she turned to look at him, knowing that her mother had been referring to the conversation the two of them had had in Wales three weeks ago, when Bryn had insisted the man she loved wasn't suitable.

She gave a shake of her head. 'It doesn't matter anymore. I— Gabriel, I need to thank you for inviting my mother and Rhys here tonight. It's made my evening so much more special.'

'So much so you fainted, damn it,' Gabriel grated self-disgustedly.

Bryn held on to his hand as he would have pulled away and stood up. 'I want you to stay right here,' she told him firmly as he looked at her questioningly. 'I need to say some things to you, and I want you to be next to me when I say them.'

A frown appeared between his eyes. 'Am I going to need some of my single-malt whisky to get through this?' he drawled.

'I don't believe so, no.' She smiled ruefully, drawing in a deep breath before speaking again. 'I'll admit, when I first realised my mother and Rhys were really here—rather than just a figment of my food-deprived, champagne-induced imagination—that I wondered why you had done it. I only wondered for the briefest of moments, Gabriel,' she assured as his frown darkened. 'The very briefest of moments,' she repeated firmly, 'before my knowledge of you told me that your reason for doing it would be a good one rather than a bad one.'

'Actually, it was purely selfish.' Gabriel grimaced; he wanted this woman so badly he was willing to do anything—anything—to get her.

Bryn gave a firm shake of her head. 'I don't believe that.'

'Oh, but it was. You kept insisting that there could never be anything between the two of us because of how your mother might react if she knew, and so I decided to eliminate that objection, at least.'

Bryn looked at him searchingly for several long seconds before a slow smile curved her lips. 'I accept that might have been one of the reasons, Gabriel—'

'Oh, believe me, it was the prime reason,' he assured her grimly.

Her smile didn't even waver. 'You like people to think you're tough and uncaring, don't you?'

'I am tough and—'

'You are most certainly not uncaring,' she insisted firmly. 'And you may manage to convince other people that you are, but I think you should know I haven't fallen for it for some time now. Not since I realised I was in love with you,' she added softly.

'Bryn?' Gabriel's hand tightened about hers.

'Don't worry, I'm not saying that with any expectation of you returning the sentiment,' she assured ruefully. 'I just think you should know, before we start our affair, that I've realised since meeting you again that I fell in love with you five years ago—'

'You— What affair?' Gabriel demanded sharply as he released her hand before standing up.

'—and that I'm still in love with you,' Bryn continued determinedly. 'And that I have no intention of having any sort of relationship with you now and pretending that I'm not—'

'Bryn, did you really just say you fell in love with me five years ago?' he repeated dazedly.

'I did, yes,' she admitted wryly. 'And the reason I'm telling you this now is because I want you to know how I feel before you tell me in what way you helped my mother and I five years ago. It's time for us to be honest with each other, Gabriel,' she encouraged softly. 'As such, I don't want there to be any misunderstandings about why and when I fell in love with you.'

His eyes widened. 'You heard your mother and I talking just now?'

'Yes.'

Gabriel looked down at her searchingly, Bryn meeting that searching gaze unwaveringly. 'You really fell in love with me five years ago?' he finally murmured.

Bryn nodded. 'On sight, I think. But it was all such a mess after my father was arrested. At the time I wondered how I could possibly still be in love with the man who had helped to put my father in prison,' she added heavily. 'I know the truth about that now, Gabriel,' she assured him firmly. 'I know that you tried to stop him, to save him from himself, and my father's answer to that was to inform the press, and so making it impossible for him to walk away as you wanted him to do. I do believe that, Gabriel.'

'Thank God,' he groaned with feeling. 'You really love me, Bryn?' He looked at her searchingly.

She nodded. 'In fact, I realised a couple weeks ago that you're the reason I'm still a virgin at the grand old age of twenty-three,' she acknowledged self-derisively. 'No other man quite matched up to my first love.' She looked up at Gabriel uncertainly as he still looked stunned. 'Too much honesty for you?'

Too much? It was perfect as far as Gabriel was concerned. Bryn was perfect. For him. She always had been.

'I have no words to tell you how much it…pleased me, to know there's been no one else for you.' Gabriel gave a rueful shake of his head. 'But you should know now that I don't want to have an affair with you.'

She blinked. 'Okay.' She nodded woodenly. 'More fool me for having believed you still did.' She drew in a deep, steadying breath. 'That makes all of this a little embarrassing, but it doesn't change any of what I've said—'

'Bryn, would it surprise you to know that I fell in love with you five years ago too?'

She stilled, staring up at him with wide eyes, a gaze that Gabriel now returned with the same directness as she had a few minutes ago. 'I know you said something like this before but—you couldn't have done,' she finally managed to protest dismissively. 'I was chubby,' she reminded him. 'I wore those unbecoming dark-framed glasses. I was so ungainly I fell over my own feet all the time—' She broke off as Gabriel gave a slow shake of his head.

'To me you were voluptuously sexy,' he corrected firmly. 'And you had—still have—the most beautiful dove-grey eyes I've ever seen, glasses or no glasses. I found your occasional lack of balance endearing rather than ungainly. And I wanted you so damned much I could hardly think straight! You were only eighteen years old, and too damned young for me, but I wanted you anyway. Fell in love with you anyway. Plus,' he continued firmly as she would have spoken, 'after your father was arrested and you refused all my attempts at trying to speak with you again, I also had every reason to believe you hated my guts.'

Bryn stared up at him dazedly, sure that she couldn't have heard him correctly. Gabriel couldn't really have just said— 'I never hated you, Gabriel.'

'Of course you did.'

'I hated the situation, not you,' she corrected. 'Would rather none of it had ever happened. But I know, I accept now, that my father was far from perfect, that he was responsible for what happened to him, no one else.' She looked up at him again. 'Gabriel, what did you do to help us five years ago?'

He grimaced. 'Do we really have to talk about that now?'

'Yes, we really do,' she insisted stubbornly.

He sighed. 'I'd rather not.'

'And I would rather you did.'

'You are so damned stubborn,' he sighed.

'Takes one to know one,' she came back ruefully. 'And if you don't tell me then I'll just ask my mother to tell me instead.'

Gabriel scowled his defeat as he sighed deeply. 'I—' He breathed deeply. 'I paid all your father's legal fees.'

Bryn just stared at him. All this time she had thought— Believed— 'What else…?' she breathed softly.

'Isn't that enough?' he drawled.

'What else, Gabriel?' she persisted.

His mouth thinned. 'I gave your mother enough money for the two of you to be able to move back to Wales. I wanted to give her more, enough to pay for you to go to university, but Mary wouldn't hear of it.'

'I should hope not!' Bryn was absolutely stunned at learning how Gabriel had helped them all those years ago. 'You really live up to your name, don't you?' she said wonderingly.

'Don't give me a false halo, Bryn,' Gabriel rasped harshly. 'I helped the two of you because someone had to.'

'And it had absolutely nothing to do with the fact that you had fallen in love with William Harper's overweight daughter?' she chided, an emotional catch in her throat for the man that Gabriel was, and always had been.

'Voluptuously sexy,' Gabriel insisted. 'Which is exactly how you'll look when you're pregnant with our child. You do want children, I hope?'

'Stop changing the subject.'

'Just thinking of you all round with our child,' he continued gruffly, 'with your breasts so big they spill over the top of your bra, is enough to make me hard.'

'Gabriel!' Bryn stood up abruptly, her breathing uneven as she realised what he had said, what his words implied. A baby? Gabriel was talking about the two of them having a child together?

He quirked a self-derisive brow. 'Too much honesty for you?'

Not enough. Not nearly enough!

She moistened her lips with the tip of her tongue, feeling a thrill run through her as she saw the way Gabriel's eyes instantly darkened at the provocation. 'I— When exactly do you intend us having this baby?'

'I think, for your mother and Rhys's sake, and my own parents', that we should probably wait until after we're married.'

'Married?' she squeaked.

'Married,' Gabriel confirmed decisively.

'But you wanted an affair.'

'You *assumed* I wanted an affair,' he corrected. 'When we met again four weeks ago and I obviously couldn't keep my hands off you, I decided to just take whatever you were willing to give me. But following on from your own honesty just now, you should know from the outset that I am very much in love with you, more so now even than five years ago, and that I won't settle for anything less than the two of us being married to each other.'

Happiness swelled so big and so wide inside her that Bryn felt as if she might actually explode from trying to contain it. Gabriel loved her. Had always loved her. He wanted to *marry* her. Have babies with her!

'I— You haven't asked me yet,' she reminded him breathlessly.

He grimaced. 'I've learned that asking sometimes isn't the right way to go about things where you're concerned.'

'Try me,' she encouraged huskily.

Gabriel looked searchingly into the glowing depths of her deep grey eyes, noting the flush in her cheeks, those slightly parted and oh-so-kissable lips. 'Will you marry me, Bryn?' he prompted huskily.

'Oh, yes, Gabriel. Yes, yes, yes!' She threw herself into his arms. 'Whenever and wherever you want.'

'As soon as it can be arranged.' His arms closed tightly about her.

'We've already wasted five years. I don't want to waste any more, want to spend the rest of my life telling you, showing you, how much I love you, will always love you!'

Bryn glowed with happiness as she imagined the future, a lifetime with Gabriel, years and years together, when they would show and tell each other how much they were loved.

* * * * *

'Alex Arlov.' He tipped his sleek head and to her intense relief released her hand.

How could I ever not have seen how arrogant he is? Angel grabbed a napkin from a passing tray and wiped it against the heel of her hand.

'The name seems familiar...'

She gnawed lightly on her full lower lip, pretending to search her memory, before producing a bright smile and pausing to stretch the moment, hoping he was worrying that she might reveal all. If it wasn't for her daughter she would, and who cared if people knew what a total fool she was.

But he didn't look concerned, just vaguely amused as he elevated one dark brow. 'That happens to me all the time...an instantly forgettable face.'

And so full of yourself, she wanted to scream as she smiled back, unable to repress a shudder as she looked directly into his ice-blue dark-framed eyes.

She willed herself to relax. Her life had moved on, and if time hadn't completely healed the wounds it *had* allowed her to see things from a different perspective. She had made a mistake, but that mistake had given her Jasmine. This man had given her a gift and he didn't know.

ONE NIGHT
WITH CONSEQUENCES

A high price to pay for giving in to temptation!

When succumbing to a night of unbridled desire,
it's impossible to think past the morning after!

But with the sheets barely settled that little blue line
appears on the pregnancy test—and it doesn't take
long for you to realise that one night of white-hot
passion has turned into a lifetime of consequences!

Only one question remains:

How do you tell a man you've just met that
you're about to share more than just his bed?

If you enjoy A SECRET UNTIL NOW
why not try

A DEAL WITH BENEFITS by Susanna Carr
and

PROOF OF THEIR SIN by Dani Collins

A SECRET
UNTIL NOW

BY
KIM LAWRENCE

MILLS &
BOON

Published in Great Britain 2014
by Mills & Boon, an imprint of Harlequin (UK) Limited,
Eton House, 18-24 Paradise Road, Richmond, Surrey, TW9 1SR

© 2014 Kim Lawrence

ISBN: 978-0-263-25413-6

Harlequin (UK) Limited's policy is to use papers that are natural, renewable and recyclable products and made from wood grown in sustainable forests. The logging and manufacturing processes conform to the legal environmental regulations of the country of origin.

Printed and bound in Spain
by Blackprint CPI, Barcelona

Though lacking much authentic Welsh blood—she comes from English/Irish stock—**Kim Lawrence** was born and brought up in North Wales. She returned there when she married and her sons were both born on Anglesey, an island off the coast. Though not isolated, Anglesey is a little off the beaten track, but lively Dublin, which Kim loves, is only a short ferry-ride away.

Today they live on the farm her husband was brought up on. Welsh is the first language of many people in this area, and Kim's husband and sons are all bilingual—she is having a lot of fun, not to mention a few headaches, trying to learn the language!

With small children, the unsocial hours of nursing didn't look attractive so, encouraged by a husband who thinks she can do anything she sets her mind to, Kim tried her hand at writing. Always a keen Mills & Boon® reader, it seemed natural for her to write a romance novel—now she can't imagine doing anything else.

She is a keen gardener and cook and enjoys running— often on the beach, as living on an island the sea is never very far away. She is usually accompanied by her Jack Russell, Sprout—don't ask...it's a long story!

Recent titles by the same author:

CAPTIVATED BY HER INNOCENCE
MAID FOR MONTERO *(At His Service)*
THE PETRELLI HEIR
SANTIAGO'S COMMAND

For my dad, Roy,
who was always proud of his writer daughter.

PROLOGUE

London, Summer 2008, a hotel

ANGEL'S EYES HAD adjusted to the dark but from where she was lying the illuminated display of the bedside clock was hidden from her view, blocked by his shoulder. But the thin finger of light that was shining into the room through the chink in the blackout curtains suggested that it was morning.

'The morning after the night before!'

She gave a soft shaken sigh and allowed her glance to drift around the unfamiliar room, the generic but luxurious five-star hotel furnishings familiar, especially to someone who had slept in dozens of similar suites; someone who had imagined at one point that everybody ordered their supper from room service.

Since she'd had the choice Angel had avoided rooms like this as they depressed her. Depressed... Smiling at the past tense, she raised herself slowly up on one elbow. This room was different not because it boasted a special view or had a sumptuously comfortable bed. What was different was that she was not alone.

She froze when the man on the bed beside her murmured in his sleep and her attention immediately returned to him—it had never really left him. She gulped as he

threw a hand above his head, the action causing the muscles in his beautiful back to ripple in a way that made
her stomach flip over. She couldn't see his face but his
breathing remained deep and regular.

Should she wake him up?

The bruised-looking half-moons underneath his spectacular eyes suggested he probably needed his sleep.
She'd noticed them the moment she'd looked at him, but
then she had noticed pretty much everything about him.
Angel had never considered herself a particularly obser-
vant person but crazily one glance had indelibly printed
his face into her memory.

Mind you, it was a pretty special face, not made any
less special by the lines of fatigue etched around his
wide, sensual mouth or the dark shadows beneath those
totally spectacular eyes. There was a weary cynicism
reflected in those electric-blue depths and also in that
first instant anger.

He had been furious with her, but it wasn't the incandescent anger that had made her legs feel hollow or even
her dramatic brush with death or that he had saved her
life. It was him, everything about him. He projected an
aura of raw maleness that had a cataclysmic impact on
her, like someone thrown in the deep end who from that
first moment was treading water, barely able to breathe,
throat tight with emotion as if she were submerged by a
massive wave of lust.

It wasn't until much later that she had recognised this
as a crossroad moment. She didn't see a fork in the road;
there was no definable instant when she made a conscious decision. Her universe had narrowed into this total
stranger, and she had known with utter and total conviction that she had to be with him. She wanted him and then
she had seen in his eyes he wanted her too.

What else mattered?

Did I really just think that?

What else mattered? The defence of the greedy, absurdly needy and just plain stupid! Angel, who was utterly confident she was none of those things, was conscious that this particular inner dialogue was one it would have been more sensible to have had before, not *after*… After she had broken the habit of a lifetime and thrown caution, baby, bath water and the entire package out of the window!

The previous night there had been no inner dialogue, not even any inhibition-lowering alcohol in her bloodstream, no excuses. The words of a novel she had read years before popped into Angel's head. Although at the time they had made her put the gothic romance to one side with a snort of amused disdain, now she couldn't shake them. 'I felt a deep craving, an ache in my body and soul that I had never imagined possible.'

The remembered words no longer made her snigger and translate with a roll of her eyes—*yes, he's hot!*

Which the man in bed beside her was and then some, but Angel had met hot men before, and she had been amused by their macho posturing. She was in charge of her life and she liked it that way. History was littered with countless examples of strong women who had disastrous personal lives, but she was not going to be one of them.

Admittedly the macho men she was able to view with lofty disdain had not just saved her life, but Angel knew what she was feeling hadn't anything to do with gratitude. Beyond this certainty she wasn't sure of anything much. Her life and her belief system had been turned upside down. She had no idea at all why this was happening but she was not going to fight it. In any case, that would have been as futile as fighting the colour of her eyes or her blood type; it just was…and it was exciting!

'*Dio*, you're so beautiful.' Her husky whisper was soft and tinged with awe as she reached out a hand to touch his dark head, allowing her fingers to slide lightly over the sleek short tufts of hair. Her own hair was often called black but his was two shades darker and her skin, though a warm natural olive, looked almost winter pale against his deeply tanned, vibrant-toned, bronzed flesh. It was a contrast that had fascinated her when she'd first seen their limbs entwined—not just skin tone, but the tactile differences of his hard to her soft, his hair-roughened virility to her feminine smoothness. She wanted to touch, taste…

Angel couldn't understand how she felt so wide awake. Why she wasn't tired. She hadn't slept all night, but her senses weren't dulled by exhaustion. Instead they were racing and her body was humming with an almost painful sensory overload.

Languid pleasure twitched the corners of her full, wide mouth up as she lifted her arms above her head, stretching with feline grace, feeling muscles she hadn't known she had. Who wanted to sleep when it had finally happened? The man of her dreams was real and she had found him!

It was fate!

Her smooth brow knitted into a furrowed web. *Fate* again—this sounded so *not* her. When she had once been accused of not having a romantic bone in her body she had taken it as a compliment. She had never thought she was missing out; she'd never wanted to be that person— the one who fell in love at the drop of a hat and out again equally as easily. That was her mother who, despite the fragile appearance that made men want to protect her, had Teflon-coated emotions.

Angel knew she did not inspire a similar reaction in men and neither did she want to; the thought of not being independent was anathema to her. As a kid she had been saved from a life of loneliness and isolation by two things: a brother and an imagination. Not that she ever, even when she was young, confused her secret fantasy world with real life.

Angel had never expected her fantasies to actually come true.

She stretched out her hand, moving her fingers in the air above the curve of his shoulder, fighting the compulsion to touch him, to tug the sheet that was lying low across his hips farther down. She was amazed that she could have these thoughts and feel no sense of embarrassment. It had been the same when she had undressed for him—it had just felt right and heart-stoppingly exciting.

No fantasy had ever matched the fascination she felt for his body. Her stomach muscles quivered in hot, hungry anticipation of exploring every inch of his hard, lean body again.

'Totally beautiful,' she whispered again, staring at the man sharing her bed.

His name was Alex. When he'd asked she'd told him her name was Angelina, but that nobody ever called her that. Apparently when she was born her father had said she looked like a little angel and it had stuck.

She tensed when, as if in response to her voice, he murmured in his sleep before rolling over onto his back, one arm flung over his head, his long fingers brushing the headboard.

Angel felt a strong sensual kick of excitement low and deep in her belly as she stared, the rapt expression on her face a fusion of awe and hunger. She swallowed past the emotional thickening that made her throat ache. He was the most beautiful thing she had ever seen or imagined.

In the half-light that now filled the room his warm olive-toned skin gleamed like gold, its texture like oiled satin. A tactile tingle passed through her fingertips. Perfect might have seemed like an overused term but he was. The length of his legs was balanced by broad shoulders and a deeply muscled chest dusted with dark body hair that narrowed into a directional arrow across his flat belly ridged with muscle. There wasn't an ounce of excess flesh on his lean body to disguise the musculature that had the perfection of an anatomical diagram. But Alex was no diagram. He was a warm, living, earthly male, and he was sharing her bed.

A dazed smile flickered across her face as she felt all the muscles in her abdomen tighten. Last night had been perfect—perfect, but not in the way she had expected. There had been hardly any pain and no embarrassment.

Angel has still failed to grasp the concept of moderation. There is no middle ground—she is all or nothing.

The words on her report card came back to her.

Her form teacher had been referring to her academic record littered with As and Fs, not to sex, but there had been no middle ground last night either. Angel had held nothing back; she had given him everything without reservation.

'I know this is bad timing, but there's a problem.'

The words had been music to Alex's ears. 'Tell me.'

They had and he had acted. Crisis management was something he excelled at—it was a simple matter of focusing, shutting out all distractions and focusing.

He had gone straight from the funeral to his office, where he'd pretty much lived for the past month. He'd

washed, eaten and slept—or at least snatched a few minutes on the sofa—there. It made sense, and it suited him.
He had nothing to go home to any longer.

Then the crisis was over and Alex had been unable
to think of any reason not to go home, where he had, if
anything, less sleep. He did go to bed but by the small
hours he was up again, which was why it felt strange
and disorientating to wake up after a deep sleep and
find light shining through the blinds of…not his room…
Where the hell?

He blinked and focused on the beautiful face of the
most incredible-looking woman. She was sitting there
looking down at him wearing nothing but a mane of
glossy dark hair that lay like a silky curtain over her
breasts—breasts that had filled his hands perfectly and
tasted—

It all came rushing back.

Hell!

'Good morning.'

His body reacted to the slumberous promise in her
smile, but, ignoring the urgent messages it was sending
and the desire that heated his blood, gritted his teeth and
swung his legs over the side of the bed. Guilt rising like
a toxic tide to clog his throat, he sat, eyes closed, with
his rigid back to her. This was about damage limitation
and not repeating a mistake no matter how tempting it
might seem.

She was sinful temptation given a throaty voice and
a perfect body, but this had been his mistake, not hers,
and it was his responsibility to end it.

'I thought you'd never wake up.'

His spine tensed at the touch of her fingers on his
skin. He wiped his face of all emotion as he turned back
to face her.

'You should have woken me. I hope I haven't made you late for anything…?'

'Late…?' she quavered.

He stood up and looked around for his clothes. 'Can I get you a taxi?'

'I…I don't understand… I thought we'd…' Her voice trailed away. He was looking at her so coldly.

'Look, last night was… Actually it was fantastic but I'm not available.'

Available? Angel still didn't get it.

He felt the guilt tighten in his gut but he had no desire to prolong this scene. He'd made a massive mistake, end of story. A post-mortem was not going to change anything.

'I thought—'

He cut across her. 'Last night was just sex.'

He was speaking slowly as if he were explaining something to a child or a moron. The coldness in his blue eyes as much as his words confused Angel.

'But last night…'

'Like I said, last night was great, but it was a mistake.' A great big mistake, but a man learned by his mistakes and he didn't give in to the temptation to repeat them.

She began to feel sick as she watched him fight his way into his shirt, then he was pulling on his trousers. She responded automatically to pick up the object that fell out of the pocket and landed with a metallic twang on the floor just in front of her toes. She bent to pick it up; her fingers closed around a ring.

'Yours?'

He was meticulously careful not to touch her fingers as he took it from her outstretched hand.

'You're married?'

For a moment he thought of telling the truth, saying

that he had been, but no longer, that the ring was in his pocket because friends kept telling him it was time to move on. Alex doubted this was what they'd had in mind.

Then he realised how much easier and less painful a lie would be. It wouldn't ease the guilt that was like a living thing in his gut, but it would make this scene less messy and allow her to say when regaling her friends later that *the bastard was married*.

'I'm sorry.'

Her incredible green eyes flared hot as she rose majestically to her feet and delivered a contemptuous 'You disgusting loser!' followed up by a backhanded slap that made him blink. He opened his watering eyes in time to see her vanish into the bathroom, the door locked audibly behind her.

Angel ran, hand clamped to her mouth, across the room, just making it to the loo before she was violently sick.

By the time she returned to the bedroom he was gone.

Angel found herself hating him with more venom than she thought she was capable of. She hated him even more than her mother's creepy boyfriend, the one who had tried to grope her when she was sixteen. The only person she hated more than Alex was herself. How could she be so stupid? He had treated her like a tramp because that was how she had acted.

By the time she left the hotel room later that morning, her tears had dried and her expression was set. She had decided she would never, ever think of him again, not think of him or last night.

It never happened.

He never existed.

It was a solution.

She could move on.

CHAPTER ONE

'THEY ARE THE second biggest advertising firm in Europe and—'

'There is something in it for you?' Alex, who had been listening to Nico's pitch while he read the small print on a contract, made the silky suggestion without rancour. He liked his big sister's son and why should his favourite, actually his only, nephew be any different from everyone else?

The younger man acknowledged the point with a self-conscious shrug. 'Well, I had heard there might be an internship going…?'

Alex finished reading, wrote his signature on the last page of the document and laid it on top of the done pile before pushing his chair back and stretching his long legs out in front of him. He flexed his shoulders and thought wistfully about the run he had promised himself as a reward for spending the morning at his desk. Not that he begrudged the youngster his time—Nico was a low-maintenance relative, unlike some who looked on him as their own personal bank. He was philosophical about the role but family was important.

'Consider the decks cleared. You have my attention.'

'Good of you.' But not entirely comfortable for him as his uncle Alex's eyes had always reminded Nico of ice chips. It wasn't the colour, although that was an un-nerving pale blue, as his own mother shared the same strangely coloured eyes with her much younger brother. It was the impression he'd had as a kid that those eyes had always been able to see right into his head. He was no longer a kid but he was always painfully honest around his uncle—just in case.

'You know that Dad's offered me a job and I'm grateful,' came the hasty assurance.

Alex voiced the unspoken addendum. 'But?'

'But I'd like to do something that didn't have anything to do with being his son or your nephew.'

'I admire your intentions if not your practicality, and you seem to forget I was born with a silver spoon.'

'And you turned it gold,' the young man said gloomily.

There was no firm on the brink of the financial abyss for Nico to save. Thanks to Alex the shipping empire founded by his Greek great grandfather had recovered from years of mismanagement and had gone from strength to strength to be hailed as one of the success stories of the global recession.

Of course even if it hadn't his uncle would still be fabulously rich as Alex had inherited the Arlov vast oil fortune a few years earlier from the Russian great grandfather that Nico had never met. That was when Alex had delegated the day-to-day running of the shipping business to his brother-in-law, Nico's father.

'And that is a bad thing?'

'No, of course not, but no one thinks of you as a little rich boy who's never done a day's work in his life.'

A direct quote? Alex wondered, feeling a stab of sympathy for his nephew, who was all of the above but also a rather nice kid.

'You don't have anything to prove.' His eyes fell. 'Just

forget it,' he mumbled. 'I knew I was talking out of my…
I guess I knew you wouldn't be up for it. I just wanted
to impress the guy from the advertising firm and you
should have seen his face when I mentioned your island,
Saronia. He lit up like a firework. Pathetic or what.' He
reached out for the tablet he had opened on his uncle's
desk and drew back as Alex withdrew it from his reach.

'You were trying to impress. Why apologise? Unless
your interest is more personal? I am assuming the new
face of this cosmetic firm is not ugly—one of your actress friends perhaps? Are you still dating…?' The name
of the pretty girl from the soap escaped him as he idly
scrolled down the screen that showed the logo of the cosmetics giant that was apparently launching a new perfume.

It was not a world that Alex knew much about. 'A big
thing, is it, a new perfume?'

'Massive,' his nephew assured him. 'They're planning to make a series of ads to promote it using the same
couple, six ads in all, really glossy and high produc-
tion values, like a kind of serial each with a story and a
cliffhanger like a romantic minisoap. They've got a big-
name director and this guy from Hollywood to star in
it—though he must be at least thirty-five.'

Alex fought a smile. 'That old!' Good to know he
had three years to go before he was classed as elderly
by his nephew.

'They want to film the first three in an exotic setting—
sand, sun and palm trees on an island paradise thing.'

'And a connection with the golden age of Hollywood
would not hurt,' Alex inserted. He could see why Saronia would appeal to them as a location.

In its day the island had been the setting for his grandfather's famous parties. Spyros Theakis—a man with a

well-documented taste for starlets—reaping the financial rewards of his successful Greek shipping empire, had hosted lavish parties attended by all the stars of the day on his private island. The photos of those legendary events still surfaced from time to time, as did the tales of wild parties, torrid affairs and general excess. Most left out the fact that the mansion had been burnt down during an electrical storm. By some miracle none of the guests had been seriously hurt but the place had never been rebuilt. His grandfather's fortunes, like those of the island, had gone into decline and the place had become uninhabited.

Alex had visited out of curiosity when the resort hotel he had commissioned was being built on the mainland just a few minutes away by boat. Emma, who had come with him, had been fascinated by the romance of the place. They had always planned to build a house there but the plans had been put on hold when she'd become ill and had been shelved permanently after the diagnosis.

He had gone back to Saronia for the first time a few months after her death, camping on the beach for a few days that had stretched into several weeks. Later that year he had commissioned a house, not the family house that he had planned with Emma but a small place, minimalist, no frills—though not the monk's cell his sister had called it. It was his own retreat; he went there once or twice a year to recharge his batteries…. God knew there were few places where he could guarantee there were no photographers lurking around the corner, no phones, no news—he was off the grid when he was there.

As much as he admired his nephew's enterprise he would sooner have invited cameras into his own bathroom than allow a film crew to invade this precious private sanctuary.

'Louise,' the younger man said suddenly as he took a seat on the edge of the big desk. 'She had a really tough upbringing and she thinks I'm…spoilt.'

'This is your soap star?'

Nico nodded.

'And you want to impress her.' Alex, who had been idly scrolling through the tablet, stopped. 'Who is that?' The lack of inflection in his voice might have made those who knew him better wonder…but Nico's attention was on his own troubled love life, not the sudden tension in his uncle's body language.

His nephew bent over, scanning the inverted image that filled the screen. It was a studio shot of an extremely beautiful young woman pouting provocatively at the camera with lips that were glossy and scarlet. Everything about her was provocative, from the swathe of dark wavy hair that fell artistically across one half of her face to the smile in her heavily lidded eyes, a smile that seemed to invite you to share a secret that gleamed in the shimmering emerald depths as she leaned forward displaying a large amount of cleavage in a gold sheath dress that clung like a second skin.

'Angel. She's a model.'

Angel… Angelina? 'A model.'

It did not surprise him. What did surprise him was the instant effect of a face he had last seen six years ago…. An incident that had not been his finest hour, but one he had consigned to the past. The instant surge of sexual hunger that tightened in his belly had a very *present* feel to it.

His nephew nodded and looked amazed by his uncle's ignorance. 'You must have seen her in that underwear campaign last year. She was everywhere.'

'I must have missed that one,' he mused, seeing the

beautiful sleek brunette not in underwear…not in anything. He went to stand but, not wanting to draw attention
to the testosterone that had suddenly pooled in his groin,
he sat back down again like some hormonal teenager,
resenting his lack of control—or at least the cause of it.

'Gorgeous, isn't she?' the young man continued, oblivious to any undercurrents in the air. 'All that hair and
those green eyes. They are going to build the campaign
around her. It's a calculated risk, they said, not to choose
a big celebrity to be the new face for a perfume, but they
want to build the campaign around someone who—'

Alex tuned out the explanation of the thinking behind
employing a relative unknown—she was not unknown
to him. Seeing that face, those eyes, remembering the
sleek, sinuous body, the undulating curves, the golden
toned skin, brought that night back so clearly that he
could smell the scent of her shampoo.

Lust slammed through him again like an iron fist.
With it came the guilt…always the guilt. Emma dead how
many weeks…? And he had jumped into bed with the
first available woman. She had led but he had followed.

His lips curled in self-disgust. He had moved on since
then, when he'd felt ready. Not one-night stands, that
was not his thing, but he had enjoyed a series of satisfying relationships with women who enjoyed sex but not
drama, and none had been tainted with guilt. If that required he maintain a certain emotional distance it was a
price worth paying.

'Yes.'

He had no desire to revisit that place of agonising guilt
but to recapture that…? It was not so much a *thing* he
was trying to recapture but an absence that he was trying to fill. He gave his head a tiny shake, aware that he
was guilty of the sin of overanalysing. She had been the

best sex of his life, so why not make a push to sample it
and her again?

Nico, who had taken his ringing mobile phone from
his pocket intending to turn it off, dropped it. It lay where
it had fallen as, jaw slack with shock, he scanned the face
of the man who sat behind the big desk, a pointless exercise because he never could read his uncle.

'Whaddaya… Yes…?' he said, unable to believe he
was this lucky.

Behind the desk Alex brought his formidable mental
control into play and pushed the increasingly erotic images from his head.

He raised one dark brow. 'Yes.'

Nico surged to his feet, radiating the sort of youthful
excitement that made Alex, who was all of what, twelve
years his senior, feel old. 'Seriously…? This isn't a wind-
up… No, you don't—'

Alex quirked a dark brow and suggested, 'Have a
sense of humour?'

Maybe the boy was right; maybe he had eradicated
that along with his conscience.

A conscience was an inconvenient thing, he thought,
seeing the expression in those big eyes. He needed to
draw a line under what had happened, and this was an
unexpected opportunity to do just that. A girl who adopted a 'jump into bed first and ask questions later' policy should have expected a few surprises, yet innocence
was an odd word to use with someone who had been so
sexually uninhibited. But for some reason…? Again, he
was overthinking this.

Take away the acrid taste of guilt and she remained
the best sex he had ever had, and due to pressures of
work it had been months since he had enjoyed any sex,
which might go some way to explaining the strength

of his physical response. He didn't try to justify it. He didn't just need sex, he needed a question mark in his life; he needed highs and lows, not a predictable flat-line monotony.

Wondering where that thought had come from, he was aware he sounded like a man who was not satisfied with his life. He was; of course he was. Alex got to his feet and picked up the jacket he had slung over the back of the chair.

'You going to pick that up?' He nodded towards the phone.

Looking dazed, his nephew nodded. 'What...? Oh, sure...'

'You will keep me up to speed?'

'Me? You want me to... Great, of course... So should I run the details past...?' Though tall and blessed with an athletic build, the younger man was forced to tilt his head back to look up at his uncle who, at six-five, was a couple of inches taller than him, and significantly more than a couple inches broader across the shoulders.

'Me,' Alex said, shrugging on a fine wool jacket that was tailored to fit across his broad shoulders so it fell into place without a crease.

'You really mean this? You'll actually let them film on Saronia?'

He'd made the pitch but in his wildest dreams Nico had never seriously expected it to work. Everyone knew how jealously Alex Arlov protected his privacy, even more so since someone had hacked into his wife's medical records not long before she died. It was after the resulting tear-jerking newspaper article that he had gained the reputation of being ferociously litigious, someone prepared to go after perpetrators who crossed the line in the sand regardless of the cost. Some people suggested that this meant he had something to hide, and pointed out the lives he had ruined by taking legal retribution, but they did so in very small voices and only after taking extensive legal advice!

Nico, who was not averse to seeing his own picture on the pages of celebrity magazines, privately considered that Uncle Alex took it a bit far. The paparazzo who had ended up fully clothed in a swimming pool at his mother's birthday bash last year, camera and all, might have agreed with him.

'With certain restrictions obviously. They stay on the mainland and make the daily commute. I don't want them anywhere near the house. I can leave the details with you?'

'Wow… Yes, absolutely and, thanks, you won't regret this.'

Alex watched the boy bounce from the room oozing enthusiasm and incredulous joy. If Alex had been the type to dwell on the motivations behind his decision he might have spent the next hour doing so with increasing frustration. But he wasn't, so he spent the next hour running instead.

Angel poked her head around the door of the lounge where most of the people involved had congregated. Used to the handful involved in a fashion shoot, she thought there seemed to be an awful lot of them.

'I think I'll go for a walk. Anyone fancy some fresh air?' She was an active person, and being cooped up in the claustrophobic atmosphere of the luxury hotel was getting to her.

Several astonished pairs of eyes turned her way. Someone whose name she had forgotten replied, his tone indulgent, 'It's raining, Angel, honey.'

It never rains in August.

Angel had lost count of the number of times she had heard this statement since they had arrived at the resort, but the fact remained that, despite the lack of precedent, it was raining and it had been for two days solid. In fact, it had been ever since they had arrived at the island paradise, this paradise they had yet to set foot on.

The delay to the photo shoot had caused tempers to fray and the money men to start muttering. For Angel it was two days she could have been at home with her daughter, not hundreds of miles away.

'It's just water.'

Her response drew blank looks. 'But you'll get wet.'

'I need the exercise.'

'I'm just off to the gym,' said India, the actress playing her mother in the ad—though the woman was only ten years older than Angel. 'Come with me.'

'I don't really do the gym thing. I'm allergic to Lycra.'

'Seriously?'

'No, not seriously, India, she's joking,' Rudie, the lighting man, explained.

'Your hair will get wet.' The objection was made by the man responsible for making her hair look perfect. He was still recovering from the shock of discovering that, not only was the waist-length ebony hair all her own, but the glossy colour had never been enhanced or altered.

'It will dry.'

'What's that smell?'

'Me, I'm afraid.' Angel brought her concealed hand out from behind her back. 'I can't resist lashings of onions.'

'Is that a hot dog?'

Angel glanced at the item that was causing the executive from the cosmetic company to look so shocked. The only person in the room who didn't seem horrified was the handsome young Greek, Nico. She assumed from his appearance he was one of the Theakis family who owned the luxury resort and any number of others around the world, and probably the shipping line of the same name, but she wasn't sure what his connection was with the owner of Saronia who he was representing.

'I really hope so.'

Again the young Greek was the only one to laugh so she winked at him and murmured, 'Tough crowd to play,' in a terrible New York drawl.

'But you had a full breakfast.' The critical follow-up came from the stylist.

Walking in the rain had clearly not been received well, but she could tell from the general air of disapproval in the room that eating an actual meal was considered ab-errant behaviour by those present. But Angel coped with their disapproval by refusing to recognise it.

The same way she had refused to recognise the broad hints earlier that she might be better selecting a pot of low-fat yogurt rather than a full English. She was all for a peaceful life.

'And it was delicious.' Angel could feel the woman staring at her as though they expected to see her devel-oping unsightly bulges as she watched.

Her grip on her hot dog tightened as she fought the urge to say something that would make everyone look at her with the opposite of their current disdain. It had taken time, but she had conquered her need to seek ap-proval, recognising late in the day that the one person— her mother—from whom she wanted that approval was never going to give it.

Only very occasionally these days did she find that eager-to-please tendency resurfacing. When it did she quashed it ruthlessly. Needy was just not a good look, and not the sort of example she wanted to set for her daughter.

She lifted her chin and embraced them all with a brilliant smile. 'Then it's just as well I'm going to go for a walk.'

The figure who had been hiding behind a newspaper lowered it, revealing the lived-in features of a photographer who was more famous than the A-list people who posed for him.

'Relax, guys, our girl here never puts on an ounce. Do you, darling?' His brows lifted as his glance slid down the supple curves of the young woman framed in the doorway. 'Looking particularly lush this morning.... Purely a professional observation, you understand, Angel, luv.'

Alex nodded to a gardener whose eyes widened as he recognised the person who had manoeuvred his way past the ladder he had set up against the trellis.

Alex liked to fly under the radar when he could. He had arrived the previous night in a private jet that had landed at a private airport and had made the short crossing alone in the rain that had been falling ever since. It was, according to the information supplied by his spy in the camp, Nico, playing havoc with the filming schedule.

The rain had just stopped and the dampness underfoot was already being turned to misty vapour by the late-afternoon sun. Someone had forgotten to adjust the sprinkler system, which was adding to the moisture, but a few of the holidaymakers had already begun to venture out of the hotel, including a large family group who were playing a boisterous game of cricket on the beach.

Alex had a few hours to kill before the meet-and-greet cocktail party Nico had arranged later that evening. The young man thought that Alex was making the effort to attend as a favour to him. Alex, whose motivation was far less selfless, had seen no harm in letting his young relative—and by association his older sister—think just that. It was always handy to have a favour in hand with his sibling.

Heading towards the noise on the beach, he made his way down the flower-filled terraces that led to the tree-lined walkway above the beach. Normally at this time of day it would have been dotted with parasols and su-pine brown bodies, but the weather meant it was almost empty except for the family group in the midst of their raucous ball game.

Alex was conscious of an uncharacteristic impatience as he anticipated the evening ahead. The tall, luscious brunette had been the best sex of his life, and he had felt nothing that had approached that level of carnal passion since. But would the incredible chemistry between them still be there?

Seeing her face had definitely aroused the dormant hunting instincts in him, and, though Alex had no inten-tion of investing emotionally in any relationship, he had normal appetites.

He shook his head and decided he would spend the re-mainder of the evening running through the details of the extension project with the contractors that would double the size of the spa. He was a firm believer in multitask-ing; to combine business with pleasure was a pragma-tism he was comfortable with, but he was considerably less comfortable with the inescapable scent of obsession attached to moving heaven and earth to engineer a meet-ing with a one-night stand from six years ago.

Thinking it over did not remove her face from his head. Instead, it was the ball that was hurtling towards him at great speed that did that. It would have hit him had not some sixth sense made him turn his head and, without thinking, he shot out his hand to catch it.

There was a ripple of applause to congratulate this display of lightning reflexes and natural coordination, followed by a chorus of apologies from the beach. He nodded acknowledgment and responded to the light-hearted invitation to join in the fun from the players with a negative motion of his head before he tossed the ball back and continued along the wide boulevard.

'Go deep, go deep!'

Someone was yelling, and he turned his head and saw a figure who was doing her level best to follow the in-struction. It was a figure who... He stopped dead. Alex had imagined the object of his lustful machinations sun-ning herself, maybe topless? Sipping a cocktail or taking advantage of the spa facilities, but not pelting across the sand barefoot in a pair of shorts and a cut-off T-shirt, her hair flying and yelling wildly.

'I've got it!'

Before he had a chance to assimilate this extraordinary turn of events she caught the ball, released an exultant whoop, jumped high in the air and was promptly wrestled to the ground by one of the male players. Alex watched with distaste as they rolled around on the ground, the man's hands seemingly everywhere. It was one of those moments when a man felt the layers of civilisation peel away, and he wasn't aware until he had begun to walk rapidly away that his hands were clenched into fists.

Angel, hot, sweaty and deeply involved in the match, didn't see the throw but she did see the distant figure fling the ball back with an accuracy that caused a sec-ond ripple of applause.

There were millions of tall, dark, athletically built,

handsome men in the world and some of them projected
an aura of authority and, well…sex. So over the years
she had experienced a few heart-thudding, stomach-
clenching moments of shocked recognition only to discover after all the breathless anticipation that as the object
of her antipathy got nearer it was not HIM, but a pale
imitation who did not possess that level of raw sensuality that she had responded to on a primal level.

But she was a mother now and her primal days were
in the past. The chances she would ever meet HIM—she
always thought of Jas's father in capital letters—again
were remote, and if she ever did it was not likely it would
be here, she thought, tearing her eyes from the tall figure. Even though she knew it wasn't HIM, her heart was
still racing as she followed the bellowed instruction to
go deep from the bowler, a ten-year-old who had a well-
developed competitive streak.

When she did catch the ball a few moments later she
found herself rugby tackled by the handsome husband of
the woman who had invited her to join the game. When
she disentangled herself and emerged triumphantly holding the ball aloft the suited figure on the broad walkway
who had dredged up memories that were better left un-
disturbed was gone.

CHAPTER TWO

AT THE END of an exhausting game the friendly family invited her to take afternoon tea with them as they were celebrating the grandparents' diamond anniversary. Refusal, they told her, was not an option, so after nipping back to her bungalow to quickly shower and change she joined them in a private lounge where she ate cakes and no one pointed out the fat content.

It was the first time Angel had enjoyed herself since she had arrived, or even come close to relaxing, though watching one of the grandchildren who was Jasmine's age did make her throat swell with emotion as she wondered what her daughter was doing.

As a result, she ate more cake and stayed longer than she'd intended. So after the lively afternoon the silence and emptiness of her bungalow felt rather depressing. Not that it wasn't a lovely room—actually it was a two-bedroom suite furnished in a very expensive version of rustic, with dark, chunky wooden furniture and floors with splashes of colour provided by the original art displayed on the white walls.

All the bungalows had flower-bedecked private terraces with spa tubs, some with a view of the pool with its mountain backdrop; others, like the one that Angel had been allocated, had a sea view. The sand lapped by the turquoise waves was sugary white and dotted with palms. The storm of the previous day seemed a dim and distant memory this evening.

Before stepping back into her room Angel dusted the sand off the soles of her bare feet. It was not hard to see why the place was popular with honeymooning couples lucky enough to be able to afford the prices the very up-market resort charged. But then paradise didn't come cheap. As gorgeous as it was, the place lacked a vital ingredient that was essential for Angel's paradise.

God, she thought, giving her head a tiny shake before she crossed the room to the side table, her bare feet silent on the wooden floor. Her chest tightened and she felt the sting of tears in her eyes as she picked up the framed photo of Jasmine.

'Here five minutes and homesick already! Your mum is a wimp,' she told the picture of the laughing child before she kissed the glass, swallowed the emotional lump in her throat and with a brisk, 'Pull yourself together, Angel,' she replaced it carefully on the side table.

Then after a last wave to the photo she straightened her shoulders and headed for the open French doors, pausing to slip her feet into a pair of flat sandals as she headed for the bedroom. It had been made very clear that the drinks party was not optional! And she was… She glanced at her wristwatch. Yes, she was running late.

So no time to change.

'Drinks and butter up the rich owner…?' She pursed her lips, staring as she aimed a frown at her reflection in the full-length mirror.

The frown was for the rich owner who would most likely have a monumental ego, and the question was purely rhetorical. The thin cotton dress she was wearing was not by any stretch a cocktail dress. It was little more than an ankle-length cover-up she had chosen earlier, a deep cobalt blue shot with swirls of green. It left her smooth brown shoulders bare, or they would have been if it hadn't been for the straps of her halter bikini.

Angel might move in the world of high fashion but she was no slave to the latest trends. She knew what suited her; she had an individual style and the confidence to carry off anything she wore.

Poise, the scout from the talent agency had called it. It was, he had told her later, the reason he had picked her out from countless pretty girls in the park that day, that and the length of her legs. Her legs *were* quite good, and Angel and the scout were quite good friends these days despite the fact that her brother, witnessing the first encounter, had warned the middle-aged man off in no uncertain terms. Her brother was the only male of her acquaintance who thought her incapable of taking care of herself. Exasperating, but she tolerated it because she knew his intentions were good, though his methods sometimes a bit Neanderthal.

She reached the bow behind her neck and, tongue caught between her teeth, managed to unclip the fastener of her bikini. She gave a grunt as she managed to whip it off without disturbing the dress. Already moving towards the door, she slung the top on the bed as she twitched the neckline, pulling it a few modest centimetres higher over the slopes of her breasts as she glanced in the mirror.

'Or should we add the pearls?' She chuckled to herself before warning her mirror image darkly, 'First signs of madness, Angel.' Snatching up the string of pretty green beads she'd bought at a crazy cheap price from an enterprising trader before a security guard had given him marching orders from the private stretch of beach, she left the bungalow at a trot, looping them around her neck as she went, reflecting it wasn't what you wore, it was the way you wore it. A cliché but true nonetheless.

It was rare that Alex felt the need to rationalise his own actions, and why should he now? Looking at the situation objectively, all he had done was agree to Nico's request. He'd helped out his nephew, which was what families did. Plus, he had business here. It was called multitasking, he told himself.

He was curious, no crime. It wasn't as if he had engineered the situation solely for the purpose of meeting with the woman who had spent the night in his bed six years ago.

Sure you didn't, Alex—you were just passing.

Of course, if he took advantage of a situation that had fallen into his lap, who could blame him?

The last time she had not fallen in his lap, she had jumped!

Alex, who believed contrary to popular belief very few people were capable of learning from past mistakes, was an advocate of living in the present. But as a pulse of hot lust slammed through his body he found his thoughts being dragged back to a moment six years ago, when, driven by the need he'd had then to fill his every waking moment with action, he had left his car and driver stuck in rush-hour traffic and walked instead along a crowded London street.

If he hadn't been…?

She had stepped off the pavement into the moving traffic and he had literally dragged the young woman from underneath the wheels of a bus.

The memory, a moment frozen in time etched on his brain, was so vivid he could smell the exhaust fumes in the air now, hear the tortured squeal of brakes and the cry of a solitary onlooker who, alone among those busily going about their own business, had witnessed the moment of near disaster.

Alex's reaction had been pure reflex, not related in any way to bravery, and his body's response had been equally involuntary when he'd turned the figure around and looked down into the face turned up to him...and carried on looking.

His anger had melted.

She was stunning!

He could remember thinking what a crime it would have been for that face to be marked. A delicate, slightly tip-tilted nose; wide, full, luscious lips; a natural pout even in repose and incredible deep green, heavily lashed, almond-shaped eyes set beneath thick, darkly defined, arched brows, and all that general gorgeousness set against flawless satiny skin that had glowed pale gold in the grey city street.

He'd found himself holding the breathing embodiment of sensuality and his body had responded accordingly and instantaneously.

Fighting the impulse to keep her plastered against his body for longer—there was no way she couldn't have picked up on how hard he was—he'd released her, but retained a steadying hold of her elbows as he'd pushed her a little away. His nostrils had flared as the scent of her shampoo had drifted his way.

She had been breathing hard and blinking in a dazed way. Even in the flat, unattractive boots she'd been wearing she'd been tall for a woman, reaching a little past his shoulder. Her slim but voluptuous curves had made the generic jeans and T-shirt she wore look anything but common.

'Are you all right?'

She'd nodded, sending the magnificent waist-length curtain of hair that shone like polished ebony silk swishing around her face. He'd watched as, head tilted forward, she did a sweep of her feet upwards.

'It's all still there and in one piece,' she'd murmured, sounding dazed. Her voice had had a delicious throaty rasp. 'You really do see your life pass before your eyes.' She'd tilted her head back and looked at him, breathing a soft 'Wow!' as her eyes widened.

He had found himself grinning, amused by her total lack of artifice, then watched in fascination as a visible wave of heat travelled up the long graceful curve of her neck, adding an extra tinge of colour to her smooth cheeks. He could not remember ever encountering a woman who wore her emotions so close to the surface. Yet despite the blush, the glowing, gorgeous young creature had held his gaze steadily.

'I think you saved my life.'

He'd given the faintest of shrugs. 'Do you make a habit of throwing yourself under moving vehicles?'

She'd then been staring as hard at him as he was at her. 'It was a first for me.'

When not breathless, the throaty, sexy quality of her voice had intensified.

He'd felt her trembling. Post-trauma or was she feeling the same clutch of lust he was…?

There'd been more than a hint of provocative challenge in her attitude as she'd lifted her chin and asked, 'Can I… Let me buy you a coffee, to thank you…? It seems the least I can do, unless you're…?'

'Coffee would be good,' he'd heard himself say.

She had expelled a tiny sigh and beamed up at him in undisguised delight, and when he'd kept a guiding hand on one of her elbows she hadn't pulled away. He'd felt her shiver and that time he'd known why.

Alex pushed away the memory; as always it was inextricably and painfully linked in his mind with guilt. On one level he recognised the guilt was irrational. He had no longer been married at that point, hadn't cheated, he'd been free to have sex with a total stranger.

Even when Emma had been alive he could have taken a mistress with her blessing. Alex was not easily shocked but on the first occasion she had brought the subject up he had been—deeply. He'd known she'd had something on her mind and had coaxed her to tell him what was bothering her but he hadn't been prepared for the incendiary suggestion she had made.

'You're a man, you have needs that I can't...and you've been so patient with me, never said that I should have told you about the MS. I wanted to, but it might have been years before it came back or even never.'

'It wouldn't have made any difference if I had known,' he had told her, hoping it was true. Even wondering had felt like a betrayal.

'I know that, Alex, but the fact remains you didn't have the choice. I didn't give you the choice. So if you need to, you know...date other women, that's all right with me. I don't have to know, I don't want to know, so long as you stay with me while I'm— I hate hospitals so much, Alex...'

And there it was, the real fear, that he would send her to some anonymous nursing home. It had cut him to the core to know his wife had been willing to endure infidelities for the security and promise of staying in the home that she had enjoyed furnishing in those first months of marriage. She had enjoyed a lot of things before the disease that had finally killed her resurfaced.

A short year later she had been confined to a wheel-chair and eaten up with guilt because she hadn't told him before they'd got married. The constant apologising had been hard to hear and sometimes had made him angry with her. Guilt piled on top of more guilt. It had been a vicious circle.

'This is your home, Emma, our home.' Her hand had felt so small under his, the bones fragile as he'd squeezed. 'There will be no hospitals and no other women, I swear.'

And he had kept his word to the letter if not the spirit. He might have been legally free but in his mind, in his heart, Alex had still been married when he had spent the night with Angelina. Though not once during that night had he thought of Emma. How could he have forgotten, even for a moment? The next morning he hadn't been able to get out of there quickly enough.

If he had encountered the stunning Angel when Emma had still been alive would he have found it so easy to keep his promise? The question wouldn't go away and he would never know the answer, but he was pretty sure that if he had it wouldn't have given him any comfort.

Alex liked to think he was able to forgive weakness in others, but he set higher standards for himself. Though he'd got out of there as fast as he could the morning after, memories of the night before had haunted him. Well, he was about to lay that ghost—literally if things turned out as he intended—to rest.

'Only the star is missing.' His inability to prevent his eyes going to the doorway sent a surge of irritation through Alex. 'Does the lady like to make an entrance?'

Beside him Nico responded defensively to the disdain in his uncle's voice. 'She's really nice.'

The balding executive whom he had directed his sar-donic comment to nodded in agreement with his nephew's assessment. 'She certainly doesn't stand on ceremony and the last thing you can accuse her of is being a diva.' He laughed at some private joke and took a sip of the orange juice he was nursing. 'And if she wanted people to notice her she wouldn't need any stunts. With Angel in the room no one else exists.' He drew a line in the air and pronounced with utter confidence, 'End of story.'

Alex recalled Angelina, or Angel as it seemed he must learn to call her, in his room, an anonymous hotel room. For him that night, no one else had existed. He clenched his teeth in an effort to eject the image of her sitting on the bed gloriously naked and utterly unselfconscious, acting as if they had just shared more than lust, acting as if there would be a tomorrow.

Dragging himself into the present, he wondered if the executive's admiration was purely professional. Was the man sleeping with the model? He knew little of the world they occupied but he supposed it would hardly be a revelation if they were.

'Rudie says Angel simply doesn't have a bad angle. The camera loves her,' Nico, the new president of her fan club, informed him.

'And Rudie is?'

'Our lighting man, one of the best.'

The guy was probably in love with her too, Alex thought sourly.

Oh, God, she was the last to arrive. Angel fought the impulse to step back into the shadows, then smiled to herself at the irony that she made her living posing for a camera, having her image stared at by the public, though she genuinely hated being the centre of attention.

She didn't retreat but paused in the doorway, her eyes sweeping the room, the light breeze pulling the silky fluttering fabric of her dress against long legs until Ross spotted her. The photographer grinned, giving a thumbs-up sign, in the process slopping what she knew would be tonic water down his front. People assumed he had a drink problem, and he let them think that. He had once confided to Angel that he simply didn't like the taste of alcohol, but being thought an ex-alcoholic made him seem more interesting.

Angel's spontaneous burst of throaty laughter alerted the others to her presence and she was immediately involved in a lot of luvvie air kissing.

Well, she'd been right about one thing: she was underdressed. The men, with the exception of Ross, were wearing suits and ties and the women cocktail dresses.

'Worth the wait,' he heard someone say and Alex could not disagree.

The late arrival's appearance had sent a rush of scalding heat through his body. Six years ago she had been stunning, possessing a natural grace and sleek sensuality that had been all the more powerful for appearing totally unstudied. She still possessed all those attributes but now she held herself with the confidence that came when a woman knew the power she wielded with her beauty, when she enjoyed it.

Every man in the room was enjoying it.

Alex's enjoyment was tempered by this knowledge and the discomfort that could be traced to the testosterone-fuelled ache in his groin. The intervening years slipped away as his blue eyes made a slow sweep upwards from her bare feet, and the pink-painted toenails—presumably the sandals dangling from her fingers belonged there.

Though it looked as if she could not have made less effort, you had to feel sorry for the women who had spent hours getting ready. Angel had stopped short of

appearing in her shorts or arriving with a group of sali-
vating half-dressed holidaymakers in tow, but her outfit
was more beach than drinks party. Had she deliberately
underdressed in order to stand out from the crowd? he
speculated. If so, the effort was unnecessary. As the man
had said, she would have stood out in every crowd and
he doubted any man in the room could find fault with
her choice of outfit.

She brought irresistibly to mind the archetypal image
of a Greek goddess in the semisheer column that revealed
every sinuous inch of her long, shapely legs from calf to
thigh. Bare shoulders gleamed gold above the draped
fabric that followed the lines of her full, high breasts
and was cinched in beneath by a tie before flowing out
in long, soft folds.

The fabric shimmered, Angel shimmered.

As far as he could tell she was wasn't wearing a scrap
of make-up. Her face, with the full sexy mouth, cute nose
and spectacular dark-lashed eyes, was beautiful, framed
against a silken fall of river-straight hair that dropped
to her waist.

Luckily, Angel thought, when reliving the moment
later that night, she'd had a drink already thrust into her
hand when the billionaire who had granted them exclusive use of his private island to film the series of com-
mercials was pointed out to her.

'Now, that's what I call a face.'

If only she'd had some warning, some inkling. But
then that was, she supposed, the definition of shock, and
it hit Angel like a sudden immersion into icy water. Initially her mind went utterly blank, rejecting what she was
seeing. Then the breath froze in her lungs; there was a
solid block of ice in her chest. Was this a panic attack?
she wondered, feeling like a drowning man going down

for the final time as she struggled to mask her feelings, willed her face to stay blank.

She looked away and waited for the pounding throb of her heart to slow. Her first instinct had been to run, but that was not an option given her limbs were not acting as though they belonged to her, except for her hand, the one with the glass in it, which managed to find her mouth.

She swallowed the contents in one gulp, her eyes darting from side to side like a trapped animal. There was no place to hide and he was coming her way. Without looking, she could sense his approach.

How was she acting so normally?

She even managed to say something to Sandy, the pretty make-up artist who had initially pointed Alex out to her. What it was Angel had no idea, but she must have been funny because the other girl laughed. *That's me, funny Angel, smart Angel, lucky Angel... Scared witless Angel!*

'Are you cold? You're shivering.' The other girl sounded worried.

Angel swallowed and made herself respond to Sandy's concerned question, forcing the words past the constriction in her throat.

'No, I'm not cold.' And she wasn't. The warm glow in her stomach, the combination of champagne and brandy in the cocktail, had begun to seep into her bloodstream. 'That's Alex Arlov?' Her voice sounded as though it were coming from a long way off. Her head was still spinning as she struggled to take on board the identity of her one-night stand, the father of her child.

Sandy misinterpreted the cause of Angel's stunned expression. 'I know, he looks even better in the flesh, doesn't he? You could cut yourself on those cheekbones.'

The other woman seemed to take it for granted that

Angel recognised the billionaire by sight. And Angel did know the name, of course—who didn't? She could even have recited a potted bio of the man, not because she found money sexy or shared the popular fascination with people who had amassed a great deal of it, but because, and here the irony was so black a short, hard cough of laughter escaped her clenched teeth, her brother had tried in his oh-so-not-subtle way to set her up with the man!

The two men had met while both were driving ridiculously fast cars around a racing circuit for fun. Her brother's excuse was it had once been his day job; the other guy, as far as she had been able to tell at the time, had been there because he enjoyed pushing the limits and he could afford the sort of toys that only very rich men could.

The two men appeared to have bonded over a mutual love of speed and obviously wives had not come into the conversation or Cesare would not have tried to set her up with the man. Her brother had been oblivious, of course, to the fact they were discussing the father of her child, and the man her overprotective sibling had, on more than one occasion, expressed a desire to dismember slowly. Angel's response had been firm but dismissive. For Cesare, the habit of watching out for his little sister was deeply engrained.

'I'm not interested in dating a Russian oligarch, even one who drives well in wet conditions,' she'd said.

Her brother had grinned at the retort but protested. 'Not dating—I was simply suggesting we invite him up for the weekend some time. I think you two would get on. He'd get your sense of humour and, let's face it, that puts him in the minority. And he's only half Russian; his father died before he was born and his mother fell out with his family and moved back home. There was a

grandfather in Russia, hence the Russian oil, but as his
mother was half Greek he was brought up by that side of
his family, and actually he's taken British citizenship.'

'Fine, invite him, whatever you like,' Angel had responded, making a mental note to be away any weekend
her brother tried to play matchmaker. 'But I think one
adrenaline junkie is enough in any family.'

And it had been left at that.

It was her own adrenaline levels that presented the
most immediate problem now. Light-headed to the point
where she saw black dots dancing, and with her heart
thudding like a metronome-driven sledgehammer against
her ribs, it was taking a conscious effort to act with anything approaching normality. The muscles in her cheeks
burned with the effort of keeping her smile pasted on as
she absently licked the crystals of sugar deposited on her
lips by the decorated rim of her now-empty glass. She
watched him approach…nearer and nearer…

Her galloping paranoia saw something predatory
about his long-legged, straight-backed stride. When he
got within a few feet of them her stomach went into a
steep dive. In other circumstances she would have been
riveted, not by fear, but by admiration. Alex Arlov carried himself like a natural athlete, every action screaming
fluidity and grace, but also the arrogance that came when
someone knew they were at the top of the food chain.
Oh, and he could throw a decent pass too; she knew now
he had to have been the man she had seen at the beach.

Angel was seized by an irrational certainty that if she
took her eyes off him for even a second she would lose
her nerve and just bolt…or faint, which would be a first.
There had been a close call in the early months of her
pregnancy when she hadn't yet realised why she couldn't

stand the smell of coffee. She inhaled and closed the door on those thoughts.

By the time Alex had reached them—seconds? Who knew? It was all a blur—Angel had lost the rictus grin of fear and had her face composed into a mask of polite indifference. Bone-deep indifference, though her grip on her composure was not even a cell deep. But who cared as long as she didn't make a fool of herself by giving in to the need to tell him exactly what she thought of him?

The indulgence of venting her real feelings, though tempting, would not exactly improve the situation. Angel knew exactly what she would say. She'd had nearly six years to figure it out, which didn't make her some pathetic creature who'd been unable to move on, or someone who had spent the past six years thinking about him.

She had a life that she loved and he had no place in it. At least that was the way it had worked this morning.... Now he wasn't an unidentifiable figure; he was here and real and present. She had always dreaded the future conversation with Jasmine that began with, 'Sorry, I don't know who your dad is,' but when she thought of naming Alex Arlov as the man in question it suddenly became not such a terrible prospect.

He might not even recognise her...? No such luck, not the way this day was going, she thought, swallowing the bubble of hysterical laughter as she grabbed another drink.

But if he didn't, if he had forgotten she existed the moment he had left the room, would it be so bad to keep him in ignorance? Well, yes, it would be, Angel thought to herself. You could stretch moral ambiguity just so far but it would make life a lot simpler.... She shook her head, unable to deal with the fallout, the deeper implications now. Not falling down was tough enough, she thought, struggling to focus on her contempt and not her near nervous collapse.

Maybe she focused too hard because as his eyes brushed her face for a split second she thought she saw a flicker of shock in those ice-blue depths, but then it was gone and so was his attention.

Angel experienced a weird sense of anticlimax and thought, *Was that it?* Sandy, the recipient of a smile of practised charm, lit up when he spoke to her in the deep gravelly drawl Angel recalled so well. She winced to hear the make-up artist respond with a high girlish giggle, but she couldn't judge. Especially as someone who had gasped *wow* the first time she had seen him was in no position to judge anyone.

The memory made her cringe. Easy hardly covered how very eager she had been to be seduced. She'd been so convinced that she was feeling some deep spiritual connection that he hadn't had to lift a finger to seduce her.

While Alex's attention was on Sandy and she had pulled back from the brink of total panic, Angel took the opportunity to study him. She wasn't the only one—most of the women in the room were checking him out.

The interest was no mystery—the aura of masculinity that had taken her breath away that first time was still intact, was presumably an integral part of him. He was the sort of man whose testosterone entered the room ahead of him, and, to Angel's intense fury and eternal shame, even after being a victim of it she was still not immune to its effects.

The difference was she was not about to equate her physical response to his blatant sexuality with anything but hormones. The shameful heat between her thighs had nothing to do with love at first sight. She was almost too embarrassed to acknowledge she had ever been naive enough to believe that such a thing existed.

At almost twenty and just starting her art college course, Angel knew she had acquired a reputation for being sophisticated among her fellow students. She never could work out how or why, but the label had stuck.

'You're so independent,' a homesick friend had once remarked enviously. 'And you can talk to anyone.'

Well, Angel was certainly independent. Arriving home for the school holidays to find a cheque and a note from her mother to explain that she'd been invited to spend the week at a villa in Switzerland made a person independent. And ten schools in eight years made it essential that she could talk to people, though it had been hard on her grades and near impossible to cultivate long-term friendships.

Given her reputation, it was ironic that, unlike most of her contemporaries, at twenty, Angel's experience of the opposite sex had been limited. Her sexual experience had been pretty much nil. Angel's problem had not been low self-esteem or issues about her body or that she was a prude. No, much worse, Angel had been a closet romantic!

The fact was none of the men she had met up to that point had come close to the idealised lover she had imagined was out there waiting for her. And when she'd met the man who looked and acted like her fantasy lover he had turned out to be a lying, cheating rat!

Even though beside her Sandy was still talking, Alex was now staring at Angel. Presumably he thought that money and power negated the need for common courtesy. He probably— The contemptuous observation was not completed because he had her hand in his.... How had that happened?

Myriad half-formed, disconnected thoughts flitted through her head as she stared at his hand, noting with a tightening in her chest that he still didn't wear a wedding band. His brown hands were strong, the fingers long and tapering. Her weirdly heightened senses could make out the slight calluses on his palms. The more she tried not to think about them gliding over her skin, touching her, the more space the images took up in her head.

She squeezed her eyes closed.

Her loss of control could only have lasted a fraction of a second but it felt like a lot longer. When, a moment later, she was able to meet his eyes, what she saw there answered one question—he remembered.

She didn't fall apart. Instead she manufactured a frown as if she were struggling to place him and then widened her eyes and nodded as though she had retrieved the memory she was searching for.

She rewarded herself with the faintest of smiles.

'Alex Arlov.' He tipped his sleek head and to her intense relief released her hand. *How could I ever not have seen how arrogant he is?* She grabbed a napkin from a passing tray and wiped it against the heel of her hand.

'The name seems familiar…' She gnawed lightly on her full lower lip, pretending to search her memory before producing a bright smile and pausing to stretch the moment, hoping like hell he was worrying she was going to out him. If it weren't for Jas she would, and to hell with people knowing what a total fool she was.

But he didn't look concerned, just vaguely amused, as he elevated one dark brow. 'That happens to me all the time—an instantly forgettable face.'

And so full of yourself, she wanted to scream as she smiled back, unable to repress a shudder as she looked directly into his ice-blue dark-framed eyes.

She willed herself to relax. Let it go, she told herself, life moves on. He's just a landmark moment, not a threat.

Her life had moved on, and, if time hadn't completely healed the wounds, it had allowed her to see things from a different perspective. She had made a mistake, but that mistake had given her Jasmine; this man had given her a gift and he didn't know. Jas didn't know either, didn't know who her father was and one day… Did she have to tell him?

'Are you enjoying island life, Miss…?' He arched a brow and studied her. Her features had lost some of their youthful softness, revealing the truly lovely bone structure of her face. She was, he recognised, one of those women who would only improve with age, perfect bone structure compensating for the slight blurring of features as the years passed.

Angel could see his mouth moving, a mouth that was a miracle of stern sensuality, a mouth she had dreamed of. But all she could hear was, *You're married.* Pride had been the only thing that day that had prevented her from crumbling when she had heard him speak the words that had crushed her, words that had turned what she had thought was beautiful into something nasty and sordid.

She blinked and struggled to focus as he repeated himself. Paul, the advertising executive who had followed Alex across the room, caught the question and said, 'We're all on first-name terms here—aren't we, Angel?'

Reminded of a puppy dog eager to please, she flicked a glance his way. She felt sorry for the man, but not as sorry as she felt for herself…. This was a nightmare.

Breathe, she told herself. *You've coped with worse.*

Such as once she had got back to her room in the university residence, when she had locked the door and stood under a shower for forty minutes but still hadn't been able to wash off that feeling of self-disgust, shame and the bitterness of disillusion.

Finally she had stopped indulging in the orgy of misery and given herself a stern talking-to.

'What are you going to do, Angel? Stay in here for ever?' Wiping the steam off the mirror, she had glared at her tear-stained face. 'Your problem is you're a dreamer, a stupid dreamer. You wanted deep and meaningful, you wanted to wait, you wanted the first time to be with someone who made you feel special. Well, you didn't get the prince—you didn't even get the frog!' She quite liked frogs. 'So what? Big deal, just suck it up, Urquart.'

It had been good advice then and it still was.

Her chin lifted. 'Angel Urquart, and I'm not actually here to enjoy myself, just to work.' She failed to inject any warmth or animation into her voice, but she managed to deliver the comment with composure. *You're doing well, Angel,* she told herself as she clenched her fingers tight, driving her nails into the softness of her palms.

Now he wasn't touching her she was able to channel some cool of her own. The cool only went skin deep but that didn't matter. What mattered was showing the cheating, lying bastard that there was nothing he could do to hurt her; she had suffered the infection and built up a natural immunity.

'I hope you'll find a little time in your schedule to enjoy what we have to offer, Angelina.'

The predatory gleam in his heavy-lidded eyes shouldn't have shocked her and definitely shouldn't have produced a hot ache at the juncture of her thighs but it did both.

Why surprise? she asked herself. *You jumped into bed with him after five seconds six years ago. Why wouldn't he file you under the heading marked convenient, easy, or most likely both, since you've clearly fulfilled both from his point of view?*

Pushing away the wave of shame, she embraced the anger coursing through her veins. Smiling, she shook back her dark hair and adopted a dumb expression.

'It's Angel, and I'm not actually big on multitasking.' She was confident she could crush his expectations. She might even enjoy doing so. 'You have a beautiful home.'

A home, a wife and to her knowledge at least one child, her child. But for all she knew there could be more, possibly a dozen children…? Did Jasmine have half-sisters, half-brothers…? Not a possibility Angel had considered before, and not one she wanted to consider now!

'This isn't my home. It's a hotel, Miss Urquart.' He paused, the line between his dark brows deepening as he scanned her face. She had gone pale, her full pink lips were blanched of colour and she looked as though she was about to pass out.

'Are you feeling all right?' She heard him ask with more irritation than concern. The rushing sound in her ears made her think of the ocean, which along with a couple of continents was what she needed to put between this man and her before she felt all right. But failing that… She snatched a glass from the tray of a passing waiter, but didn't hold on to it for long.

'I don't think that's a good idea, do you?'

Her green eyes fluttered wide and she stared with utter astonishment as in a seamless motion he tipped the contents of the untouched glass he had taken from her fingers into a flower arrangement. Her jaw dropped as she felt her temper fizz. This man was totally unbelievable!

'What do you think you're doing?' The words didn't deliver the verbal punch she had intended. Instead her voice had a breathy, vulnerable quality. Teeth clenched, she continued to glare up at him, dabbing her tongue to the beads of sweat that clustered along her upper lip. She rubbed a hand across her forearm and found her skin was moist but cold.

He did not enter the debate but, after subjecting her to a narrow-eyed scrutiny, concluded with an air of resignation, 'You need some fresh air.' When he had contemplated her horizontal, a dead faint and ambulances had not entered the picture. So much for a little light flirtation. Alex preferred the woman in his bed to be sober and fully conscious!

He kept telling her what she needed—that night he had known what she'd needed before she had, and he had given it to her. She stiffened as she felt a hand in the middle of her back.

'What do you think you're doing?'

'You are repeating yourself and, in reply... Excuse me...' The small group parted like the sea in response to his soft-voiced request. 'I am saving you from yourself.'

You're six years too late for that, she thought, deciding that struggling to evade him would just draw people's attention. As it was she was conscious in the periphery of her vision of a few curious looks as they moved towards the door.

Outside he spoke to a hovering member of staff and a chair appeared. He pressed her down into it. 'Better?'

She nodded and turned her face to the sea breeze. 'It was a bit warm in there.' Actually it was warmer outside but she no longer felt as if the room were closing in on her. Once her head stopped spinning and the tightness in her chest eased she would be fine. 'Thank you. Don't let me keep you from your guests.'

CHAPTER THREE

'YOU ARE BEING irritatingly childish.'

This lofty condemnation brought her head up with a jerk…mistake! Angel closed her eyes and waited for the world to stop spinning, opening them a moment later when she found a glass placed at her lips. She responded to the terse instruction to drink; the alternative would have been choking because he did not have what could be termed a gentle bedside manner!

She turned her head away and mumbled, 'Enough.'

'You are welcome.' He watched as she dabbed the back of her hand to the excess moisture on her lips and his focus slipped as the memory surfaced of them softening and parting beneath his. The muscles in his angular jaw tensed and the sinews in his neck stood out as he forcibly ejected the memory, but not before he heard the throaty sound of her plea—*please*…!

That husky plea had been all it had taken to silence the voice in his head, the one that had been telling him he ought not to be doing this.

He had done it and he wanted to, needed to, again. The struggle then like now had been to keep his passion on a leash. Something about this woman seemed to tap directly into his primal instincts.

'What happened in there?'

My past came back to bite me. 'Other than you over-reacting,' she accused him, not willing to admit how close she had come to passing out in public. 'I've told you it w—'

His cold eyes narrowed with irritation as he cut across her impatiently. 'It wasn't the heat.'

She narrowed her eyes and fixed him with a glare. Anyone with an ounce of sensitivity would have tact-fully gone along with the heat excuse and not pried and prodded. 'Do we have to have a post-mortem? I got a bit light-headed. It happens. Now I feel much better. I'll have an early night.'

Perhaps the problem was that she had had too many early nights… The thought did not improve his frame of mind. While he was not looking for a long-running thing—there seemed little point waiting for boredom to set in, as it always did—he did like exclusivity.

He was not a possessive man but sharing was a deal breaker.

'It does not happen for no reason.'

Angel started to feel guilty as he continued to scruti-nise her face as though he would find the answer there.

'Will you stop looking at me like that?' she husked. 'You're making me feel like a criminal. I haven't bro-ken any law.'

'Are you sure?'

'I think I'd have remembered.'

'Have you taken anything?'

Still taking breaths of fresh air to clear the muzzi-ness in her head, she flashed him a confused look, then, as his meaning suddenly dawned on her, lost all colour. The heat returned in a searing wave of outrage until her smooth cheeks glowed.

And the insults just kept coming!

'You're accusing me of being a...a...a...junkie!' And then he had the cheek to look astonished when she got upset. This man really was outrageous, she fumed.

He felt relief. Her outrage might be a case of the lady protested too much but his instincts told him otherwise. 'No need to overreact.'

She clenched her teeth. The pat-you-on-the-head, patronising quality of his drawled response made her want to scream.

'I'm simply excluding possibilities before I call a doctor.'

Her eyes widened this time in horror. 'I do not need a doctor and I'm not overreacting. I'm reacting to you insulting me, interrogating me...'

'Insult...?' he drawled, his ebony brows lifting at the suggestion. 'It is not exactly unknown in the world you work in for people to...dabble.'

Her mouth twisted into a scornful smile. 'Now, that's what I admire—a man who isn't afraid to generalise or judge from his secure position of moral superiority.'

Alex blinked. She had claws and a mouth on her, this woman—a million miles from the two-dimensional sexy purring kitten of his memory. A slow, contemplative smile spread across his lean, hard face. These changes didn't make her any less attractive, just more of a challenge.

And he had always liked a challenge, or he had once. Recently he had gone for the easy option way too often, as it came with the lack of emotional commitment that was essential to him. To commit yourself to someone and risk losing them, risk losing part of yourself... A man who invited such a thing more than once was to his mind insane.

'You are clearly feeling better. Actually I was thinking prescription drugs. They can react badly when combined with alcohol.' He tilted his head in the direction of the room they had just exited. 'And you were knocking it back a bit in there.'

So not only was she some sort of junkie, he was also calling her a lush!

'Thanks for the advice.' Her green eyes glowed with contempt, aimed partly at herself. This hypocritical self-righteous creep was the man she'd waited for? She gave a short bitter laugh. Had she really been that young and stupid?

'For the record, being a model doesn't mean I'm part of some seedy subculture. I'm used to people making assumptions—the odd male who thinks that because I've advertised underwear I have no problem with being looked at as though I'm a piece of meat on a slab...' She left a significant pause and had the pleasure of seeing a muscle in his lean cheek clench. 'Not one of the perks of the job,' she conceded. 'However, you have taken insults to a new low. For the record, if I want advice on the clean life I wouldn't come to you, Mr Arlov. You're a...a... Not a nice man.' *Not nice? You're so hard core, Angel.* 'You're a rodent!'

As she finished on a breathless note of quivering contempt a memory surfaced as strong as it was unbidden: the ferociously strong lines of his face relaxed in sleep, the long eyelashes softening the angle of his carved cheekbones. Not vulnerable and not soft but more... She had never been able to put a name to the quivering sensation in the pit of her stomach. No more could she now, though she felt it again.

Alex's nostrils flared as he sucked in an outraged breath. He liked feisty but there were limits. 'And you base this opinion on what?'

'That you're a rodent?' She was already regretting the rather limp animal analogy. If there was an animal she would have likened him to it would have been a wolf, with its piercing eyes, sleek, lean body and dangerous bearing. An illicit little shiver slipped slowly like a cold finger down her spine.

'I've always thought rats got a bad press, but not nice? I'm hurt,' he mocked. Alex could live without being thought nice.

'Rodent works for me, but what would you call a married man who sleeps around? For the record, and to save you the effort, these days it takes more than being told someone *needs* me to get me into bed!'

Even if the person saying the words had a voice that was sin itself.

Six years was a long time and people change but this…! 'Thanks for the heads up,' he murmured, adding without missing a beat, 'What does it take?'

She shook her head, playing dumb because it was on the tip of her tongue to admit not much. It was true, and she was ashamed she had recognised him as her moral Achilles the second he had touched her. It had shocked her so deeply it had triggered the… Whatever it had been, Angel remained reluctant to assign a name to what had happened. She was perfectly willing to accept that panic attacks existed; they simply didn't happen to her.

'What does it take to get you into bed these days?' Whatever it was it would definitely be worth the effort. He had not been this hungry for a woman in a long time—if ever.

'I'm curious—do you work at being offensive or are you naturally gifted that way?'

'You didn't answer my question. On second thought,

don't. Let me get there by myself. It will be more satisfying than being fed the answer.'

The colour flew to her face. The effects of his purred
remark on other parts of her anatomy were too mortifying
to think about. 'You're not getting anywhere with me.'

'Oh, well, you know what they say—it's all about the
journey not the destination…' A saying that had always
struck Alex as particularly ridiculous, never more so than
in this context. He had every intention of reaching, enjoying and extracting every atom of pleasure from his destination. The anticipation of sinking into her warm body
and losing himself was strong enough to taste.

She shot him a look of utter disdain. 'Do you ever listen to anything anyone says?'

He elevated a dark brow and gave a slow smile. Without a word he hooked his hand behind her head and
dragged her face up to his. The action was deceptive,
the kiss druggingly deep, his tongue sliding between
her parted lips while his firm mouth fitted perfectly over
hers. Angel registered the heat that was everywhere; she
heard the almost feral low moan but didn't connect the
sound with herself.

When it stopped and she managed to prise her heavy
eyelids open she found herself looking up into a pair of
blazing cosmic-blue eyes. So dizzy she staggered, she
gave a choked gasp of horror and stepped backwards,
once, twice and amazingly stayed on her feet.

'The truth?'

As if she were emerging from a nightmare—one she
had shamefully fully cooperated with and not struggled
to escape—Angel fixed her blazing eyes on his face,
swallowed a bolus of acrid self-disgust and wiped her
hand across her pumped-up plump lips. Where was
her self-respect? Where was her pride? When this man

touched her she stopped being… She stopped being herself and became someone that scared her, someone whose actions she couldn't predict.

She took a deep restorative breath; she would not fall apart. Yes, he'd like to… But no way. He was acting as if it was no big deal and so could she. It was just a pity the message of defiance had not reached her trembling limbs or core temperature.

'You,' she contended contemptuously, 'wouldn't know the truth if it bit you!' Rich coming from someone who wasn't telling him he had a daughter, or couldn't admit she wouldn't fight too hard if he decided to kiss her again. She lowered her eyes over the shamed acknowledgment and heard his throaty chuckle.

'The truth is I'm more into body language.' Especially when the body in question was as lush and perfectly formed as hers. 'Words can lie…whereas there are some things that you can't hide….'

Her head came up with a guilty jerk. 'I'm not trying to hide anything.' The moment the words left her lips she knew silence would have been more convincing.

'For instance, your pupils have expanded so much there is just a thin ring of colour left.' Her eyes were the purest green he had ever seen flecked with tiny pinpoints of swirling gold. 'You really are a very good kisser.'

So long as his observations did not drop below neck level she could deal. 'Kissing is not hard.' It was the knowing when not to that was hard. 'It's a…a…reflex,' she flung back.

His ebony brows lifted. 'I've never heard it called that before.'

Hating the smugness in his voice, she snapped. 'You think you know body language? Well, study this,' she invited, pointing to her own face, pale now and set into a cold mask. 'I was ill in that room because I saw you and was reminded of an episode in my life I'm not too proud of, in fact I'm deeply ashamed of.'

'That's your problem, not mine.' Shame and guilt were not to his mind something to be yelled about. They were things you lived with; they were the price you paid for mistakes.

Angel drew in a deep shuddering breath and revealed the ultimate unforgivable crime that she laid at his door. 'You turned me into the other woman.' Her voice dropped to an emotional whisper as she realised. 'You turned me into the person I never wanted to be—my mother!'

Alex's jaw clenched but his anger almost immediately faded. He was very good at reading body language but it did not require his talent to interpret the expression in her emerald eyes as shock.

So Angel had mother issues? That was not his problem, and he had no interest in helping her work her way through them. He refused to recognise an uncharacteristic urge to draw out more details, an urge that directly contradicted his determined lack of interest.

Six years, Angel, but you got there in the end. How could she not have seen it before? *'Madre di Dio!'* she mocked softly, then gave a little laugh.

The throaty exclamation distracted him. 'Italian?'

She blinked as it took her a few moments to return from wherever she had gone. 'Half.' She didn't elaborate. It seemed, Angel thought grimly, that she had done too much show and tell already!

Economy of detail was something Alex appreciated in his lovers, actively encouraged, but even he liked a whole sentence.

Well, at least the Latin connection explained the golden glowing looks, and possibly the temper too, though if he said so she would probably not waste the opportunity to accuse him of generalising.

'I've heard of people rewriting history but this is the first time I've seen it firsthand. You're acting as though you were some passive victim. The way I recall it you were an equal and active participant, so the outraged-virgin act is a bit over the top.' Although amazingly she retained the ability to blush like one—the colour that washed over her cheeks deepened the pale gold of her skin with a rosy sheen. 'This can't be the first time you've bumped into an old one-night stand?'

Her eyes slid from his as she swallowed the insult, though she doubted he had intended it as such. He wasn't making a moral judgement. That was just who he thought she was. It was easier to let him continue to hold that opinion than tell him the truth.

What would be his reaction, she wondered, if she came out with, 'You're the only man I've ever slept with'? She almost laughed at the image of his imagined incredulity. Or worse, he might ask her the question she'd asked herself a thousand times—why him?

How could she begin to explain to him something she didn't even understand herself?

She made herself look at him and felt her insides shudder as their eyes connected. 'One like you.'

In case he decided to construe her comment as a compliment she added coldly, 'One who made me feel… cheap.' Feeling this was an admission too far, she dodged his gaze and missed the expression that flickered across his lean face. When she raised her eyes his face was stone. 'I may just be a model, which clearly in your eyes makes me a pill-popping bimbo—' she took a deep breath and made a conscious effort to control her indignation '—but I don't sleep with married men!'

Her shrill accusations might not have touched him but this last quiet comment did. 'I'm not married now.'

Was that meant to make her feel better? Or was it a lie to get her into bed? Angel told herself she didn't want to know; all she wanted was to get out of here and away from him.

'Now, why doesn't that surprise me?' she drawled. 'I really hope she took you for a lot of money...' His bank balance was probably the only vulnerable area he had, she thought bitterly.

'She's dead.'

The blunt pronouncement drew a gasp from Angel, who immediately felt like a total bitch. So this was what it felt like to have the rug pulled out from under your feet.

During the ensuing silence the mortified colour flew to her cheeks and then receded. What was she meant to say that didn't sound trite and insincere?

'Oh!'

Before she had said anything more the uniformed employee who had brought her the chair reappeared, this time carrying a tray with a cafetière and coffee cups, and at a nod from Alex he placed it on the table.

The young man spoke in Greek and Alex Arlov responded in the same language.

Questions flying around in her head, Angel watched as he poured the coffee and pushed one her way without asking. Had he loved his wife?

His expression wasn't giving any clues and in her book a man who loved his wife was not unfaithful. *But that's just me, the idealist,* she thought with a wry grimace.

'Do you want sugar?'

Angel, who hadn't been aware she'd been stirring the coffee, put the spoon down with a clatter in the saucer and shook her head. 'No, I don't take it.'

He had slept around, but she supposed that some men did and some women put up with infidelity or didn't know. It was weird to her— Actually, no, it was utterly abhorrent, but marriage meant different things to different people.

'I'm sorry, I didn't know about your wife or I wouldn't have said...what I did.' Then, aware that her comment might come across as hypocritical, she added, 'Even if it is true.'

Had the poor woman lived her life in ignorant bliss, or turned a blind eye, or had she known and cared and suffered the humiliation...? Angel didn't know which scenario was worse.

She tore her eyes from his handsome patrician profile and thought how hellish it must be to be married to a man that other women lusted after. That was one hell she was never going to know about.

Marriage to any man was not on the cards for her. These days, when it was easy to live together—and even easier to drift apart—it seemed to Angel that desire to raise a family was one of the main reasons that couples made their relationship official.

For her there would be no more children. There had been a time when the knowledge had made her sad... angry...filled with a 'why me?' self-pity, but now she had reached a stage of why not me? She had accepted it, and could not imagine a man or a circumstance that would make her walk down the aisle.

She had not discounted the possibility in the future of a man, someone nice who Jasmine liked, someone who didn't make any demands. She could live without head-banging sex but a hug would be nice, and stability. She could remember craving boring stability when she was a

child and envying her friends who had complained about
the boredom of the things she had longed for.

The expressions scudding like clouds across her face
made him wonder what thoughts were responsible for
putting that pensive look in her eyes. Then, catching
himself wondering, he experienced a flash of irritation.

It seemed a good moment to remind himself that he
wanted to bed her, not know how her mind worked.

'I seem to have put a damper on the conversation.'

Her green eyes lifted from the contemplation of the
untouched swirling liquid. 'Sorry if I'm not amusing you.'
Presumably, she brooded, he was one of those men who
expected women to tie themselves into knots being interesting and amusing. 'And we were not having a conversation.' Her eyes lowered towards her coffee and lifted
again suddenly. It was as if her resolve not to show any
interest broke at the last moment. 'Was it… Your wife…
Did she… Did it happen recently?'

'No, it didn't.'

When he offered no further information Angel took
a sip of the coffee and looked at him over the rim of her
cup. 'It must be hard bringing up children alone…?' she
murmured, trying hard not to look like someone who had
a stake in his response.

Was Jasmine an only child or did she have half siblings?
The brother or sister that Angel had always felt vaguely
guilty for not supplying. Siblings looked out for one another when things got tough. If she vanished… Angel gave
herself a sharp internal shake. Nothing was going to happen to her, and if it did she had things organised. But a
father had not featured in those arrangements.

Of course, if it turned out he had his own family he
might not be interested in pursuing a relationship with
Jasmine anyway. His loss, though from a selfish point of

view it would make life simpler. She felt a stab of guilt.
This wasn't about simple, this was about what was best
for Jasmine, and if that involved allowing her father to
be part of her life she would move heaven and earth to
make it happen. He was right; she was no innocent victim. If she hadn't thrown herself at him the way she had
none of this would have happened.

She pressed her fingers to her temples. Her head felt
as if it would explode with all the unanswered questions
swirling round in it, and there were not going to be any
of the answers she wanted until she told him.

'We didn't have any children.'

They had planned to have a family but not immediately. Of course, it had seemed as if they would have all
the time in the world, then all too soon they had had none.
A blessing, Emma, struggling to come to terms with the
rapid progress of her illness, had said, but as her denial
had turned to deep depression she had become angry and
blamed him for... Well, pretty much everything, until it
had reached the point when she had turned her head to
the wall when he walked into the room.

The doctors had sympathised and called it transfer-
ence. His wife, they said, was transferring all the guilt
she felt for concealing her illness when they married onto
to him, and as they had predicted the phase passed. But
to his way of thinking what followed was harder. Emma
had been consumed with guilt. The precious time they'd
had left together had been dominated by it.

Angel lowered her eyes but not before he glimpsed the
moisture lingering there and her expression. He reacted to
the sympathy he loathed using a tried-and-tested method
to kill off the pity that made his skin crawl.

'Turn down the empathy, Angel. I'm not a candidate
for a sympathy shag,' he drawled.

Her appalled eyes flew to his face, suddenly minus
their emotional moisture. 'You are a candidate for a kick,'
she retorted, adding in a conversational tone, 'You really can be vile.' She was almost immediately hit by a
wave of remorse, so added, 'I am genuinely sorry about
your wife.'

'But I'm vile—a rodent, yes, I get that.' The tension
vanishing from his manner along with her sympathy, he
produced a mocking grin. 'I'm enjoying living down to
your expectations of me. Relax,' he advised, 'I do not require a shoulder to cry on.' Though a warm breast to lay
his head against would not be rejected. The one in question rose and fell revealing a glitter of something shiny
in the deep valley.

'I was not about to offer one.' Offering anything to
the only man you had ever fantasised about lying naked
beneath was something to be actively avoided. She swallowed hard and dropped her gaze, wishing she had not
thought about being naked. 'And I have no expectations.'

'But some curiosity.' The speculation was pretty much
proved when she couldn't meet his eyes. 'Don't feel bad.
Everyone wants to ask. Few do—death is one of those
subjects that people tiptoe around. Emma died of MS,
an aggressive form she had been ill with for some time.'

Angel could only marvel that he could sound so de-
tached while revealing this tragic sequence of events. For
all the emotion he was displaying he could have been re-
counting the story of a stranger's life.

'It was lucky we had no children.' He sketched a sardonic smile. 'Now your turn…?'

She got that he rejected sympathy—hard not to—but
she felt it anyway, a strong surge of empathy that she
couldn't repress. She would have felt the same for anyone
in his situation; the difference was she hadn't spent the

past six years hating anyone. Not to do so, even briefly, felt odd…uncomfortable, and required some major mental readjustment.

'One.' She couldn't pretend that Jasmine didn't exist.

He stiffened. 'In most countries that is all a person can have at one time.' The joke, it seemed, was on him. Why the hell hadn't she just told him she was married up front?

Why didn't you consider the possibility, Alex?

Her bewildered-sounding response cut across his inner dialogue. 'One…?'

'You're not wearing a ring,' he clenched out, feeling cheated.

Anchoring her hair against a sudden flurry of wind, she followed the direction of his gaze and drew the hand down to look at it, turning it over as she blew away the errant raven strands that immediately plastered themselves across her face. She was of the school of thought that said less was more when it came to jewellery and she rarely wore rings when working. Her hand went to her neck where she wore her father's signet ring on a chain. Her brother had inherited a Scottish estate complete with castle, and she, being a woman, had got only the ring. She didn't resent it half as much as her brother felt guilty about it.

'Why should I…?' She stopped as the penny dropped. 'God, not a husband! I have a child, a daughter.'

This was only slightly less astonishing to him than her having a husband. His eyes went to the fingers that were rubbing the chain she wore around her neck. Through her fingers he recognised the disc he had initially taken for a pendant nestled between her breasts as a ring.

'You have a baby?' His eyes drifted down her slim body and he felt a kick of lust that made his strong-boned features clench.

Title Page

Hard not to recognise this as the perfect opportunity to speak. *So why aren't you, Angel?*

We have a baby. It didn't matter how hard she tried, Angel couldn't visualise his reaction to this bombshell.

'She's hardly a baby.' Her expression softened. Jasmine had been a lovely baby, though it might have been easier to enjoy her loveliness if she had ever slept. The first eighteen months had passed in a blur of sleep deprivation.

'But she must be young, and you're a single parent...?' Did the ring have some significance? A token from the father?

Angel instantly prickled with antagonism; her chin went up. She was pretty secure when it came to her parenting skills, able to shrug off and smile her way through well-meaning advice, but when the source of the criticism was the absent father of her daughter it turned out she couldn't.

'Yes, I am, and I really don't think my childcare arrangements are your concern,' she tossed back, realising as she spoke that this situation might change very soon. When he knew he might think that he should have a say. The idea appalled her.

Blinking at the level of belligerence in her attitude, he made a pacifying gesture with his hands. Her eyes followed the gesture—he had lovely hands.

'I am hardly an expert on the subject.'

He watched as her hunched shoulders flattened. He could almost feel her willing the tension away. Her tense smile was a clear effort and she avoided his eyes. 'That doesn't stop most people offering advice.'

'Is her father involved?'

Angel couldn't look at him. Lucky thing she was sitting down because her knees were shaking. 'No.'

'I imagine it can't be easy…?'

He imagined right, but Angel would not have it any other way. The sleepless nights were more than compensated for in a million other ways. 'I make it work.'

'I'm sure you do.'

Again, she couldn't take his comment at face value. 'And no, I'm not naive enough to think a single working parent can have it all, but I don't want it all.'

From this defiant statement he read that she wanted it but couldn't have it. The idea that the father was unavailable, most likely married, seemed a real contender. Funny how some women were drawn to unavailable men…. Was she one of them?

'We all want some things more than others.' And at that moment all he wanted, wanted so much he could taste it, was this provoking, dark-haired, green-eyed witch. His innate ability to distance himself from a situation had failed him completely—he wanted her under him, he wanted to be inside her and he knew he wasn't going to have a moment's peace until he had achieved this desire.

The expression in his eyes stopped her asking what it was he wanted more than other things. The expression in his blue eyes was explicit enough to cause a head-on collision between a fist of some unidentifiable emotion and her solar plexus.

She got to her feet. 'Well, thanks for the coffee and the little chat but I'm fine now.'

'I'll walk you back to your bungalow.'

A cold fist of fear tightened in her belly as Angel realised that she wanted to say yes. When she recognised how much she wanted to say yes the fist tightened even more.

She tossed back her hair and made her voice cold.

'That will be quite unnecessary and I'm not going back to my bungalow. I'm going back to the party.' A room full of people no longer seemed a bad thing; she didn't want to be alone with her thoughts.

'If it makes you feel any better, Emma, my wife, died several weeks before we slept together.'

The words stopped her in her tracks. She shook her head. Was she being slow...? 'You expect that to make me feel better?'

He had, but it was fairly obvious he had been wrong. 'I thought you had a right to know.' The comment had not sounded so lame or pompous in his head.

'But not before I spent six years worrying that I'd turned into my mother. Why on earth did you say you were married?'

'I didn't say, you assumed.'

'And you didn't put me right. Why... Oh, you... Oh...' Comprehension flickered into her eyes. 'It was the quickest way to get rid of me...?'

'I have a distaste of scenes.'

She sucked in a deep breath through flared nostrils. Hearing the beat of helicopter blades somewhere in the distance she could only hope that they were here to whisk him away. 'I'm going back into the party—your party, so I can't stop you coming too, but if you pester me so help me I'll report you to the hotel management for harassment and I don't care who it upsets!'

Not him, if his expression was any indicator. 'I can speak for the management when I say that we take all complaints very seriously.'

'We?' She shook her head. 'This hotel is part of the Theakis group.' Her frown deepened as his firm lips twitched. 'What is so funny? Don't you believe I would?'

'Oh, I believe you would follow through with any rash

threat you make. But before you do I should explain that my grandfather was Spyros Theakis, Angelina. I *am* the Theakis group and speaking in that role I can assure you we take all such complaints very seriously.'

The realisation hit Angel like a stone. Having deflated her, he strode off in the opposite direction without another word or backwards glance.

CHAPTER FOUR

ANGEL STAYED AT the party for another hour but by the time she reached her room her headache had become a full-blown migraine. At least it meant she wasn't going to lie awake going over the events of this evening. Instead, she was going to lie awake waiting for the medication, which she always carried with her, to kick in, willing herself not to throw up while she tried to ignore the vice crushing her skull and the metronome inside it.

Wow, it was a win-win situation!

She did throw up. In fact she spent half the night with her head in the toilet. It had been after four when she had finally crawled back to bed and fallen asleep, a fact that resulted in her spending an age in Make-up—or maybe that was normal for film? Angel didn't have a clue and as she stepped out in front of the camera she was very conscious of her inexperience.

She told herself that no one wanted her to fail, but she could imagine a few people might be amused if she did. As it was, she didn't mess up. Apparently the first full morning's filming had gone well, though to Angel the progress had seemed torturously slow.

She said as much to her co-star, if that was the right description of the actor who was to play opposite her in the soap-style series of adverts.

'Take up knitting like me, darling,' he advised.

'How long do you think we have for lunch?'

'In my humble opinion...' he began.

Angel couldn't not smile. In her opinion Clive didn't have a humble bone in his body.

'All right, not so humble.' He might not do humble, but he did have a sense of humour. 'We have finished for the day.'

It turned out he was right.

Angel had already checked it out so she knew that the narrow strait of water that separated the private island from the hotel beach was safe. So when she declined a seat on the boat in favour of swimming the short distance her co-star responded in much the same way he had when he'd found her reading a book.

'For pleasure?'

Angel, who knew he had a post-grad degree, suspected he was never off duty, always playing his part as the pretty-but-dim public school boy that most of his well-paid Hollywood roles had involved him playing.

The deep turquoise water was warm and Angel, who was a strong swimmer, was a couple hundred yards from the beach when she stopped and began to tread water, watching the people on the beach before flipping onto her back to float lazily.

It was the angry metallic buzz sound of the Jet Ski that made her lift her head. If she hadn't she wouldn't have seen the kid who had obviously drifted out farther than he intended on an inflatable toy, and she watched in horror as he fell off into the path of the Jet Ski.

Two things became immediately obvious. One, he couldn't swim very well and two, the driver of the Jet Ski couldn't see him.

Her yelled warning alerted the people on the shore, several of whom entered the water shouting, but the Jet

Ski rider remained oblivious and she was a hell of a lot closer than anyone else.

With a pounding front crawl that left her breathless, Angel managed to get to the child and make sure he stayed afloat. But it became harder to stay that way when the boy let go of the inflatable and transferred his hold to her neck, gripping tightly. Pulled under without a chance to fill her lungs, she surfaced a few moments later with the kid latched on like a limpet only to see the Jet Ski heading right for them.

At the last moment she pushed the kid's face into her shoulder and closed her eyes, not perhaps the most practical response, but it worked to the extent that they were still alive when she opened them. Though this was, it turned out, less to do with her closed eyes and more to do with the Jet Ski rider seeing them at the last moment.

He swerved and didn't quite miss them. But her shoulder only took a glancing blow, which she barely noticed, as at this point she was busy struggling to stay afloat. The kid was half strangling her with his grip, and the close encounter with the Jet Ski had seriously freaked him out so he had begun kicking out wildly with his legs.

The relief when a speedboat pulled up alongside and someone hauled him up out of her arms was intense.

'Thank you so much.' Her grateful waterlogged smile faded slightly when she saw the owner of the hand she had grabbed gratefully on to, his face a dark shadow against the sun shining directly into her eyes. But there was no mistaking his identity.

She landed in the boat in a staggeringly inelegant, breathless heap and crawled onto a bench seat.

'You're all right?'

'Fine,' she lied, finding herself nodding meekly in response to his stern, 'Don't move.' As if she could have if she'd wanted to!

* * *

Alex didn't trust himself to respond to this patent lie and maintained his silence on the way back to shore, choosing not to compete with the boy, who was now bawling in his ear very loudly.

'I want my mum.'

'She is welcome to you.'

Angel gasped. 'Don't be so mean. Can't you see that the poor thing is upset?'

He was upset! Alex was pretty sure that watching her swim directly into the path of that Jet Ski had taken six months off his life. Angel, on the evidence so far, was not destined to make it to thirty!

'I can *hear* that he's upset,' Alex retorted grimly, holding the kid with one hand and steering the boat with the other. He flashed her a look of irritation and snarled, 'Will you sit still? Because if you fall out, so help me I'll let you drown. In all my life I have never witnessed such a reckless, suicidal, stupid action!' he raged. 'Every time I see you, you are trying to kill yourself!'

Before she could defend herself against this unjust attack he cut the engine and the people who had waded out into the shallows were there, arms outstretched, to deliver the boy to his mother.

A young man wearing the logo of the hotel on his polo shirt and a label that identified him as a lifeguard on his cap climbed into the boat and, after speaking to Alex, took the wheel.

Alex himself peeled off his own shirt, dived neatly into the water from the far side of the boat and vanished under it before appearing on the shore side where the water reached his waist.

Hair slicked wetly back, looking like some impossibly perfect front cover of a men's health magazine, he squinted up at Angel, water streaming down his brown face. 'Do you want someone to take you to the marina or...?' He held out a hand.

She treated his offer of assistance from the boat with a look of cold disdain, though as she lowered herself into the water the pain in her shoulder made her wish she had swallowed her pride.

He didn't turn back once to see if she was managing so it became a matter of pride that she stay on her feet even though a delayed reaction to the drama was beginning to set in.

When she reached the shore slightly distant from the group around the child and his family, she watched Alex in action. He took charge, of course he did—it was clearly second nature to him. He was just one of those individuals people naturally turned to in times of crisis and he was good, she had to admit, as she watched him soothe, calm and casually issue instructions.

It was curious that the father of the child who had up until that moment held it together broke down and started weeping, almost as if Alex's competence gave him permission to fall apart. At that point his wife stopped crying and began berating their son, who had been on the point of enjoying all the attention.

'If it hadn't been for that lady.... She's a heroine.'

Someone clapped and someone else picked it up, then with a chain-reaction effect the ripple spread and everyone was clapping.

Angel, whose entire attention had been focused on Alex—she might even have had her mouth open—became belatedly aware of people looking in her general direction, and looked around expecting to see the heroine referred to until the penny dropped.... *Oh, God!*

With heaven-sent timing the shaken driver of the Jet

Ski chose this moment to wade ashore and, taking advantage of the distraction afforded by his appearance, Angel headed for the rocky area that shielded the main beach from the smaller, quieter cove at the far end. She gave a quick furtive look over her shoulder before she waded through the water and then down onto the beach the other side of the rocky outcrop.

The small cove was empty, and with a sigh of relief Angel flopped down onto the sand, her closed eyelids filtering out some of the brutal midday sun. It wasn't until she stretched out that she realised she wasn't only shaking on the inside but on the outside too, fine tremors that shook her entire body.

She lay still and waited for it to pass, nursing her head, which, still tender from the previous night, had begun to throb gently. Great, she needed that like a… Actually a hole in the head might relieve the pressure she could feel building.

Alex was probably the only one who had seen her slip away. He was definitely the only one to follow her. The idea of her acting like some sort of injured animal, crawling away to lick its wounds, made him furious. The woman had the self-preservation instincts of a lemming.

He clambered over the rocks, not around them, to reach the empty cove. There was a very good reason it was empty at this time of day. The water Angel had waded through was already waist deep and in another ten minutes it would be cut off from the bigger beach. Swimming around or a trek through the pine-forested strip that edged the sand were the only ways back to the hotel, a fact that was written in red letters a mile high on signs along the beach.

When he spotted her stretched out on the sand he hit the ground running, then stopped as he saw her chest lift, her breasts pushing against the black fabric of her bikini top.

At the best of times—which this was not—Alex was not well schooled in compassionate concern; he lacked the finesse and the patience. Yet as he reached the spot where she lay and looked down at her he felt his anger slip away. In his head he saw her face when she had realised the applause was for her. Many people dreamed of earning such plaudits, of being hailed a hero, but she had looked…stunned, horrified. It would have been the prefect punishment to have drawn her in to take a curtain bow, but the hunted expression on her face as she had slipped away had made him repress the malicious impulse.

Lying there, she managed to simultaneously look as sexy as hell and damned, throat-achingly vulnerable.

'Are you all right?' Concern added a layer of gravel to his deep voice.

She didn't leap out of her skin, but only because she had felt his shadow blocking the sun a fraction of a second before he spoke. Still stinging from his unfair comments in the boat, she imagined the expression of impatience on his lean face. In her head she could see him glancing at his watch, thinking, *That bloody woman again!*

She raised herself onto her elbows but didn't lift her gaze. 'I'm fine,' she said, arching her foot to rub the sand off one foot with the red-painted toes of the other.

His eyes on the top of her dark head, he wondered how she managed to make the assurance sound much the same as *go away*—it was a talent. He was sorely tempted to do just that. If she was so determined to put herself in a hospital, who was he to stop her?

Unaware that he had chosen that moment to drop

gracefully into a squatting position beside her, Angel started to sit upright. The near collision of their heads drew a tiny gasp of alarm from her throat. Rocking back on his heels, he remained, from Angel's point of view, far too close!

He still didn't have his shirt on, and he made her think of a particularly sexy pirate. How embarrassing that she couldn't stop staring at his chest; her eyes were welded there.

'I'm fine,' she croaked, thinking this comment had rarely in her life been less true.

'You're working on the theory that if you say it more than once it makes it so.' He didn't sound amused; he sounded exasperated.

'It *is* so.' Teeth pressing into the pink softness of her full lower lip, she finally managed to drag her eyes upwards and discovered that he wasn't looking impatient or even angry. He was looking worried and concerned, and instead of being mollified by the discovery she was thrown into an instant state of heart-pounding confusion. With Alex it seemed a condition she spent about ninety per cent of her time in.

From the tangled muddle of emotions lodged like a heavy stone in her chest, anger and resentment dissolved. Without them she felt oddly defenceless; she didn't know how to deal with his concern. *Who are you kidding, Angel? You don't know how to deal with him full stop!* The man was the father of her child and he was a total stranger—a pulse-racingly disturbing total stranger.

Well, one solution would be to get to know him, she thought. He's right here. Stop snarling and start talking. Was picking fights with him a way that she had subconsciously adopted to delay the moment she told him about

Jasmine? She tried to push the idea away but it lingered…
as did the scent of his soap in her nostrils.

'I really am all right. I was just escaping the fuss….
How about the boy?'

'He doesn't seem any the worse for the experience,'
Alex commented drily. 'He was posing for photos when
I left…. What's wrong?'

'Nothing.'

'You winced.'

She expelled an exasperated sigh of surrender and
snapped. 'My head hurts. It's nothing.' Compared to last
night it was true. She turned her head, giving a little grunt
of relief when she saw that the skin on her shoulder was
not broken. It was sore, though.

Growing irritation made his jaw clench again. She had
managed to make it sound as if it were his fault.

'Let me see.'

She turned her head away. 'No, I didn't hit it. I just
have a headache.'

'Headaches don't leave bruises.' His long brown fingers, their touch delicate but firm, pushed aside the sat-
urated strands of hair from her forehead, causing her
eyes to fly wide and green to his face, the frantic fluttering sensation that began in the pit of her stomach and
spread hot and dangerously fast making her pull away
while she could.

The subsequent jolt caused her bruised shoulder to
ache.

'Leave me alone.'

The words mocked Alex even as her belligerent emerald eyes taunted him.

Leave her alone!

That's your problem, Alex thought grimly. *You can't.*
Six years ago he hadn't been able to and he still

couldn't. From the moment he had seen her he had wanted her and that hunger had not decreased. If anything it had grown and it didn't matter how aggravating, how sheer bloody minded she was, no negative was negative enough to make him any less hot for her.

Around this woman his self-control was zero. Even the fact she had just been involved in an accident didn't save her from his lust. No, lust he could cope with, but this ability she had to draw emotional responses from him was something he was not willing to recognise, let alone deal with.

'You're bloody lucky all you have is a headache!'

The fresh blast of disapproval hurt but at least it enabled her to throw off the weird feeling of vulnerability.

'Do you have to yell?' She framed a pained furrow between her darkly defined brows. 'I'm not deaf.' Or needy, she reminded herself.

His jaw tightened and the memory of her putting herself between the blades of the Jet Ski and the child resurfaced to increase his rage. 'Do you ever think about the consequences of your actions?'

It was the consequences of both their actions that she had been living with for six years. 'I accept them,' she told him quietly. 'How about you?' Well, she was going to find out the answer to that one very soon.

He ignored the wry interjection and barely registered her sudden look of panic. 'We are not talking about me. I'm talking about your publicity-seeking stunt.'

Her temper fizzed. 'A stunt! You think I arranged that?'

Alex didn't, but the thought had flashed through his mind. 'No, I don't think you've got the brains....' he admitted, an edge of weariness entering his voice as he added, 'Do you ever think before you leap or jump?'

She fixed him with an evil-eyed stare. 'You're right,
I didn't think. Story of my life!' She sniffed. 'If I had
thought, do you think I'd have wasted my virginity on a
selfish, lying bastard who let me think he was married
just to get out the door?'

She closed her eyes to blot out the expression stamped
on his face. The man didn't just look shocked, he looked
as though someone had aimed a loaded revolver at him
and pulled the trigger.

The words didn't just hang in the air, they vibrated,
the volume growing with each beat of her heart. Unfortunately, there was no way she could retrieve them because, true to form, she'd done it again. She'd blurted
out the truth at the worst moment imaginable. *Way to
go, Angel, out to personally disprove the old adage that
wisdom came with age.*

CHAPTER FIVE

'YOU'RE TRYING TO tell me... No... No, you were not a virgin!' Even as Alex voiced the denial his brain was making connections that he couldn't believe he hadn't seen before.

''Course not. What can I say? I have a sick sense of humour.'

Angel's eyes were closed, squeezed tight like a little kid who thought the action made her invisible.

'You were.' He dragged a hand through his hair and got to his feet, walking several steps away before stalking back to stand over her. 'You were a virgin, and you acted like a damned...'

'Damned what?' she challenged, getting to her feet.

He just looked at her and shook his head, groaning. *'Theos!'*

She shrugged, wrapping her arms around herself, cold despite the afternoon heat. Shock, she speculated, viewing the tremors that were shaking her body with a weird objectivity. The genie was out of the bottle, the truth was out there and she couldn't get it back, so she did the only thing possible—she downplayed it like mad!

'Let's not make a big deal of it. A girl's got to lose it some time.'

'You think this is a subject for cheap jokes? It *was* a

big deal. It *is* a big deal—to me and it should be to you.'
He hadn't even been Emma's first lover, and it had not
been important to him. For some men perhaps there was
an appeal in teaching a novice the ropes, but it was a responsibility that he would have actively avoided had the
opportunity ever arisen. It hadn't—or so he had thought.

'I'm sorry if my ability to laugh at ancient history of-
fends you, but it was a long time ago and life moves on.'
And it also occasionally threw some surprises, and the
surprise today was the strength of Alex's reaction to the
news. He was still pale beneath his tan. 'There has to be
a first time for everyone—it's the second time that can
be more problematic.' She cleared her throat and, regretting the reference to her nonexistent sex life, hurriedly
tacked on a laughing, 'Even you.'

She lifted her eyes to his face and her smile faded. It
was impossible to imagine Alex being young and inex-
perienced, his face smooth, his eyes without cynicism.

'Why the hell didn't you tell me?' he blasted.

His indignation continued to strike her as pretty per-
verse. 'I don't recall conversation being very high on the
agenda.' She forced the words past the tight constriction
in her throat. 'Would it have made any difference if I'd
told you?'

Alex opened his mouth and closed it again. It was a
good question and he'd have liked to think it would, but
on that day he had not been thinking with his brain.

'I resent being made to feel like some sort of bloody
predator.'

He resented! 'Well, I'm *so* sorry I've made you feel
a victim, but I guess it's a responsibility I'll have to live
with.'

The saccharine insincerity dripping from her sarcastic retort brought a defining flash of colour to the knife-edged contours of his carved cheekbones.

'Did you set out that day with the intention of—?' He bit down on the question, but not soon enough to stop Angel's eyes sparking afresh with anger.

'Sure,' she drawled, disguising her hurt with a sarcastic tone. 'I engineered the whole thing.'

A muscle alongside his mouth clenched as their eyes connected, sizzling blue on flashing green. 'You can't leave anything, can you?' he charged. *Like the fact you acted like a total irresponsible bastard, Alex?* 'I know it wasn't your fault,' he gritted through clenched teeth. 'It was my bloody…' He stopped abruptly. 'You said the *second* time was the problem.' He shook his head, not following the crazy idea to its equally crazy conclusion.

'Did I?' she said, thinking did this man miss nothing? She adopted a sweetly insincere smile and hid behind the truth. 'Oh, yes, you've guessed it. You spoiled me for any other man, Alex.'

Responding to her mockery with a curt, unsmiling, 'Except for the father of your child,' he extended a hand to her.

Staring at the hand, not the man she nodded. 'Oh, yes, there is him.' And there was Jasmine.

And Jasmine's father.

Oh, God! She knew the delay with coming clean was not making things better, quite the opposite, in fact. With a sigh she dropped her head into her hands and began to scrub her eyes with the heels of her palms. She felt a surge of despairing disgust as she asked herself where was the woman who never avoided an awkward issue but met it head on?

As she tilted her head to look at him her hair fell back, revealing the beginning of a bruise on her temple. Staring at the discoloration, Alex felt his stomach muscles lurch and tighten with an emotion as strong as his previous anger and totally inexplicable…. Only a madman would feel protective towards this provocative witch with her smart mouth and her combative attitude.

He was not a madman. It was *her* sanity that was the issue here; *her* insane behaviour was what he was here to challenge, although the conversation had drifted somewhat. *Time to refocus, Alex,* he thought.

'That was a crazy thing you did.' Also brave; the private concession was made reluctantly. It was hard not to admire this woman's fearlessness—at least from a distance. For those close to her it must make life hell, he thought grimly. 'You could have killed yourself….'

He closed his eyes, seeing the scene again and experiencing the same awful sense of helplessness. The memory remained like an icy fist in his chest as he glared at her and spelt out the fact she seemed incapable of grasping. 'You could be dead.'

'I can't die. I have Jasmine,' she asserted confidently. It was a simple fact. Jasmine would have been without a mother and that couldn't happen…. It nearly had!

Like a tower of cards her confidence slipped away. Oh, God, he was right. She was a mother—she couldn't go around leaping in without thinking.

'I'm a terrible mother!'

Hearing the anguished wail and seeing the tears rolling silently down her cheeks cut through the righteous anger that gripped him like a hot blade through butter. He was unable and unwilling to identify the emotion that tightened in his chest as tenderness, but he dropped back down beside her. His time when he touched her she did not pull away as though he were poison. Instead she leaned into him, melted into him softly, shaking her head on his chest.

One moment he was fighting the urge to throttle her, the next he was fighting an equally primal desire to comfort her. His emotions did one of those three-hundred-and-sixty-degree shifts that seemed to happen around her.

'What if—?'

'You have lived to tell the tale. There is no point in what ifs. So how old is she, your daughter… Jasmine?' He spoke not out of genuine interest but a need to distract her. At the same time he ran a soothing hand over her wet hair, lifting it off her neck; the texture of her warm, damp skin beneath fascinated him.

'She's started school. Well, she had.'

'Had?'

'She was off a term as she wasn't well, but she's having some home tutoring and she'll soon catch up. She's smart.'

The audible pride in her muffled response caused his hand to still, though the dark strands of her wet hair remained coiled around his fingers. It was difficult for him to see her as a mother but, he thought to himself, *You don't have the exclusive on family feeling, Alex.*

'She's better now?' he asked, giving her time to regain control.

Angel nodded into his chest. 'I took some time off but this opportunity was too good—' He felt her stiffen before she pulled away from him. Tucking her hair behind her ears, she regarded him with a defiance that was echoed in her addition. 'I suppose you don't think mothers should work?'

She clearly expected his judgement. *And why not, Alex? You've done little else but judge so far.*

Quick to judge and slow to forgive. The words of his

mother, a sad observation that he had lived to understand the meaning of but that had meant little to him when she'd spoken them soon after his half-sister had appeared like a disruptive whirlwind in their lives.

'I know nothing of the pressures of being a mother... or a parent.' His brow creased as he admitted, 'I still struggle to think of you as one.'

'A mother or an actual person, not a body that looks good in a bikini?' Before he could respond to the bitter accusation she added wearily, 'Being a mother is one job where experience is not a prerequisite.'

'There's nothing on your website that mentioned you have a daughter. Is that a professional thing?'

'You're not the only one who likes their privacy.' She blinked her sooty lashes over wide emerald eyes as her voice dropped an astonished husky octave. 'You looked me up?'

'I was curious.'

So was she, and maybe it was the hint of evasiveness in his manner but she suddenly heard herself asking the question that she'd heard many people voice, but that as yet had no satisfactory answer. Everyone had theories but nobody could really understand why they were being allowed access to the private island.

'Why *are* you giving us access to Saronia?' The moment the words left her lips she regretted them, but it was too late to back off. 'They say you've refused royal requests.' Why would a man who'd refused honeymooning royals open his doors—or at least a restricted area of his shoreline—to them?

'Do they?'

She narrowed her eyes. 'You know they do.'

'So what is your theory?'

She lifted a hand to shade her eyes. It was a bit late in

the day to make out that she hadn't thought about it, but she tried anyway. 'I don't have one, but if I had to guess I'd go with those who think it's a bored, rich man's whim, unless you really are thinking of expanding into cosmetics?' Apparently the rumour had gone viral.

'Are you asking for insider information?'

'Hardly. The rumour has already sent the firm's shares through the ceiling. Even we mere models have been known to read the financial pages,' she observed, quite pleased to have surprised him. Her smug grin vanished as he hitched a brow and, holding her eyes with his, touched the sole of her foot with his finger. The light, barely there contact made her stomach dissolve and her toes curl of their own volition.

'Has no one suggested that it is because I wanted to have you at my mercy?'

She fought against the seductive quality of his deep voice, hating that he was mocking her. 'Now, that really would make me feel special.'

He shrugged and grinned. 'No mystery. My nephew asked me to further his career.'

'And you're a very nice uncle who does favours for your nephew?'

'It has been known, but I am an *adequate* uncle. It isn't hard—Nico is a nice kid, and it pays to keep on the right side of my sister, Adriana.'

'Do you have much family?' she asked, thinking to herself, *You have one more than you think.*

'My parents died some time ago in a car accident. I have two sisters.... There is Adriana—she's ten years older than me.' His mobile lips twisted into a half smile as he surprised her by confiding, 'I was an afterthought.'

'This is Nico's mother?'

He tipped his head in acknowledgment. 'Her husband,

Gus, was an international lawyer based in Geneva, but now he runs the Greek operation. They have just the one son.'

'You said you had *two* sisters?'

There was a long pause.

'Lizzie is your age.'

Lizzie did not strike Angel as a very Greek or Russian name. 'I thought you said you were the youngest?'

'Lizzie is my half-sister, the result of an affair— actually a one-night stand.' The small shocked sound that escaped her throat awoke him to the fact that he had just revealed more private details in the past thirty seconds than he had in the past... Actually ever. 'The details are not important.' Just the sort of thing that blew a family apart. 'As I said, she is my half-sister, the baby of the family.'

'And you resent her existence?'

The speculation drew a heavy frown and a flash of anger. 'Nobody in the world could resent Lizzie.' Except his mother, who could have but had not.

The softening in his expression when he spoke of his half-sister could not have been feigned. It could be envied, though she was dismayed to discover she did not envy this girl who brought the warmth to his eyes. One thing Angel did not want to be was his sister!

'So your parents' marriage broke down.' Angel, who knew how that felt, was sympathetic.

Being taken away from the only home she had ever known and the father she had adored at age eight had been a trauma that had stayed with Angel. In her youthful eyes it had seemed as if she was being punished. What other explanation could there be? Her feelings had alternated between guilt for some unknown sin she must have committed and anger at her father for sending her away.

She had been acting up during one of their short visits to their father when her big brother had sat her down and spelled a few facts out.

'You can act like a spoilt brat and ruin our time here or you can enjoy it. This isn't Dad's fault or mine or yours.'

'But Mum doesn't want us!'

'Sure.' Her brother had held the fists that were punching him in sheer frustration and explained quietly, 'But she doesn't want Dad to have us more than she doesn't want us. Do you get it, kiddo?'

Angel had, sort of, in her childish way. 'I think I hate her, Cesare.' She had whispered the confession because she knew this was a bad thing.

Cesare hadn't said she was bad; he had simply shrugged and retorted, 'Why bother? She's not worth it. Just remember when we're old enough she can't keep us and then we can live where we like.'

'Here at the castle with Dad?'

'Sure,' her brother had agreed, handing her a tissue and advising her to wash her face and brush her hair because she looked like a banshee.

'My father betrayed my mother, she forgave him, there was no divorce.' Angel sighed a sad smile, curving her lips as she dragged her thoughts back to the present. They had gone back to the Scottish castle of their childhoods but there had been no Dad. He had died and Cesare had inherited the ailing highland estate along with responsibility for its debts.

'You were lucky.'

His astonished stare fastened on her face as he sneered, 'How do you figure that one?'

'Divorce is not a good thing and a mother who forgives is…' Head tilted a little to one side, she studied his face. 'But you didn't, did you?'

'What?'

'Forgive him.' He was quick to hide it but Angel saw the shock move at the back of his eyes, followed by a cold, closed look.

'It was not my place to forgive.' And now it was too late to tell the father he had idolised that he understood the weakness… How could he not when he was staring at his own in the face? 'Though, yes, with the arrogance of youth I did judge. Having indulged in a one-night stand, I am in the classic glass-house-stone-throwing position.'

There was a delicious dark irony that he had blamed his father for not taking responsibility for the consequences of his actions…. Unprotected sex—how stupid is that? He heard the scornful words of his younger self and they still had the power to make him flinch.

The only reason he had not found himself in a similar situation was not down to higher moral standards or even basic common sense, but pure luck!

'So it isn't normal— You…you don't—' She broke off, flushing.

'Sleep with women I have just met? Actually no. Though I can understand why you made that assumption given how we met. That makes you unique on two levels—my only virgin and my only one-night stand,' he remarked bleakly. 'How about you?'

'I thought you'd already decided that a model is an easy lay.'

He winced and frowned at the crudity while uneasily accepting its factual accuracy. 'I was not enquiring about your sexual history.'

'Oh, I see, you just want to know the *real* me?' She widened her eyes. 'Where do I begin? My political views or my favourite author? Let's see, I'm a Pisces, I drink too much coffee and my favourite colour is green….'

'Do you always make a joke when things get too personal?'

Shocked that he had recognised the self-defence mechanism so easily, she shook her head in an angry negative motion, but before she could follow up with a firm denial he asked a question that, even though she knew was inspired by idle curiosity not suspicion, almost tipped her over into outright panic.

'Where is she, your daughter, now?'

Not here, thank goodness.... Angel shuddered to imagine how she would have reacted if fate had thrown this man in her path when Jas had been with her.

'At home, in Scotland, with Ce...' She stopped, remembering that he knew Cesare and not wanting him to make the link between her and her brother until she was ready. 'I always know she's safe with him.'

The mention of the other man and the perceptible loosening of the tension in her body language when she mentioned him caused muscles along Alex's taut jaw to clench.

He rarely found himself taken by surprise but he was. Having established that the father was not involved in the upbringing of the child, it had not occurred to him to question whether another man was. And considering he was a man who was justifiably famed for factoring in all possibilities when he approached a project, in retrospect it seemed astonishing that he had not foreseen any other outcome, when engineering a situation where their paths would cross, other than them falling into bed together. He had not been willing to contemplate failure.

It had genuinely not once crossed his mind that Angel might be with someone. He struggled to readjust to these facts.

While he recognised it was totally irrational, he could not shake the feeling of being cheated.

So what did you expect, Alex—that she'd spent the past six years waiting for you to reappear? The glaring immaturity of his reaction annoyed him, and, continuing in the immature mindset, he found himself blaming her for the situation.

His slightly narrowed eyes went to her left hand, but the long tapering fingers were bare of everything but sand. To leave a child with someone implied a great deal of trust but there was no ring. He half closed his eyes but he could still see her fingers on his skin. He inhaled and fought his way through a rush of hot lust...*a virgin*!

He still could not get his head round the fact that the best sex in his life had been with a virgin! Everything was successfully conspiring to up his guilt levels: the wife he had watched suffer barely in the ground and he had jumped into bed with a green-eyed witch...then that temptress had turned out not to be a siren but a virgin! Effectively making him feel like some sort of predatory sleaze. What was it they said—ignorance was no excuse in the eyes of the law?

It was certainly no excuse in his eyes.

He had been staring so long at her hands that Angel had to fight an impulse to hide them. Instead she dug them into the sand before rubbing them against her thighs and dragging them through her wet hair.

'You're with someone?'

This was good, he told himself. It was always good to focus on a known quantity. A partner meant there was no chance of becoming involved once more with her. That was one line in the sand he did not cross.... *Unlike virginity, Alex?*

'Does the child's father mind her being brought up by another man?'

'Would you?' she countered.

He thought about it—but not for long as it was a no-brainer. 'Yes, I would.' Little Lizzie—not so little these days—had spent the first few years of her life farmed out to relatives and friends before her father had claimed her and given her the home that had always been hers by rights. To allow that to happen to a child of his…?

It would never happen! His child would not suffer an identity crisis. She would always know where she belonged, she would always feel safe, loved and secure.

The instant response sent a flurry of panic through Angel. She brought her lashes down in a concealing sweep to hide her response. Exhaling a slow, measured, calming breath, she told herself there was no way he could know—and he didn't.

She looked up. There was no shocked realisation, not even a shade of suspicion in his bright eyes.

'I am bringing my daughter up alone.'

'So you make the calls and your boyfriend of the moment acts as a childminder, providing he has no problem with your work taking you away from your family?' It amazed him that any man trusted her enough to let her out of his sight, let alone halfway across the globe.

An energising rush of anger surged through her body as, with lush lips compressed in an angry rose-tinted line, she retorted, 'I would never ever farm my daughter out!'

'Why do you constantly assume I'm judging you?'

'And you're not?' she flung back.

'Or do you judge yourself?' he speculated.

'And for the record there's nothing wrong with a man being the carer.'

He arched a brow. 'Did I say there was?'

'You implied it,' she contended. '*If* I had a boyfriend who wanted to stay at home and look after Jas I'd consider myself lucky.' But she'd refuse. Angel would never allow her child to become fond of someone who could vanish. 'And I don't enjoy being away from Jas.' She swallowed, her voice thickening with emotion she couldn't hide as she added, 'But it won't always be this way. I've given myself five years to make enough to start my own—' She stopped and thought, *You are telling him this why, Angel?*

Out of this information one detail jumped out at Alex. '*If*… You do not have a boyfriend?'

'Why? Are you thinking of applying for the vacancy?' As jokes went this one fell pretty flat. Did the man even have a sense of humour? 'That was a joke. My brother is good at helping out with Jas.'

'You have a brother?'

'We share…' She paused and lowered her gaze from his interrogative stare. She felt disinclined to explain the circumstances that had led her to be living in a wing of the highland castle that her brother had inherited. She had tried to replicate for her daughter the idyllic childhood there that had been snatched away from her and Angel was not about to let anyone tear it away from Jasmine.

'He was available to take care of Jasmine.'

She took a step away from him towards the rocks, taking care to avoid the tideline of broken shells and seaweed that was coarse underfoot. 'Look, I'd better be getting back.'

'Not that way.'

She looked at the hand on her arm, feeling a worrying disinclination to break the contact.

'You can't get back along the beach at high tide.' His hand fell away, leaving Angel conscious of the tingling imprint. 'It is nearly high tide.'

Absently rubbing the spot where his fingers had been, she fought another tide—this time one of rising dismay. Alone on a beach she could have coped—she was resourceful and it appealed to her spirit of adventure—but she wasn't alone!

'We're trapped?'

'Another instalment in your dramatic life.' For a split second he was tempted to say they were trapped, but he stifled the impulse. 'Relax, there's a path through the trees.' He pointed to the pines that lined the beach. 'Slightly longer, but quite well marked. Come on, I'll show you.'

Side by side but not touching, they walked towards the tree-shaded area. The pine needles underfoot crunched as they walked beneath the fragrant canopy. In the softer light the bruise on her forehead was much more evident.

'I think you've escaped a black eye.'

'It's my shoulder that I'll feel tomorrow.' She rotated her shoulder, feeling the stiffness that was bound to get worse before it got better. Her hand went to her head, which she dismissed with a casual, 'I bruise easily.' She stopped, her eyes widening as she turned to him, and she grimaced as she realised the implications of his comment. 'There's a bruise? You can see it?'

He nodded, picking up the concern in her voice and wondering why she was bothered about something she had previously shrugged off.

'Terrific!' Wincing slightly, she traced the slightly raised outline on her temple with her finger. It was not vanity or the pain that gathered her brows into a worried straight line above her tip-tilted nose, but the prospect of what the women in Make-up would say when they saw her, and the horror would likely not be limited to them.

The last thing she needed as the new girl was people questioning her professional attitude.

'It's not *that* bad.'

She slung him a gloomy look and continued to walk. 'It is *that* bad if you have lights and a camera pointed at your face. There's only so much even the best make-up and lighting can disguise.'

And even less could she disguise her growing feeling of confusion around him. Life had been simpler before she'd had any insight into the man who had for six years been the focus of her anger. Not a shiny, perfect hero—although he did have a habit of being in the right place to snatch her from the jaws of, if not death, definitely discomfort—but not, it turned out, a serial seducer. He was a man with a family and a history that had left him with his share of emotional scars and even, it seemed, the odd moral value.

Struggling to lift his eyes from the long, sinuous curves of her sleek brown body, his gaze drawn to the tiny slice of paler skin where her bikini bottom had slipped down over the angle of her hip bone, he shrugged.

'Can they not film around your scenes?'

Angel laughed. She could not imagine that this would be the response from the team when she appeared looking this way. 'This is an advert, not a blockbuster. I'm in all the scenes and, as they keep telling me, time is money.'

'No, time is a luxury.'

They had reached the point where the trees thinned and the hotel came into view.

'A luxury I don't have.' She expelled a deep sigh. 'Ah, well, I'd better face the music.' She turned to him. 'I might not have said it. In fact, I know I didn't, but thank you for fishing me out of the drink. I really am grateful.'

He looked down at her with an odd expression. 'I do not want your thanks—I want this!'

Without warning, he bent his head and covered her mouth with his. A primitive thrill shot through her and she moaned into his mouth, responding to the hunger of his lips, melting against him as she was carried along on a dizzy tide of raw need. Not fighting it, not questioning, just sinking into all the warm darkness that only he seemed able to tap into and going with it. The relief... the release, it was incredible! She had stopped being the person she tried so hard to be and let herself be the person she was—with him.... *Why him?*

As abruptly as it had begun, it ended.

They stood there staring at each other. Angel saw wariness in his blue eyes then, with a muttered imprecation, he turned away.

She remained where she was, her eyes wide, her hand to her mouth as he stalked away back along the path they had just walked along.

CHAPTER SIX

AFTER HER FACE had been viewed from all angles and all light conditions by all interested parties, including the dermatologist who had been shipped in when Clive had developed a spot, it was decided that the situation was not as bad as originally feared. In three days' time the swelling would be gone and the bruises that make-up didn't disguise could be airbrushed away.

Three days was not long enough to fly home and see Jas, but long enough to miss her like hell. With nothing to fill her day, Angel found sheer boredom set in very quickly. Sunbathing on a beach might be many people's idea of bliss, but Angel had never been good at sitting still doing nothing.

With no other suggestions after she had been banned from doing anything that might injure her and delay the schedule further, she ended up armed with a pair of knitting needles, a ball of bright blue wool and instructions from Clive, who assured her a child could do it. He predicted she'd be amazed at how relaxing it was so she sat beneath a palm tree and set about being creative.

Half an hour later, her teeth aching with tension, she grabbed the tangled lot and flung it across the beach. She knew she was acting like a spoiled child, if you discounted the adult expletive that accompanied the action.

She knew it wasn't the minor frustration that made her want to yell and stamp her feet, it was everything that had gone before and what was to come. Her teeth ached with the tension that was tying her body in knots. Not thinking was exhausting. If she could have rid herself of the decisions she had to make in the same way she had that damned wool—the colour reminded her of his eyes—she might have been able to enjoy a moment's peace.

Before the voice, the prickling on the back of her neck had warned her she wasn't alone. Even so, she flinched when he spoke.

'It's an instant fine for littering here.'

How long had he been watching her?

She turned her head in the direction of the mocking drawl but sat rigidly, watching as he gathered up her rejected knitting and walked back towards her. It was just her luck. Miles of beach and he had to walk along the stretch that she had chosen. Ashamed of the ache of longing that made her throat dry, she followed his progress across the sand.

Alex was in no hurry, but as he got closer her heart rate became more erratic. Pressing a hand to her chest, she lowered her gaze and trained her eyes on his bare feet. It seemed a relatively safe part of his anatomy to focus on until, unable to stop herself, she lifted her gaze up over his hair-roughened calves and muscular thighs. The khaki shorts he wore were belted low over his narrow hips and his short-sleeved shirt hung open, revealing his lean ribbed brown torso.

'So are you here to arrest me?' She extended her hands, wrists crossed for imaginary cuffs. 'I'll come quietly.'

'Now that I find hard to believe.' The idea of her giving up without a fight brought a grim smile to his face as he dropped her knitting needles onto her lap. 'Actually I'm here to save you.'

The comment drew a sardonic laugh from Angel. The only thing she needed saving from was standing right there, sending her entire nervous system into a state of chaos, with his long, greyhound-lean limbs, oozing sex from every perfect pore.

'From death by boredom.'

'Who says I'm bored?'

He reached down and picked off a fibre of bright blue wool that clung to his shorts. He arched a sardonic brow and let the fibre blow away. 'You're bored.' And unless he was totally out in his assessment, as eaten up with burning frustration as he was.

Bored...much worse, thought Angel. She was hopelessly aroused—just looking at him made her nerve endings tingle. She pressed a hand across her middle to ease the heavy dragging sensation low in her pelvis. There was no place to hide except behind the big floppy hat she wore and the sunglasses that hid her eyes from him.

She produced a scowl. 'Isn't that littering or are you a special case?'

His white teeth flashed. 'I like to think so.'

She stroked a restless hand up and down her smooth calf. 'I'm not good at sitting still.' Catching the direction of his gaze, she stopped stroking and pushed her sunglasses back up on her nose.

The admission did not come as a surprise. She was not exactly what could be termed a restful woman: stubborn, aggressive, confrontational... As he mentally made a list of her less desirable qualities his eyes followed her hand to her face. All that was visible was her firm, rounded chin and her mouth, and there was nothing at all restful about those plump, luscious lips. An unfocused glaze drifted into his eyes as he struggled and failed to suppress the memory of those lips parting beneath his.

The silence stretched and he stood there looming over her like a statue until she could bear it no more.

'I think you're the one that's bored.' She aimed for cool and haughty but achieved something more akin to sulky.

In response he flopped down on the sand beside her, intensifying her cowardly impulse to run. His shoulder was an inch from hers. If she could have figured out a way of widening that gap without being obvious she would have.

Maybe what people said was right: that you could run but you couldn't hide...? On the other hand you could try, at least when it came to examining your own feelings.

Angel jammed the tangled mess from her lap into the massive holdall, managing to jab one of the needles into her leg. 'Ouch!'

'Been for a swim?' He could see the outline of her bikini under the thin thigh-length cover-up she wore.

'I'm not allowed. In fact I'm banned from pretty much everything apart from breathing and I'm in everybody's bad books.'

'They can't blame you for saving a kid's life.'

'Why not?' she countered. 'You did...and saving his life is a bit of an exaggeration.' She jammed her unread paperback on top of the knitting and clicked the clasp of the big raffia bag closed.

'Ever modest.' And ever a temptation. He stared at her mouth, wanting to slide his tongue between those beautiful, provocative lips. The need was so strong that for the space of several heartbeats he lost track of his real objective.

She sniffed and pushed her sunglasses up the bridge of her nose, flashing a small, tense smile. 'That's me...

it's just a shame I'm not the creative type.' She nodded
at the bag.

He adopted an expression of innocent surprise. 'Really? I thought you went to art school.'

'I didn't finish the course—' Her expression tensed as
she flashed a suspicious look his way. 'How did you know
that?' she demanded, whisking her knees up to her chin
and wrapping her arms protectively around her calves.

He shrugged casually. 'Someone must have mentioned
it.'

Or something, namely the bio in the short report provided by the people who normally did background checks
on prospective employees for him, a report that concerned specifically the months prior to the birth of Angelina Urquart's daughter…and most importantly that date.

It had been 3:00 a.m. when the seed of the idea had
first entered his head. It had spent the next hour insidi-
ously burrowing in, taking root while he had spent that
period by turns becoming totally convinced he was right
and equally totally convinced that the idea was a combined product of his overactive imagination, sexual frustration and sleep deprivation.

He needed to know—he needed to know at what point
a nightmare became a premonition and for that he needed
information. Alex had not bothered to work out time
differences. He would not have used a firm who were
not available on a twenty-four-hour basis and the person
whose direct line he rang sounded alert and helpful—he
expected nothing less.

They could not supply the information he really desired, but what they could supply and did was information that could confirm that it was possible.

The details that popped into his email box at 5:00 a.m.
gave the bare facts he had requested: Angelina Urquart

had given birth to a daughter eight months to the day after they had spent the night together.

He could be a father. Statistically speaking it was probable he was guilty of the crime that he had found it so easy to condemn his father for.

That it was possible to have a child, be a father and not know... He could have walked past his own daughter in the street and not guessed who she was. The idea utterly appalled him, but did fatherhood?

Running normally cleared his head. Facing the idea of being a father while covered in sweat and breathing hard, it still remained totally shocking but not the nightmare he had expected it to be. Was he feeling what his own father had the day that Lizzie's aunt had turned up with the child and a stack of letters that the child's dead mother had written but never sent, to dramatically inform the stunned man in front of a room full of party guests that it was his turn now to take responsibility for the child he had fathered?

At least he had some privacy to get his head around the concept and his big reveal would be at a time and place of his own choosing...if there was a reveal. After all, the question mark remained.

If he was right, why hadn't Angel told him? Did she ever plan to tell him? As he felt his anger mount the sense of loss he experienced, thinking of the years he had missed and would never get back, made it tough to see the situation from her point of view...but he was trying.

She came across as confident, but how much of that was window dressing? Six years younger, alone and presumably scared out of her wits at finding herself pregnant, had she tried to find him? Thoughts of her in that state of mind increased the guilt that gnawed away at him like acid. On one level he recognised that she wouldn't

have known where to start to look for him, and in that
case he knew that she hadn't set out to deprive him of
parenthood. But on another level, he wondered if she
hadn't been secretly relieved. Her opinion of him was
so bad that she probably thought he would make a cata-
strophic parent.

His jaw clenched. For a man who rarely found himself not in a position of control to be forced to recognise
that his position as an unmarried father gave him precious few rights, let alone control, was tough for Alex.

He was going to be part of his child's life no matter
what it took…. The thought of another man thinking access to Angel's bed gave him the right to become a father
to her child was a situation that he could not contemplate.

'So why didn't you complete your course?'

The question was casual but something in the way
he was looking at her made her uneasy. Angel dodged
his gaze and shrugged. Maybe she was getting paranoid
but Angel responded to the alarm bells. 'I had some distractions.'

A baby.

His baby?

It had been several hours now since he had faced the
possibility; the emotional impact had felt like a ten-tonne
truck landing on his chest. Three hours to run, pace,
speculate and plan…the weight remained but his brain
was now clearer. The solution was there and he would
do whatever it took to get the information.

Information that was stored in one place—her beautiful little head.

Not for nothing had the business world named him
the perfect poker player. There were no 'tells' to even

hint at an agenda behind his casual invitation. 'And how about now?'

She shook her head and gave a shrug of incomprehension.

'Could you do with some distraction?'

She clamped her lips tight over an outraged gasp. 'Well, no one could accuse you of subtlety, could they? Thanks for the offer but no, thanks.'

He gave a throaty laugh. 'Actually I wasn't propositioning you. Don't be embarrassed.'

She stuck her chin out. Embarrassed did not cover the toe-curling mortification that made her want to literally bury her head in the sand. Anything was preferable to seeing his smug face. 'This,' she gritted, circling her face with a finger, 'is relief.'

He took her chin between his thumb and forefinger and with the other hand pushed her shades up into her hair. The action was casual, confident, as though he had the right to touch her. *You're not doing much to disabuse him of this massive misapprehension, are you, Angel, just sitting there like some sort of mesmerised rabbit?* she thought to herself. When she ought to be… What…?

'No, this is beautiful….' he husked.

Trying to kick-start her brain felt like wading through warm syrup. *This is not me…. Why does he make me act this way? Why do I let him do this to me?*

Because you like it?

The crazy thought almost made her laugh. She pulled her sunglasses down again.

'I'd love to discuss your idea but—'

Angel dug her fingernails into her palms, focusing on the pain to help her fight her way to control. She turned her head and his hand fell away.

Digging her heels into the sand, she said, 'It wasn't an

idea.' Her voice sounded very small, the scornful laugh weak— Well, actually, pathetically unconvincing.

'Don't sulk,' he said, drawing an outraged gasp. 'Obviously I want to have sex with you.'

He delivered this piece of information in a manner she associated more with ordering a pizza than propositioning. The violent lurch in her chest was possibly, Angel mused, her heart stopping. Despite the possibility of her imminent expiration she somehow—it was a miracle—kept her expression blank. Thank goodness for sunglasses.

'I get that a lot.'

Not a lie, but she'd never felt in danger of requiring CPR before. Or…best to treat the comment as a joke— the alternative was not something she felt equipped to cope with.

She saw something flash in his eyes—anger?

'I'm sure you do,' he countered smoothly, 'but on this occasion I was thinking more along the lines of lunch.'

Lunch with Alex Arlov? Now, that was a crazy idea.

Or was it? Wasn't this an opportunity to get to know Jas's father in the nonbiblical sense? She still needed to decide if he was a man she wanted to be involved in her daughter's life. For that judgement she had to put her personal feelings aside.

And what were her personal feelings?

She gave her head a tiny shake and pulled her hat more firmly down on her dark hair, glad that he could not hear her thoughts or, thanks to the tinted lenses, see her confusion. Normally someone who had a head-on approach to life, she had been skirting around that question since he had reappeared in her life.

And with good reason. Feelings… It sounded so simple but how was she meant to analyse something so, so…

visceral? It was easier to accept it. What was the point of delving deeper? At its most basic, she was attracted to him, but that hardly made her special. She had seen the way women looked at him…all women. He was a man who inspired lust and around him she dropped several IQ points; her brain just didn't function at full capacity. In fact sometimes it just didn't function full stop!

Well, they were welcome to him, she told herself. At least she had the maturity now to be able to differentiate between lust and deeper, more profound emotions.

Tell that to your nervous system!

'Eating is not one of the things you are barred from doing, is it?' He unscrewed the bottle of water he had been carrying. Halfway to his mouth he paused and extended it towards her. 'Want some?'

'No, thank you,' she responded, primly polite.

'Is it?' he said, wiping his mouth with his hand.

She started guiltily—her eyes had been riveted on the muscles working in his brown throat as he swallowed. 'What?'

'They haven't banned you from eating?'

'That depends on the calorie count. They are worried about my hips.' She was regretting the flippant remark even before she had finished speaking, but managed not to make the moment any worse by successfully resisting the impulse to tug the spangled, jewel-bright fabric of her cover-up lower over her hips. As his head tilted to one side his eyes slid over her sleek, smooth curves, lingering on the supposed problem area.

After a nerve-shredding moment his gaze lifted, his expression blank, but the glow in his eyes made her stomach flip. 'Yes, I can see you must need to be careful,' he delivered in a deadpan tone, thinking that he had never met a woman who so totally encapsulated all things erotic and sensual.

Wide and indignant, her eyes flew to his face. A moment later her tension fell away and she was laughing in response to the gleam in his blue eyes. Then the gleam changed, became not amused, and she looked away quickly, her heart thudding, her mouth dry.

'How would you like it if I drew attention to your flaws?' He didn't have any—at least not physical ones.

'You brought your hips into this discussion,' he reminded her. 'Not that I'm complaining, and if you're going to tell me you have any self-esteem issues don't waste your breath.'

His heavy-lidded glance moved from her lips, sweeping downwards over the length of her sinuous, sleek, leggy frame. No woman could be as unselfconscious in bed as Angel had been if she was not happy in her own skin. She had taken pleasure from her own body as much as she had from his, and he had never known a woman to display such fascination with his body before or since.

Without warning a piercing stab of pure lust sliced through him, raising the level of his arousal painfully as he allowed the door in his head to open a crack for the memories to push through, not in a controlled way but in one hot, steamy rush. His brilliant eyes darkened and glazed with licking flames as he saw…felt…her hands gliding over his skin, the moisture of her tongue.

Her lovemaking had been as generous as her cushiony soft lips… It had never crossed his mind for a split second that she had been a virgin, not even when she had been so tight when he had entered. There had been that shocked little cry, but he had taken that as a compliment.

Maybe you didn't want to know, Alex?

The sudden audible crack of his finger joints made

Angel's questioning gaze shift from his extended fingers to his face. The golden skin was pulled taut across his magnificent bones; his angular jaw was tensed; his eyes remained hidden by the luxuriant sweep of his preposterously long eyelashes.

She could see the tension in the rigidity of his powerful shoulders as he reached down and took her hand.

'You shouldn't be sitting here in the midday sun.'

She didn't react to his impatient tone; she reacted to an unacknowledged desire to make contact and to the fizz of electricity through her body that made her head buzz as she allowed him to pull her to her feet.

When she pulled her fingers free they continued to tingle. She held her hand against her chest and struggled to take control of her breathing…and then found she was virtually panting! Acting like some sort of sexually deprived bimbo was sending out all the wrong messages.

Or, more worryingly, the right ones!

Her laughter was as uninhibited as her lovemaking had been in his thoughts.

'I will personally guarantee your physical safety.' He arched a brow and held out a hand towards her. 'I have said something that amuses you?'

She looked at the hand and thought, *You don't make me feel safe. A lot of other things, but not safe.*

'I don't require a bodyguard.'

Their glances connected and suddenly the fizz between them made it hard for her to breathe.

'How about a charming companion and lunch?'

'Really?' She made a pantomime of looking around. 'Where would I find one of those?' she asked, before adding almost shyly, 'Lunch would be good.'

When her desperate attempt at humour did not produce even a half smile Angel huffed a sigh. 'I am hungry,' she admitted, thinking, *Where is the harm?* And she was doing this for Jas. She wasn't looking for a soulmate, but that was no reason to deprive her daughter of a dad. Though that did depend on the dad.... And how was she meant to judge if he was good enough for Jas if she ran away every time she saw him?

What sort of man was he?

Oh, she'd read the stuff on the internet and knew about the wealth, the enigmatic reputation that had resulted in some wild speculation, and she took all that with a pinch of salt, but the man did come across as a mass of contradictions.

They walked in silence along the path that led from the beach through sweet-scented pine trees. Once or twice she looked up at the tall man walking beside her and he seemed lost in thought and showed no inclination to engage her in conversation. This suited Angel, who made no attempt to break the stalemate, though, as she mockingly told herself, in order to get to know him she might have to speak at some point.

As they reached the place where the path entered the hotel's gardens Alex took a left turn instead and opened a gate marked Private that had always previously been locked.

'Where are we going?' She had her answer as they rounded the bend and a small cove came into view. It was empty but for the motor launch moored off the rocks.

'For lunch. Careful, the rocks are slippery.'

'I thought we were going to the hotel.'

'We're not.' He did not elaborate.

'I can see that,' she returned, ignoring his hand. She was making a point, a trivial one perhaps, but it felt important to emphasise the fact that she could cope alone. Or was she simply prepared to fall rather than risk experiencing the electrical surge that occurred whenever she touched him?

With a frown she pushed the intrusive suggestion away and, with one hand out to balance, the other holding the heavy swathe of her hair out of her eyes, she inched her way cautiously down the rocks, aware that landing on her bottom would prove both painful and humiliating.

Her refusal to accept a helping hand, literally, brought a small ironic twist to his lips. The action encapsulated the woman: stubborn, reckless and damned irritating. But he conceded as he watched her from the vantage point of the boat that she really was the most incredibly graceful and alluring creature he had ever seen.

There were very few people who could make slipping and slithering look elegant, but she was one of them. His jaw clenched as he restrained himself from flying to her rescue after a particularly spectacular lurch.... If she fell and broke her beautiful neck it would serve her right.

This was no path, thought Angel, more a free climb, and the appeal of clinging to a rock face with nothing to harness you for pleasure passed Angel by. She decided it was a case of practicality over pride, but a few feet from the end of the rocky path she did not refuse the hand he reached out. She'd made her point and it was quite a leap into the boat.

He had made it look easy, of course.

'Thank you.'

His ironic grin broadened as he clasped her hand, then vanished as she landed. The momentum of her landing sent her crashing into his body and the flash of heat that slid down his front caused his smile to fade. His heavy eyelids lowered, hiding the hard, hungry look in them, as his hands on her elbows pushed her away and he directed a cool, 'Steady!' to the top of her head.

Concealing the fact that all his instincts were telling him to grab that gorgeous behind and mould her to him came at a price, in the form of the pain in his groin and the slick of sweat that lay like a fine sheen over the surface of his skin. Despite appearances and the Northern blood running in his veins, he was immune to the heat, but the same could not be said of a soft warm female, at least not when it came in the dangerous form of Angel Urquart.

'We're eating on Saronia?' she speculated, experiencing mixed feelings about this journey into the unknown. The caution was sensible, the excitement was not!

'Don't you like surprises?'

'Only some of them.'

'Come on, Angel,' he urged, mocking her with his electric-blue eyes. 'Live dangerously.'

Angel looked away, remembering what had happened the last time she had lived dangerously. Now she was a mother who was going to provide her daughter with what she had craved as a child: a calm, nurturing environment to grow up in. Combustible relationships were not on the agenda and there was no escaping the fact that sparks flew every time she came within the same square mile as Alex.

Unlike yesterday, she was in a position to actually appreciate the wind-in-your-face experience of cutting through the water in the fast speedboat. She sat back, knowing the journey would not last long, though it turned out to be a little longer than she anticipated. Instead of mooring where the film crew were dropped off, he continued on, following the coastline.

The filming had all taken place at the side of the island that faced the mainland. They had been requested not to leave the immediate area so she had never seen this side of the island, and she immediately saw how different it was—much greener and more lush.

He cut the engine and brought the boat expertly up to the edge of the small wooden pier.

'There used to be a road from the other side of the island but it fell into disrepair. The only access now is by water or helipad.'

It turned out there was no road this side either. The stony, near-vertical route he drove the open-topped four-wheel drive along barely deserved to be called a track. Halfway up the hill Angel, who was hanging onto the overhead strap, turned her head and yelled, 'If you're going to drive like this, you might at least put two hands on the steering wheel.'

He threw her a lazy smile. 'You're a back-seat driver.'

Angel didn't respond. They had just topped the crest of the hill and she was staring at the scene revealed in front of her. The pristine sand was as silver white as the Hebrides, the long waving grass behind it dotted with wild flowers, and set in the middle of the green rippling carpet was a white marquee and pitched under it was set a long table. Two figures were unloading items from the four-wheel drive vehicle parked close by.

'If I'd known I would have dressed.'

She half expected the couple who were unloading food to wait on them, but they drove away after a quick word with Alex. As she watched them vanish and responded to the light touch between her shoulder blades that made her conscious of every prickling inch of her skin she realised just how alone they were.

She gave a laugh to cover her nerves and approached the shaded table covered with a white cloth laid with silver and crystal.

'This is your idea of a picnic?' It might be some people's idea of a seduction scene. Discounting the possibility and the flip of excitement low in her pelvis, she was sure that he wouldn't have gone to this much trouble for nothing. The question remained—a lot of effort, but why?

'I don't like sand in my food.'

'You could always concrete over the beach.'

'An idea, but I have to think about my eco credentials.'

'Especially as they're so profitable.'

The muttered response drew a thin smile from him. 'You are, as always, eager to assign the worst possible motives to my actions.'

She opened her mouth to deny this charge and closed it again, her eyes sliding from his as she mumbled, 'I can be a cynic.'

'If you're interested in all things eco you might like to look around my house sometime.'

Following the direction of his gesture, she frowned, seeing only a grassy hill above the high-tide mark, but then a glint of light reflected off glass caught her attention.

'Goodness!'

'Yes, it's easy to miss at first, isn't it?' The architects had fulfilled their brief and made the structure blend in with the landscape, but they had gone one step further—they had made it part of the landscape.

Excavated into the hillside, his sanctuary with its turf roof and no manufactured walls was invisible from most angles, but the clever design meant that every room was flooded with light from the massive glass panels that faced the sea.

'You live there?' It was not the power statement that she had assumed any home of his would be.

'I stay there occasionally. It suits my needs, but it is

not equipped for entertaining, hence…' He gestured to the table.

'Won't you sit down?' He pulled out one of the chairs and, feeling both awkward and anxious, she took her seat.

The first fifteen minutes did not give her any insight into him as a person. His conversational skills were as she had expected but he managed to avoid any personal questions, instead turning them back on her. It was deeply frustrating.

'You do not care for seafood?'

Angel, who had been pushing her food around her plate, set her fork down and decided the best approach was a direct one.

'Why did you ask me here? Not to talk about the food, I'm sure.' Nibbling on her lower lip, she caught hold of one of the crystals that weighed down the cloth, rolling it between her fingers.

'Why did you come?' he countered.

She set her elbows on the table and stared across at him. 'Do you always respond to a question with another question?'

His brows knitted as he forked a large prawn into his mouth. 'I am resisting the temptation to say pot, kettle, black.'

'Not very well,' she inserted sourly.

'The answer to your question is, yes, I do, when the answer interests me.'

'I was bored and hungry.'

'You haven't eaten much.'

'I'm watching my weight.'

'Do you ever worry about your part in the message that the media sends out to young girls?' His tone was deceptively casual but the eyes that met hers were anything but.

'Message?'

'The pressure to achieve an impossible level of perfection, like the women they see in the magazines. The message that equates beauty with happiness. Of course, I was forgetting you have a daughter of your own. I'm sure you are well aware of the pressures facing young women.'

She stiffened, her heart beating fast as she twisted the linen napkin between her fingers. He knew, somehow he knew! Or he thought he knew….

'Jasmine is not a woman. She's a child.'

'True, but they grow up so quickly and I believe that anorexia sufferers are getting younger and younger.'

She shook her head, angry now, and got to her feet. Looking down at him lessened the feeling of being a mouse being toyed with by a large feline. 'Why are you suddenly so interested in my daughter?'

He laid his own napkin down with slow deliberation, holding her eyes as he got to his feet. 'Because I had this idea… It's crazy, but in my experience those are the ones that it pays not to ignore. So I did a little research and a few surprising things came up, like the fact that your daughter was born eight months to the day after we spent the night together and there was no one before.'

'Or after.' *Did I really say that?*

He didn't react, but she could feel the emotions rolling off him.

Angel didn't blink; she didn't breathe. She shrugged and struggled to hold on to her manufactured calm.

'So you want to know if you're Jasmine's father? Couldn't you just have come out and asked? Did it really require all this elaborate stage-managing?'

'It occurred to me that you might be waiting for the right moment to tell me…?' He had really tried hard to think of this from her point of view but her expression was not saying she appreciated the effort. He had been her only lover.... Only... He experienced a stab of sheer primitive possessive satisfaction, and breathed out, letting the air escape in a slow, measured sigh.

'I thought I'd provide it.... I thought if you were relaxed—'

'You thought you'd get me drunk,' she countered, pointing to the second bottle in the ice bucket. 'And trick me into saying things!'

The comment hit a raw nerve. First she threw his consideration back in his face, now she tried to make herself the victim. 'I shouldn't have to trick you into anything. If I've got a bloody child I have a right to know.... I have a right to know her!' It was the first time she had heard him use Russian but she was guessing she wouldn't find the translation of what he snarled in any phrase book.

As angry now as he was, she heaved in a taut, angry breath of her own. What did he know? Parenthood wasn't a right—it was a privilege!

'Rights? You have no rights! You see Jasmine only if I say so, and I don't. I came here wanting to find out if you were the sort of person I want in Jasmine's life, the sort of person who would be good for her to know. Well, now I do know, and you're not. I wouldn't have you near my daughter...for...for...anything! You're a manipulative bastard who treats people like chess pieces... You're the last father I'd choose for my daughter.'

Breathing hard like duelists, they stood either end of the table facing one another, firing angry words, not bullets, though the words could inflict considerable damage and once they were out there they were impossible to retract.

Even though she was still furious Angel was already beginning to regret the things she had said.

He leaned forward, his hands flat on the table, and fixed her with an icy blue arctic stare. When he spoke it was in a voice that was several decibels lower than the hot words shouted in the heat of the moment. Cold, considered and chosen to inflict the maximum level of fear.

Angel was seeing the man that made powerful men tremble with fear.

'You have picked the wrong man to challenge. You will not keep my daughter from me. Attempt to prevent me seeing her and it will be me you come begging to for visitation rights. If you have a skeleton... If you have a bone fragment in your cupboard I will find it and my lawyers will use it.' He hardened his heart against her pale, stricken expression and added, 'You started this, but I will finish it. That much is a promise.'

Without another word he walked away.

Angel didn't react. She just stood there, frozen. She roused only at the sound of an engine and she turned in time to see him vanishing in a cloud of dust.

He had driven away, leaving her stranded.

Not quite able to believe the situation she found herself in, she looked from the dust cloud to the food and wine spread out and with a laugh she slumped down into the chair.

'At least I won't starve.'

She was still sitting there twenty minutes later when one of the men who had earlier been laying out the food appeared. If he found the situation strange nothing in his manner suggested it as he framed his meticulously polite question.

'Are you ready to return to the mainland?'

She was ready to kiss the feet of her rescuer but she was much more circumspect in her icy state, and responded to the respectful enquiry with a nod and a smile.

CHAPTER SEVEN

ALEX PULLED THE car over after a mile, leaning his elbows across the steering wheel. He thought he knew every inch of the island but he struggled to get his bearings as he pushed his head back into the padded headrest and looked up through the open roof at the trees that blocked out the sun.

'Well, that worked out well, Alex.'

He'd had it all planned. While he had rejected all Angel's charges at the time, had she been so wrong?

Driving like a lunatic, while satisfying, was not going to solve anything. He had blown it; he had acted while the emotive impact of discovering he was a father was still fresh. When she hadn't said what he'd wanted to hear he had launched into attack mode and made a tough situation ten times worse.

Back at the bungalow the only thing she wanted to do was… Actually there were two things she wanted to do: throw herself on the bed and weep, and break something. The first she didn't do because she was due to have her prearranged chat via the internet with her daughter in less than half an hour, and the second… Well, she was supposedly a grown-up and grown-ups did not throw their rattles out of the pram, unless of course the supposed grown-up was Alex Arlov!

Things hadn't gone his way and he'd simply gone off in a strop. Admittedly, a pretty magnificently broody strop, but the fact remained that she had refused to play by his rules so he'd walked away, issuing threats that had made her blood turn to ice. Not to mention that they revealed what a truly ruthless man lurked beneath the urbane exterior.

Would he adopt the same sort of parenting style? When the going got tough would he opt out?

Her hands balled into clawed fists at her side as she paced the room. The man made her so mad! She took a deep breath and reminded herself that this was not about her or her feelings, or, for that matter, Alex. It was about Jas and she was not going to run the risk of laying her precious girl open to hurt or rejection.

It was after her chat with Jas that Angel did cry—tears of regret more than anger. Her little girl was so lovely. She deserved a father, someone who would take her as she was, and not weigh her down with unrealistic expectations. Did Alex even know what having a child involved? Or would Jas just be another possession to him?

Had he meant those threats?

Should she get legal advice? The thought of anyone trying to take away her daughter… She shuddered as she recalled his lethally soft-voiced threat, aimed with dagger-like accuracy to inflict the maximum fear and panic.

She wouldn't panic; she would fight!

The last thing she felt like later that evening was being sociable, but Angel knew that her no-show would be construed as standoffishness by the others so she was forced to sit around the big table and smile her way through the evening. She responded good-naturedly to the teasing about her heroics until she realised why the ad-agency man who had been the most vocal in his exasperation after the resulting delay now seemed quite jovial about the subject.

She expressed her relief to Clive, who was sitting beside her. 'I'm glad he's calmed down.'

'Of course he's calmed down, darling—all that free publicity!'

Angel shook her head. 'Publicity?'

'Seriously?' The slightly tipsy Hollywood actor scanned her face for signs of irony, then, finding none, laughed hilariously, causing someone at the opposite end of the table to request being let into the joke.

'It turns out that our Angel is one of life's innocents. She doesn't know that someone recorded the whole hero thing on their phone and uploaded it onto the web.' He turned back to Angel and explained with a touch of envy he didn't quite disguise, 'You have gone viral. All that free publicity is better than sex as far as our Jake is concerned, and the only thing the world loves more than a heroine is a heroine that looks like you do in a bikini.'

The other man raised a glass at the charge.

'Oh, God, no!'

Her genuine horror made Carl laugh even more. 'Of course, there are some theories the whole thing was staged. Don't you just love conspiracy theories?'

'No.' She huffed out an exasperated sigh. Clive's blend of superficial charm and malicious humour was beginning to pall. Compared to Alex's far more abrasive, abrupt and in your face— God, why was she even thinking about Alex, let alone using him as a measure of male perfection? She couldn't think of anything less perfect. She closed down the inner dialogue with a resounding snap and produced a clear, focused smile. Nobody could accuse her of being obsessed. 'I don't, but I believe in respecting a person's right to privacy.'

The actor gave a shaky smile, clearly in two minds. Was she being serious…? 'Ever thought you were in the wrong line of work, darling?'

'Frequently,' she admitted, permitting herself a dry laugh before she turned her attention to Sandy on her right. Her present career was a means to an end, something she had fallen into rather than planned. She had given herself five years, and if at that point she had not made enough money to set herself up with the fashion-design label she had mapped out in her head then she would walk away with no regrets and possibly more than a little relief.

Angel made it through the meal, avoided the copious free-flowing wine, but not even her sweet tooth gave her the appetite to make it through the pudding course. Pleading tiredness, which was not a lie, she made her excuses early and during her walk back to her bungalow found fifty messages when it occurred to her to check her phone!

She only replied to the two from her brother. It took even longer than she had anticipated to calm and reassure him, and she agreed with his decision not to keep Jas up to speed with her mother's newfound fame. In the back of her mind she wondered if being an internet heroine would be a plus or a minus if the fight got to court?

Her brother hadn't laid a guilt trip on her; it wasn't his style. But even so, Angel was feeling pretty much a failure as a mother by the time she reached her bungalow and searched for the swipe card for the door.

'It's not locked. Anyone could have walked in.'

Angel yelped and spun around as the tall figure

emerged from the shadows. Even without the moonlight that illuminated his face, revealing the strong syb-
aritic slashing angles and spine-tinglingly strong bones,
it would have been impossible to mistake the identity of
the person who was lurking there.

'And did you?' She managed to project a level of cool
she knew she didn't have a hope of sustaining for long.
The sound of his voice had begun a chain reaction that
she had no control over; his physical presence made the
feelings that were surging unchecked through her body
even more urgent and mortifyingly obvious.

How could you hate someone and want them at the
same time?

She crossed a hand over her chest, unable to restrain
a wince when it brushed the shamelessly engorged nipples she was attempting to hide. Her heart was in her
throat, the dull, thunderous clamour echoing in her ears
drowning out the more peaceful sound of the waves as
she lifted her chin to an imperious angle and repeated
her accusation.

'Well, did you?'

'I thought I'd wait to be invited.'

'Then you'll have a hell of a long wait.' A predictable
response and, she realised, shamefully untrue. Where
this man was concerned, instead of locking doors she
had a terrible tendency to fling them wide open and drag
him in!

He didn't react to the belligerent challenge. Instead
his narrowed eyes followed the hand she wiped across
her face. 'You're shaking.'

Acutely conscious of the unblinking blue stare, she
responded to the note of accusation in his voice with a
resentful, 'Probably because the last person who jumped

out from behind a bush as I was trying to open my door now has a restraining order against him.'

The mocking smile vanished from his face. 'A restraining order?' A relationship turned sour, violent…? His hand clenched. 'Who was… Is this man?'

Angel, already regretting she had mentioned the incident, shrugged. 'Just a sad man. He was harmless really.'

A nerve clenched in his cheek as Alex stared at her in stunned disbelief. She sounded so calm, so casual!

'So harmless you took out a restraining order against him.' His sardonic statement was shot through with audible anger, the same anger that made his blue eyes burn as he focused on it instead of the sick lurch in the pit of his belly as he imagined her defenceless, vulnerable and at the mercy of some crazed lunatic. Yet today he had ripped into her himself, issuing every kind of threat he could think of…trying to hurt her.

'It turned out all he was carrying was a bracelet.'

'What did you think he was carrying?'

'A knife,' she admitted, adding with an embarrassed grimace, 'What can I say? I watch too many cop shows on telly.'

'You thought I was a knife-wielding maniac?'

She moved her head in a negative motion. 'You surprised me, that's all. And he didn't have a knife and he wasn't really a maniac, though obviously not entirely right in the head.' She accompanied the explanation with an illustrative tap on her own head, thinking as she did so that perhaps she was in no position to throw stones.

After all, sane did not exactly describe her own reaction when she had seen him as being that of someone in full possession of all her mental faculties. Her stomach muscles were still quivering. She had spent the best part of the evening calling him every name under the sun, inside her head of course, but the moment she had seen him her throat had thickened and her traitorous heart had started to thud.

'A person who serves you coffee and decides your smile means you are soulmates has issues. Obviously if I'd realised it was just another of his presents I wouldn't have hit him over the head with the plant pot, though maybe it was a good thing I did,' she mused. 'Because the plant pot actually proved a lot more effective than a police warning and he decided that I was not his soulmate after all.'

'Plant pot?' he echoed, struggling to wade through this information.

'It was the only thing there.'

The note of apology drew a choked sound from his throat and he realised it was impossible to judge Angel by the other women he knew. She was clearly a creature who acted on instinct.

Combine that sort of reckless impetuosity with youth and a passionate nature and it wasn't hard to see how she had ended up pregnant. But then the mystery was how he had been the first. He still struggled to get his head around that knowledge.

Alex had no excuse, which was why he was here and he couldn't allow himself to be distracted.

'The things you said this afternoon... You were right. You were not telling me anything I don't already know.... I just wasn't ready to hear it.' She watched as he dragged his hand through his dark hair, which, she noticed, was already tousled. He was still wearing the same clothes he had been in earlier that day, though they were a lot more creased, and for the first time since that night six years ago she was seeing his jaw shadowed with dark stubble.

'From me?' She anticipated a savage rebuttal and got instead a thoroughly and totally disarming tip of his head.

'This is your call and I will abide by your decision. The threats I made were…selfish. I'm sorry, you were right. You have every reason to hate me. I slept with you, I took no precautions, it was thoughtless, I've never…' He just stopped himself producing the classic 'I've never done it before' line. After all, why should she believe it? Actions, he reminded himself, spoke louder than words. 'I want to make things right.'

Angel was shaken by the depth of self-loathing in his voice, but she forced a laugh and framed her ironic rebuttal in a voice as cold as she could make it. 'You want Jasmine.'

The goad made the lines bracketing his mouth tighten but he managed to hide his frustration, well aware that once already today he had barged in like the proverbial china-shop bull, issuing threats when he should have been asking questions, building bridges.

'It's true, I want to be a father to my child. But you were right—I'm in no position to call the shots.'

Not being in a position to call the shots, as he termed it, had to be a new experience for him. But Angel was not totally trusting of this new Alex, and she refused to be lulled into a false sense of security. She would not lower her defences just yet.

'That's a pretty big U-turn for someone who was talking custody battles not a few hours ago.'

'I told you about Lizzie…'

'Your half-sister?'

He nodded. 'She was ten before she knew who her father was, before she knew *she* was wanted…. I want Jasmine to know she is wanted.'

The soft addition sliced through her determined stance

of wary hostility. There was no question of his sincerity. 'She does!' Angel rushed to protest earnestly. 'I know what it feels like to think you're nothing but a nuisance.' Feeling awkward at the admission, she dodged his glance and added, 'I've never let Jas think for one second she isn't wanted and loved.'

'I'm sure you're a great mother, but that isn't the issue.'

He thinks I'm a great mother? 'What is the issue, Alex?' It was pretty obvious that the superficial simi-larities had dredged up some old issues for him. 'This isn't about your relationship with your father. You can't allow the things that happened in the past to colour the present.'

He emitted a laugh of disbelief. 'So it's purely acciden-tal that your mothering style is the complete opposite of your own mother's? That's not a criticism, it's a fact. It's what people do. We try to avoid our parents' mistakes. Some of us fail….' He gave a snort of self-disgust. 'Talk about history repeating itself.'

'That's not true! The situations are totally different,' she protested.

'In as much as Lizzie's mother chose not to tell my father she was pregnant because she knew he was mar-ried. You didn't even know my name. My dad had always been my hero. He made a real effort with me, maybe to compensate for the fact he'd been estranged from his own father. We did everything together, then afterwards… It was never the same between us. I didn't hold back. I let him know I despised him. I never lost an opportunity to twist the knife. Pretty ironic considering that I ended up emulating him.'

'But you didn't!' she exclaimed. 'You're not—!'

His blue eyes lifted and Angel could see that they blazed with self-contempt in the half-light. 'Married…?

My wife had been dead weeks! Tell me how that makes me any better?'

The pain in his voice made her wince. 'People do things when they're grieving that they wouldn't do normally.'

A sound of astonishment escaped his lips as he moved towards her out of the shadows. 'You're trying to excuse what I did...?' He swallowed, the muscles in his brown throat visibly working as he finished on a note of raw incredulity, '*You* of all people!'

'You're not being fair on yourself, Alex. You loved your wife, you were hurting, grieving... You had been for a long time....'

'I knew it was going to happen.'

'And is that meant to make it easier? For goodness' sake, Alex, cut yourself some slack.' She registered his startled expression but didn't let it faze her or allow him the space to protest. Some things needed saying, especially when they were so obvious, and he was too close to it. 'You were there when your wife needed you, weren't you?'

'I think so.... Yes, I was, but I couldn't...'

'I know that's hard, but you tried and you did your best. And when she was gone you did something out of character, not because you loved her any less, but because you wanted to stop...thinking.' She shook her head sadly. 'I don't know what your wife was like, but I'm willing to bet she would have understood what you did and not considered it any sort of betrayal. I wouldn't, if it had been me.'

She was displaying a generosity of spirit that made him feel humble. 'I think you are a better person than me.'

'I wish I was. You lost yourself in one night of sex and I...I...' She choked with a bitter laugh. 'I was kind of in love with the idea of being in love. Relax,' she added, seeing his expression. 'I have grown up.'

'Being a single parent will do that to a person.' She might have relieved some of his guilt over that night but not over the repercussions. 'I want my child to know she is wanted, Angel.' He doubted very much he could be as good a father as Angel was a mother, but he would try.

'So why didn't you just say so instead of... It's obvious your sister had a tough time, but Jasmine knows she is wanted, Alex.'

'She doesn't know she is wanted by me.'

The words made her heart give a heavy thud of empathy. In the fast-falling dark she struggled to read his expression. Now his figure was little more than a dark outline, backlit by the moonlight reflected off the silvered ocean surface.

'You wanted me to listen.... Angel, I'm listening. I want to help, I want to be involved. Is that selfish? I don't know....' He took a deep breath, a soft sibilant hiss escaping through his teeth before he said quietly, 'No threats.'

'I wasn't threatened.' Not true—she had been. But not nearly as much as she would have been had she not had the security and the confidence of a brother with all the ruthlessness and resources to face Alex on equal terms. To fight on her behalf, should she ask him.

'I need to be part of her life...whatever it takes.'

Angel's restless covetous glance was drawn and then lingered on the sculpted contours of his wide, sensual mouth.

There was a big difference, she reminded herself, between wanting and needing. She needed to rediscover that mouth about as much as she needed a boil on her nose, but, God, she wanted it so much it hurt.

Angling her chin defiantly, she cleared her throat.

'I suppose you think all you have to do is kiss me and I'll agree to pretty much anything?' she challenged. 'Your problem is you think you're irresistible!' she tacked on, realising as she spoke that she was halfway to believing he was!

Maybe more than half, she thought. She recalibrated as she lost the ability to move, actually to breathe, as he surged towards her, taking the shallow steps of the bungalow veranda two at a time. He was at her side before she had an inkling of his intentions and then it was too late to stop him.… Did she actually want to?

He framed her face between his big hands. His stare had a soul-piercing intensity and she couldn't look away, afraid that a blink might break this spell.

'Kiss…?' The flash of his white grin was predatory as he bent his head and kissed her slowly, extending the erotic pleasure, taking his time as he slid his tongue deep between her parted lips, tasting her. There were no words to describe the sweet, hot ache between her thighs.

Angel was left gasping, open mouthed, for air when his head finally lifted. She felt his hands at her waist supporting her; her knees sagged; her legs felt as though they belonged to someone else.

'I'm planning to do more than kiss you, Angel,' he rasped, the promise making her tremble in anticipation. Still holding her eyes, he ran his tongue across the plump, trembling outline of her lower lip before tugging it gently with his teeth and asking, 'You have a problem with that?'

His problem is he thinks he's God's gift!

My problem is he's right.

In her head Angel saw herself pushing him away, defusing the situation with a few well-chosen words interspersed with the odd acid barb.

Outside her head, she was melting into him, pushing

her aching breasts up hard against his chest, absorbing his heartbeat, his heat and the sheer maleness of him. She drew his head down so she could take the initiative and move her lips slowly across his, sampling the texture, breathing in his scent as, with eyes half-closed, she whispered into his mouth, 'No problem.'

His eyes flared and the primal incandescence made the breath in her lungs catch and burn. She stood trembling and passive, her heart thudding like a drum as he pushed his fingers deep into her lush hair so that they cradled her skull, dragging her head back to expose the long line of her throat.

Her eyelids squeezed tightly shut as he pressed his mouth to the pulse at the base of her throat. Her deep sigh became a long moan, the sound slipping past her clenched teeth as his tongue and lips progressed up her neck until he reached her mouth again. By this time her skin was slicked with a layer of moisture and she was panting short, shallow gasps as if she had just run a marathon.

Alex was breathing hard too as he brought his face in close. His nose grazing hers, she wrapped her arms around his neck, conscious of the rasp of each laboured inhalation. He was close enough for her to see the faint pinpoint marks left by sutures running either side of the thin white scar that was almost hidden by his hairline. His forehead was creased in a frown of intense concentration as he stared into her upturned features; the skin of his own face was drawn tight, pushing against the perfect bones, emphasising each individual plane and angle. He was breathtakingly beautiful, but it was the raw, rampant hunger stamped on his face that sent a fresh, explosive surge of sheer need coursing through Angel's body.

Struggling to articulate what she was feeling, simultaneously frightened and helplessly excited by the desire roaring like an out-of-control forest fire, in a voice that was hers, yet not hers, she whispered, 'I need this. I need you.'

Not her voice, but it was definitely his mouth that came crashing down on hers. Her body arched as she kissed him back, responding to the pressure with a wild frenzy of need that drew a deep, throaty moan from Alex.

'Hell, I don't have… We need to be careful.'

'No, it's fine. I'm on the pill.'

'Thank God!'

Still kissing frantically, they stumbled backwards. Angel was dimly aware of the sound of the door closing behind them a split second before she lost her footing and stumbled. Before she fell she was in his arms, swept quite literally off her feet, and being carried, a novel experience for a woman who was five-ten in her bare feet! A woman who had never before wanted to feel weak or helpless and out of control… That so wasn't her.

In the bedroom he rested one knee on the bed before he sat her down in the middle of the soft downy quilt. She rested there looking dazed and so beautiful that the box he had locked his feelings away in cracked wide open.

'You're beautiful,' he said, looking into the luminous, passion-glazed eyes lifted to his. He touched the side of her soft cheek with his thumb and felt her shiver. Her eyes drifted closed as she turned her head and, catching his wrist, pressed her lips to his palm.

The speed with which she had gone from hating him to feeling his pain and then wanting him more than oxygen was disorientating. Actually it was scary. 'This is me, not the airbrushed version.'

The warning drew an amused grunt. Alex abandoned the pretence he was in control as a wave of emotion moved through him. Instead he decided to enjoy it…and her.

'I have seen you naked before.'

Her eyes opened as he rose to his feet. She grabbed the front of his shirt and, falling backwards, pulled him with her.

She felt rather than heard his throaty chuckle as he raised himself on one arm and warned in a voice thickened by passion, 'I'll crush you.'

Still holding his shirt, she tugged—hard—smiling as pressure caused buttons to fly in all directions across the room. Hands flat on the delicious, warm golden skin of his chest, she leaned up to kiss him, tugging at the flesh of his lip with her teeth as she whispered, 'I'm kind of hoping you will.' The torrent of need he had awoken in her was elemental, out of control… *She* was out of control. The raw passion left no room in her head for any thought. She was driven, focused on one thing: to lose herself in him, to be totally consumed by his raw power.

Kneeling over her now, he didn't take his eyes off her face as he fought his way out of his shirt before flinging it across the room.

Her skin was so sensitised that even a light shiver made her conscious of every point of contact between her and her clothes. They felt heavy; she felt too hot…. She tugged at the neckline of her dress and tried to smooth the fabric bunched around her middle, barely able to breathe now as her eyes drifted hungrily over his naked torso and her quivering stomach muscles cramped. The heat crackling under her skin burned as she absorbed the details. He was utterly perfect: lean, hard, gold-toned skin gleamed with a slick of sweat; his broad chest had power and strength and was marked by whorls of dark hair and sharply defined with slabs of muscle; his belly was washboard flat and bisected by a directional arrow of dark hair. Her chest lifted in a deep, voluptuous sigh of appreciation.

The shirt long gone, moving quickly and urgently, Alex reached for the buckle on the narrow belt that was threaded through the waistband of the linen trousers he was wearing. But Angel was there before him, driven by an all-consuming need to feel him, see him, her fingers shaking but surprisingly nimble as they unclipped the belt.

Before she could follow through with the action, he took her hands and lifted them high above her head. He kissed her with slow, erotic thoroughness before he took hold of the thin top she wore and, taking the hem, lifted it over her head.

She was wearing a tiny pair of panties and a bra that was little more than a couple of triangles of lace in a matching pink.

Alex gave a low appreciative growl in his throat and reached for the catch on her bra.

The underwear was gone before her head hit the pillow and he was bending over her, stroking her, his hands moving down her sides and over her ribcage and up to cup the quivering flesh of her breasts. Her body arched up to meet him, her arms wrapping themselves around his neck, as she struggled to anchor her aching core to him, all the while pressing increasingly ardent kisses to the strong brown column of his neck.

Angel squeezed her eyes closed and sank her fingers into the deep lush pelt of his hair, extracting and relishing every individual sensation, but somehow it wasn't enough.

She wanted more; she needed more.

Maybe if she said it?

'I know.' His breath was moist and hot on her cheek, on her neck then her breast, and the air left her lungs in one open-mouthed gasp. His hands were moving up over her ribcage as his tongue traced the outline of her areola, before drawing the engorged peaks into his mouth first one, then the other.

In a fever of need she only distantly registered him sliding her panties down over her hips, gasping but not resisting as he parted her legs. She moaned low in her throat, pushing against his hand as he slid his fingers between her legs, parting the swollen and incredibly sensitive folds, making her pant and gasp as he rhythmically stroked the swollen flesh. Her gasps turned to deep feral moans as he touched the tight nub at her core and her body lifted off the bed.

'You like that?'

She nodded. It made her dizzy to look into his burning eyes but she knew that the trust required to let him touch her went way beyond the merely physical. She had a connection with this man who was the father of her child, and that made it neither shocking nor shameful.

She lifted her head and kissed him back hungrily, no longer even attempting to retain control. She didn't want control; she wanted wild and elemental. She wanted Alex, wanted to be devoured, absorbed, to become one with him.

'I want you too!'

Had she spoken out loud?

'Hell, I haven't been able to think straight,' he groaned, 'since I saw that photo of you.' Holding her eyes with his as they lay side by side, he took her hand and curled her fingers around his hard, smooth shaft. 'That's how much I want you, Angel,' he slurred thickly.

He felt so good, and his half-closed eyes gleamed fe-

verishly bright as she touched him. His expression turned
raw and predatory and aroused her more than she had
imagined possible.

Her lips parted as he lowered his mouth to hers, the
deep, probing kiss draining her, sending her deeper and
deeper into a vortex of sensation. As he moved over her
she reached down and guided him into her, holding his
gaze until that last moment when he slid thick and hard
inside her.

Her eyes squeezed closed as every cell of her being
focused on the feeling. She heard herself gasp.

'Oh, please!' As they began to move together his hands
anchored her hips to the bed and she wrapped her long
thighs tightly around him. Breathless, Angel moved with
him, her sweat-slicked skin gliding and sliding against
his. Their gasps and cries merged into one as their bodies
came together, until she gave herself up to the firestorm
of wild sensation that rocked her body.

As she began to float back down to earth Angel felt
light. The secret burdens she had carried all her life were
gone. She had slain her demons, she wasn't her mother—
she loved him.

She lay in the dark, appreciating what had happened
to her, not being afraid of it any more than she was afraid
of her own heartbeat. He was as much a part of her as
that. That he didn't feel the same way, that he couldn't,
made her sad, but it also made her determined to extract
every last atom of pleasure from the moment.

There were more moments during the night, less urgent, less bruisingly raw perhaps, but each one more
shatteringly sensual than the last.

Angel woke feeling cold. The sheet was crumpled on the
floor and Alex was lying on the other side of the bed.

He woke as she shuffled across the bed and shivered as she pushed closer to the warmth of his body. Streaks of light had appeared along the wide horizon where the sea met the sky. It would soon be morning and what then…?

She shivered again and felt her chest tighten with an emotion she identified as loneliness. How crazy. She wasn't alone—she had Jas. A sigh hissed from her lips.

'Are you cold?'

'I'm fine,' she said, her voice muffled against his shoulders. He threw his arm across her and it lay big and heavy and reassuring across her shoulders. She liked the feel of his hair-roughened thigh against her smooth leg.

Don't get to like it too much, Angel, the voice in her head advised. Turning a deaf ear to that voice, she focused on the fingers that were moving in slow, lazy, circular movements across her belly.

Then the hand stilled and she sensed the tension in his body. 'What is that?'

She shivered, this time with pleasure as the heel of his hand rested on the sensitive mound of her pubic bone, though he ran his thumb along the thin white line not quite obscured by the soft fuzz of curls at the apex of her long legs.

'Complications during labour. I had an emergency C-section.'

He felt as if a hand had reached into his chest. So much had happened to her that he was responsible for and he'd been totally oblivious.

'You could have died?' Guilt rose like bile in his throat. What had he been doing at the time? Driving a fast car? Signing off on a deal and congratulating himself? Enjoying technically perfect sex with a beautiful woman…?

There had been nothing technical about last night.

Raw, explosive, elemental—yes; as addictive as a nar-
cotic—definitely! He knew now why he had gone to such
lengths to bring her back into his life. He'd been trying
to recapture this feeling, this emotional connection that
only a single one-night stand had given him.

'If I'd been living in a Third World country possibly,
but I wasn't. It was all routine.' And scary as hell.

He didn't believe a word of it. He had taken her innocence and got her pregnant. *A prince among men, that's
you,* Alex told himself.

'You were alone?'

She shook her head.

'Your mother was with you?'

The suggestion drew a chortle of laughter from Angel.

'I thought maybe having a baby would have brought
you together.'

Her hands curled over his. Drawing his fingers to
her lips, she kissed them, then his mouth. Some breathless moment later she admitted with a laugh, 'Being old
enough to be a grandmother is a crime my mother has
still not forgiven me for. I'm not even sure what country
she was in when I gave birth. She bores easily.'

He said a word that sounded vicious.

'Will you teach me to swear in Russian? That sounds
really satisfying.'

'If you teach me to make love in Italian, *cara.*'

'It works for me.'

'Tell me you weren't alone when you gave birth.'

'I wasn't,' she said, hearing the guilt in his request.
'My friend, Clara.' Who despite her very good intentions
had spent the first few hours of Angel's forty-eight-hour
labour flirting with a young doctor, and when things had
started happening had fainted away gracefully. While
the labour had gone disastrously wrong, Clara was

being diagnosed with concussion and even got admitted overnight. Angel had been her maid of honour when her friend had married the handsome young obstetrician six months later.

'And my brother flew back from Dubai as soon as he got the news I was in labour. Jas arrived a month early, so he was there to hold her before I came around.' According to the midwives he had worn a trench in the floor walking up and down, waiting for her to recover from the anaesthetic.

That should have been me. The thought surfaced, the strength of it taking him by surprise. He should have held his baby, and now he never would. His loss, not hers. It was obvious that Angel put her child above all else.

She omitted a few details from her potted history, such as that she'd come around in a high-dependency unit, or that her first recollection when she had surfaced from the anaesthetic had been hearing her forceful sibling who had no doubt bullied the information out of the doctor asking him if he was sure she would never be able to have children in the future.

'Is there no hope? IVF...?'

'Not impossible but extremely unlikely,' had been the medic's response. 'Would you like me to tell the father...? Or will you...?'

'If I ever find the scum who did this to her I'll do better than that! I'll make sure he doesn't do this to any other woman! Is she awake yet?'

Angel, who had closed her eyes and pretended to be unconscious, had almost immediately drifted back into a drug-induced slumber.

But when she'd woken she had remembered the conversation she had overheard, which had helped when Cesare had broken the news to her later; she had been able to make it easier for him by responding calmly as she'd told him honestly that she was fine. When she'd been discharged a few days later everyone had considered her to be coping remarkably well, though Angel had been unable to dispel the feeling that they were waiting for her to fall apart.

When they'd realised she wasn't going to—it had taken a while—it had been a relief that everyone had stopped walking on eggshells around her and she could get on with looking after her baby. She had happily left the anger to her brother, who had deduced with no help or confirmation from her that the father was married.

She had genuinely believed she was all right until that morning six months down the line when she had been folding away the clothes that Jasmine had outgrown, smoothing the fabric of a hand-knitted, exquisite, tiny newborn cardigan that it was hard to believe her robust bouncing daughter had ever fitted into. The reality had hit her with no warning.... Why was she storing the tiny garment so carefully in layers of tissue and lavender bags for the future? There would be no brother or sister to wear it.

No more babies.

The tears had begun to leak from her eyes, silently at first, then had come the muffled sobs and finally the awful wrenching wails. A lot later she had dried her eyes and the next day had delivered all the baby clothes to the local charity shop, reminding herself sternly that she had a precious child and many people were not that lucky.

She had not thought of it since, but now she realised that she had needed to cry, needed to mourn a future that was lost, she thought sadly. But she had done her mourning and moved on; now she was getting on with her life.

Had Alex? Was he still mourning the future with his wife that had been denied him?

'Was your wife ill a long time?'

She felt him stiffen a moment before he rolled away from her. 'Yes.'

'I know mourning is a very personal process.' She reached out to stroke his back before taking a deep breath and beginning tentatively, 'My friend had grief counselling when her—'

'I don't need a grief counselor. I have you. You were right—I have been eaten with guilt because I buried my grief in anonymous sex. I'm not proud of it but you helped me see…I have moved on, Angel. The question is,' he said quietly, 'have you?'

In the space of a heartbeat Angel experienced the disorientating sensation of a total role reversal. One second she was feeling supportive and understanding, the next she was the one being asked to face her demons, and it was too soon.

CHAPTER EIGHT

ANGEL HAD LAIN with her eyes closed, pretending to be asleep, as she heard him getting dressed. But when she heard Alex moving around in the other room she got up. She didn't want him to leave without doing something to close the distance that had opened up between them.

Belting her robe, she walked quietly into the adjoining room. Alex, who hadn't heard her, was holding the photo of Jasmine in the silver frame. It was the expression she saw etched on his face in the brief moment before he realised she was there that swung it—the longing mixed with pain that vanished the moment he knew he was not alone.

Swallowing the lump of emotion in her throat and ignoring the small voice in her head that told her she'd live to regret opening this door, she responded to his cautious good morning with, 'You can see Jas.'

He went rigid for a moment, his face a total blank, then he smiled and tipped his head. 'Good.'

'If you agree that when and how to tell her who you are is my call.'

Slowly he nodded. 'That seems fair.'

Angel expelled a deep sigh and hoped like hell once more that this was going to work out.... She had to make it work. 'Right, I'll make arrangements. Another thing

I think that—no!' She backed away shaking her head, one arm extended as if to fend him off as he approached, the gleam in his eyes sending her nervous system into meltdown. 'Don't!'

His fingers that had moved to loosen the knot on her robe stopped; he was frustrated but not alarmed. He bent his head towards her. 'What's wrong?'

Wrong, yes, she thought, that was the right word. He'd been the wrong man at the wrong time for all the wrong reasons.

'I can't.'

The furrow on his brow smoothed. 'You have an early call? That's a pity,' he murmured, thinking it was a disaster! Unable to stop himself, he dropped his eyes to the thrusting profile of her nipples. He had never wanted a woman as much as he did Angel. It was a struggle to present a casual attitude about this delay when every cell in his body was pumped and primed to peel back the layer of silk and explore the even silkier delights beneath.

'I don't have an early call. I mean… What I mean…' She stopped, squeezed her eyes closed and groaned. 'Don't look at me like that,' she pleaded.

'Like what?'

His display of innocence drew a growl of frustration from Angel. 'Like you're…'

'Thinking about making love to you…?'

When wasn't he?

His eyes narrowed as he struggled to contain a flicker of shock. Sex no longer came with a big guilt trip. It had become a normal part of his life again, but it was not something that occupied his thoughts exclusively. Or it hadn't been until Angel had come back into his life.

This frank translation made her flush and press a hand to her heaving chest.

'I can't focus!' she choked. 'I'm trying to tell you we can't…ever do…' she jerked her head in the direction of the open bedroom door where the tumbled bedclothes were visible '…that.'

'That?'

She lifted her chin and responded to his taunt with an unintentionally loud reply. 'Sex. That's part of the deal. If you want to be part of Jas's life then we have to get our act together.' She expelled a breath. It was over with; she had said it. This was the point where the tension was meant to flow from her body. She had told herself she'd feel better once she got this over with, but she didn't.

'You just lost me.'

She struggled to preserve her calmness, aware in the face of this pretence of ignorance that with his steel-trap mind he got the point half an hour before most people. 'A child needs continuity…security.'

What she did not need was a constant stream of 'uncles' at the breakfast table; she did not need slammed doors, raised voices, dramas played out at volume at all hours of the day and night; she did not need spurned lovers who turned nasty or even the ones that turned pathetic.

'You expect me to argue with that?'

'I put Jas's needs ahead of my own,' she said quietly.

There might not be a definitive rule book that told you how to be a good mother—Angel had discovered everyone had to work it out for themselves, and there were times when she frankly got it wrong and worried about just how much mothering skills were down to genes—but at least she knew how not to be a bad mother, or at least an uninterested one.

Growing up, she would have settled for her mother remembering once in a while that she had children! Her beautiful and erratic parent had lived her life exactly as she had wanted and her children had been the ones who had done the adapting.

'And you need me.'

The smug insertion proved to Angel that they were still not on the same page. 'This isn't about your ego,' she flared, tightening the belt on her robe, thus unwittingly causing the neckline to gape.

Jaw clenched, Alex dragged his gaze off the heaving contours of her bosom and the effort made his tone abrupt.

'Then what is it…?' He stopped as the penny belatedly dropped. He could see where this was going.

'You mean you want to get married?'

The cynic in him was not surprised. It was not the first time a woman had looked at him as prospective husband material. He was normally alert to the subtle signs that signalled attempts to manoeuvre him into matrimony, but he hadn't seen this one coming. For some reason, neither could he summon up his well-rehearsed smile, the one that softened his harsh response.

And none of the women he had let down gently had been the mother of his child.

His eyes narrowed. That made a difference. And now that he thought of it, was it such a bad idea from a purely practical point of view? Of course he was old-fashioned enough to prefer to be the one making the proposal, but Angel's horrified exclamation suddenly cut into his stream of thought.

'M-marry? Of course not!'

The unmitigated horror in her voice was reflected on her face. It seemed he could always rely on Angel to deliver a kick to his ego.

'That would be ridiculous.' She gave a laugh, wincing

when her effort to convince him she was neither crazy nor an idiot made her sound both. 'I'm not wife material, believe me.'

'What, parents getting married?' His jaw clenched as he resisted the childish impulse to inform her that there were more than a few women who would not consider the idea of being his bride a nightmare. 'Hell, yes, you're right, crazy…that would never catch on,' he drawled, swinging away from her, his feet silent on the floor as he stalked towards the window. He reminded her of a caged tiger on a short leash as he traversed the room.

'Please, this is not a joke,' she reproached to his retreating back.

He spun back, spearing the fingers of both hands deep into his hair as he rocked back on his heels. 'Sorry.'

Her eyes narrowed. 'Thanks for that sincerity.'

'I'm sincere—sincerely tired of this ridiculous discussion.' His sarcasm made Angel clench her teeth. 'Just tell me what is bothering—'

'My pretty little head?' she jumped in, glaring.

A spasm of irritation crossed his patrician features. 'You are not pretty.'

Angel was not particularly mad about her looks. Given the choice she would have chosen blonde and petite, but she had no body-image issues and she was well aware that she was considered by most people to be more than averagely attractive, so it made it all the more crazy that the comment hurt. 'So I'm ugly!' She could not believe this childish response was coming from her own mouth.

'No, you are beautiful,' he countered. Midglare his eyes broke contact with Angel's and slid to the photo. 'So is she. She looks so like you….'

The husky observation successfully refocused Angel's attention. 'She has a much sweeter temperament.'

'Maybe she takes after her father...?'

Alex Arlov, sweet? Any other time the two words in the same sentence would have had her in hysterics but Angel didn't crack a smile.

She made an effort to channel calm. 'I can't have an affair with you, Alex.'

Even if she could have stomached the idea of sex without an emotional commitment it wouldn't have worked. She simply lost all sense of perspective when it came to Alex. She could never maintain any sort of simple sexual relationship with the way he made her feel.

She had never understood women who would risk everything for a man. She didn't want to understand, but what she did know was that if such a man existed Alex Arlov was the living, breathing embodiment of it.

'Who's saying I want an affair?'

She flinched at the growled rebuttal and, lifting her chin, defiantly murmured, 'My mistake.' Presumably an affair was too formal a footing for what he had in mind. 'As a matter of interest, what did you have in mind?' She arched a delicate brow and suggested in a sardonic drawl, 'Friends with benefits?'

'We are not friends.'

'Thank you for reminding me.'

A look of regret slid across his lean face. 'I didn't mean it that way.... I just...' He dragged a hand through his dark, tousled hair. 'I just... You're driving me crazy.'

There's a lot of it around, Angel thought grimly. 'Don't worry, I appreciate bluntness,' she said instead. Hopefully he could take it as well as dish it out. 'I can't have sex with you at all. We need to keep our relationship uncomplicated for Jasmine.'

He struggled to follow her logic and realised there was none. 'How is us sleeping together bad for Jasmine?'

'I want my daughter to learn about relationships based on mutual respect and—'

'Our daughter.'

The correction made her grate her teeth. 'For five years she's been my daughter, Alex.'

'And you resent the fact it has to change,' he flung.

The suggestion that this was a *fait accompli* annoyed her. He was failing to recognise that she was the one making an effort.

'I'm an example to my daughter. I don't want her to think casual sex is all she can have. I watched my mother sleep her way around the fashionable spots of Europe. I had her boyfriends drift in and out of my life and I don't want that sort of instability for Jasmine.'

'So you *are* holding out for marriage.' He seized on this evidence triumphantly.

'I'm holding out for a relationship based on more than lust,' she countered. 'One that is…safe.'

His heavy-lidded gaze slid over her sleek, sensuous curves and the fist of desire in his belly tightened. 'Safe!' he spat in disgust. 'And what is so terrible about lust? Lust is not a bad place to start….' he commented in a deep throaty drawl that made the surface of her skin tingle.

The deep, drowning blue of his eyes made her dizzy and it was an effort to break the contact. 'Only if both participants want the same thing.'

'I thought I gave you what you wanted.'

His inability to see what she was saying drew a frustrated grunt from Angel.

'My mother changed her lovers the way some women change their shoes. I know what it feels like to grow fond of someone and have them vanish or to hear arguments when you're trying to go to sleep, to have a sleazy boyfriend of your mother's make a pass at you.' She saw the outrage flare in his eyes and added quickly, 'Only once and my brother walked in.'

'So how is the fact your mother was a lousy parent relevant?'

'I know what bad parenting is.'

'And good parenting involves being some sort of born-again virgin? I'm curious—are you planning on not having any sex or is it just sex with me that will emotionally scar our daughter?'

'You're deliberately twisting things.'

'So untwist things and tell me you're not saying I can either be part of my daughter's life or sleep with you?'

'It is not an either-or situation, Alex.'

He exhaled a frustrated hiss through his teeth. 'What is it, then?' Without waiting for her to respond, he shook his head and, drawing a sharp line in the air with his hand, said, 'You know, I really don't want to hear, because none of it is true. You know what I think? I think this isn't about Jasmine, it's about you. You're using her as an excuse because underneath that facade you're scared. What of? Becoming your mother?'

'Of course not,' she answered too quickly.

'From what you've told me you are the exact opposite of your mother.'

'This isn't about my mother. It's about us…. You.'

'You're scared of me?' A look of shock chased across his lean face. 'It never occurred to me you were… Why would you be?' His eyes narrowed as her eyes slid from his, shifting to a point over his shoulder. It was a telling gesture.

'Of course not.' It was true, she wasn't afraid of Alex, but she was afraid of the way he made her feel. The emotional impact of meeting him again had felt like having a tourniquet removed from a deadened limb and the abrupt resumption of circulation and feeling had been agonising. But as hard as she'd tried she couldn't reapply the tourniquet to her emotions.

She loved him and he was going to break her heart. It was as inevitable as night following day. But it wasn't the broken heart precisely that she was avoiding—it was Jasmine witnessing it breaking, seeing the slow disintegration of the relationship and thinking, as Angel had, that that was all there was to look forward to in life.

'We all have issues in our childhood....'

The insensitive attempt at amateur psychology brought her resentful gaze back to his face. A second was all it took for him to capture and hold her.

'What made you so scared of enjoying a normal healthy sex life?'

'I'm not afraid,' she replied, hiding her discomfiture behind a cool mask.

'Did your father cheat on your mother?' he speculated.

'My dad adored my mother even after she walked out on their marriage and took us with her, then did her level best to forget we existed.' In a small corner of her head a voice was saying, 'Too much information, Angel!' but she couldn't stem the flow of revelations. 'And in answer to your question, I'm not scared, I'm determined— determined that my daughter will always be my first priority.'

She gave a weary sigh. 'It's simply the way I want it to be. Don't you see?' she appealed to him. 'This,' she said, moving her hand in an illustrative sweep from her chest to him and back again, 'is exactly the situation I want to avoid.'

'This is a situation that you have engineered,' he countered grimly. 'You've created a self-fulfilling prophesy. Do you even know how unrealistic you're being? Do you really think you're going to find some guy you'll never fight with? You'd be bored within a week,' he predicted.

'I'm not looking for a guy. This is just the way it's going to be, take it or leave it.'

It was the torment in her green eyes that made him hold his tongue—that and the realisation that she genuinely believed all the rubbish she was spouting. Her logic was totally crazy but he recognised this might not be the time to point it out. This was the time for a tactical retreat...but he would be back.

Alex closed the door behind him as he left, which should have made her happy. It was what she wanted, but as she picked up the phone to arrange Jasmine's trip over to meet her father happiness was not the emotion that was uppermost in her mind. She might never have sex again, and that was reason enough to feel depressed.

She had had the most gorgeous man in the universe ask her to be with him, and she had sent him away! More significantly, he had gone without even putting up much of a fight.... Probably, she thought gloomily, he'd been secretly relieved.

But she'd done the right thing, almost definitely she'd done the right thing. They'd made a great child, but living together... No, she had made the right decision... totally!

Wasn't the right thing meant to make you feel good?

She didn't feel good; she felt like someone who had just slammed the doors of paradise shut and stayed on the wrong side, which was mad because paradise was a cool, calm place of serenity. Serene and Alex… No, she had made the right decision, hadn't she…?

She lifted her chin and took a deep breath. *For God's sake, Angel, you've made your bed and now you have to lie in it…alone.*

Things happened faster than Angel had anticipated. The young woman who was standing in for her nanny was available to accompany Jasmine on the next flight, and she seemed eager to. So it was less than twenty-four hours later that she was thanking her for accompanying Jasmine on the journey and saying goodbye, leaving her to wait for her return flight.

Jasmine, strapped into the seat beside her, was so excited she chatted constantly all the way from the airport, unable to keep still in the seat. When they reached the bungalow she was visibly flagging.

'You like your bedroom?' Angel asked as the little girl did her umpteenth circuit of the room.

'Love it loads,' she said, taking a seat on the bed, watching while Angel unpacked her small suitcase. Jasmine began to swing her legs metronome style, her heels hitting the wooden frame with a regular dull thud.

'These shorts are too tight,' she remarked as Angel took out a blue denim pair with cute ducks on the patch pockets. 'But we didn't have any time to buy some more.'

'Don't worry, we'll buy you some new ones. There you go—all done,' Angel said as she put the last T-shirt in the drawer and closed it. 'How about a nap?'

The little girl looked offended. 'I'm not a baby, and I want to go in the water. You promised.'

Angel sighed. Like an elephant, her daughter never forgot. 'Everyone has naps in the afternoon in warm countries.'

'Even grown-ups?'

Angel nodded. 'Absolutely.'

'So you're going to take a nap too...with me?'

The logic was inescapable, and Angel, knowing a rash promise once made was hard to escape, dodged the issue.

'Why don't you change into your swimsuit and we'll have a swim first?' She floated the idea, knowing what the response would be. Watching her daughter leap up and down like a crazy thing on the bed made her realise how quiet her life was without Jas in it, how much emptier.

This was her. This was what she wanted, but did Alex, with his billionaire jet-setting lifestyle, have a clue what he was asking for?

Having left Jas to change into her swimsuit, Angel changed into her own one-piece—a black halter that she double tied at the neck. The last time she had been wearing it in a public pool, Jas had thought it funny to unfasten the bow and Angel had found herself in a very embarrassing topless situation.

He was nervous.

Alex gave a self-derisive smile. He was nervous of meeting a five-year-old child! Maybe nervous was not the best word to describe the combination of excitement, anticipation and trepidation in his gut. Carrying the gift—it had been a novel, actually a unique, experience for Alex to pick out a gift personally and not delegate the task to his excellent PA—he walked along the beach towards Angel's bungalow. He was a few hundred yards away when he heard the sound of laughter.

He did not consciously follow the sound but he ended up on the shore, oblivious to the waves lapping over his leather shoes, watching the two playing a game that involved much splashing and lots of noise. The first glimpse of his daughter was as Angel lifted her high out of the water, a wriggling laughing figure whose high-pitched chuckle he could hear above Angel's husky contralto tone.

There were few perfect moments in life, the really golden ones that stayed with you until the end. Alex had read somewhere that witnessing the birth of your child was considered by many to be one of them. He had not been there for the birth of his child so in some ways this was it: perfect. She was perfect.

'Who is that man, Mummy?'

Angel, who had just surfaced from the water and was kneeling, turned her head and saw him. Her stomach flipped. She had never associated the word lonely with Alex Arlov but standing there he looked... She swallowed the boulder lodged in her aching throat and slowly got to her feet.

'That's my friend.' She extended her hand to Jasmine. 'Shall we go say hello?'

Alex remembered a friend who had described how unreal it had felt to take his newborn home from hospital for the first time. He had spoken of the shock of overnight becoming, not a couple, but a family.

Times that by a million, Alex thought, and you might get somewhere near the complex swirl of emotions he was feeling.

He wasn't seeing a new baby. His daughter was not a blank slate; she was a fully formed little person with a store of experiences that he knew nothing about, a personality. Was she scared of the dark? He resented that he didn't know, but he was going to find out, and the only way to do that was to be a family.

Alex believed that only fools rushed headlong into important decisions, and allowing emotions to become involved was just so obviously a massive mistake that it did not even warrant debate. It turned out there were exceptions to this rule and standing on the beach he discovered one. He made the most important decision in his life without a second's debate or hesitation.

He was going to marry Angel and they were going to be a family. It would happen.

CHAPTER NINE

JASMINE ACCEPTED THE explanation without question. 'Does he want to play with us?'

Angel shook her head. 'I don't think so, sweetheart, and I think maybe we've had enough now too.' She took her daughter's hand and they waded out of the shallows and onto the beach where Alex, his dark hair fluttering slightly in the breeze, was standing looking gorgeous. This was obviously a given, but he was also incongruous in this setting in a tailored pale grey suit. The top button of his white silk shirt open and his tie hanging loose around his neck were the only minor concessions to the sun beating down.

His appearance was not lost on Jasmine.

'Your shoes are wet. It's really stupid to wear shoes on the beach.' She wriggled her own bare toes in the wet sand and directed her critical gaze to the rest of him. She didn't seem impressed by what she was seeing. 'Or a suit. It's not p-pract...?'

She looked to her mother, who automatically supplied the word, 'Practical,' before adding, 'Don't be rude, Jas.'

Alex stepped back out of the shallow water, barely giving his handmade Italian-leather shoes a glance. His daughter had a Scottish accent; the highland lilt was unmistakable. It brought home forcibly the extent of his ignorance. He didn't even know where she had lived her five years. He had assumed London, but clearly he couldn't have been more wrong.

'She's right. My outfit is not beach appropriate.' His outfit was appropriate for the discussion of oil leases. If the change of venue had been considered unusual by the oil executives who had expected to be in London, they had not said so when he had met the fleet of helicopters personally. 'But I've been working, and you, I see, have been swimming.'

'I can't swim yet. Mum has tried to teach me but I'm not a natural.'

Her sigh and serious expression drew a smile from Alex. While he did not know a lot about five-year-olds it seemed to him as a not-totally-objective observer that his daughter was pretty advanced for her age, and she not only looked startlingly like her mother but she was also not afraid of speaking her mind.

'Perhaps I could teach you?'

He turned his head towards Angel to gauge her reaction to his suggestion. She was bending forward to pick up a towel from the sand, a wet swathe of her hair concealing her face.

'Mummy?'

Angel dropped the towel around her shoulders. 'That's very kind.' The little girl skipped ahead.

'So do you mind?'

'That's not the point. You made it impossible for me to say no, and I don't appreciate that. Don't manipulate me, Alex.'

'It wasn't intentional. She didn't look to be afraid of the water.'

Angel laughed. 'Jas isn't afraid of anything. That's the problem—she has very little sense of danger. I don't want to make her scared but it's a hard balance.... She's not afraid of water. It's the cold—she hates it. I first tried to teach her at home when she was a toddler—we have the white sand and the clear seas, but the water is not warm at any time of the year and she is a warm-blooded little creature. She loves the sun.'

'So I see. The accent came as a surprise—charming, but a surprise.'

'I don't even notice she has an accent. We have an apartment in the castle....' She saw Alex's expression and added a quick explanatory footnote, 'My brother inherited the estate when our dad died—beautiful, remote and a lot of rain. Isn't it every little girl's dream to live in a castle?'

'Is it?'

'I was happy there when I was her age.'

'You have no accent.'

Her smile faded. 'No, I lost it and my roots, but Jasmine won't.'

'Roots are less about places and more about people.'

'There speaks someone who didn't grow up in a series of hotel rooms.'

'You said she had been ill? Was it serious?'

'It took a while to diagnose, a thing with her hip. It required a lot of bed rest and that was tough. They thought she might be left with a limp but she's fine. Are you all right, Alex?'

He tore his eyes off the playing child and nodded. 'Fine.' As fine as any man could be when he knew the woman he loved had faced all those things alone.

'Are you sure?'

He nodded. 'I should have been there.'

The burning intensity of his gaze made her look away. 'You're here now.'

'Yes, I am.'

They caught up with Jasmine, who, to Angel's maternal eyes, was showing visible signs of flagging. 'Want a carry, sweetheart?'

'No, I'm okay. What's that?' She stared curiously at the parcel in Alex's hand.

He withdrew the book from behind his back. 'A book. I thought you might like it. It's about a princess who marries a handsome prince after he saves her from a dragon.' A far simpler time when all a man had to do to prove himself was slay the odd dragon. Life was much more complicated these days.

'I already have a book about a princess. She rescues the prince and she hates pink.'

A lot more complicated—he couldn't even impress a five-year-old. 'It seems,' Alex said in a soft rueful aside to Angel as she took the book from him, 'that I am not politically correct enough.'

They had reached the steps to the bungalow and Angel opened the book. 'Look, Jas, this book has such lovely pictures, really beautiful.' How crazy that she wanted to save his feelings. He was trying so hard that it made her heart ache to watch him.

'Are there any cats in it?'

'I'm not sure,' Alex admitted.

'I like cats. Thank you very much.'

He inclined his head. 'You are most welcome, Jasmine.'

She allowed herself to be led up the steps to the veranda, where she jumped directly onto a bench. 'I could look at the pictures now.'

'Nice try. We had a deal. A swim and then a nap.'

With a show of reluctance she got up.

'Say goodnight to Alex.'

'Goodnight, Mr Alex.'

'Goodnight, Jasmine.'

'There's a bottle of wine open in the fridge if you want some. I won't be long…if you want to wait.'

'I want…'

He stood up when Angel walked back into the living room a few minutes later and pulled out a chair for her, wincing as it scraped on the wooden floor. 'Sorry.'

'Don't worry. Nothing will wake her now.'

'She's quite a character. You have done a good job.'

Angel felt herself blush with pleasure at the compliment. 'I've had a lot of help….'

'You have a nanny?'

Her chin lifted defensively. 'Luckily.'

He watched, one brow raised, as she ignored the wine he had poured and filled her coffee cup from a Thermos jug. 'It was not a criticism.'

'My brother is great and my normal nanny is sporting a leg plaster. Her really great stand-in flew over with Jas and then back.'

'So what does your brother do—?' He broke off, frowning. 'Is that a good idea?' She looked at him over the rim of her cup. 'You do know you're displaying all the classic signs of caffeine overload?'

'Am I?'

'You're jumpy as hell, you can't sit still… Look,' he broke off to say as the cup she had put back down on the table rattled. 'You're trembling and I bet your heart is racing and you're dizzy? Am I right?'

Oh, he was right. 'And that's because I drink too much coffee?' A man with a mind like a steel trap, but it turned out he didn't know everything. She was beginning to think that where she was concerned he knew nothing!

'If you're not careful…'

She gave a sputtering laugh and drew his frowning disapproval.

'This isn't funny, Angel.'

'Oh, I know it's not, believe me,' she said, looking at his mouth hard enough to memorise it. She picked up a magazine from the table and wafted her face with it. 'But don't worry, I know my limitations with coffee.' It was her limitations with Alex that were her problem. Her internal red light just failed to activate with him.

'You've met him, I think.'

He watched as she topped up her coffee cup. 'Who?'

'My brother. I believe you played with cars together. Cesare…?'

A look of utter astonishment spread across his face. 'You are Cesare Urquart's sister?' Meeting someone with a public persona in the flesh could, Alex knew, be disappointing when that person fell far short of your mental image. But that hadn't been the case when he had met the ex-racing driver whose career he had followed. He had liked the man and the feeling seemed to have been reciprocated.

She nodded.

'Does he know about me?' Alex asked, imagining his own reaction if the situation was reversed and he discovered the identity of the man who had got his young and beautiful sister pregnant.

'Not yet.'

'I'm assuming there will be no place to run,' he observed sardonically.

She flicked him a glance, resenting the fact he could look amused when she was genuinely worried about what her brother would do. Wade in all guns blazing probably.

'That settles it,' Alex said. 'I'll have to marry you.'

She struggled to match his flippancy. 'You really

know how to sell the idea. Of course I'll marry you. Name the day.'

'Tomorrow, unless you want a big wedding?'

The joke was beginning to grow tired. 'Very funny.'

'Why would you think I'm joking?'

She turned to him with an astonished stare. 'Because if you weren't that would make you insane.'

'It is insane to think a child is better brought up within the confines of a marriage?'

'We're not talking about Jasmine.'

'Yes, we are, Jasmine and us. You won't be my lover, so be my wife.'

Feeling the panic begin to build, she pressed a hand to her tight chest. 'There is no us.'

A spasm of impatience moved across his lean face. 'Don't be ridiculous. I'm the father of your child and I'm the only man you've ever slept with. That adds up to a big fat us.'

'It doesn't add up to marriage.'

'I'm not talking a paper marriage, if that is what is bothering you. Not a sterile, convenient—' He saw her flinch and stopped. 'What have I said?'

Pale as paper, she shook her head. 'Too much.'

He shrugged and forced himself to stifle his impatience. He had given her enough to think about, planted the idea, now it would grow.

He allowed himself one final parting shot.

'You don't want Jasmine to be an only child, do you?'

She was glad he couldn't see her face, or the tears that began to slide down her cheeks. She was grateful to him; she needed that. For a moment there she had started to let herself think that the crazy things he said were possible.

CHAPTER TEN

THE MOMENT ALEX walked into the hotel foyer, a trail of assistants behind him, he realised that something was wrong—it did not take a genius to work this out.

The area was crowded, some people talking, others gawking, and in the middle of them was Angel, white faced, wild eyed and she was shouting.

'What is wrong with you people? I don't want to sit down. I don't want to fill in a form. I've told you I can't find my daughter. My little girl, she was there and now she isn't. I need help, not tea!'

The shrill words stopped Alex in his tracks. He felt a cold hand close around his heart, then a moment later he was surging forward and the crowd was parting.

'Angel.'

She spun around; her expression when she saw him would stay with him for ever. 'Thank God, Alex, it's Jas, she's—'

He laid his hands on her shoulders and held her eyes with his. 'I heard. Just tell me what happened.'

Angel expelled a deep shuddering sigh and focused on his eyes, trying to block out the rest of the room and the white noise of panic in her head. 'We were walking back after lunch.' She gave another deep sigh and shook her head.

'Look at me, Angel.'

She responded to the firm voice, taking comfort from the calm in it. 'She'd spent the morning at the shoot with me watching. We had lunch, yes, I already said that, and…I really should get back outside.'

'In a moment.'

'I saw Nico, he asked me about… I don't remember. I only turned away for a moment, really only a moment, and when I turned around she was gone, vanished!'

'And when was this?'

'A couple of… I don't know, just now.' She clutched her head and struggled to think straight, fighting her way through the panic.

'Fine. Show me where you last saw her.'

The next few minutes were a blur for Angel, who retraced her steps and repeated the sequence of events for what seemed like the thousandth time, then sat and watched, feeling helpless and more scared than she had imagined possible, while Alex divided up the volunteers into teams and gave them areas to cover.

'She can't have gone far, and ten teams can cover a lot of ground. We will find her.'

She caught his arm. 'I want to go too.'

'No, I need you and Nico to stay here in case she makes her own way back, and everyone has Nico's number.' Nico held up his phone. 'He's the contact so you'll be the first to know.'

'You're afraid you'll find something bad—that's why you don't want me to go!' she accused shrilly.

Alex took her by the shoulders. 'You can't think that way, Angel, and you're not going to fall apart. You're strong. Look at me, Angel.' Her wild restive gaze settled on his face. 'We are going to find her.'

She swallowed and took a deep shuddering breath. 'I'm not strong, Alex.'

He gave the most tender smile she had ever seen and touched her face. 'You are as tough as old boots.'

Then he was gone.

Nico's phone rang exactly ten minutes later, the longest ten minutes of her life.

Still holding his daughter's hand, Alex dropped into a squatting position beside her and pointed towards Angel, who was belting across the sand with Nico and several staff trailing in her wake. 'There's your mummy!'

As Angel reached them he released Jasmine's hand and, rising to his feet, took a step back as Angel, panting, tears streaming down her face, dropped down on her knees and grabbed Jasmine, hugging so tightly the little girl protested and wriggled to escape.

'Sorry…sorry…' Angel pushed her back, one hand patting her own mouth to hold back the sobs that struggled to escape from her throat as her anxious green eyes scanned her daughter's face. 'You're all right?' She lifted her eyes to the tall figure who stood over them both. 'She's a-all right? Oh, God, my teeth won't stop chattering.'

To witness the emotion she was leaking from every pore was making his throat ache. 'She's fine,' Alex promised huskily. 'She's just had a little adventure, haven't you, Jasmine? And none the worse for it, excepting a few scratches.'

'I was very, very brave.' She looked to Alex for confirmation of this proud boast and he tipped his head gravely.

'Just like your mother.'

Angel, shaking with the force of her relief, impelled to touch Jasmine every other second just to prove she was real, was not feeling brave. She was still fighting the nightmarish images in her head. As her distress began to communicate itself to the little girl the proud smile vanished and her lip began to tremble. 'Mummy...?'

'Don't do that again...ever...promise me.!'

Jasmine's face crumbled. 'You weren't there!' she wailed.

The words pierced Angel's heart. 'Don't cry, darling....' Angel sniffed, hugging her daughter's rigid body. 'It's all right now.' She stroked her daughter's head and Jasmine's arms went round her neck. Carrying her, Angel rose awkwardly to her feet and over the top of Jasmine's head she smiled at Alex and mouthed 'thank you'.

Cool focus and the ability to empty his mind of everything but what he needed to do had got Alex through this, had kept his darkest imaginings at bay. All it took was the gratitude in her shining eyes and those self-imposed barriers crumbled. He tipped his head, his own smile giving not a hint of the rush of powerful emotions locked tight in his chest, the primal need to protect the two women in his life from all the dangers that lurked out there.

He moved to stand protectively beside them and kissed the top of the curly head pressed to Angel's shoulder and said quietly, 'Will you be all right?'

Angel felt her face drop. 'You're not coming with us?' Hearing the wobble in her voice, she pinned on a weak smile in an effort to retrieve the situation, and she struggled to display some of the self-reliance she prided herself on.

All in all it was a pathetic effort.

His fingers tightened on the bones of her shoulder; his hand felt heavy, reassuring. Angel closed her eyes, sucked in a deep breath, before throwing her head back to meet his eyes.

'I'll be fine,' she pronounced, thinking, *Don't get used to leaning on him, Angel. He won't always be there.*

'I won't be long. I just want to make sure that this section of beach is fenced off by the morning. We don't want this happening again.' He sketched a bleak but determined smile and beckoned his nephew over. 'Nico will see you back to the bungalow and wait until I get back.'

Nico nodded. 'Of course.'

Jasmine raised her head. 'I want my kitten back.'

Angel arched a questioning brow and angled a glance up at Alex. 'Your kitten, darling?'

'She saw a stray cat and it looks like she followed it through the hole in the fence, crawled through after it. The cat led her back to her litter of feral kittens and Jasmine decided she wanted to take one home.' He skimmed over the struggle he had had to convince her that this was not a good idea. His daughter had, it seemed, inherited her mother's stubborn disposition as well as an underdeveloped sense of danger.

Life for a man in a household with two such females was not to be envied, but it was what Alex had discovered he wanted for himself, what he would do anything to achieve.

'Hence the scratches.'

'Scratches?'

He took one small grubby hand, turned it over, and Angel saw the scratches on the chubby wrist and arm. They looked red and angry. 'Hold on…' He pulled his mobile phone out and glanced at the message on the screen. 'Mark Lomas.'

Recognising the name of a man whom she had exchanged the odd good morning with during the week, Angel felt a stab of resentment that Alex should consider taking a message from a guest a priority at such a moment.

He gave a nod of satisfaction as he slid the phone back into his breast pocket. 'Mark should be there by the time you get to the bungalow.'

'Why?'

He felt a stab of anxiety as he studied her face more closely. Angel remained dramatically pale, her skin the colour of wax, her eyes dark emerald bruises nestled among the pallor.

He wanted to urge her to sit down before she fell down and give him Jasmine, but he knew it would be a futile exercise. Angel was holding on to her daughter as if she would never let go and would definitely resist any efforts he made to lighten her burden.

His jaw tightened—a burden she had been carrying alone for too long because of him.

'I thought you might have spoken the other night. He's in the next bungalow to you. A doctor...?'

'I might have.'

'He's coordinating the medical backup on the charity race,' he explained, referring to the charity Ironman event that was currently causing a buzz in the hotel.

'I sent a text when I found Jasmine and explained the situation. I thought he could take a look at her, clean up those scratches and do what is necessary. He asked if her tetanus is up to date. I didn't know.' His jaw clenched as he looked away. He would know...next time. Not that he wanted there to be a next time, but there would be other times...other crises, and he would have the knowledge a father should.

'She's covered.' She kissed her daughter's tear-stained cheek and realised that she herself probably didn't look any better.

'Shall I take her?' Nico offered.

Angel shook her head and held on to her baby. Life would be so much simpler if she could never let go, could keep her safe from the big bad world for ever. She heard people say that the hardest part of parenting was letting go, but it wasn't until now that she knew what that really meant.

With Nico by her side she walked away from Alex, thinking that it felt wrong to be doing so. What was so important that he couldn't come with them? She wanted to tell him he should be with them but didn't—he ought to know.

They reached the bungalow two minutes ahead of the doctor, who arrived apologising for his tardiness, wearing shorts and little else but a reassuring air of calm competence.

As Alex had predicted he cleaned the scratches, applied some antiseptic and managed to distract Jasmine while he gave her a shot of broad-spectrum antibiotic. He advised Angel to keep an eye on the scratches as cats' scratches, he explained, were more prone to infection than dogs', and told her to contact him if she had any concerns at all.

Angel had managed to adopt Alex's what-an-adventure-you've-had tack with Jasmine, who was displaying a youthful resilience that Angel envied. After having a bath and a sandwich or two from the tray that had arrived at the room Jasmine had barely been able to keep her eyes open. She was asleep before her head hit the pillow.

Going back to the living room, Angel persuaded a reluctant Nico that he didn't need to stay.

'Are you sure?'

'Totally. I'm just going to take a shower and head for bed myself.'

Finally alone, she checked on Jasmine before she padded over to the shower, leaving all the interconnecting doors open so that she would hear should Jasmine wake. She didn't, of course, but Angel spent more time stepping out wet to check for some imaginary sound than she did washing off the sand and grime.

Not bothering to dry her hair, she squeezed out the excess water and brushed it back off her face with her fingers. It fell in a heavy rope-like twist down her back. Pulling on the silk robe hung behind the door, she belted it and hurried back to Jasmine's room to double check, her heart suddenly pumping double-time as she stepped into the room.

Angel felt the panic leave her with a soft whoosh. Her daughter hadn't moved since she'd last looked, which was probably all of five minutes ago. It wasn't as if she had expected Jas to have vanished.... Her knees shook a little as she made an effort to gather her composure.

Walking back into the adjoining room, she started on hearing a knock on the door. It wouldn't be Alex—he wouldn't have knocked and maybe he wouldn't even come. Nico would have reported that they were all right. Why should he come?

Because I want him to!

Pull yourself together, Angel. Since when did you need a shoulder to cry on? Impatient with herself, she went to the door where a smiling maid in the dark blue hotel uniform stood holding a tray.

'The coffee you ordered, miss.'

Did I?

Angel thanked the girl and didn't pursue the forgetfulness. Amnesia registered pretty low down in the day's events, so Angel asked the maid to put the tray down on the coffee table.

Two reviving cups later Angel was standing on the veranda when she saw him.

She watched him approach, shading her eyes against the glare of the setting sun that threw pink fingers of light across the silver water. He was too far away for her to make out anything, but his silhouette and his long-legged elegant stride were unmistakable, the way he moved as distinctive as a fingerprint.

Post-caffeine hit she was thinking more clearly, and as she squared her shoulders she knew what he had come to say. Not the words precisely, but definitely the senti-ment of the things he would not say in front of Jasmine. And she wasn't going to fight him on it. He was here to blame her, call her a terrible mother and he was right. She had no defence against the truth any more than she had defence left against her feelings for him.

She loved him.

It had taken her long enough to work it out. When it came to personal relationships she was a blank page. Un-like her, Alex knew about relationships. He'd been in love enough to get married, enough to be devastated when he lost the love of his life, enough to sleep with the first... Well, maybe not the first woman he met but probably the first one who had begged him to take her to bed.

One night of escaping his nightmares, seeking obliv-ion in mindless sex and who could blame him? It would take a harsh critic to judge him for that but he had clearly judged himself and struggled to wipe the shameful mem-ory from his mind. Marry him.... Yeah, sure, they really were the foundations of a great relationship!

Obviously she knew that Alex was physically attracted to her, and his devotion to Jasmine was not in question.

But Angel knew that wasn't enough. Easy thing to say now when she was clear headed, but in his presence—and certainly in his arms—she rarely felt that way.

Then keep out of his arms, Angel!

Alex slowed and paused, one hand on the wooden balustrade, coming to a dead halt at the bottom of the shallow flight of wooden steps. The sight of her standing there stole his breath away, the same way she had stolen his heart.

She had every reason to hate him but her generous heart had let him in. She'd given him a second chance, and of course he understood she was wary of trusting him, but if it took him the rest of his life he would convince her.

Her heart started to thud heavily, the echo loud in her ears as he mounted the steps. She could feel the acid taste of self-recrimination in her mouth. He could not possibly blame her more than she did herself.

And she'd lectured him on the responsibilities of being a parent! It was on her watch that this had happened. It didn't matter how many times she went over it in her head, she still couldn't figure out how it had happened; her attention had only been distracted for a moment—and that had been enough.

The blue pedal pushers and white shirt were gone. She now wore a black silk kimono emblazoned with humming birds that ended midcalf to reveal her endless golden legs. His eyes slid hungrily down her body, over the soft, sinuous, sexy curves, and he swallowed, losing his focus as his body surged lustfully. When his gaze settled back on her face her slicked-back hair revealed her face as a perfect oval.

'Is she asleep?'

Angel nodded, lifted her chin and launched into a pre-emptive apology. 'I know it was my fault, totally and—'

He touched a finger to her lips. 'You talk so much rubbish.'

Angel had steeled herself for his accusations; she was totally prepared for his anger. She could have taken that, but what she had no protection from was the incredible tenderness in his face, the concern in his blue eyes and the caressing warmth in his vibrant voice as he took her by the shoulders and looked down into her face, not judging her but offering her support.

'Sorry I was so late but I wanted to be there when the police arrived and explain the situation. And I didn't want to leave until we'd checked the perimeter fence for holes, a classic case of after the horse has bolted, I know, but—' He stopped. 'Here's me babbling and you...you poor baby, you look like hell.'

Her lip quivered. 'I... For God's sake, don't be nice to me, Alex!'

Ignoring her plea, he slid his arms slid around her back. 'Come here.'

Her face crumpled and she stepped into him, feeling his arms close around her as the tears began to flow.

She almost choked on her shame and sense of inadequacy as she struggled to communicate her guilt to him. 'It was all my fault. I—'

'Don't be ridiculous,' he condemned roughly as he passed a hand over her slick wet hair. 'You can't watch a child every second. Even I know that.'

Her teary face lifted. 'I can and I will,' she flashed fiercely, fighting against every instinct she had as she pulled away, dabbing her wet face with her hands and sniffing.

Who'd have thought a sniff could be sexy...? Not Alex,

but with Angel there had always been a steep learning curve. Fighting against the temptation to haul her back into his arms, he took a couple deep breaths to conquer and beat the dangerous need into submission. She was shattered physically and emotionally; this was not the time.

'So what did Mark say? You didn't mind me calling him? I just thought it would be less traumatic than a trip to the hospital. I explained about her hip.'

'He was great with her and she's fine. Just superficial scratches and she was very thirsty. He gave her an anti-biotic jab to be on the safe side.' Angel's eyes darkened as she shuddered and whispered, 'When I think what could have happened.'

'Don't!'

She closed her mouth over the smart 'easy for you to say' retort, realising with a stab of remorse that it wasn't easy for him. If she still needed it she'd had ample proof today that Alex loved his daughter deeply. Today he had been a rock.

'It is a totally pointless exercise to torture yourself this way.'

She exhaled a long shuddering sigh. 'You're right.'

Some of the gravity left his face as he gave a crooked half smile. 'I am?'

She didn't smile back. 'I don't know how I'll ever thank you for what you did today.'

Alex shook his head, embarrassed by her shining-eyed gratitude. He did not want her gratitude—he wanted her. 'There is nothing to thank me for.'

Her green eyes widened in protest. 'If you hadn't found her before it got dark it could have been hours be-fore she was discovered and anything could have happened.' There were a lot worse things out there than kittens.

He touched her chin, drawing her face round to his as his fingers moved to frame the side of her face. 'You weren't going to do that, remember...?' She nodded, her throat too thick with emotion to speak. 'I was only doing what a dad is meant to and, let's face it,' he added bleakly, 'I have some time to make up for.'

The regret in his voice brought a lump to her throat. No matter what pain it cost her it was worth it for Jasmine to have her father in her life.

'Can I see her?'

Her reply was husked with emotion. 'Of course. You don't have to ask.'

'Since when?'

She gave an uncomfortable half shrug. 'I know I've been defensive and suspicious. It's hard for me to—'

He filled in the blank. *Trust.* And he had played a big part in any trust issues Angel might have.

A strange expression flickered across his face. Taking her totally by surprise, he leaned down and kissed her mouth softly. 'I'll hold you to that promise.'

Balling her hand into a fist to stop it going to her trembling lips, she went with him, but paused at the bedroom door and let him go inside alone.

When he dragged himself away from the sleeping child—it still seemed a total stunning miracle that he had had anything to do with her creation—Alex found Angel outside on the veranda. Night had fallen and the white fairy lights wrapped around the branches in the trees had sparked into life, their glow lending the scene a twinkling other-worldly quality.

'It's a beautiful evening....'

Angel turned and she looked so magnificent that for

a moment he couldn't breathe. He stopped midsentence and, loosing a low growl of frustration, he dragged a frustrated hand through his hair.

'This is ridiculous!' His dark brows drew together in a straight, uncompromising line above his hawkish, masterful nose. 'I have so much to say and I'm discussing the weather with you, as if we've just met in the street!'

From where she was standing Angel could feel the waves of emotion rolling off him. She shook her head urgently. 'No, Alex!' She knew what he was going to say—today could only have convinced him more that his duty was to marry her. Everyone thought she was cool and capable and it was an opinion she liked to encourage. Sometimes even she fell for the act, but today had outed her as a spineless, needy wimp who, when the going got tough, fell apart.

'I can't marry you, Alex.'

Aware of how fragile she was, he struggled to control his impatience but he knew it was a battle he was losing.

Pale but composed now, she took a step backwards, widening the gap between them, but not the growing tension. As she continued to hold his gaze she explained the situation in a distant expressionless voice.

'Marriage,' she explained carefully, 'isn't meant to be a penance.'

His eyes darkened with outrage at the suggestion. He started forward and then stopped himself. 'You think marriage to me would be a penance?'

'Oh, God, no!' She took a deep breath and waited for the urgent need to walk into his arms to pass. 'Marriage to you would be...' She stopped, lowered her gaze, thinking, *Too little too late, Angel.*

Way too late. She had been standing there, not wearing

her heart on her sleeve, but instead painted like a neon sign across her face!

Still, she mused darkly, she was not telling him anything he didn't already know.

She made herself meet his eyes. 'I know you think it's your duty to marry me.' Feeling the pressure of a future without Alex, a future where she waved goodbye as he drove off with Jasmine for the weekend pressing in on her, heavy and dark, she struggled to maintain eye contact as she told him bluntly. 'I'm not what you need.'

'What I need!' he grated through clenched teeth before swearing in several languages. To hell with this not being the right time, to hell with her being fragile. He had to challenge her blind, wilful stupidity. 'You know nothing, Angel Urquart, but I do. I know that you love me, so why the hell don't you stop putting us both through hell and admit it?'

'Love has got nothing to do with it,' she flared back. 'And don't you dare yell at me. And even if it did…' She shook her head and said firmly, 'There are very good reasons why I can't marry you.'

'Name one,' he challenged, looking unimpressed.

'Well, you don't love me.' Hard words to say without sounding terribly vulnerable and needy but Angel liked to think she pulled it off. 'You don't even like me most of the time….' Taking a moment to flick the damp tail of her hair over one shoulder, she left ample room for him to jump in, but he didn't. He just stood there being unhelpful and looking so gorgeous that she wanted to weep.

'You make me laugh, when you're not making me yell.'

She slung him a reproachful look. Did he have any idea how hard this was for her? 'You think that you should marry me because of Jasmine. I know you mean well…!'

His lips curled in dismissive scorn. 'I am not some misguided do-gooder!' He took a purposeful step towards her. 'I am a man who wants you, and I intend to have you….'

This outrageously arrogant pronouncement should have made her do many things: laugh scornfully, realise what a lucky escape she'd had, but no. Where on that list of responses came a surge of heavy, hot, toe-curling excitement?

His confidence was total, impregnable. The gleam in his dark eyes as they looked down into her face was hungry.

The urge to melt into him, to lift her face to receive the kiss she could almost taste, was so compelling that resisting it drew a tiny moan from her lips. His silence seemed to be willing her to make that move.

'You know you want me, so why are you fighting it?'

'Yes, I want you.'

The admission upped the tension several more notches. His eyes glowed an incandescent, dizzying blue. The combustible quality that was always there just beneath the surface was no longer buried beneath a veneer of sophistication but right there in her face.

'But you're not talking about wanting, you're talking about marriage. I can't marry you, Alex.'

'I keep hearing that—'

She was unable to retreat any more as the back of her legs had made contact with the small rail that ran around the veranda. She held up her hand, more in hope than any real expectation it would stop his advance, and if he touched her she'd…!

'I can't marry you,' she blurted, 'because I can't have

any more children.' His reaction to this information was hard to read because he didn't display any reaction at all.

She had been quiet too when they'd told her the details. She'd thought the overstretched professionals had been relieved when she hadn't broken down, and they had spoken of her healthy attitude.

'Do you understand what I'm saying?'

He tilted his head to one side and surveyed her through narrowed eyes. He didn't buy her supernatural composure for one second. He could feel the pain she was struggling to hide as sharply as if it had been his own. He fought the urge to haul her into his arms and tell her everything was going to be all right. He needed facts.

'How about you tell me what you're saying?'

She responded to the quiet request with a minimal shrug. 'I told you that I needed a Caesarean when Jas was born.' He nodded. 'I might have implied that it was straightforward.'

He hefted out a deep sigh. 'And it wasn't.'

Her shadowed gaze flickered upwards. Remote was the word that came to mind when she tried to read his expression. 'I lost a lot of blood,' she admitted. 'And, well, technical stuff aside, the long and short of it is the chances of me conceiving again are pretty remote.'

He heard her out in silence, his expression growing colder the longer she spoke. 'You could have died— something that slipped your mind, I suppose.'

She was not surprised he was angry. 'Childbirth is very safe these days and my life was never in any real danger. It's not something I think about too often. I have Jasmine, I don't need… It's a closed chapter for me and I didn't see how it could affect us. I mean, how was I to know that you were so ridiculously old-fashioned? I wasn't expecting you to propose.'

'I really don't see... If what you're saying is true...'

Her spine stiffened. 'If!' she ground out tautly. 'Why would I lie?' Did he think she got a kick out of revealing intimate medical details?

'Get down off that high horse, Angel. I'm just trying to make sense of you taking the contraceptive pill unless you were just saying...'

'Oh... I am on the pill, the doctors advised it. Although the chances of me getting pregnant are pretty much the same as winning the lottery, it still is technically possible.' With further tests he had said he could be more precise but Angel, who had had enough of being poked and prodded, had refused.

'Why am I getting the impression that you are giving me only half the story?'

The consultant's final comments came back to her.

'I cannot emphasise how important it would be for you to seek medical advice immediately, *immediately*, Miss Urquart should you even suspect you might be pregnant.'

'If I did by some miracle get pregnant I'd need to be monitored.'

Under his tan Alex paled. 'By that you mean it would be dangerous for you to have a baby...as in life-threateningly dangerous?'

'That,' she said, dodging his gaze, 'is an overstatement. If it did happen—'

'No!'

She gulped at his tone. 'Yes, I know, like I said, the likelihood of it happening is a bit like winning the lottery.'

'I mean you will not try.' His hands landed on her shoulders and she could feel the tremors running through him. 'Not now, not ever, will you put your life at risk that way.' It would be just like Angel to pull some stupid stunt like that. 'Do you hear me? Ever!'

Hard not to hear him, not that he was yelling. His voice had dropped to a low bass rumble, the way she'd noticed it did when he was particularly annoyed, but there was nothing wrong with his projection.

His blazing blue eyes burnt into her as he groaned and slid his big hands down her back. She could feel his fingers, warm through the fabric, as they came to rest on her hips, his thumbs on the indent of her waist. 'I've only just found you again. Do you think I'd run the risk of losing you? It would be selfish—Jasmine needs her mother, she needs you.... I need you, Angel. There was a time when I thought about you as my weakness...now I know you are my strength.'

Tears of emotion filled her eyes, spilling like crystal drops down her cheeks. 'You need a woman who can give you everything. You need to wait. I know it might seem impossible now,' she told him gently, 'but one day you'll love someone the way you did Emma. Imagine how awful it would be if, when that time came, you were tied to me. You need love in a marriage, Alex, and you deserve it. And you deserve babies with that person. I've seen you with Jasmine. You'll want a family of your own one day and I can't give it you.'

'You stupid woman.'

She blinked.

'You really are a stupid woman!' The insult was delivered in a voice that held so much love that her eyes filled. 'You already have given me a family—you have given me Jasmine. You and Jasmine are all the family I want or need, my bolshy, belligerent, beautiful Angelina, my very own Angel. I love you.'

She swallowed and covered the bottom half of her face with her hands. 'But I'm not…'

'You're not second best.'

Her eyes widened at this display of perception. 'I loved Emma,' he agreed quietly. 'And I was glad I was there for her, but we barely had a relationship before I became her carer. We were never really a couple. I think if things had been different we could have been happy but you… you…' He touched her cheek, wonder shining in the incandescent blue of his eyes as he bent to kiss her lips. 'You are my soulmate.'

Joy exploded through her. 'I love you, Alex.'

At the words the tension drained from him and he smiled. Taking her hand, holding her eyes with his, he placed it palm flat against his chest, against the beat of his heart. 'If life took you away from me, it would break. I would break,' he told her in a voice thick and throbbing with the strength of his emotions.

Tears of joy seeping from her eyes, Angel took his hand and kissed the palm lovingly while she looked up at him, vision blurred with tears of joy. 'I won't let you break, Alex,' she promised huskily.

He brushed the tears lovingly away from her face with his thumb. 'Marry me, my Angel.'

'What are you doing tomorrow?'

His grin blazed as he bent his head to claim her lips. 'Becoming the luckiest man on the planet!'

EPILOGUE

'DADDY!'

It was a title he never tired of hearing. 'Yes, Miss Jasmine?'

'Can we go now?'

'Homework done?'

Jumping up and down impatiently, Jasmine nodded vigorously. 'I've been ready for hours.'

Alex shrugged. 'Don't look at me—so have I. We're waiting for your mother. Blame her.'

'Blame me for what this time?' Angel asked, walking into the room.

'Keeping us waiting,' Jasmine supplied.

'What's the hurry? The snow isn't going to melt anytime soon.' It had been one of the longest winters on record.

'It might! The sun is shining and I want to show Daddy my snowman. He doesn't believe it's taller than him... nearly taller than him.'

'Well, I'm sorry, but getting this one ready is not a five-minute job.' Angel looked down at the bundle in her arms who was barely visible beneath the layers he was cocooned in. His eyes were closed; his dark lashes lay like a fan across his cheeks. Looking at him it was hard to believe he had kept them awake half the night.

Amazing to think now that when she'd first discovered she was pregnant she had really thought it might split them apart. It was the thing they had both agreed on: no more children. But it had happened anyway, her little miracle, and in the end it had drawn them closer than ever.

She had been more worried about telling Alex than about the pregnancy itself, and she would never forget the look on his face when she had told him. She had never thought to see her big, bold, impossibly brave husband scared, but he had been. She never saw that look again, but she knew the fear was there and the memory of the terror in his eyes would stay with her for ever. Now though, when she thought of it, she was able to see it beside the expression on his face when he had held his newborn son for the first time.

But Alex had been there for her every step of the way. She didn't think she could have made it through those months with her sanity intact; his wildly overprotective instincts had been in overdrive.

But if ever she became impatient with him when he wrapped her in cotton wool, Angel had reminded herself of that look.

Appearing at her elbow, Alex twitched aside a fold of blue blanket to reveal his son's face. 'His first trip out.'

'Are you sure he'll be warm enough?'

Alex's rich warm laughter rang out. 'In that lot he's more likely to suffer heat exhaustion.'

It still didn't seem real to Alex that he had a son, and, while he loved little Theo more than life itself, the pregnancy itself had been the worst months of his entire life.

The fear of losing Angel had never left him for a single instant. He had felt as though he were walking around with a stone in his chest. He had tried to hide his fears, for Jasmine's sake he had struggled to maintain an illusion at least of a normal family life, but the strain had been immense.

Angel had been amazing. She had sailed through the pregnancy serenely; despite two stays in hospital and intense monitoring she had never once complained.

His wife was truly amazing. He kissed her, a long and lingering kiss that brought a flush to her lovely cheeks.

'What was that for?'

'A man has to take what he can when he can.'

The reminder of the previous afternoon when they had not used the time to catch up with lost sleep but with lost lovemaking brought a deepened flush to her cheeks and a sparkle to her eyes.

'Can I push Theo?' Jasmine asked. 'I'll be very, *very* careful.'

'We'll take turns,' Alex decided as he took control of the pram and zipped up the protective covering, then in a soft aside to his wife added, 'My turn on top later, I think.'

'Marriage is all about give and take.'

And she had married a man who gave a whole lot more than he ever took!

* * * * *

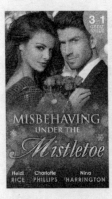  

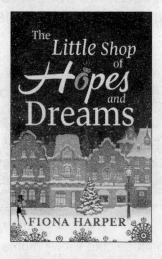

MILLS & BOON®

Want to get more from Mills & Boon?

Here's what's available to you if you join the
exclusive **Mills & Boon eBook Club** today:

✦ *Convenience – choose your books each month*
✦ *Exclusive – receive your books a month before
anywhere else*
✦ *Flexibility – change your subscription at any time*
✦ *Variety – gain access to eBook-only series*
✦ *Value – subscriptions from just £1.99 a month*

So visit **www.millsandboon.co.uk/esubs** today
to be a part of this exclusive eBook Club!

15_INSHIP